W9-ATD-780

ALSO BY TARA SUE ME

The
Exposure

The Submissive Series

TARA SUE ME

BERKLEY
New York

BERKLEY
An imprint of Penguin Random House LLC
375 Hudson Street, New York, New York 10014

Copyright © 2016 by After Six Publishing Co.
The Chalet copyright © 2014 by Tara Sue Me

Library of Congress Cataloging-in-Publication Data

Names: Me, Tara Sue, author.
Title: The exposure/Tara Sue Me.
Description: First edition. | New York, New York: Berkley, 2016. |
Series: The submissive series
Identifiers: LCCN 2016012990 (print) | LCCN 2016019595 (ebook) |
ISBN 9781101989319 (paperback) | ISBN 9781101989326 (ebook)
Subjects: | BISAC: FICTION/Romance/Contemporary. | FICTION/Romance/
General. | FICTION/Contemporary Women. | GSAFD: Erotic fiction.
Classification: LCC PS3613.E123 E98 2016 (print) | LCC PS3613.E123 (ebook) |
DDC 813/.6—dc23
LC record available at https://lccn.loc.gov/2016012990

First Edition: October 2016

Printed in the United States of America
1   3   5   7   9   10   8   6   4   2

Cover art by Madga Indigo/Moment/Getty Images

To my readers, who allow me to do what I love.

Acknowledgments

This is the ninth book in the Submissive Series. I know that's not a lot comparatively speaking, but considering *The Submissive* was only supposed to be a writing exercise, I think it's safe to say no one is as surprised as I am that the series has grown to what it is today.

Many thanks to Elle Mason, who is my crit partner, my beta reader, and the president of the Cole Johnson fan club, and she basically keeps me sane. Couldn't do it without you, Twin!

To the entire staff at Penguin Random House: Claire, Jenn, Erin, and everyone who has touched this series, you all are the best!

Special thanks to my dad, who, at my request, doesn't read my books, but nonetheless was extremely beneficial in helping me brainstorm and plot the blackmail piece in this book. Dad, as I wrote the manuscript, I discovered the finer points often veered from our initial discussions, but I've found it's best not to argue when the characters tell me to change something.

Many thanks to Fiona, Christine, and Tina for their continued support and e-mails that make me smile.

Thanks as always to Mr. Sue Me. It's because of you and your support that I'm able to continue to do what I love.

Finally, to all my readers and the numerous book bloggers who read my stories, it is truly an honor and a privilege to have you read my words.

The

Exposure

Prologue

ABBY

Meagan looked up from her desk. "You found these where?"
I shook my head. "It wasn't me. You remember Cole
and Sasha? From opening night at Luke's place?"

"The submissive with the short dark hair and the hot Brit?
Not likely to forget him."

I laughed—a lot of people had that reaction to Cole. "That
hot Brit actually collared her a few months ago. He also recently
bought a house and they were in the attic cleaning when Sasha
came across those." I pointed to the stack of magazines.

I hadn't recognized the cover model immediately. The young
woman staring up at us from the front page had teased blond
hair and ice blue eye shadow. She was worlds away from the
woman sitting across from me now with sleek, straight hair and
natural makeup that subtly enhanced her features.

"Look at me. I don't even remember being that young." Meagan shook her head. "Well, now you know part of my history with Luke. We did a photo shoot another lifetime ago."

She sighed and organized the magazines into a pile on the corner of her desk, but she didn't look up immediately and something lurked in her eyes when she did. "Thank you for bringing these by. I somehow misplaced my copies."

I got the distinct impression she'd misplaced them on purpose. "I'm sorry," I said. "I didn't mean to upset you. I just thought you should know we found them."

"It's okay. It was just a shock seeing these. It's been so long."

"I had no idea you used to model."

"*Used to* being the important part."

I took a step back and studied her. "I can see it, though. You have that look about you. I never noticed it before, but now? Definitely. You probably could still do it."

Meagan raised her eyebrow. "Model? Please."

"Or anchor the news. Something in front of the camera."

"I don't think so," Meagan replied. "I'm very happy sitting behind a desk. Besides, do you have any idea of the stress that comes with modeling? And I'm sure it's only gotten worse in the last few years."

"One could say you're older and wiser and could handle it better now."

"Or one could say I'd work myself into an early grave."

"I think you've pretty much got that one covered with the job you already have."

Meagan laughed. "You're probably right."

She changed the subject and I went along with her, not wanting to pry too much. It was obviously a subject she didn't want to discuss.

Yet, when I stopped by her office two weeks later, the magazines were still on the corner of her desk.

Chapter One

Meagan Bishop should have taken the paper cut as a sign. A sign with flashing red lights that read *OPEN LATER*. But instead, she shook her finger and tried to open the invitation without getting blood on the fine linen paper. And since she insisted on opening the envelope, she really had only herself to blame when the contents punched her in the gut.

Guy Ferguson had been nominated for an Emmy and he'd invited her to his celebratory dinner. Because, as he'd made a note in his flawless script, *"I couldn't have done it without you."*

She hated the Emmys.

No, that wasn't it. She hated that Guy Ferguson had been nominated for one. Guy Ferguson, the man she'd groomed years ago for a correspondent position doing human interest stories. She already worked for the news organization and even though she secretly wanted the job, she instead helped Guy, an acquaintance she knew from college, in his quest. She remembered his smile and hug when he'd received the offer. And in the years that followed, he'd always drop her a note when he climbed another rung on the corporate ladder.

She told herself she was settled in her executive position for the same media corporation, but the truth was, she still yearned to be in front of the camera.

Her phone rang, and she shoved the invitation into her desk drawer and answered without looking to see who it was.

"Meagan Bishop."

"Ms. Bishop, this is Officer Smyth at the front desk. There's a Mr. DeVaan here to see you."

DeVaan . . . Luke was here? To see her?

She almost told the security guard that she was too busy and to send him away. But she was insanely curious as to why Luke would be stopping by.

"Send him up," she said. She pulled a compact out of her purse and checked her hair, smoothed the platinum blond strands and made sure there was nothing between her teeth. She reapplied lipstick and chided herself the entire time.

She'd just popped a breath mint in her mouth when he knocked on her door.

"Come in," she said.

He opened the door and stepped inside. As always, the sight of him made her heart beat a bit faster and her stomach flip. He, of course, didn't look affected at all. Damn the man. He simply stood there smiling at her with his cocky grin and his gray eyes dancing with amusement.

"Luke." She waved toward an empty chair. "What brings you by today?"

"Thanks for seeing me, Meagan." He sat down. "I know you're

busy and we're past mindless small talk. I won't take up too much of your time."

"I appreciate that."

"I've been asked to collaborate in a book of erotic artistic photographs. A coffee-table book. It's a promising project, but I've been rather busy with the clubs lately and I don't have the contacts I used to."

Meagan knew Luke had a side business taking erotic pictures. It wasn't shocking he'd be asked to do a book. The question was, why did he think she needed to know?

"Sounds like an amazing opportunity," she said.

"I'm glad you think so. I'd like for you to be my model."

He spoke it so matter-of-factly, so by-your-leave, she wasn't sure she heard correctly. "What?"

"I'd like to showcase you. I want you to be the model in the pictures."

It didn't make any more sense when he said it the second time.

"Are you out of your mind?" she asked.

"Not the last time I checked."

She leaned back in her chair and glared at him. "I think you have some nerve traipsing into my office and asking me to model for you. Correct me if I'm wrong, but we tried that once before and it was *you* who said we shouldn't do it again."

"That was over fifteen years ago, Meagan."

"Some things a girl doesn't forget."

Like having his body hot and hard against hers. His smooth voice whispering sexy little nothings in her ear.

And, days later, his insistence that not only could they not see each other anymore, but that it would be for the best if she found a new photographer.

"I had no idea you could hold on so tightly to something that happened so long ago," he said.

"Forgive me if I'm trying to abide by the boundaries you set up."

"Fifteen years ago."

She stood up. Luke had consumed enough of her time today. "If you don't have anything else, can I walk you out?"

He stood, ready to leave, she was certain, but then he looked down and his lips curled into a smug smile. "Boundaries, huh? I haven't seen that cover in years."

Those damn magazines Abby brought. She'd forgotten they were on the corner of her desk. Of course he would see them. Of course he would. If she'd only spent her time cleaning her desk instead of touching up her lipstick.

"Abby brought those by. Someone she knows found them and recognized me."

His finger traced the image of her face. "Is that right?"

"Yes, your name wasn't even mentioned." She added that just to show him how little she thought of him and his visit and his photography skills.

He lifted his head and the grin that had started out in the corner of his mouth spread to his entire face. "The lady doth protest too much, methinks."

"I don't know what you're talking about, Shakespeare."

Still smiling, he moved to her side of the desk and stood much too close. "You see, sweetheart, when you have to constantly say something, it comes across as if you're trying to convince yourself of the fact."

She rolled her eyes. "I forgot. Not only are you a photographer—you're also a freaking mind reader. Tell me, is it your experience behind the camera or as a Dom that makes you think you know everything?"

He chuckled and the sound was warm and inviting and seductive. "Now, you know I don't claim to know everything. But I know this." He stroked her cheekbone with the back of his hand. "I still make your blood race and your heart pound. You and I have unfinished business and one of these days, we're going to see it to completion."

Damn him for knowing her so well. She jerked away. "In one of your better dreams, maybe."

He ignored her barb. "I know because *you* make *my* blood race and *my* heart pound and I'm not going to ignore it forever."

She breezed past him and opened the door. "I don't expect you to ignore it forever. Ignoring it for the next fifty years will suit me just fine."

"Keep telling yourself that, sweetheart. No need to walk me out. I know the way." He hesitated at the door and turned back. "We were great together once, Meagan, and frankly, I think we'd be even better now. If you change your mind . . ."

"If I change my mind, I'll have myself committed."

He tipped an imaginary hat and left.

She thought that would be the last she heard or even thought about Luke for a long time. Since she'd already made up her mind not to go to his club anymore, she wouldn't see him there and the truth was, they really didn't travel in the same social circles.

But even though she didn't see him, she wasn't able to banish him from her thoughts quite as easily as she thought she should. After the day he stopped by, he popped into her mind at the

most inopportune times. Like when one of the Doms she casu-
ally played with happened to call. She told herself she turned
down his offer of playing because she was really busy with work,
but deep inside she knew better. It was because of Luke.

Since he'd mentioned taking erotic pictures of her, whenever
she thought about playing with anyone, an image of *him* came
to mind.

A week after his visit, she finally got around to putting the
magazines away.

That, she decided, was that.

But two days later, she sat at her desk, trembling, as she reread
the e-mail on her screen for the fifth time.

> It's reckoning day, bitch. I bet after all these years, you
> thought no one knew what you did seventeen years
> ago. That's exactly what I wanted you to think. But
> now it's time to pay up or be exposed for the lying
> whore you are.
>
> Luke DeVaan has some things I want and you're
> going to get them for me. I don't care how you do it. I'm
> sure a slut like you can think of something.
>
> We'll start easy with a little test. Find out the location
> of his next building site and reply to this e-mail. You
> have three days. If you fail, you will be punished.
>
> Don't fuck up,
> The Taskmaster

Seventeen years ago? She swallowed. She had been so certain
only her brother knew what happened that summer. If the person who sent the e-mail had any idea, it could not only damage

her life and her brother's, but also ruin the reputation her father had worked so hard for.

The e-mail address was generic. She drummed her fingers on her desk and tried to think of someone she knew who could discreetly look into who it belonged to. The problem was she'd have to let them read the e-mail and she did not want to go into what happened that summer seventeen years ago.

Damn it.

She wasn't going to the police, obviously. Not without thinking this through more. And she wasn't about to give in to the demands. Which left her doing nothing.

It was probably no more than a game of chicken and she wasn't interested in playing. With a nod of her head and few quick keystrokes, she deleted the e-mail.

She tried not to think of it in the days that followed, but it was difficult. She kept wondering who it could be, what exactly they knew, and what they were going to do at the end of three days. Hadn't she always heard that you weren't supposed to give in to blackmail demands? That things would only escalate?

At times, that thought was enough to convince her she'd made the right decision. Unfortunately, that wasn't the case the majority of the time.

On the third day after receiving the e-mail, she admitted she couldn't focus on anything. She jumped at every unexpected noise, looked over her shoulder constantly, and dreaded every moment her e-mail indicated a new message had arrived.

When her phone rang shortly after lunch, she almost didn't answer it. But a quick glance at the display told her it was Abby calling. With a sigh of relief, she hit the CONNECT button.

"Hey, girl," she said. "What's up?"

"Umm, I'm not exactly sure." Something in Abby's voice,

along with her words, set off her internal alarm. "I just got this e-mail."

Meagan's stomach fell to the ground. She didn't want to ask, but she had to. "What kind of e-mail?"

"It's, ah, a naked picture of you."

Her grip tightened on the phone. "What?"

"I don't recognize the e-mail address and the message says, 'Your boss is a slut.'"

Meagan closed her eyes. Shit. "Forward to me," she managed to get out.

"Do you want me to try to figure out who sent it? I'm sure Nathaniel—"

"No." Meagan couldn't even fathom bringing Abby's husband into this. For starters, the man didn't like her. And there was no way she wanted him to see her naked. She shivered. "No, thank you. I'm pretty sure I know who it is."

She was surprised how easily the lie fell from her lips.

"Okay." Abby didn't sound convinced. "If you're sure."

"Yes, completely. Just forward it to me and I'll take care of it."

"Let me know what you find out."

"Will do." But Meagan wasn't sure she wanted to involve Abby.

Abby didn't waste any time getting off the phone and within seconds of disconnecting, the e-mail arrived in Meagan's in-box. She looked at it, not really wanting to open it, but knowing she had to. With a sigh, she clicked on it and watched as it opened on her screen.

In the brief moments since Abby mentioned the picture, she'd wondered what sort of naked picture it was and was horribly afraid of the answer all at the same time. That weekend with Luke, their first and only, he'd taken some shots of her. Did those pictures even exist anymore? She didn't know, but she sure as hell would find out.

The truth, when she saw it, made her heart skip a beat. It was definitely her and she was naked, but the most alarming thing about the photo—she was in her house. And from the date stamp, it was taken this morning as she got ready for work.

She reached for the phone to call the police, but her fingers hovered just over the numbers. How could she bring up the picture without telling them about the blackmail? And if she mentioned the blackmail, she'd have to confess about her brother. Shit. She couldn't contact the police after all.

She drummed her fingers on her desk, trying to figure out what to do next when her laptop pinged with a message.

> *I see you decided to go about this the hard way.—The Taskmaster*

Beyond the message, what freaked her out more was that it was sent via interoffice chat. Holy fuck, did the blackmailer work for NNN? Her fingers flew over the keyboard.

> **Who are you? How did you get that picture? Do you work here?**

The reply was almost instant.

> *I don't think you're in a position to ask questions.*

She was typing out a reply when the next message popped up.

> *You have 24 hrs to get me the next club's location. You think that picture's bad, wait until your entire office sees the ones you actually posed for.*

He knew and he had the pictures. *Damn it, Luke.* But in reality she should have been cursing herself. She was the one who allowed him to take the pictures in the first place.

Fine. You win, she replied.

I always do.

The interoffice chat box disappeared and she picked up her phone to call the IT Department.

"Hello, Ms. Bishop. How can I help you?"

"Can you tell me which employee has the chat name Task-master?"

"Management doesn't allow nicknames like that."

She took a deep breath so she wouldn't take her anger out on the poor guy who had the bad luck to take her call. "I know that. Can you do a quick search anyway?"

"Sure, I don't have anything better to do. Hold on."

From the other end of the phone came the sound of typing and then silence.

"No, ma'am. No Taskmaster." He made no attempt to hide his *I told you so* tone.

"Thank you," she said and hung up.

What were the odds someone hacked into the company's computer system? It would make sense. Especially since the chat message arrived almost immediately after she opened the e-mail. Or had someone simply hacked into her computer?

Either way, it looked as if she was going to have to talk to Luke sooner than she'd anticipated. With a sigh, she reached for her phone and dialed.

"Hello?"

"Hello, Luke?"

"Meagan?" His voice was tinged with disbelief.

"What the hell did you do with those pictures of me you took fifteen years ago?"

There was silence from the other end of the phone. She got up and closed her office door. "I'm waiting."

"Which pictures?"

"Don't *which pictures* me. The ones of me naked. Do you have them?"

"Jesus, Meagan. What's this about? Of course I have them."

"Can anyone get to them?"

"Not unless they go through me first."

His assurance didn't ease her panic. "I want them."

"Okay. No problem." He paused before continuing. "Is everything okay?"

Her heart had stopped pounding once he told her she could have the pictures. She took a deep breath and tried to sound normal. "Yes, it's only someone I know had some pictures leaked and I thought about the ones you had."

"Should I bring them by your office?"

"No." She made up her mind quickly. It wasn't that much of a decision: her life versus talking with Luke about his offer. "Why don't we get together and talk about the photo book thing. You can bring them then. Can you meet tonight?"

Luke shook his head as he shoved his phone back in his pocket, but he couldn't keep the grin off his face. Meagan called. And she said she wanted to talk about the shoot. He couldn't fathom what had changed her mind, but he was glad it did. He knew there was a reason he never got around to telling Rick, his partner bankrolling the book, that she wasn't interested and they'd have to find another model.

Even better, she'd asked him to dinner. Granted, she insisted it was a business dinner and not a date. "So don't go getting any ideas," she'd said.

Useless words, he'd almost told her. When it came to her, he had nothing but ideas. Still, for the time being, he'd play it her way. The important thing was they were going to have dinner and at least talk about the upcoming photography project. He smiled. It was more than he thought possible after visiting her office.

He'd never quite forgiven himself for the way things ended with Meagan all those years ago. Young and relatively inexperienced, he'd taken the cover shots of her and later that night invited her to dinner, which led to round after round of hot and heavy sex. He had been on top of the world: his photography was doing well and he had Meagan in his bed. She'd been his every fantasy come to life: smart, sexy, and willing to experiment in bed. He'd never been in love before, but during those short few weeks with Meagan, he'd fallen hard and fast. So much so that he didn't stop to think about anything other than how perfect things were.

But a more experienced photographer, one he considered a mentor and friend, found out about his affair with Meagan and strongly suggested he call an end to it. Luke didn't regret ending the relationship. Looking back now, it was unprofessional and sent the wrong message to any potential models. He did, however, regret that she'd been hurt. Seeing it from her perspective, he'd gone from hot to cold in a matter of days.

He couldn't change the past; all he could do was make the present better.

He pushed open the door to his latest BDSM club and nodded at the security guard. Nathaniel West had messaged him earlier, asking for a brief call, and Luke expected his phone to ring any minute. If he had to guess, he'd assume it was about the club the two men planned to build in Wilmington, Delaware. Damn, he hoped it didn't interfere with the picture book. He knew Meagan said she only wanted to talk, but he knew he could convince her to do the job if he could just talk to her about it some more.

Construction in Delaware might throw a kink in his plans.

His phone rang as soon as he sat down at his desk. "Nathaniel, hello."

"Hey, Luke. Thanks for agreeing to talk on such short notice. We're heading out this afternoon and I'm not going to be easily accessible for the next week."

"Going somewhere fun with Abby?"

"And the kids. We're going to our chalet in Switzerland. First time we're taking the kids."

He felt a ping of jealously. Nathaniel was one lucky SOB with his gorgeous wife and submissive, and they had two great kids. But he also knew that, just like anything worth having, the Wests worked hard on their relationship.

"I hope you and Abby manage to get some alone time," he half joked.

"That's what nap time is for, my friend."

Luke laughed. "I hear you. So tell me what's going on."

He heard Nathaniel sigh and a chair squeak as he leaned back. "I heard back from Fritz Brose."

Fritz was the contractor they wanted for the Partners Club in Delaware. He'd been recommended by Cole Johnson, one of the senior group members. Luke had never worked with Fritz, but had heard of him and, after talking with Fritz in person, both he and Nathaniel knew he was the man for the job.

"What did he have to say?"

"His schedule isn't going to allow for him to be in the States for any length of time, much less to start on the club, for at least another six months."

Luke breathed a sigh of relief. "To be honest, that's not bad news for me. I potentially have a project that's going to take up a lot of my time. Six months would allow me to complete it."

"Same for me. I'm rearranging my executive staff in New York and I need to focus on that. Well, when I get back into the country, that is."

"Do you want me to call Fritz back and tell him we're okay with the time frame?"

"No, I can take care of it."

After he got off the phone with Nathaniel, Luke leaned back in his chair and smiled. For the moment, everything was going his way. Now he just needed to get Meagan on board. . . .

That night, Luke sat in a Manhattan deli waiting for Meagan to show up. Everything had been her idea, from the time they met, to the location. Had it been up to Luke, he'd have picked her up and taken her to a nice restaurant. But instead, he'd let Meagan have her way and that meant the entire vibe for the evening screamed, *This is not a date!*

As if he needed the reminder.

She must have felt the need to prove she wasn't lying the least bit, because she walked in ten minutes late, talking on her cell phone, and barely acknowledged his existence. Without giving any sort of indication that she even knew he was there, she slid into the corner booth he'd selected, sat down, and continued her conversation.

"Right," she was saying to whoever was on the phone. "That's the angle I thought we should take." She paused to let the person on the other end talk. "But what else would you expect?"

Luke cleared his throat. She glanced his way for the first time and held up a hand.

"Yes," she continued. "I agree. Talk it over and call me back."

"Don't let me keep you from anything," Luke said.

"You're not." She put the phone in her purse, and placed her hands in her lap. "Thank you for agreeing to meet with me."

"I'm at your disposal whenever you need me." Was it just him or did she look uncomfortable? She fidgeted in her seat and her eyes swept the deli. "Are you okay?" he asked.

"Yes. Sorry. It's been a strange week. Nothing major."

He didn't believe her. There was something going on. Something more than just a strange week. But for the moment, he would let it slide.

"I was surprised to get your call," he said, bringing the conversation back to why they were sitting at the same table on a *definitely not a date* get-together. He passed her the envelope containing the nude pictures he'd taken of her years ago. "That's all of them. I don't even have copies. Now, what additional information can I give you about the art project?"

"Can you give me a feel for the pictures? Will I be alone or will there be a Dom in the scene with me? Will I be naked? Is there any way to conceal my identity? I really don't want people to know I'm doing this. *If* I agree, that is."

Luke bit back his laugh. "One question at a time, sweetheart."

She flopped back in her chair and crossed her arms, but didn't say anything. Clearly, she was waiting for him to say something.

"You'll probably be naked for some of the photographs, but don't worry. This isn't pornography. It's an art book. And as of right this second, I don't foresee bringing a Dom in, but you never know. And we can work it out to where your name isn't listed and your face isn't visible."

She nodded. "What's your time frame?"

"I would like to get the project wrapped up in the next few months."

"And if I agree to this, how long will it take and when will you need me?"

"I know you're busy and have a demanding job. I think we could get together weekends only. Maybe Saturdays?"

"It's because of my job that I don't want it public that I'm the model."

Her request made perfect sense and shouldn't be a problem. He could only imagine how difficult it might make her job if word got out she'd posed for a BDSM photography book. No matter how artful it was. "Of course, Meagan. I wouldn't want to do anything that caused you trouble or made you uncomfortable."

She didn't answer right away, but pulled out her phone. He assumed she was checking her calendar. Since her attention was elsewhere, he could study her without her feeling uncomfortable.

She was a stunning woman, and the way she sat with her head bent down made her hair swing forward. The late-afternoon sun rays touched the blond strands, bringing out such beautiful hues, he doubted there were names for all of them. His fingers itched to pick up his camera and capture everything.

Their time together had been short-lived, but left a permanent impression on him. She'd been relatively inexperienced sexually when they were together, and he'd already been heavily involved in the BDSM scene. He'd thought he'd surprise her that weekend when he brought the rope out. But the real surprise turned out to be her and how much she enjoyed everything they did together. The sight of her discovering her submissive nature had been one of the most beautiful and erotic things he'd ever witnessed.

Damn, he'd been an idiot to leave her.

He'd been wrong to walk away from her the way he had. It had been for the best they broke up, but he'd gone about it the wrong way. She'd been vulnerable, trying to come to terms with her newly discovered sexuality. He knew that now. He might have called himself a Dom, but he'd still had a lot to learn.

"Okay," she said, looking up. "I'm not saying I'm definitely going to do it, but I'll agree to one session to see if I want to continue."

He nodded and tried to cover up his excitement. He'd get her in his studio and do everything within his power to make sure she'd come back. "I can work with that."

"Can you start this weekend or will you be busy with your club?"

"I can start this weekend. The New Jersey club is doing well and the staff can handle a day without me."

Her head tilted. "I was sort of surprised you ended up building clubs, what with you being artsy and all."

"Photography became a side venture for me. I like managing the clubs, providing space for people to play safely."

"How many do you have now?"

"Two as of today. Nathaniel and I are planning to build one in Wilmington, Delaware, but the contractor isn't available at the moment, so the timelines for that one have been moved back."

"That'll be good for the Partner's Group. I'm assuming that's who it's for?"

"Yes, Nathaniel said they needed a place to get together. Apparently, at the moment, they normally get together at another member's house." Luke recalled she worked with Abby; he needed to remember that. Something had happened between the two women early in Abby's employment. From the pieces he'd been able to put together, whatever it was hadn't been completely Meagan's fault, though she had been negligent. To this day, Luke could tell Nathaniel didn't care too much for her.

"I can see how they'd want to get the new place built quickly," she said.

"Yes, well, some things can't be helped." And he'd put off working on the club for years if it meant he would be able to have Meagan in front of his camera again.

"Anything in particular I need to do or bring this weekend? And where are we going to shoot?"

"I'll have everything we need. And"—he watched her carefully for the next part—"I have a studio at my house. If you're comfortable with that, we could do everything there."

She sucked in the corner of her lip and bit it. "That should be fine."

"If meeting at my house makes you uncomfortable, I can book a studio." It wouldn't be optimal, but he'd do it in order to have her.

"No, it's okay. That'll be fine." Her voice dropped to a whisper. "I trust you."

Her words hit him squarely in the chest. That she could trust him, even after the botched-up way he'd left things years ago, touched him deeply. "Thank you, Meagan."

Damn. Damn. And triple damn. Meagan glanced at the time on her laptop. It was almost midnight and she had to get the e-mail to The Taskmaster. She wasn't about to have a naked picture of herself sent out to every person who worked at NNN.

Truthfully, she hadn't anticipated being out so late. Dinner with Luke had run a bit longer than she planned. After agreeing to do the one session and getting the information about the club he was building with Nathaniel, she couldn't just up and leave the table. She hated to admit it, but Luke had been right when he came by her office that day. There was unfinished business between them and she really wanted to do at least one photo shoot with him.

It would be useless to deny how thoughts of their last one affected her still. The way he'd looked at her with an intensity so strong he may as well have been touching her. Then, when he did touch her, even if he was only positioning her . . . God, she was an idiot, but she wanted to feel his hands on her again.

After dinner, she made a spur-of-the-moment decision to work out of the office the next day and to check in at the bed-and-breakfast near the Hamptons she often visited when she wanted to get out of New York City. Traffic had been horrible, though, and it took her almost double the amount of time it normally did to arrive.

She typed out a response to The Taskmaster's last e-mail as quickly as she could.

> *The next club is in Wilmington, Delaware. Timelines have been pushed back. No opening date at the moment.*

She didn't acknowledge his Taskmaster nickname or include her own. She looked back up at the time: eleven thirty-six. Close, but she'd made it.

The reply came back almost instantly.

Cutting it awfully close, aren't you?

Anger pounded in her veins.

You said by midnight. I obeyed.

He didn't reply and that made her restless. There was only one person who could keep her mind off The Taskmaster and that was Luke. She sat back in the chair and closed her eyes. Remembering.

Chapter Two

Fifteen years ago

He asked her out to dinner not long after taking the last photo. In fact, he came up behind her as she was taking off her makeup, their eyes locked in the mirror, and simply said, "Will you have dinner with me?" And just like that, with those six words, he started her down a road that would forever color how she looked at the world.

Hours before he was to pick her up, she made a mess in her bedroom. She emptied her closet, not liking anything she saw. The outfit had to be perfect. He was a photographer, for crying out loud. He looked at beautiful women every day.

The pile of discarded clothing on top of her bed climbed to ridiculous heights, matching the panic that grew within her with each passing second. The date was going to be disastrous. Seriously, she couldn't even find something to wear. He'd show up and she'd be naked. Wouldn't that be the perfect way to start the date?

She posed the question to her roommate, Tessa, who only smiled and nodded and said, yes, it sounded like the perfect date to her. Meagan threw a sweater at her. Tessa finally grabbed her arm and dragged her down the hall to her room.

"I've been saving this outfit for a special date." Tessa opened her closet. "But since Lloyd and I broke up, it won't be happening anytime soon, so I want you to wear it tonight. For your photographer."

Meagan didn't know Tessa had such a beautiful dress in her closet. Most of her clothes were grunge, but the dress she held out was a classically elegant black sheath.

Meagan ran a finger over the V neckline. "Are you sure? I mean, I'd love to. But if it's that special . . ."

"No, it's not. Please. It's more suited for you anyway."

She didn't want to let on how much she'd like to wear the dress. "If you're sure."

Tessa smiled. "Positive. There's only one condition."

"What's that?"

"You have to let *him* take it off," she said with a devious twinkle in her eye.

Like that would happen, Meagan wanted to say, but instead nodded. "Sure thing."

Tessa pushed the dress at her. "Go. Change. Be fabulous."

Her roommate's advice repeated in her head hours later as she stood in Luke's apartment. He'd taken her to an upscale steak house in the city and when they finished their entrees, he oh so smoothly asked if she'd like to go back to his place. "For dessert."

"Depends on what you're planning to serve," she replied with a slight smile and a tilt of her head. In that moment she was on top of the world and she felt as if she was invincible. She was a goddess and had the world in the palm of her hand. In the last week, she'd had her first photo shoot for the cover of a magazine, she'd been asked out by Luke DeVaan, the up-and-coming photographer everyone was talking about, and he'd just asked her to his place.

This, she decided, was living.

But when he looked her square in the eyes and answered with "You," she realized she had no idea what living was.

It was as if she had been born that night. Or something inside her was born. Sure, she'd had sex before. But it'd been with guys, boys, really, who were all fumbling fingers. Too eager to get off to even bother seeing if she was satisfied. Much less to try to find out what she liked.

Luke, though, was no boy. And, in all honesty, *guy* didn't fit him either. No, Luke was one hundred percent man. The first time he took her slow and easy. He was so intent, it almost seemed as if he wasn't concerned with his need. Every question he asked, every touch of his hand, was about *her*. Did she like it when he stroked her here? Was this area sensitive?

At times she felt as if he was a student and his final exam was her. She learned things about her body she didn't know. Especially after they recovered from that first time.

They spent the entire weekend in bed. And Luke called in and canceled his meetings on Monday.

He got up from the bed after making the call, gloriously naked and not embarrassed at all. It was somehow soothing, the ease and comfort he found in being naked. She wondered if it had to do with his being a photographer. Whatever it was, it made her feel confident, too. When he got up from the bed, she sat up, not even caring she was naked. She didn't even attempt to cover her breasts. If Luke could do it, she could, too.

Odd. Before, with anyone else, she felt all sorts of uncomfortable at being naked after sex. There were times she couldn't get her clothes on fast enough. And her partners hadn't been any better.

Yes, she decided. She could get used to a man like Luke.

She'd assumed he was going to the bathroom, and when he went out the bedroom door instead, she decided he must have needed a glass of water or something. She almost called out to him to bring her a glass, but before she could, he was walking back into the bedroom with something in his hand.

He held it out and her heart jumped up in her throat. *Rope.* "I'd like to try something," he said. "You don't have to. I won't push it or anything. But if you're open to a little bit of experimenting, I think you'll really like it."

He'd been right, of course. At first, she wasn't sure she wanted to be tied up. The sex had been incredible by itself and she'd always been one to believe that if it wasn't broken, there was no reason to fix it. More times than not, if you messed with something needlessly, it only created havoc.

But with Luke, the rope became an extension of him. He was so knowledgeable and, though it didn't seem possible, his focus grew even more intense. As he worked the rope around her body, she didn't feel restricted at all. She felt secure and safe. She fell into what seemed like a trance while he worked. He moved hypnotically with the rope, binding her for his pleasure.

He told her not to move and she didn't dare disobey. She feared if she did, he'd stop and she didn't think she could stand that. When he finally stepped away and held up a mirror so she could see herself, she nearly hummed in pleasure.

She looked sexy and grown-up. What's more, she *felt* sexy and grown-up. Like a woman. The rope wrapped around her upper body, twisted around her breasts, leaving her nipples exposed, and then went behind her back like a halter top.

"Beautiful, isn't it?" he asked.

She nodded and brushed her fingers over the soft coils. "I never knew you could use rope for something like this."

"I'm just learning," he said.

"People *teach* this kind of stuff?"

He gave a little laugh and she felt a bit silly, not at all like the sophisticated woman she'd told herself she was. Of course people taught this sort of thing. You had to learn somehow.

"Yes," he said in confirmation of what she'd already decided. "I'm a member of a club and they have special classes teaching things like this." His smile grew wider. "According to them, since I just tied you up, you should be calling me 'Sir.'"

She wrinkled her nose at the thought of that.

"What's that look for?" he asked.

"Call you 'Sir'? Really?" She shook her head. "Never. It reminds me of my dad and that kills my mood."

"Mmm, I see." He didn't seem to have thought of it in quite that way before. "Look at it like this. It turns me on when you call me *Sir*."

"It does?" She thought about it some more. "It doesn't make you feel like you're my dad?"

"In no way does it make me feel like I'm your dad." He moved a bit closer, that smile of his hinting at wickedness. "Maybe more like that hot teacher you had a crush on in high school."

"I didn't have a hot-teacher crush in high school." She did actually, but she wasn't about to tell him about it.

"No?" His eyes seemed to pierce right through her and she knew he realized the truth. "I don't think I believe you. Tell me who he was."

She crossed her arms as best she could over her chest. "No."

"Now I can tell you're lying." His smile grew even bigger. "I spank girls who lie to me."

Her mouth dropped open. *"Spank?"* Now she knew for certain he had a daddy fantasy going on. "I thought you said you didn't do the daddy thing."

"I don't."

"But you want to spank me and have me call you Sir."

"Which has nothing to do with a daddy fantasy."

"What does it have to do with then?"

"Have you heard of BDSM?"

She told him no and for the next twenty minutes, they talked. She still wasn't sure she understood everything, but it made a bit more sense. And the way he talked about it made it sound hot.

It became even hotter when he took her over his knee and spanked her.

She lost track of the number of times she came that day. And when she woke up in his arms on Tuesday, he took her again. Tessa laughed when Meagan called her over breakfast and told her she wouldn't be home just yet.

"Seems like the dress worked," Tessa said.

Something certainly did, Meagan had to agree. She wasn't so sure it was the dress, though. Probably, it was that shirt made out of rope.

She ended up begging him to put her in bondage again and he gladly did so. On Wednesday, he wove the rope around the lower part of her body. It was during that hypnotic time that he was binding her, that she began to imagine their future. They could work together as a team: he'd take the pictures and she'd model. Then at night, he could tie her up and have his wicked way with her.

She'd even call him *Sir*.

It was so perfect. So right. Together they'd be unstoppable. They'd be on top of the world. Heck, they'd *own* the world.

"Why are you smiling so big?" he asked at one point.

But she wasn't ready to share her dream just yet. It seemed too soon and she didn't want to freak him out. Maybe in a month or two. Or six. When they'd been together for long enough that he'd see how good they were together. How much better they would become. Then they'd talk and he'd agree how perfect they were, and then they'd be together forever.

She got giddy just thinking about how wonderful it was all going to be.

"Nothing," she answered. "Just happy."

"Me, too," he said, and her heart soared because it sounded as if he was already well on the way to seeing how good they were going to be.

"Kiss me," she whispered, needing to feel him.

He pulled her close and gave her one of those kisses that made her entire body feel electric. She wondered idly if any of the crew at their next photo shoot would be able to tell they were together.

"Do you have another job lined up?" she asked when he pulled back.

He resumed working the rope around her left ankle. "I have a few meetings set up later this week that I can't blow off. Do you have anything?"

"No." She didn't, but she knew the pictures from their shoot were going to be fantastic. It was only a matter of time before people came knocking on her door. She just had to be patient.

She looked down and caught Luke staring at her. He leaned down and nibbled on the inside of her ankle bone. *Gah. That felt good.* She sucked in a breath and leaned her head back.

She had no problem being patient. No, not at all. Not with Luke here to distract her.

She finally made it back to her apartment on Thursday. Tessa laughed and shook her head when Meagan headed straight to the bathroom for a long, hot soak in the tub.

When he didn't call that weekend, she told herself it was because he had all those meetings he'd brought up. And she knew how those could be. Get a bunch of creative people together in a room with a bunch of number crunchers and nothing was getting done anytime soon.

He'd call soon, though. She felt certain.

On the following Monday night, she called her answering machine herself, just to make sure it was working. He had to be really busy, right? It was getting harder and harder to believe.

She was torn when Friday night came and Tessa invited her to a club. She didn't want to go out. What if he called while she was gone? So she told Tessa that Luke came down with the flu and she was staying home.

When Tessa gave her that *I can see what you're doing* look, Meagan explained that she couldn't go out because her throat was scratchy and it wouldn't be very responsible of her to spread germs around all of Manhattan, would it?

Either Tessa couldn't come up with a counterargument, or she saw the truth and didn't want to push. She gave Meagan a hug, told her not to wait up, and left.

As soon as she was gone, Meagan raided the freezer and downed an entire pint of chocolate chip cookie dough. Through her tears, she thought back to their time together, trying to figure out what she'd done wrong. She couldn't think of anything. Everything had been so wonderful. So fulfilling. And she hadn't done anything stupid like talk about the future.

All she could come up with was that he wanted someone with more experience in the bondage scene. He probably wanted someone who wouldn't balk at calling him 'Sir.' For all she knew, he might have taken it the wrong way when she asked about the daddy fantasy thing. With that remark, maybe she'd disrespected him.

She hadn't looked any further into the BDSM scene, hoping that he'd be the one to instruct her in everything. If she had truly scared him off, should she research the topic more herself? Was it something she'd want to pursue without him?

She decided to think about it later, when it became obvious he didn't want her.

Damn it, her heart hurt just thinking about it and she couldn't help but hold out some sort of hope that she was wrong.

By the time he showed up at her apartment unexpectedly a week later, though, she knew the truth. He didn't want her. And that was unmistakable when she opened the door at his knock and let him in. His eyes said everything before he even spoke. She was glad Tessa had gone away with her sister for the weekend. Meagan had the feeling she was going to have an ugly cry when Luke left and she'd rather be alone for it.

She let him in without saying a word and neither one of them said anything until she closed the door.

"Meagan——" he started, but she cut him off.

"You know," she said. Fuck, he looked so guilty. "You could have called. I'm a big girl."

"I know you are." He hung his head, as though he didn't want to look at her. "It's just that after that week . . ."

She waved her hand, telling herself to act as if those days and nights together were something she did all the time. Pretend she had torrid affairs every night of the week. "Please, it was just sex. You didn't propose or anything."

His head shot up in surprise and he studied her with those eyes that had been so inquisitive before. She schooled her features and forced her body to remain neutral. She could do this. She refused to show him how hurt she was.

"Oh," he finally said.

"You feel the same, right?" she asked. "I mean, I just assumed you did. Especially after I didn't hear from you."

He ran a hand through his hair. "It's complicated."

She snorted and it sounded so real, she was proud of herself. "Complicated? Come on. We were two horny people who scratched an itch. What's complicated about it? Nothing."

He looked bewildered. "It's complicated because of the work we did together. It wouldn't do either of us any good to have the reputation of sleeping with people we work with. Well, it might do you some good. Get you more offers, but they probably wouldn't be the kind you wanted or be from the people you wanted . . ."

He continued rambling and she tuned him out. Basically, she just smiled and nodded. Thank God she beat him to the *this isn't going to work* speech. She was so glad he didn't call sooner. What if he had and she'd blurted out something stupid? Yes, it was much better this way.

"He was the one who helped me see how bad it would be for us to be together." Luke was still talking. Truthfully, she had no idea what he was saying or who he was even talking about.

Suddenly, she just wanted him out of her apartment. Enough

already. What was done was done and it was time for her to accept it and move on.

"Listen," she said, cutting off whatever it was he was saying. "I hate to cut this short, but I need to get ready."

He lifted an eyebrow. "You're going out?"

"Yes, and"—she looked at her watch—"I'm running a bit late now. So, sorry to cut this short, but . . ."

"Right," he said. "I'll just be going."

He turned to head to the door and, at the last second, looked over his shoulder. For the briefest moment, it looked as if he was going to say something further, but when he spoke all he said was, "Good-bye, Meagan."

She steeled herself. Five more seconds and he'd be out the door. Then she could break down. Four seconds. "Good-bye, Luke."

Three.

He opened the door.

Two.

He walked out.

One.

The door closed behind him. She dropped to her knees on the floor and let the tears fall.

Chapter Three

Tired and cranky, she woke up the following morning only to see whoever The Taskmaster was hadn't replied. Fine, she thought, let him be that way. At least there wouldn't be a naked picture of her sent out. She tried to work a few hours, but thoughts of her and Luke and the camera wouldn't allow her to concentrate.

Before they parted ways the night before, Luke had asked if Saturday was too soon to start. She didn't have any plans for the weekend and, since The Taskmaster had insinuated that there would be more information he wanted from Luke, she thought it for the best she do something to speed the relationship up a bit. That way, it wouldn't seem so strange to approach Luke whenever her next order came through.

She fucking hated that she was allowing herself to be used the way she was. But she had no choice. Not if she wanted to protect herself and her brother. She felt bad about using Luke as well, but in this war, he was just a necessary casualty. Besides, it wasn't as if she was hurting him in any way. If she looked at it from a different angle, she was actually doing him a favor. After all, he'd been the one to approach her, not the other way around. That was the way she was going to look at it going forward. She wasn't doing anything to hurt him. She was helping.

She did wonder briefly about the timing of the first e-mail following so closely with Luke stopping by to see her. Were the two related somehow? She tried to picture Luke as The Taskmaster, but nothing about that fit.

She rolled her shoulders. What she needed was a good hard scene with someone. Unfortunately, she didn't want to play with any of the Dominants that came to mind. She could always call one of the girls she played with, but what she needed wasn't to take control from someone, but to give it. Besides, after the dream last night, she was hot and bothered and wanted sex. If she played with one of the girls she Topped, she wouldn't get her own release. Sure, to take control of someone else's pleasure was heady, but tonight she wanted someone to take control of *her*.

When Luke left her years ago, she had no idea what to do with the new understanding and knowledge she had about her sexual nature. Wanting to prove to herself that it was more than just Luke, she'd gone to a local club and, within two hours, found that she enjoyed Topping as well.

What followed was a year of self-discovery and by the time Luke had been out of her life for twelve months, she'd found what she needed. When playing with men, she craved being submissive. But when it came to women, she preferred the other side of the crop. With the girls she played with, though, she always made it very clear she didn't have sex while Topping.

Many of them wanted the release that came from pain and a few just had the need to serve.

She gave them what they needed and took what they would offer her. It was a mutually beneficial arrangement. But today, that wasn't what she craved. Unfortunately, she knew she wasn't going to get what she wanted, so she did her best to put Luke, sex, and any combination of the two out of her mind.

Wednesday night, she knew she had to do something. She didn't think she'd be able to submit to anyone with Luke fresh in her mind, so she slipped on her black leather and went to a nearby club.

It wasn't as nice as Luke's, but surely it would do for the night.

"Mistress B," the bouncer working the door said when he saw her. "Been a while since we've seen you. How are you?"

"I'm well, Master C. Hope you are."

The tall, muscular man nodded and looked her up and down. "I'd be better if you weren't here as a Top."

Meagan had played with him once and that had been enough. He was competent enough, but something about playing with him didn't work for her. Unfortunately, he didn't feel the same and ever since that one time, he'd been bugging her to do another scene with him. She'd told him she didn't get the same vibe he got when they were together, but he seemed to think if they just tried again, she'd feel it.

Eventually, she got tired of saying the same thing over and over, and she made up her mind to visit that particular club only as a Top. So far it had worked and Master C no longer asked her to play.

"Some nights being submissive isn't what I need—know what I mean?" she asked.

He shook his head. "Being submissive is never what I need."

"Maybe you should try it sometime," she said. "Most subs I know like it when their Dom has been on the other side."

He gave her a smug smile. "I think you just want me on my knees before you."

Which just proved that he didn't know her at all. "I only Top women, Master C. I'm totally submissive when I play with men."

Someone else came up behind her and Master C turned his attention to them. Meagan scurried into the club before he finished business and wanted to continue the conversation.

Once inside, she breathed a sigh of relief, but it was short-lived. It took only one look around the club to know this wasn't going to make her feel better. Seeing the various women she'd played with before look her way with the hope in their eyes that she'd pick them for a scene, left her feeling nothing.

She tried telling herself to give it a few minutes; that it would look odd if she left immediately after showing up. She made her way to the bar and ordered a drink; maybe the alcohol would loosen her up enough to get her in the mood for a scene.

It wasn't to be, though. She could blame it on the drink that didn't loosen her up at all. Or she could blame the bartender for not using enough alcohol. But she did neither of those things. Instead, she blamed herself. It was her fault for thinking she needed to be the one in charge when, in fact, it was the opposite. She made herself a promise that the next time she went out to a club, she'd go as a sub.

Before she could finish her drink and discreetly leave, a Dom she was friends with came up to the bar and sat down beside her.

"Mistress B," he said with a nod, "how are you doing?"

"Hey, Master G. To be honest, I was just thinking about heading home."

She decided he must have seen her sitting by herself and thought she wanted company. She most certainly did not, and she really didn't want the company of someone who just came over because she looked lonely.

He wasn't a close friend; they only talked when she visited this particular club. He was about her age, though, and she knew Melissa, his collared submissive. Melissa worked part-time at the bed-and-breakfast Meagan went to occasionally. She looked around the room, trying to find her. Master G and Melissa were normally together. Meagan finally saw Melissa on the other side of the room, talking with a group of submissives.

"Leaving so soon?" Master G asked. "You just got here."

"I know." She took a deep breath and figured she might as well tell him the truth. "I've had a lot on my mind this week, and I thought it'd be a good idea to come here. But I'm not in the proper headspace to Top tonight."

He nodded in understanding. "That makes sense. Too bad, though. I heard some of the single submissive ladies whispering about how long it'd been since you've been here and how they hoped you'd pick them to play with tonight."

Great, she thought. *Now on top of everything else, I'm letting more people down.*

"I hate that," she admitted. "But it truly would be a bad idea for me to Top anyone tonight."

He didn't say anything, but studied her in that way Doms did. As if he was slowly peeling back the layers of the mask she showed the world in an attempt to get to her true self. She schooled her features, determined not to give anything away. But he kept studying her, and she dipped her head.

"I overheard you say once that you're a switch?" he asked.

"Yes," she confirmed, and then to keep the conversation from going in the direction she thought it was headed, she added, "But I don't submit here. I only Top."

He held his hand up. "I wasn't going to suggest you sub. Not here, anyway. Though I do think *that's* probably what you need."

She allowed herself a terse laugh. "That obvious?"

"Only to those of us with eyes."

"Oh, well, good. That leaves out . . . let's see, no one."

"But they have to actually use them, and that, as you well know, cuts out quite a few."

She nodded in agreement. "Unfortunately, I'm not dressed as a sub tonight, and I'm not in the mood to go home, change, and then head out to another club."

"What if I propose something a little different?"

Master G often shared Melissa with other Doms. Meagan didn't think he was contemplating anything like offering her to Meagan. She would hope not anyway. Not after she'd explained her current frame of mind.

But he must have given his sub some sort of signal, because Meagan saw the other woman's body shoot to attention and she whispered something to the group she was with.

"I would like for Melissa to have some experience in switching roles. She's expressed a desire, and though I don't think she's a switch"—he shrugged—"I've been wrong before."

"How do I factor into this equation?" Meagan asked.

"If you're open to it, we can grab a private room, and I'll take on the submissive role tonight. You can instruct Melissa in the use of a few implements."

This was something new. Meagan had often given advice and worked with other women in the lifestyle before. However, she'd never worked with a submissive Topping her Dom before.

He must have sensed her hesitation, because he replied before she could get a word in. "Don't think of it as Topping me. Trust me, you won't be. I'll be in charge. But it would really help me out. I can instruct her while I'm submitting, but it'll be difficult."

She should agree. She always enjoyed teaching others, and though she didn't Top men, she knew Master G was being honest when he assured her that he would be in charge. It wasn't the same as playing in a scene, but maybe it would help her frame of mind to do *something*.

"Okay," she said, decided. "I'm in. What's the plan?"

A genuine smile broke out across Master G's face. He'd obviously thought she was going to tell him no. "Thank you. This will be a big help." He signaled Melissa to come to him. "I think something simple for tonight. Maybe a crop or flogger?"

Meagan's brain was already working on what she'd do as she listened to Master G's instructions. Yes, she thought. There was no doubt about who was in charge.

Melissa approached them and dropped to her knees before Master G. "You called me, Master."

The Dom reached out and touched her shoulder. Immediately, the submissive's body relaxed and she looked up.

"Yes, dearest. Mistress B is going to join us in a private room. I asked her if she'd help us introduce you to being a Top. You may feel free to talk with her and ask any questions you have. Just keep in mind that even though I'm acting as a submissive, this is still my scene. Understand?"

Meagan could tell Melissa was working hard to contain her excitement. It flashed in her eyes and seemed to pulse throughout her body.

"Yes, Master," Melissa said. "Thank you. And thank you, Mistress B."

"You're welcome, dearest." He stood up. "I'll go find an empty room upstairs. Why don't you ladies talk for a few minutes and then meet me in about ten?"

Meagan nodded.

They waited until he moved out of earshot before talking.

"Thank you so much for doing this," Melissa said.

"It's no big deal," Meagan said. "I'm glad to help."

"It's something I've wanted to do for a long time. I finally got up the nerve to talk to Master about it a few months ago."

"Really? Because you were afraid of how he would take it or because you didn't think he'd be interested in letting you try?"

Melissa gave a nervous laugh. "Both, I guess. Maybe a little bit afraid to change the status quo? But I finally realized I wasn't being honest with myself. And that meant I wasn't being honest with him. That's what made me decide to tell him."

"And see?" Meagan asked. "He took it okay, didn't he? And he's arranged for you to learn."

"Can I ask you a question?"

"Of course."

"How did you know? That you were a switch?"

"I was new in my BDSM journey. I had only recently discovered that I was a submissive. I went to a club, not unlike this one, to learn more about the lifestyle. There was a training class for newbies, and I went. We had to put down which role we mostly identified with. All I had known at that point was being a submissive, but the instructor wanted us to at least experience both sides, so I did a few scenes where I Topped and I found out I enjoyed it."

"It's a little scary when I think about being the one in control. What if I mess up?"

Meagan patted her hand. "You will. It's inevitable." Melissa looked as if she'd had the wind knocked out of her at that, and Meagan rushed to add, "Go ahead and accept the fact that you aren't perfect and never will be. Tell yourself you will mess up. Give yourself the freedom to mess up."

"I like that. Giving myself the freedom to mess up." She took a few deep breaths and then looked at Meagan. "I'm ready. I think."

"Don't worry. Nothing bad will happen. Master G will see to it."

The mention of her Master made Melissa smile. "You're right about that."

"Tonight we're just going to go over a few implements. Nothing too hard-core."

"I think I can handle that."

"I know you can." Meagan stood up. "Let's go."

They made their way past several scenes. The crowd was picking up, and Meagan started to feel better. Maybe being in her element was helping. She nodded and spoke to a few people she knew as they went up the stairs. Melissa was quiet, having only been given permission to talk to Meagan.

Several private rooms were located off the hallway at the top of the stairs. A few of them had closed doors, so they ignored those and peeked into the first room they came to with the door slightly cracked.

Master G was kneeling, facing away from the door. He had removed all his clothes, except for his boxer briefs. Meagan pushed the door open a bit more so Melissa could pass, but she stood frozen in place.

Meagan tried to imagine how off it must feel for her to have their primary roles reversed. "Go stand in front of him," she whispered, but loud enough for Master G to hear.

Melissa silently nodded and made her way into the room. Meagan closed the door behind them and then joined the couple in the middle of the room.

"Aside from the oddness of it," Meagan said to Melissa, "how do you feel at this moment?"

Melissa was still staring at the bowed head of her Master. "It's . . . I don't know . . . so many things." She took a deep breath. "I guess if I had to pick one word, I'd go with humbled. I feel very humbled at the moment."

"You seem surprised by that," Meagan said.

"I am."

"Why?"

"It's crazy, I know. I've always heard Doms say submission is a gift, but it didn't click until right now." She looked up at Meagan, and her eyes were filled with unshed tears. "It really is, isn't it? He's so vulnerable in that position. And he's staying there for me. For me to do with him what I want. It's . . . wow."

Meagan wondered if seeing her Master kneel before her would color the way Melissa viewed being a Top. She remembered the first time she experienced the emotional realization Melissa just had. How it had transformed into the need to care for the submissives she scened with. There was an element of control to be sure, but for her, like for Melissa, it was the longing to ensure the trust they gave was cared for and attended to.

As it turned out, she didn't have to wonder for long. Melissa sniffed. "I can't."

Meagan almost didn't hear, her voice was so low. "What?"

"I can't be a Top."

Meagan eyed Master G, but he didn't move. "Do you think you could do it with someone who wasn't your Master?" she asked.

Melissa shook her head. "I don't think so. Standing here, seeing Master like that? I don't think it would be different with anyone else. I don't want that much responsibility. It's too much."

Meagan recalled Master G saying earlier in the evening that he didn't think Melissa was a switch. Looked as if he was right.

"I'm sorry I wasted your time," Melissa said to Meagan.

Meagan gave her a hug. "Oh, honey, you didn't. My role was to help you see what you needed to see, and you have."

"Thank you," Melissa said, but her attention was already off Meagan. She knelt beside her Master, put her arms around him, and whispered, "And thank you for doing this to show me what you already knew."

Master G pulled his submissive into his arms and whispered something in her ear that made her giggle. Though she really hadn't done anything, Meagan felt a bit more content. And judging by the way the couple on the floor was kissing, they didn't need her any longer.

She turned and started on her way out.

"Meagan," Master G said from behind her.

"Yes?"

"Thank you. I'm really glad you were here tonight."

And though she knew she wouldn't feel the blissful peace that followed a scene, she was glad she was in the club, too. She took her time going down the stairs, thinking.

What if she changed clothes so she could submit tonight? The night was young, and the scene with Melissa and Master G had invigorated her a bit. Made her feel more alive. She could take her boots off and walk barefoot. It wasn't optimal, because she hated the feeling of dirt under her feet, but she could do it for a night.

She could keep her skirt on and maybe either go topless or

just wear her bra. Yes, that would work. Moving faster, she hurried to the women's locker room. On her way, she noticed Master C standing by the front desk.

Damn.

She'd told him she was here as a Top tonight. If he saw her, he'd want to play, and if she was with someone else, he'd think she lied to him.

As she stood watching, a couple approached the door. There was really nothing overly noticeable about either of them, but something about the man seemed off. He kept looking around as if he expected someone to be following him.

Very strange.

The woman with the man said something to him, and he grabbed her arm so tightly, she winced. He leaned his head down and whatever he said made the woman shake her head. Meagan disliked the guy on sight. She typically thought herself to be a good judge of character and this man had *bad news* written all over him.

They had made it to the door, and Master C very animatedly refused to let them in. The man argued, but Master C stood his ground, and within seconds, two security guards rushed past her. One look at the rather large and well-built security guards, and the man backed down. He shouted something to Master C, but grabbed the woman and walked back to his car.

Master C and one of the guards stayed where they were. She supposed to ensure he stayed away. But the second guard came back inside.

Meagan couldn't stop herself from asking, "Who was that?" as he went by.

"A troublemaker, Mistress," he replied. "He's been blackballed from every club in the area. Don't know why he keeps trying to get in one, and for the life of me, I don't understand why a woman would be with him."

"Oh?" She raised an eyebrow. "Why?"

"Word is he's not one to follow safe, sane, and consensual rules."

The woman at the man's side flashed in her mind. Why would she be with him? She didn't like any of the answers that came to mind.

"No need to worry, though." The man had obviously mistaken her silence. "I'll keep you and everyone else safe. He won't be back anytime soon."

Suddenly, she felt sick and the elation she felt earlier had disappeared. All she really wanted to do in that second was go home, put on some pajamas, and eat ice cream.

"I know you will," she assured him. "But I've had a long day and don't feel in the mood anymore. If you know what I mean."

"Yes, indeed." He looked over his shoulder. "I'm sure he's long gone, but it'd make me feel a lot better if you'd let me walk you to your car."

"I'd appreciate it. Thank you."

Saturday came with no further word from The Taskmaster, but Meagan still found herself out of sorts. She told herself she was an idiot. All she was doing was posing for Luke. Which, she begrudgingly agreed, she hadn't done in fifteen years.

She pulled up to the driveway of the address he'd given her and gawked at the house. Either photography or building clubs or the combination of both had been good to him. His house was a grand contemporary wooden structure. Slowly, she proceeded up the drive, taking in as many details as she could of the manicured yard.

Luke met her at the door.

"Your place is beautiful," she said, instead of saying hello.

"And you're surprised about that?" he asked, a hint of amusement tickling his lips.

"No, well, yes, I mean . . ." She took a deep breath. "It's just not how I pictured a bachelor who builds BDSM clubs to live."

"Then come on inside." The amusement wasn't even a hint anymore; a grin covered his entire face. "I have the living room set up as a harem and a padded table and St. Andrew's Cross where the kitchen should go. But in order to get there, we'll have to step over all the mattresses I put out along the hallway to accommodate the many orgies I host."

"You are such an ass." She pushed his chest to move him out of the way and stepped into the foyer.

He captured her wrist. "You're on my turf now, sweetheart."

She didn't want him to see how the veiled warning made her knees weak and her heart race. "I'm here for you to photograph, nothing else, so drop the Dom attitude."

He looked as though he wanted to say something else, but instead he nodded his head. "Let me show you where you can put your things. Then we can go ahead and I'll take you to the studio."

From the way he sounded, he wanted to get this over and done with as quickly as possible. Fine. That was fine by her, too. She followed him down a hall that didn't have any mattresses, but rather pottery pieces and paintings that gave the impression of an art gallery. With the number of windows the house had, the natural lighting was stunning. She sort of wished he'd walk slower so she could take it all in.

But he was a man on a mission and didn't stop until he came to the end of the hallway. "I have the clothes I want you to wear in the bedroom." He pointed to the door on his right. "There's a bathroom in there you can use to get ready. When you're dressed, come out this door and go across the patio, and I'll be waiting in the studio."

With that said, he headed outside. Meagan put a hand to her stomach in a useless attempt to calm the butterflies. Holy shit, she was really going to do this. Taking a deep breath, she walked into the bedroom and hurried to the bed to see what he'd selected for her to wear.

She stood, staring at it for several long seconds. Then, with a sweep of her hand, she picked it up and carried it outside and into Luke's studio.

"What the hell is this?" she asked, lifting the scrappy material up to his face.

"It's what I want you to wear."

"You said clothes. This isn't clothing."

He walked toward her with long strides, never moving his eyes from hers, and when he stood before her, he took hold of her wrist. "Let's agree on some ground rules, why don't we?"

She was afraid to speak. If she didn't say anything, maybe he wouldn't know what the tone of his voice did to her. To counteract the delicious shivers running through her body, she lifted her chin. "Depends on what they are."

"We both agree you're not here as my submissive; however, I *am* the one in charge of these photography sessions and because of that, you're going to listen and follow my directions."

"That doesn't sound so much like ground rules. Maybe more like you spouting things off and me blindly following."

"Whatever you want to call it, sweetheart." He nodded back toward the house. "Go change."

She didn't move. "You are such a pigheaded ass."

"Turns you on, doesn't it?"

Damn him for knowing the truth. "You'll never know."

"I already do."

She didn't know how to respond to that, so instead of goading him anymore, she went back into the bedroom to change. Once there, she unfurled the skimpy lingerie from the tiny ball she'd shoved it into, and was shocked at what she found when she held it up in front of her.

It was a high-end brand, known for their delicate handmade lacework. Its subtle sensuality hit her. It was really a gorgeous piece. But did he have it here, or had he bought it for her?

She wasn't sure she wanted to know.

Moving quickly, she splashed water on her face and then applied light makeup, doing her best to ignore the way her hands trembled. Stupid nerves. She decided to leave her hair down, but brushed it until it snapped with electricity and fell softly around her shoulders. Something about the process of getting ready for Luke to photograph her reminded her of getting ready for a scene with a Dom, and the ritual of it eased her anxiety, leaving only excitement behind. By the time she slipped the short lacy gown over her head and stepped into the tiny panties, she felt calmer.

In fact, she was so calm, so prepared, and so ready, she had to stop herself from kneeling in front of Luke when she made it back to the studio. As it was, it felt as if he'd turned the heat up fifteen degrees.

She was certain he noticed, but he simply nodded. "You look perfect, Meagan." He pointed to a wrought iron bench. "Go have a seat and we'll get started."

The cool metal soothed her heated flesh and she had only a moment to take a deep breath before she heard his footsteps. He didn't give her instructions on how he wanted her to pose; he simply moved her himself. Within a few minutes, she was sitting straight on the bench, her hands folded in her lap, and her head bowed.

"Close your eyes." His whisper was rough, but his hands were gentle as he swept her hair to one side so it fell across her right shoulder. "That color looks magnificent on you. Just like I thought it would."

Her heart jumped up to her throat. Did that mean he'd bought it for her?

"So many people think of black when they think of lingerie and I agree, it has its place." He trailed a finger along the lace skimming her breasts. "But I like this hue. The palest pink. Just a shade different from your skin. An alluring combination of innocence and seduction."

He stepped away from her and she wondered if he was picking up his camera.

"It's not the gown itself, of course," he spoke, and she couldn't hear anything from the camera. "That color could wash some women out or make others look too young. But on you, it's almost regal."

Surely he was taking pictures; she couldn't imagine him standing there just *talking*. Not when he had photos to take. But damn it all, she didn't recall him talking when he'd photographed her before. Back then, he'd been like your standard photographer—directing and shooting. The man he was now . . .

She'd vastly underestimated both him and his ability to affect her. And she had a feeling that was a big mistake on her part.

"I'm going to print these in both color and black and white." He kept on talking as though he was having an everyday conversation. "I bet in black and white you'll have to look really close to see what's skin and what's silk."

As he spoke, she felt transformed. With his words wrapping themselves around her, she became something beyond herself. She was more than a model, more than a woman; she was a muse. Greater still, for those few short moments in time, she became *his* muse. And the shocking part was, she didn't want to be anyone else.

She didn't want the session to end either, because she knew once it did, she'd go right back to being plain Meagan Bishop.

"Lift your head, but keep your eyes closed," he spoke softer. She hoped she was getting to him, even if it was only a little bit. It seemed only fair. "Tilt your head back, just a bit. Part your lips. Slightly."

Following his direction was effortless. The muse in her pictured how she looked and was pleased.

"That's it." His voice was rougher. He was definitely bothered by her. The side of her that was plain Meagan Bishop smiled. "Keep your eyes closed and move slowly."

Freed by his words, she moved slowly and seductively. The muse became an enchantress. Luke didn't speak, but she heard the faint clicks of his camera and his footsteps as he moved around her. For a few moments, it was as if they moved in unison as one: her, Luke, and his camera.

It was one of the most sensual things she'd ever experienced and she wasn't going to examine it or try to figure it out. She freed herself of any inhibitions and just let her body move along with the feeling, wishing whatever magic they created could last forever.

But, of course, it couldn't and much too soon, she heard Luke's heavy sigh. "That's enough for today."

Was it her imagination or did he sound as if he didn't want it to end either?

As if she could somehow delay the inevitable, she took her time opening her eyes. She scanned the room for Luke, desperate to know if he felt something, too, or if it was only in her mind. But when she found him, his back was to her.

She wondered if he was hiding.

"Should I get dressed?" she asked, surprised at how husky her voice sounded.

"Yes, that's fine."

She waited for several long seconds to see if he'd turn around so she could find some sort of hint in his expression about how he felt. But he never did and she decided to leave before the quiet moment turned awkward.

Once she'd changed back into her clothes and hung up the beautiful gown, she slowly made her way into the hallway. He must have heard her, because he called, "I'm in the kitchen."

Following the sound of his voice, she met him in the house's expansive kitchen. Luke stood, looking out the back window, turning only when she entered the room. He nodded at the table where two water bottles sat.

"I got you some water," he said. His expression was veiled and she couldn't help it—it pissed her off.

"Do you typically provide aftercare for your photography sessions?"

It was the wrong thing to say; she knew it as soon as the words came out of her mouth. He moved to stand in front of her.

Hell, she'd forgotten how tall he was.

"I thought you might be thirsty," he said. "It has nothing to do with aftercare. If it were aftercare, you would be in my arms, both of us basking in the joint pleasure we'd experienced. I'd be stroking your hair, telling you how much you pleased me and turned me on. I might even kiss you. Run my lips across your shoulders, taste your skin, enjoy the hint of salt that remained." He picked up a bottle of water and gave it to her. "This is merely water. However, if you'd like to experience my aftercare, we can look for a mutually beneficial time to further explore what would be involved."

And just like that, he'd thrown the gauntlet down in the most matter-of-fact way possible.

"I think we'd better stick to photography," she managed to get out.

He nodded and took a sip of his water. "Consider it a standing offer."

She was fresh out of snappy comebacks. Probably because the photography session had her wondering what a BDSM session would be like with this older Luke. She had a feeling it would be nothing like what she had experienced with the younger Luke and *that* was nothing short of spectacular.

Luke breathed a sigh of relief as Meagan's car pulled out of the driveway. The photography session had been a lot more intense than he'd bargained for. Meagan obviously thought so too, or else she wouldn't have made the comment she did about aftercare.

Damn, but he didn't remember things being so fiery with

her the last shoot they did. Then again, maybe they had been. After all, they'd spent the following weekend in bed.

He took a big sip of his water. No, there was no way in hell the chemistry between them had been so palpable fifteen years ago. No way had she played to the camera all those years ago the way she had today. He'd known she'd look incredible in the silk and lace he bought for her, but he had no idea she'd become the very embodiment of every fantasy he ever had.

Fuck, just thinking about it made him hard.

He was going to spend a lot of time in a cold shower if today was any indication of how future sessions would go. What he needed to do was to get his mind on something other than Meagan Bishop and how she looked wrapped in the tiny bit of almost nothing.

His phone vibrated on the counter where he'd left it and he gladly went to answer it. Finally, he could talk about something that wasn't Meagan.

Except it was the gentleman behind the book, Rick Campbell, and Luke knew he'd be calling for an update. He had to admit, he'd been surprised when Rick approached him about the project. Apparently, Rick had been at his latest club's grand opening and had been captivated by the pictures Luke had decorated with. Rick called him the next day to inquire about them and when he found that Luke was the photographer, he brought up the book.

The book itself was to be published by a small press that specialized in nonfiction coffee-table books. Luke had been tempted to snicker at the thought of a BDSM book being considered a coffee-table book, but Rick had been completely serious.

"Hello, Rick," he said with a smile. "How's it going?"

"Great. I'm calling to see if the session went as expected."

"It did. Ms. Bishop is everything I told you about and more. Definitely the right model for the job."

"Then I'm glad she agreed to work with you. Would you be able to send over a few shots from today?"

"Of course. She just left, so give me a few hours to go through what I have and pick some out to send."

Rick agreed and after they disconnected, Luke sat the phone back down with a groan. Looked as if he wasn't going to get a break from Meagan after all. Instead, he was going to spend the evening with images of her barely covered body.

First things first, though, he decided. And the first thing up was an ice-cold shower to show his body who was boss. As he walked past the bedroom Meagan had changed in, he saw the skimpy gown hanging where she'd left it.

First thing up was a *longer-than-long* ice-cold shower.

Later that night, he stood in his New Jersey club, just a few minutes from his home in Princeton, and hoped the sights and sounds would help keep his mind off Meagan. So far it wasn't helping. He wasn't sure why. It was a Saturday night and the place was crowded. From the looks of it, everyone was having a great time. He smiled and nodded at a few people, but didn't stay in one place long enough to strike up a conversation, because he didn't feel like sitting around and talking. He felt restless and unsettled.

Which he partially blamed on Meagan and partially on himself. After all, he was the one who'd picked out that damn gown. But it was all her fault she looked so damn good in it.

He thought about finding a willing submissive and escaping off to a private room. He'd never played at his own club, but that didn't mean he couldn't.

Maybe a nice long, hard session was just what he needed to clear his head. He walked toward the check-in desk, planning to look through the submissive list to see who'd showed up alone tonight, when a soft, seductive laugh had him changing his direction. He knew better, but for some reason it sounded like Meagan.

In all likelihood, it wasn't her, but rather his mind conjuring her up because she was so heavily on his mind. The sound was coming from a nearby lounge area. He made his way toward it as quickly as possible and came to a full stop.

Damn it all to hell and back. It was Meagan.

She didn't see him and he almost smiled. He couldn't wait to make his presence known. But as he grew closer, he saw who she was talking with and froze.

A man who went by the name "Master V"; a man who was removed from the membership roll. He'd been dishonest to Meagan months ago the night Abby was almost assaulted. Though many things bothered Luke about the man, at the moment two held the top position in his head: why was Meagan talking with that asshole?

Regret, anger, and jealousy boiled inside him, but they all dimmed in comparison to his second question: *What the hell was Master V doing in his club?*

Both Meagan and Master V heard him approach at the same time and turned. Meagan looked surprised, but Master V just looked smug.

"How did you get in?" Luke asked, seeing no reason for pleasantries.

The so-called "Master" answered with a confident "I just gave them my name."

Luke stepped closer, the *just-what-are-you-going-to-do-about-it* expression on the other guy pissing him off more with every second. "What name would that be?"

Meagan stepped in between the two men. "Luke, you're being rude."

Luke held up his hand. "Meagan, this is none of your business. Stay out of it."

"What do you mean it's none of my business? It was my conversation you interrupted."

Standing slightly behind her, Master V simply snorted in enjoyment. Was he enjoying a scene he had orchestrated?

"Meagan," Luke said. "I'm telling you one more time—"

"Do you need help, Boss?" The head of his security team appeared at his side.

Luke didn't move his eyes from the couple in front of him. "Find out what name *Master V* used to get in tonight."

He'd given explicit instructions that the so-called Master V was not to be allowed in his club. He knew for a fact his employees would not let him in. It only made sense the man used a different name to get into the club.

He was mad at himself now. Somehow there was a loophole in his database that allowed members to be listed more than once, under different names. It was his mistake and he'd own up to it.

"Excuse me?" Meagan said.

But before he could fix the security issue, though, he had to deal with Meagan. He turned to his security lead. "I'll let you take care of him. I'll handle her."

"You'll handle me? Handle me?" Her voice was filled with ire. "What the—"

"Enough." Luke stepped closer to Meagan as Master V was

led away by security. Luke took her wrist and held it up, his thumb stroking the red bracelet there. "Unless it's escaped your attention, you're here as a submissive tonight and you are being disrespectful to me, not only as a Dom, but also as the club owner. Not for the first time, either, I'll remind you."

She jerked her hand out of his, put both on her hips, and tipped her head. "And?"

"And since the Dom you were with is no longer here, your discipline falls to me."

Understanding swept across her face and she went pale. "I loathe you. I don't even know why I come here. Every time I show up, you follow me around just waiting for me to mess up. It's like you're looking for a reason to get your hands on my ass."

"Why do you come here?" he asked. "I can remember at least five times you swore you'd never come back and yet you still show up."

"There was nothing on TV tonight."

He could almost laugh at her thin attempt at bravado. Almost, but he wouldn't; he had an image to protect and he didn't want the other submissives to get any ideas. "You'd think with as much trouble as you're in, you'd be just a bit more respectful."

"I don't see the point. You're going to do what you're going to do anyway. Might as well let you know how I really feel."

"Still with the backtalk, sweetheart?" he asked. "It's like you're looking for a reason for me to get my hands on your ass." She opened her mouth to object to his slight restatement of her words, but his next words stopped her from doing more. "And trust me, by the time we're finished, everyone in here will have no doubt about how you really feel."

For the first time he could ever remember, Meagan looked

unsure of what to do or say next. No worries, he told himself. For the next however long it took, she didn't have to concern herself with what to do or say. He would be the one to direct her. And it started with one word.

He narrowed his eyes at her. "Kneel."

Meagan kept her eyes on Luke as she went to her knees. She recognized she was in enough trouble without disobeying him more, but she wanted him to see her eyes. To feel her anger.

Though, truly, she really had only herself to blame. She *had* been disrespectful to Luke. Many times. And with her display tonight, she'd basically pushed him into a corner until he had no choice other than to do what he did. She did know better, but damn it, it was as though his very presence egged her on.

Unless he was right and she really just wanted his hands on her.

She didn't feel like walking down that path at the moment.

When she made it back to her apartment after the photography session, she'd been surprised to find her earlier restlessness had dissipated, leaving her calm and at ease. It was as if she'd spent the last few hours in an actual scene instead of merely being photographed.

Then another e-mail from The Taskmaster had arrived and all her calm went straight to hell.

I knew you wouldn't disappoint me. Keep up the good work and I'll be in touch.

The anonymous man had taken pictures of her in her home; she didn't know why it shocked her that he knew how she'd spent her afternoon. But it did and she found herself antsy and out of sorts. When Master V called and asked her to meet him at the club, she jumped at the chance. She hadn't talked to him since that fateful night at the club, and the way she saw it, she'd finally have the chance to grill him about what really happened. Sure it was Luke's club, but her need to get out of the house exceeded her need to keep her vow never to step foot into one of his clubs again.

She found Master V waiting for her inside when she arrived, so she didn't know what name he used to get in. She had to admit, if he was listed twice using different names, Luke had every reason to be upset. Truthfully, as soon as she'd met up with him earlier tonight, she knew it had been a mistake. He had no interest in talking and she had no interest in playing. Still, when Luke had interrupted their conversation, all she could think about was how the entire evening was just a colossal waste of time and she hadn't found anyone she wanted to scene with.

Of course, now she was going to get a different kind of scene.

The short time she'd been with Luke in the past hadn't allowed him the opportunity to do anything resembling a punishment session. And the few times she'd observed him play, either in a demo or in a public setting, he'd always been participating in pleasurable scenes.

Funny, even though she'd imagined playing with him over the years, *this* was one scenario she'd never thought of.

He stood in front of her, watching her with questioning eyes, as if he was trying to read her mind.

"Do you have anything you want to say?" he asked.

"I'm sorry for disrespecting you, Sir."

He looked relieved that she hadn't argued. Surely he knew her better. But then again, she hadn't exhibited her best side the few times he'd seen her as a submissive. With that thought came the determination that no matter what, she would take what he dished out and she'd be the best damn submissive he'd ever disciplined.

She bowed her head.

"Thank you, Meagan."

Because she did Top on occasion, she was familiar with the decisions Doms faced. She had no issue with Luke's decision to call her on her disrespect and correct it.

On the other hand, she was irritated with her traitorous body for being turned on at kneeling at his feet.

"Stand up and strip," he said.

She couldn't look him in the eye as she followed his command and folded her clothes neatly. After the photo session, it seemed too intimate to do so and she wondered if she'd feel the same if he'd had her naked in the studio.

Fuck, it turned her on being naked in front of him.

"Very nice, Meagan," he said, but his voice was strained. "Now, go sit at the bar. I'll meet you there soon."

Sit at the bar? What the ever-loving fuck?

Still, she'd told herself she was going to be the best submissive he'd ever punished, so she made her way to the bar and sat on one of the stools. Almost every eye was on her, but out of respect to Luke, no one touched or talked to her while she waited for him to return.

She didn't hear him come up behind her and she jumped when he placed a laptop in front of her. Maybe he was going to video something?

"I've decided your punishment is that you're going to sit naked at the bar and you're going to go through the membership of the club, looking for duplicates like your friend V. I want everything cross-checked: names, numbers, employers, photos. Find the duplicates and forward them to me."

He wanted her to what?

"There are faster ways to accomplish this, Sir." She didn't want to argue, but this was borderline ridiculous. There was software he could install. Programming he could run. Anything but the way he was suggesting. "Doing it this way will take forever."

"I'm aware of that, but I want you to do it this way. And if you don't finish tonight, I want you back here tomorrow. Naked and working. And you will sit here, checking my database until you've finished and I've approved your work."

Forget borderline ridiculous; he'd just crossed over into completely ridiculous. There was no telling how long it would take to complete the task. "I'd rather you spank me."

"I'm sure you would. You think I didn't see how turned on you were standing before me, naked? But I need the database checked, so that's what you're going to do." He leaned down and whispered in her ear, "I'd rather be spanking you, too. But know this, Meagan. If I got my hands on your ass, I wouldn't stop until I had you on your hands and knees, legs spread, begging me to fuck you."

Hot. Damn. And. Yes. Sir. The visual his words brought to mind were enticing. So much more desirable than what she currently had to look forward to. If she closed her eyes, she swore she could almost feel him behind her, his warmth pressing against her. She swallowed a moan.

He chuckled. "Get to work."

With a resolved sigh, she turned her attention away from the man behind her and opened the listing of members, trying to work out in her head what would be the best way to go about checking everything. She decided to pull up V's information first to see if she could find the second name he was listed under.

After she'd been working a few minutes, Luke stepped away. She was surprised to find she missed his presence. Determined not to dwell on it, she refocused on the spreadsheet before her, though she felt as if she was looking for a needle in a haystack.

She scrolled through the list of addresses. Would V have listed the same one? After several minutes of looking, it didn't appear he had.

"Meagan?"

She had focused so intently on the computer, she jumped at the sound of her name. "Damn it, Sir." She turned to face the interruption. "You scared me half to death."

"I'm sorry. I thought you heard me." He held out a slip of paper. "Here's the name he used to get in. Thought that might help."

"Yes, thank you." She looked at the paper and frowned. She didn't recognize any of the information. Interesting. But opening up the alternate name on the computer, she saw the connection. "There we have it."

"What?" Luke peered over her shoulder.

"He listed his real name as a reference. Talk about a 'fuck you and your security system, too.'"

"Shit."

"Right?" She clicked through the rest of the information. V really was a disgusting pig. She felt even worse than before that she'd agreed to be with him tonight. Before she could allow herself time to think about that, she had to take care of Luke's request. "And the thing is your staff never would have caught it. Nothing else matches. You're going to have to start collecting driver's license information, Social Security numbers, or something."

He pulled up the stool beside her. "This is worse than I thought."

"I have to say it and, trust me, it's not that I'm trying to weasel my way out of anything, but you need someone with a lot more knowledge and experience than me to fix this."

"I thought we'd taken care of security when we reopened."

"You didn't have the members reapply, or at least, I wasn't asked to. Did you have anyone run background checks?"

He ran his fingers through his hair. "Not yet. I was going to ask Jeff Parks to do it in a month or so."

"Might I suggest you have him do it sooner rather than later?"

"Yes. Definitely." He shook his head. "I thought it was okay to wait since almost everyone had been a member for so long. But I see now a clean sweep is in order."

She nodded. It was scary when she thought about it. If no one had ever done a background before . . .

She didn't want to dwell on that.

"Meagan," he said, and she lifted her head to find him holding out a robe. "You can get dressed if you'd like. I don't see the point in you doing anything further."

"Thank you." She slid off the stool and slipped the robe on. "And, Sir, I am sorry for how I acted. Truly. I've Topped in a scene before. I wouldn't have put up with my attitude either."

"I appreciate you saying that." He nodded. "I was thinking. Would you have time to have lunch next weekend before we start shooting?"

She raised an eyebrow and he laughed.

"Honestly, I just thought it'd be a good idea for us to talk. Get to know each other." He waved toward her. "When we both have our clothes on."

It would be dangerous to accept his invitation. She could already see how easy it would be to fall back into the schoolgirl crush she'd had on him years ago. And how much more would this grown-up Luke appeal to her?

But, on the other hand, it would be a good idea for her to get closer to Luke in ways other than photography. There was still The Taskmaster to think about, after all. She would have to keep in mind that being with Luke this time was the means to an end. Nothing more. If she did that, she should be able to have lunch with him without getting any emotions involved.

She hoped anyway. "I think that would be fine. Should we meet somewhere?"

"You could come by the house. Might be easier than going somewhere and then having to go to my place. Just do it all in one location."

"I'll do it on one condition."

"What's that?"

"You have to give me a tour of your house. It looked fascinating."

His laugh was easy. "It's a deal."

Luke always regretted that he wasn't much of a cook. It wasn't because he didn't try; he did. It just seemed as though everything he cooked tasted like cardboard. Cooking should be simple. All he had to do was follow the recipe. But it never was that easy.

Before Meagan came over on Saturday, he went to the local farmers' market and got fresh produce for a salad. He had some cooked chicken left over at the house from the night before. He'd throw it all together for a quick lunch. It probably wouldn't be a good idea to eat anything too heavy, anyway.

Meagan arrived on time, stepping out of the car and looking incredible. He couldn't help but remember how she looked the weekend before, naked and needy before him. He'd wanted so badly to touch her, but to punish himself along with her, he'd given her that ludicrous spreadsheet to work with.

He shook his head and watched her walk to the door. She'd pulled her hair back into a ponytail. Interesting choice. He hadn't told her anything about the way he wanted her to wear her hair, but the ponytail worked perfectly for what he had planned for today. And unlike last week, she didn't have any makeup on. Perfect. Though he thought he might have her put on some red lipstick after lunch.

He opened the door, expecting to see her smile, and was caught off guard by her frown.

"Is everything okay?" he asked.

"Sorry. What?"

"You look distracted and you're frowning. Is everything okay?" He moved to the side to let her pass by him and enter the house.

"Yes, just a message that came through on the way over. It's okay. I can handle it." Her phone rang with an incoming message and she stopped to read it.

He closed the door and watched as she typed back a reply.

"Meagan," he said softly.

"Hmm." She didn't look up.

"Meagan," he said just as soft, but she continued messaging. "Hand me the phone."

Her head snapped up. "What?"

He held out his hand. "Hand me the phone."

"I'm finished now."

"Yes, you are. Give it to me and you'll get it back before you leave."

"That's okay. I'm fine."

He shook his hand. "Give it." She sighed, but put the phone in his hand. He turned it off. "Thank you. I know it's hard to believe, but the world won't grind to a screeching halt if Meagan Bishop doesn't answer her phone or reply to a text for the next few hours."

"I know that, you know."

"I'm sure you do, but I'm a jealous, jealous man." He closed the distance between them and lifted her chin so she met his eyes. God, she was gorgeous. "I only have you here with me for a few short hours. Don't make me share."

She blinked and her cheeks turned a light pink, which made her only more appealing. "So greedy," she said, her voice husky.

He shouldn't be touching her the way he was. She had been very clear about what she did and did not want from him. But at the moment, her eyes were dark and her lips slightly parted. When she looked at him the way she was, he couldn't keep his hands off her. "Always," he said in agreement with her earlier statement and ran his thumb along her bottom lip.

She drew it into her mouth and nipped his fingertip, looking him straight in his eyes the entire time.

Damn, but if that didn't send sparks down his body and make his cock beg for more. "Vixen," he said, but didn't move his finger.

"Ass."

He chuckled and dropped his hand. "Maybe I better give you the tour before we do something we said we shouldn't."

She looked just disappointed enough that he seriously contemplated changing his plans for the afternoon and giving her exactly what they both wanted. But no sooner than the thought came to him, he disregarded it. To do something that radical would be to follow the path that had brought them heartache all those years ago. He wanted them to start new.

Which meant he needed to take her on a tour of his house. "Come on, I'll give you the grand tour."

The disappointment fled, replaced by curiosity, and he led her down the hall. "This part of the house you saw last week." He walked past the bedroom she'd changed in, pointed out his bedroom, and made his way into the living room.

As soon as they entered, she made a beeline for the two oil paintings he had displayed in the middle of the far wall. "I saw glimpses of these last week and couldn't wait to see them close up. They're obviously the real deal." She looked up at him. "Maxfield Parrish."

He looked at her with surprise. "You know of him?"

She nodded. "Art minor. I'd tell you these two pieces belong in a museum or an art gallery, but I have the feeling you know this."

"I do. In fact, these spent the last few weeks in my gallery downtown. I brought them home so I could enjoy them before trying to find a buyer."

She turned, clearly surprised. "You're going to sell them?"

"Yes, there's so much artwork I like, if I kept everything, you wouldn't be able to walk in the front door."

Her resulting laughter took him by surprise. Had she ever

laughed at something he said before? He wasn't sure, but he didn't ever want her to stop.

But she did when she noticed him staring at her. "What?"

"Your laugh."

"What about it?"

"I'd like to hear it more often."

"I guess I'm not the kind of person who laughs a lot." A strange look crossed her face. "I don't know why."

Damn it. How could telling her that he liked her laughter cause all the joy to leave her face? That hadn't been his intent. "Hey, did I say something? I didn't mean to upset you."

"It's nothing." She exhaled and gave him a sad smile. "I wish I were the type person who laughed a lot, that's all."

"Maybe you are and you've just been hanging out with the wrong people."

"That's a definite possibility."

"Let me show you the rest of the house." He motioned for her to follow him out. No sooner had they stepped into the hallway than the kitchen timer he'd set for the bread went off. "Tour and then eat or eat, then tour?"

"Eat and then tour."

"A woman after my heart. Let's go."

They walked back to the kitchen where she insisted on helping him set the table. He wasn't in a mood to argue with her and he rather liked having her be all domestic in his house. She looked as if she belonged and the thought made him smile.

She put two bowls on the table. "You're looking at me funny."

"Am I?"

"Mm-hmm."

"How?"

"Like you're a dog and I'm a bone you've just been given."

"I'd never look at you like you're a *bone*." He leaned back on the countertop and crossed his arms. "Maybe a juicy steak."

She smiled and he *thought* he heard a giggle. That was progress. Maybe it wouldn't be too much longer before he was getting full-fledged laughs routinely. He should make that a goal, to have her laugh, *really laugh,* once a week.

"I guess a juicy steak is better than a bone," she said. "Though I can't imagine by much."

"It is, trust me." He pushed back from the countertop. "Let's eat and you can tell me all about how you went from cover model to TV executive."

"Really?" She sat down as he brought the salads over. "Why would you want to talk about something so boring?"

"The camera loves you and you were once quite passionate about modeling. I'm trying to figure how it is you're satisfied sitting behind a desk."

She took a bite of salad and, once she'd swallowed, replied, "What makes you think I'm satisfied?"

Her words struck his heart, just like she probably knew they would. "Aren't you?"

"Most days, yes." She shoveled her lettuce around the bowl. "But then others . . . Like, take this invitation I recently received. One of the NNN anchors has been nominated for an Emmy and he invited me to his celebratory dinner. I helped him get his foot in the door eons ago when I was fresh out of college. Days like the one I got the invitation? I'm not so satisfied then. I feel unsettled."

"Why?"

"Because I wonder what my life would be like if I'd made other choices. If I'd decided not to help him, that it was every man for himself. If I'd gone for the job instead of coaching him for it. If I sat in front of a camera rather than sitting behind a desk."

"Do you want his job?"

"I wouldn't turn it down. The invitation really shouldn't bother me the way it has. He's done a good job. He should be recognized for it. But, like I said, most days I'm content. Truly."

There was so much more to life than merely being content, especially since from where he sat, she was trying to convince herself she was even that. He'd tell her that one day, but now wasn't the time. "Will you go to his celebratory dinner?"

"Yes, I will. Not so much because I want to, but because it would hurt his feelings if I didn't. I've always been there for him in the past. This is a big deal. I should go. Besides, if I don't, people will talk about how I'm jealous and couldn't swallow my pride enough to go to a lousy dinner."

"Sounds like an absolute fright."

"It will be." She stopped shoveling her food around and tilted her head. "Will you go with me?"

Just as soon as the words left her mouth, she clamped her lips shut, as if she couldn't believe she'd asked the question.

"To the absolutely frightful celebratory dinner?" He lifted an eyebrow. "Are you sure you want *me* to go?"

"Yes." She nodded, apparently having decided not to renege on her offer. "It'll be so much better with you there. I hate going to functions like that alone."

Even though there had been less animosity between the two of them, he knew she wasn't asking him as a real date. No, she simply didn't want to show up alone. He would be acting as her support, not her date. Frankly, he thought she'd spent enough time by herself; she needed to get out more. Enjoy life.

"When is it?" he asked.

"Next Saturday night. Oh, I wasn't thinking. It's a Saturday. In Manhattan. Damn. We might need to move our session up so I . . . we . . . can go. If it's okay with you."

Her words sent his imagination into hyperspeed. Forget having the session before. All he could think about was Meagan in the moonlight. First in her evening gown and then totally nude, bathed by the light of a thousand stars. "Yes, I'll go with you." His voice sounded rough and he cleared his throat. "Except we'll do the session outside, afterward."

Chapter Four

Meagan looked at her reflection in the full-length mirror on the back of her bathroom door and frowned. Not because she looked bad, but because she actually *cared* what she looked like. But it was more than that. She wanted to know what he would think. Would he like the gown she'd selected?

Normally, everyone wore black to these functions. There was the occasional woman who wore silver or red. In fact, she'd planned to wear a silver gown herself. But she had been window-shopping and this gown had caught her eye. She'd marched into the store and asked for it in her size, telling herself the entire time it had nothing to do with *him*. Luke.

But of course, deep down, she knew it had everything to do with Luke. She ran her hands down her sides and took a deep breath; then she looked at herself again.

The gown was a pale pink, with delicate sheer fabric covering one shoulder. And though the bottom of the gown barely brushed the tops of her heels, there was a slit on the left side that rose dangerously high up her thigh. Luke had been right—the color was fabulous on her.

She turned to look at the back and gave a nod of satisfaction, right as her doorbell rang. She'd told Luke that she could meet him at the party, but he'd said no, he would come by her apartment and pick her up. Inside, she'd been secretly thrilled, even though she scowled at him and said, "Fine."

Her heart raced as she made her way to the door and she waved her hands so she wouldn't get sweat on the gown. It was absurd she was nervous. She was a grown-ass woman. Attending a dinner party with a man shouldn't fill her stomach with butterflies. But maybe, if it were any other man, there wouldn't be any butterflies.

She took a deep breath and opened the door.

Luke's eyes grew wide, first with shock and then with something else. He didn't say anything as his eyes traveled over her body. She lifted her head just a bit, letting him look his share.

"My God, Meagan," he finally said. "You are magnificent."

He liked it. From the looks of it, he more than liked it. "Thank you. Someone told me I looked good in this color."

"Someone has a good eye."

She looked him up and down, not sure she'd ever seen him in a suit and tie. He looked sexy as hell and then some. "Someone has a good everything."

He made a noise that sounded like something between a moan and a growl. He took a step closer to her, but didn't touch her. "We'd better be on our way before I'm tempted to rip that gown off you and show you just how good my everything is."

Promise? danced on her lips, but she bit it back. "Let me grab my purse."

As she turned to get her things, he gave a low moan she couldn't help but smile at.

Oh yes, the back of the gown was almost nonexistent.

Guy had rented out the entire restaurant for the evening and even though she and Luke were a few minutes early, when they stepped inside, she was surprised by the number of people present. Everyone had their nose in the air, as if silently judging the people around them. The decor was contemporary and uninspired. From what she could tell, the dinner appeared as if it was going to be just as stuffy and boring as she had feared. At least she had Luke to liven up her evening.

He took her coat and gave it to the hostess to check; then he placed his hand low on her back, right where skin met the fabric. The warmth of his touch felt good and her body relaxed. Yes, inviting him had been the best decision she'd made in the last few months.

"Do you know all these people?" he asked in a whisper.

"Only about fifteen percent."

Across the room, Guy saw her and waved. She put on her fake smile and waved back, groaning softly when he spoke briefly to the people he was standing by and headed her way.

"What?" Luke asked, but there wasn't time to tell him anything because within seconds Guy stood in front of them.

"Meagan." Guy gave her cheek an air kiss and looked her over. "Wow, you look great. And who is this?" he added with a nod toward Luke.

"I'm Luke DeVaan, an old friend of Meagan's," he replied before she could get anything out.

Luke stood about two inches taller than Guy's six feet, but

Guy still looked her date up and down in appraisal. "Old friend? I'm one of Meagan's old friends and I don't remember her ever mentioning you."

"Isn't that funny?" Luke asked by way of an answer. "I don't remember her ever mentioning you before, either."

The two men kept on staring at each other as if silently trying to determine who'd known her the longest. Meagan rolled her eyes. Men. Honestly.

"Luke, Guy and I met in college," she said. Guy's smile got bigger seconds before she took him down a notch. "Guy, Luke and I met shortly after I graduated from high school."

It was Luke's turn to smile big and Meagan decided maybe the dinner wasn't going to be so boring after all. She turned to Guy. "I never mentioned Luke to you because we only dated for a short while. In fact, I went out of my way to ignore him for the last several years."

"But I'm persistent," Luke added.

"That you are."

Guy tipped his head. "I'm glad you could make it," he said, but his voice didn't sound as if he meant it.

Luke started rubbing her back with only his thumb and she could have hummed in pleasure. How in the world had she forgotten how good his hands felt? More important, how had she managed to live without it for so long?

"Congratulations on your nomination," Luke added.

"Thank you." Guy lightly brushed Meagan's bare shoulder. "I wouldn't be here without Meagan."

Luke tensed beside her. Because Guy touched her? He would have to get over it; they weren't in a club, after all. No one had to ask his permission to interact with her.

"Now, Guy," she chided. "I just gave you a push. You did all the hard work yourself."

"That's kind of you to say. What do you do, Luke?"

"I run an art gallery downtown and a few clubs in the city."

"Oh, diversified. Interesting. What kind of clubs? Maybe I've been to one."

"Trust me. You haven't."

Guy opened his mouth to reply, but Meagan beat him to it. "Luke, come with me over to meet Mr. Black. He's the CEO."

She dragged him a few feet away. "What are you doing? What was that?"

"What was what? I simply told him there was no way in hell he'd ever been to one of my clubs."

"He may have. You never know."

"He hasn't. I know."

Whatever. It wasn't worth a fight and she didn't want to ruin the evening. If that meant breaking up their little testosterone battle, she would. She peered around the crowd, trying to find Mr. Black, but he was so short, he often got lost in groups. "Well, I seem to have lost my boss."

"No worries. We can go pick on Guy some more."

"No, we can't. Honestly, what's gotten into you?"

"I didn't like the way he looked at you and then touched you. More than that, you let him kiss your cheek. You haven't even let me do that."

"It was an air kiss. You want to give me an air kiss?" She lifted her head slightly, offering him her cheek.

He dipped his head, as if he was going to take her up on the offer, but instead he simply whispered, "No, thanks, sweetheart. I have my sights set on a different kind of kiss. I'll bide my time until then."

"You sound sure of yourself, Mr. DeVaan."

"I like it when you call me Mr. DeVaan." His hold on her waist grew rougher. "And I—"

"Meagan Bishop, you sly dog. Who do we have here?"

Meagan held back a sigh and turned toward the office flirt. "Robin, this is my old friend Luke DeVaan. Luke, this is—"

"Robin Skye." The petite woman with curly hair the color of wet sand held out her hand. "Nice to meet you."

"The pleasure's mine."

"Not yet, but the night is young."

Meagan coughed. Robin batted her lashes. Luke looked faintly amused.

Meagan was getting ready to suggest to Luke that they go get a drink when a server came by with a tray of shrimp. Robin picked one up and held it up to Luke's lips with her other hand cradled underneath. To the casual observer, she would appear to be preventing spills, but in reality, she was probably getting ready to touch him the minute he opened his mouth.

"Want a bite?" she asked in a way that suggested she was offering a whole lot more.

Meagan felt certain if she looked in a mirror, she'd have steam coming out of her ears. Seriously? Was the woman drunk or just immature and stupid? And Luke, what the hell was going through his mind?

"No, thank you." He turned his head, his voice flat. "Shellfish allergy. Though I would love a glass of wine." He held out a hand to Meagan. "Come with me?"

She placed her hand in his and heard his sigh of relief as Robin headed for her next victim.

"Damn, Meagan. Who are these people you work with?" he

asked as they approached the bar. "First the man with the easy lips and then the woman with the easy everything else."

"Television's a weird business."

"I run multiple kink clubs. Television isn't weird—it's borderline harassment."

"Guy was just being charming. Robin is . . . well, Robin."

He didn't say anything else about the guests. He ordered two glasses of wine, passed one to Meagan, and downed his own in three gulps.

And she'd thought the dinner would be stuffy and boring.

"Want another?" Meagan asked him, eyeing the empty wineglass, barely able to keep the laughter from her voice.

"No, I'm good now."

Damn, but he had anticipated a much quieter evening. Between the man who obviously had eyes for Meagan to the petite woman who'd made no doubt about how much she wanted him, the night was shaping up to be interesting.

"What time are we actually eating?" he asked.

There were tables set up in the back of the restaurant. From where he stood, it appeared there were name cards at each seat. He never understood why people thought name cards were necessary. Weren't they all adults? Couldn't they be trusted to pick out their own seats?

Meagan looked at her watch. "Probably in about thirty minutes."

"Did you tell anyone I was coming as your guest?"

"No."

He groaned inwardly. "Great."

"What?"

"The tables have name cards. If you didn't tell anyone I was coming, I either don't have a seat or I'm seated next to *her*." He smiled over at Robin, who was watching them. She lifted her hand and waved.

"Truly a fate worse than death," Meagan said in a deadpan voice.

"Sweetheart, if I didn't want to sit next to you at dinner, I wouldn't have agreed to come tonight." He brushed her cheek with the backs of his knuckles. "I've been looking forward to this all week—don't pawn me off."

She closed her eyes and leaned into his touch. He told himself it was probably the alcohol, though really, she'd had only the one glass.

"I have an idea," she whispered.

"What's that?"

"Let's leave."

"Before dinner?" At her nod, he replied, "Scandalous."

She opened her eyes. "I'm game if you are."

"Think anyone will miss us?"

"Robin."

"Let's go."

She giggled and he took her hand as they made their way to pick up her coat.

"You aren't really allergic to shellfish, are you?" she asked.

They stepped outside and he helped her slip her arms into the sleeves. "No, it just seemed to be the quickest way to get rid of her. Most people aren't going to argue with a food allergy."

"Quick thinking on your part."

"Speaking of quick thinking, we need to eat. Let's grab something quick and eat it in the park."

"A picnic in Central Park?" She raised her eyebrow. "Dressed like this?"

"Where's your sense of adventure?"

He knew that'd get her. She threw him an *I know what you're doing* look, but replied, "Let's do it."

"Excellent. I know just the place. It's right off West Fifty-seventh, not far from here."

Tucking her arm against him, they started off. But, of course, she was full of questions.

"Are we going to sit on the ground? I really don't want to get all dirty. Should we get a blanket? Where can we find one? Maybe we just skip the picnic and go back to your place. You still wanted to fit a session in today, right?"

He pulled her out of the flow of pedestrian traffic and brought them both to a halt. "Meagan. This is supposed to be fun. Stop stressing out about it and leave the details to me. All the details. To me." She started to say something, but he hushed her by bringing a finger up to her lips. "I mean it. I'll take you over my knee right here."

And though her eyes darkened with desire, she only nodded. But he wanted more.

"Say, 'Yes, Sir.'"

Her entire countenance dissolved into sweet submission. "Yes, Sir."

Fuck, what those two words did to him when they came out of her mouth. He wanted to take her in his arms and crush his lips against hers. He wanted her lips and her kiss so badly he could taste it. And he wondered, not for the first time, if her lips still tasted the same.

Damn it all to hell, he was going to find out. Not right this second. Maybe not even tonight, but soon. Soon, he'd taste her kiss again.

Using all the self-discipline and self-control he could muster, he lowered his head, bypassed her lips, and whispered in her ear, "Thank you, Meagan. I've never heard sweeter words."

Was it his imagination or did she look *disappointed* that he hadn't kissed her?

Regardless, it wasn't the time or the place to give her the type of kiss he wanted, so he took her hand once again and started walking toward his favorite pizzeria. It wasn't a long walk, but he was thankful it was long enough to cool his blood and keep him from doing something he wasn't quite ready to do.

Meagan didn't say anything while they walked. More than likely she was fuming over his threat to take her over his knee, but he really didn't care. She might identify as a switch, but she needed to understand she wasn't going to Top him.

The owner of the pizzeria hurried to the front of the restaurant as soon as he saw Luke enter. He gave only a passing glance to their finery before punching Luke on the shoulder.

"Good to see you, DeVaan. What can I do for you tonight?"

"Good to see you, too, Angeleno." Luke raised an eyebrow. "Meagan?"

"Thin crust. All the veggies."

"Give us a large thin with all the veggies, a bottle of your house red, and a tablecloth. To go."

Angeleno snapped his fingers. "It is done. Give me fifteen minutes."

Luke turned back to Meagan. Fifteen minutes was long enough for her to decide she didn't want an impromptu picnic in Central Park. But she was watching him with curious eyes that held a hint of laughter and Luke couldn't help but smile.

"What?" he asked.

"Do you do this often?"

"First time, actually."

He was going to tell her she could ask Angeleno when he came back, but she seemed satisfied with his answer.

"I've walked by this place, but never stopped," she said, looking around.

Luke tried to imagine it was his first time entering. It was difficult; he'd been to the tiny restaurant often over the years and the owners were like a second family. To him, the entire space gave a warm and comforting vibe. Soft candlelight, crisp tablecloths, and the inviting aroma of brick oven–baked pizza. "If you haven't eaten the pizza here, you haven't had real pizza yet."

"I'll hold off on making that decision until I've tasted it."

"You'll be singing its praises by the time the night's over."

A large family came in and they were all so packed in the small area, there wasn't much opportunity to talk anymore. Right as the group was seated, Angeleno appeared with the pizza and two bags.

"I have everything you need in the bags," he told Luke while he rang him up. "And Teresa insisted on sending cannoli. On the house."

"You truly married an angel. Be sure to tell her thank you for me."

The older man grinned. "I certainly will. Now you two go and have fun."

"He seems really nice," Meagan said once they were outside again and headed toward the park.

"I swear he's half saint. He and Teresa have always been there for me. They're great when you just need someone to listen."

He didn't mean to say that; it just spilled out. Hopefully, she wouldn't push and want to know more about what the sweet couple had listened to him talk about. Namely because it was her. During those awful days that followed their breakup, they'd listened and didn't pass judgment.

Perhaps Meagan could tell, because she didn't pursue it any further. "Where should we have the picnic?"

"I think just inside the park," he said, thankful that she'd picked up on his unspoken desire. "Much more likely for me to behave if there are people close by and a chance we'll be seen."

She cut her eyes at him, probably in an effort to see if he was teasing or telling the truth. Because he didn't want her to know just how close to the truth he'd been, he made sure his expression gave away nothing.

They had lucked out. The weather was perfect for a picnic, and though there were several couples and families who had the same idea they did, Luke was able to find a somewhat secluded spot. He handed the box and bags to Meagan and spread out the tablecloth on the ground.

She placed the items on the red-and-white-checkered fabric and then lowered herself to sit as gracefully as she could. "I can't believe we're doing this."

They were getting quite a few double takes from their fellow Central Park visitors. Let them look. Luke imagined every guy who walked by was wishing he was the one sitting across from Meagan. Angeleno had packed some paper plates, so Luke took one and put two slices of pizza on it before handing it to Meagan.

"Thanks." She bit into her first piece and her eyes nearly rolled to the back of her head. "Mmm, damn. This is seriously good."

Luke refrained from saying, *I told you so.* "Bet it beats what Guy had on the menu."

"No doubt, but Robin will be upset we left early. I think *you* were on her menu for the evening."

"She should go with pizza. Much more likely to happen."

Meagan snickered.

"Is she like that with everyone?" he asked.

"Only the men who are really hot." She stopped and tilted her head. "No, scratch that. She's like that with anyone who has a penis."

"I fear for all the males in the world."

They ate in silence for a few minutes, watching the people passing by. A little girl walking with her mom and dad saw them and pulled her parents to a halt.

"Mommy, look. Daddy, look." Her voice dropped to a whisper. "It's a princess."

Luke glanced at Meagan to see if she'd heard. She had. She waved at the child, then blew her a kiss and waved.

The little girl squealed with delight and waved back. "You're so pretty."

Meagan smiled and nodded in acknowledgment, looking exactly like the princess she'd been mistaken for. The mom bent down and whispered in her daughter's ear and the child nodded enthusiastically.

"'Bye, 'bye, princess." She waved as her parents led her down the sidewalk.

"So sweet," Luke said when the trio was out of sight.

"She was," Meagan said wistfully. "I love how children see the world for all its good and believe everything is full of magic."

"Damn shame anyone has to grow up."

"I never pictured you as the Peter Pan type."

"I don't want to stay a child, but when you see a little one like that? I hate to see them lose that sense of wonder."

"That's rather telling." She reached for another piece. "When did you lose yours?"

"I was ten."

"What happened?"

"My parents got a divorce."

Meagan nodded. "That'll do it. Nothing like the two people who mean the most to you to decide they can't stand each other anymore."

"I guess it's hard for anyone at any age, but I felt totally blindsided."

"Do you see them a lot now?"

He twisted the plastic cup Angeleno had given them for the wine. "My mom died of breast cancer six years ago. Dad remarried and is living in Texas. I don't see him often." Another subject he didn't want to talk about. "How about you? How are your parents?"

"My father was a fireman and died in the line of duty. My mom was never the same after and died a few years ago."

His heart ached for the grief he heard in her voice. "I'm so sorry."

She shook it off. "Now, my dad's parents are still alive. They've been married eighty years."

Luke gave a low whistle. "Eighty years?"

"Don't be too impressed. I'm certain they only stayed married to piss the other off."

"I don't care. That's a long-ass time to stay married out of spite. We should change the subject—this is depressing," he said.

Meagan took another slice of pizza. "Let's talk about how it's possible I've lived in New York for as long as I have and I've never tried this pizza."

"Don't forget we have cannoli."

"I never forget dessert."

He waited until she'd finished the slice she had in her hand before opening the container holding the pastry. But when she reached for it, he shook his head. "Nope. Let me."

She narrowed her eyes slightly, but parted her lips.

"There we go," he said, slipping it into her mouth.

"Oh, man. This is better than the pizza and I didn't think that was possible." Her tongue darted out and licked her lips, capturing the sugar gathered there. She gave a happy sigh and he wished he could join her, but the sight of her licking her lips made him too damn hard to join in and act content.

"I don't know about the session tonight," she said. "All these carbs."

"You'll do fine." He reached over and encircled her wrist with his thumb and forefinger. "Besides, you're too skinny. You won't even notice the carbs on you."

"Bet I will."

He stroked her wrist with his thumb. "Bet I can make you forget all about them."

Meagan shivered from the faint contact Luke made with her skin. The way his fingers moved against the sensitive area on the underside of her wrist gave her just enough of a hint of how they would feel along other parts of her body. More than that, though, it made her want his touch. Want him.

If she closed her eyes, she could pull from her memory how his fingers felt years ago. Then, his touch was certainly knowledgeable, but it had lacked a certain confidence that he clearly had now. She had a feeling that as much as he had rocked her world all those years ago, he would put her in such a spin now, she might never recover.

He sat beside her, watching her with those observant Dom eyes that didn't miss anything. She couldn't help but notice that his eyes had grown dark. Touching her affected him just as much as it did her. His touch grew lighter and lighter until his fingers left her wrist completely.

"Are you finished eating?" he asked, his voice husky.

"Yes," she answered, and she had the strange feeling she was agreeing to something else.

He stood and helped her to her feet; then they both collected the litter. Luke folded the tablecloth and tucked it under his arm, saying he'd return it to Angeleno later. When the area was clean and they left the park, it was dusk.

By the time they reached Luke's house, it was dark, though the clear sky allowed the full moon to show off. Luke appeared pleased with the light it provided. He stepped out of the car and nodded. She thought she heard a murmured "Perfect" as he helped her out.

Since he'd said they'd be doing the session outside, she waited for him to give her instructions.

"I'm going to step inside and get my equipment. Do you mind waiting out here?" he asked.

"I'll be fine out here," she said. "It's pretty tonight."

He wasn't gone long. When he returned, he'd removed his jacket and tie. His top button was undone, exposing his neck and chest. Damn, she wanted to touch him. Wanted to unbutton his shirt, peel it off his shoulders, and run her hands over his chest.

Either he didn't notice her desire, or else he chose to ignore it. "Stand right there," he said, setting up the camera. "The moon's at the perfect angle."

She didn't know the first thing about angles and lighting, but if he was happy with it, she was, too. For several minutes, she swayed in the moonlight, brushed her hair back, and looked up at the sky. She'd never been photographed outside before, much less at night. There was something almost surreal about it. *Magical* would have been a good word if she believed in such things. Whatever it was, she felt alive.

"Can you unzip the dress by yourself?" he asked.

"I got it on alone," she reminded him.

"I figured," he said. "Just didn't know if you needed help."

"If you helped, we probably wouldn't get any more photographs taken tonight."

"Are you stalling?"

Maybe she was. He'd seen her naked before. Recently even. But this somehow seemed different. More personal. More intense. Just *more*.

Because they were alone? Or because they'd gotten to know each other better since then?

She turned so her back was to him and, looking slyly over her shoulder, she ever so slowly reached behind to her back and tugged the zipper down.

The only negative to having him as her photographer was the inability to see his eyes. Of course, maybe that was for the best, because *this way* she could pretend his expression held anything she wanted it to. *Yes*. Tonight she would play his moonlit muse and he would love her for it.

She looked off to her side as the gown slowly slipped from her shoulders and bit her lip as if unsure about what she was doing. In her mind and for the camera, she became someone else. She was an inexperienced siren gradually becoming aware of the power she held over the men around her. She turned her body slowly, brushing her hair over her shoulders, and twisted her hips so the gown fell softly to the ground.

Forget holding power over men—there was only one man she cared about. Luke.

He was silent as he worked, but she didn't mistake the sharp intake of breath when she was finally naked and faced him fully. Even then, she wouldn't look the camera in the eye for fear it would break the spell they were both weaving.

Together in the moonlight, they became the creators of an untold story. Making magic with the way she moved her body and the way he captured what he saw through his lens. No words were spoken while they worked. None were needed. For whatever reason, when he picked up his camera and focused it on her, they moved as one. It had been that way before and the years hadn't diminished that.

Though she wasn't watching him, she sensed when he stopped and put the camera down. She was surprised he'd finished; time seemed to have flown. But even more surprising was the realization she wasn't ready for the night to be over.

She heard rustling as he put the camera away.

"You can get dressed if you want," he said, breaking the silence, but not the spell. "Or I can go get you a robe."

"No."

"You don't want a robe?"

She turned to face him. The moon had slipped behind a tree; it was hard to make him out. "I don't want to get dressed."

"Meagan?"

She wasn't sure she'd heard him so unsure before. "Come to me, Luke."

He struggled; she could sense it from where she stood. The man versus the gentleman. The Dom versus the professional photographer.

"You've put the camera down," she told him. "It's just us. Meagan and Luke."

Part of her knew she shouldn't tempt him. It was too similar to what they'd done before. But she was older now and wouldn't let her emotions get involved this time. She was a grown woman, not a girl. She took what she wanted and tonight, she wanted Luke.

"Just for tonight," she whispered. "Tomorrow we can go back to being working partners. Tonight we're just two people who want each other and are finally doing something about it." She tilted her head. "You do want me, don't you?"

He didn't answer, but crossed the distance between them with quick steps until he stood before her. There was just enough light for her to make out the desire in his eyes. "Hell, yes, I want you."

"Then what are you waiting for?"

"Nothing." He framed her face. "I'm not waiting for anything."

He kissed her and it all came back to her with the touch of his lips. His taste. His commanding presence. His artistry. They were all present in his kiss and though she remembered them, she didn't recall them being exactly like this. So overwhelming. So completely intoxicating. Surely, it wasn't this good before.

He lifted his head, just long enough to murmur against her skin. "I don't think I could have waited another day without having you." He licked her neck. "Your taste. I've never forgotten. So damn good."

She hummed in pleasure as his lips trailed across her collarbone and his hands dipped low to rest right above her ass. He pulled her close, pressing hard against her and leaving no doubt in her mind that he wanted her.

"Feel what you do to me?" he asked in a growl. "What watching you in the moonlight did to me?"

Feeling inspired, she pushed on his shoulders and he took a step backward in surprise. "What the hell, Meagan?"

She slowly rocked. Swayed back and forth. Dancing for him. "You like watching me in the moonlight?"

"God, yes."

She ran her hands over her hips. Cupped her breasts. "Like what you see?"

"I'll tell you what," he said, and the smirk on his face was evident in his tone. "You can do what you like out here, but once we cross that threshold, you do what I say."

She was still moving seductively when she replied. "What if I don't want to go inside?"

"I'm not fucking you outside."

"Why not? Afraid of what will happen if I take charge? Afraid you'll like it?"

"Nope. I'm afraid of bears. Afraid they'll come up on me unaware and maul me to death when I'm deep inside you."

She laughed. "But what a way to go."

"You plan on spending your entire time talking?"

"Bossy. Bossy. Bossy." She stopped dancing and placed her hands on his shoulders. "I think I'll start by undressing you. See what you have underneath all those clothes."

"You've seen it."

"It felt bigger when it was pressed up against me just a few minutes ago."

He chuckled. "I'm yours for the next ten minutes."

"What happens after ten minutes?"

"Then it's my turn."

She didn't waste any more time. With quick fingers, she unbuttoned his shirt and pushed it off his shoulders. He was magnificent with his shirt off. "All those clothes hide a damn fine body. You work out."

It wasn't a question, but he answered it anyway. "Almost every day."

She ran an appreciative hand over his biceps. "Push-ups?"

"Yes. So I have complete control over my body when I have you underneath me. Your legs spread to give me access. Your pussy wet and ready. Your breasts pebbled and waiting for my mouth."

"All that from push-ups?"

"Perhaps I'd better show you."

"Not yet. I still have ten minutes."

"Now. I'm not waiting ten minutes."

Chapter Five

"Damn," Meagan said. "You're still bossy."

Luke swallowed his laugh. "And you still like it."

"I'll go inside on one condition."

"Negotiating, are you?"

"How badly do you want inside?"

He dragged a finger down her belly, stopping right above the apex of her legs. "I want inside so, so bad."

To her credit, she didn't bat his hand away or try to get him to move it lower. "Then you have to agree you owe me ten minutes. To be collected at the time of my choosing."

"Deal. Now inside."

"Where do you want me?"

The correct question was where didn't he want her because he wanted her everywhere. "We'll start traditionally. In the bedroom."

"On the bed?"

"Not that traditional. I want you bending over the bed."

She sighed. "I didn't even get to take your pants off."

"Inside. Now. Not another word."

"You said I could do what I wanted out here."

Oh yes, she was going to be fun. He loved a submissive with sass. "That was ten words. You get ten spanks. I suggest you be quiet and go wait for me like I asked."

She turned and headed toward the house, but he heard her mutter, "Dominants."

"That's eleven." He laughed as she scurried inside.

He followed right on her heels, afraid if he didn't, he'd change his mind and he didn't want to change his mind. He was doing exactly what he'd done years before and he'd broken her heart then. But this was different, wasn't it? She'd insisted it was only for tonight and he believed her. After all, no matter how much he wanted a relationship with her, he wasn't even sure she liked him most of the time. He was a handy scratch for her itch tonight. No need to overanalyze it.

He stepped into his room, saw her waiting for him, exactly like he asked, and his ability to analyze anything left him. He'd seen her naked at the club and even minutes ago in the moonlight. But damn. Seeing her in his room, bent over his bed, at his command, left him breathless.

She didn't move a muscle as he approached her. Didn't react in any way when he lightly ran his hand across her ass. It occurred to him at that moment, the last time they'd been together, she was new in her submissive journey and he'd never observed her in a scene. This experienced submissive Meagan was a new person altogether.

He couldn't wait to get to know her.

"Very nice," he said, giving the flesh of her backside a squeeze.

Just because he wanted to. "I owe you eleven spanks and I'm going to round it up to an even twelve. But because you followed my commands so well once you made it inside, I'll let you pick the implement."

"If it pleases you, Sir, I'd prefer no implement. I'd prefer you use your hand."

He couldn't hide the shock in his voice. "Why is that?"

"Because I like the feel of your hands on me, Sir."

He'd be more than a fool to turn her down. He'd be a crazy-ass fool.

"That would please me very much. My hands like being on you." He moved into position behind her. "No need to count."

Instead of starting right away, he slid a finger between her legs. Damn, she was soaked. "Someone really likes my hands on her."

To keep her on the edge, he decided to tease her a bit more. "I'm trying to decide how I'll spank you. Slow and methodical, so you feel every swat? Or hard and fast, so I take your breath away? Do I slowly turn your ass pink or do I master your flesh at one time and really show it who's boss?"

Her legs started to tremble, just a bit. "You're thinking about it now, aren't you? Wondering what I'll do. How I'll do it. You're imagining both scenarios, trying to decide which one you want. I tell you what. I'm feeling extraordinarily generous tonight, so I'm going to let you decide. Either I spank you slow and fuck you fast or I spank you fast and fuck you slow. Your decision. And you have five seconds to decide and if you don't, you get all spank and no fuck."

He'd barely got the words out before she was answering. "Fast spank. Slow fuck, Sir."

So as not to disappoint, he moved quickly. Not even giving

her a chance to take a breath before he rained twelve of his hardest on her pale backside. After each one, she gave a gasp of pain/ pleasure that made him so hard, he feared he'd come before they even started.

"Holy fuck," she gasped when he'd finished. Her ass was a flaming red, and his hand felt sore.

"That's holy fuck, *Sir*." He gave her one last stinging slap, this time on her exposed pussy, and was rewarded with a desire-filled moan.

"Holy fuck, Sir."

"That's better. Now on your knees before me." He waited until she'd moved into position before continuing. "You wanted to take my pants off earlier. I'm going to let you do it now. Then you're going to thank me for your spanking by sucking my cock. I hope you know how to deep-throat because I want that mouth open and your throat taking every damn inch of my dick."

She moved quickly and without hesitation until she'd stripped him and saw the size of his erection. Then her eyes betrayed her and he sensed uncertainty in her for the first time.

He gave himself a tug. "All for you, sweetheart. Open wide and thank me for that sore ass."

She placed her hands on his thighs and opened her mouth.

"I'll let you do it at your pace, but we're not moving on until you've taken it all. And if you stop, I'm taking the lead and I won't be slow or gentle."

She took her time, but to her credit, she didn't stop. He found himself unable to look away from the sight of her taking his dick in her mouth. He reached the back of her throat and when she relaxed, he slipped all the way inside.

"Damn. You took all of me, just like I asked. Feels so good, I'm tempted to throat-fuck you. The only thing is that sweet pussy has been teasing me all night and I can't wait to bury myself to the hilt inside."

He reached down, grabbed a fistful of blond hair, and pulled her head up so she had no choice but to look him in the eye. "Like the feel of my dick in your mouth? Are you imagining how it's going to feel once I get it inside another part of your body?"

She nodded around his cock. He lightly slapped her cheek before slipping out of her. "Back on the bed. How flexible are you?"

"I'm not Gumby, but I'm not a lightweight either, Sir."

"Good enough. On your stomach. Knees near the edge and I want you to reach behind your back to grab your ankles."

In that position, she'd be completely spread for him with the added benefit of giving him the ability to use her arms for leverage. He waited, even after she'd arranged herself the way he asked, so she could sense her vulnerability. She needed his touch; her body trembled with pent-up desire. And though he wanted nothing more than to thrust into her and take them both to completion, it'd been too long to rush.

So against his own urges, he simply stroked her legs. The soft skin of the inside. The sensitive area at the juncture of her thighs. Then, with the lightest touch possible, he brushed her clit.

"Oh, God. Please, Sir!"

"Please, Sir, what?"

"Please, Sir, do something."

He gave her clit another barely there brush. "Isn't this something?"

"I meant something . . . more."

"Something more?" He slapped her ass. "I think you've been playing Top so much you've forgotten who's in charge tonight. Try to Top from the bottom one more time and all you'll do is watch me get myself off."

She mumbled something.

"What was that?"

"Sir. Yes, Sir."

Right. Like he bought that. He spanked her again. "I don't believe for a minute that's what you said, but as long as you understand the consequences, I'll let it go."

She wisely didn't say anything further. He blew on the reddened skin of her ass, making her shiver, and it struck him that while he liked her in this position, he didn't want to take her like this the first time. For damn sure if they had only the one night, he would take her more than once.

"Flip over onto your back," he said. He wanted to see her face as he possessed her. More than that, he wanted her to see his. There was no way he could change the past, but perhaps it would ease her mind about the present if she saw what she did to him.

She turned quickly and raked her eyes over his body, a faint smile playing on her lips. He was pleased to find her looking at him. All in all, it seemed only fair; he'd certainly looked his share at her.

"Like what you see?" he couldn't help but ask.

"Yes, Sir," she replied, shocking him with her honesty. "Very much so."

"That makes two of us. Every inch of you is fucking beautiful."

"Thank you, Sir."

He wanted to tell her she was more beautiful now than she was all those years ago, but didn't, thinking it would probably not be in his best interest to bring up the past. Focus on the present, he told himself. The past was unchangeable, the future uncertain. All he had control over at the moment was now and he was going to make the most of it.

"You ready for me?" he asked, rolling on a condom. "Ready for me to fuck you—how did you pick? Slow?"

"So ready, Sir."

"Open your legs for me."

He moved between her thighs as she dropped them open. She held her breath waiting for his first penetration, but he didn't appease her. Instead he slapped her clit with his cock.

"You look so damn fuckable. Your legs spread. Your pussy glistening. Your clit aching to be touched."

She gritted her teeth and hissed as his cock struck that spot again.

"I bet I could get you off like this."

"I bet you could too, Sir." She arched her back against the continuing torment of her sensitive flesh.

"Maybe we'll try that later. We agreed to one night, but you'd better believe I'm going to ensure it's a night you won't soon forget. In fact, I hope you don't have plans for tomorrow, because I'm going to take all damn night. By morning you won't know your own name, but your body won't forget mine."

To prove his point, he shifted his hips and entered her with one long, slow thrust.

Her eyes fluttered. "Oh my God. Did you get bigger?"

It was so unexpected, he chuckled. "Not that I'm aware of."

He withdrew and started a torment-inducing rhythm with his hips. At least it was torment inducing for him. He should have thought through giving her a choice in how he took her. Though from the way she kept lifting her hips, trying to draw him closer, she was second-guessing her decision as well.

"Ah, yes," he lied. "I could do this all night."

She whimpered.

"You feel incredible. So hot and tight, and"—he punctuated his words with a hard thrust—"good."

He started moving just a touch faster. "Wrap your legs around my waist." He needed to feel her wrapped around his body. He loved the feel of her wrapped more intimately around him.

No sooner did he feel her heels on his butt than he knew he'd made a mistake. With each thrust into her, her legs tightened around him, urging him onward, pleading silently for him to take her faster.

He moved within her a few more times before he gave in to the need his body screamed for.

"Fuck slow."

"Oh, hell, yes," she said, as he drove into her harder and faster. Allowing them both to move toward what they needed. "Sir."

He slipped a hand between their bodies. He'd never come first before in his life, but if she didn't catch up to him soon, he was going to break that record.

"How close?" he asked.

"Very, Sir."

He stroked her clit. "Let it go."

She didn't give a verbal answer, but nodded and closed her eyes. A few more thrusts and her body spasmed around him. Normally, he'd have given her a second orgasm before allowing himself to take his own pleasure. But he knew he'd never be able to last that long. It was a miracle he'd lasted as long as he had.

He managed to slow his thrusts down, drawing out every sigh, whimper, and moan she had before his own climax crashed over him, drowning out her sounds of pleasure with his.

Meagan wasn't sure she could work up enough energy to move. Though, all things considered, if she never moved again, she probably wouldn't find it in herself to complain. Holy shit. She didn't remember sex with Luke being that good.

Granted, she recalled it had been pretty awesome, but there was no way it was THAT awesome.

"I'm crushing you," he said, shifting away from her.

Was he? She didn't care. In fact, she rather liked the feel of his weight on her. Odd, she normally didn't. She didn't want him to move too far away, so she found the strength to keep a hand on his shoulder.

His hard, slick-with-sweat-from-fucking-you shoulder. Just remembering the way he looked above her, his muscles flexing as he pounded into her . . .

Fuck.

She wanted him again.

And that was A Very Bad Sign for a number of reasons, beginning with the fact that they were working together professionally. They had been down this road before. It didn't end well.

Her body went cold as the second reason came to her.

Taskmaster.

Damn it all to hell and back. She hadn't even thought of the blackmailer all night. Why did he have to jump straight to her head after such an amazing time with Luke?

Because anyone who knew what was going on would assume she'd just slept with Luke to get close to him. She knew that's the way she'd look at her current situation. And she didn't even want to think about what Luke would say. Whatever happened, she'd just have to make sure he never found out.

As if she didn't already hate The Taskmaster enough, this just added to the number. He'd just managed to throw a wet blanket on the most perfect sex she'd had in . . . well, ever.

She refused to let him have that much power. Not on the one night she'd decided to give herself to Luke. Yet another reason why one night only was smart. And if she had only one night, she wasn't going to waste it.

"Hey," she said, rolling over to her side to face Luke.

He tucked a strand of hair behind her ear. "Hey, yourself."

She stretched. "That was amazing."

"I agree."

She lifted herself up on one elbow so she could see the alarm clock over his shoulder. "Night's still young."

"Is that a subtle hint, Meagan Bishop?"

"Oh no." She traced his raised eyebrow. "There was nothing meant to be subtle about it."

He laughed and rolled her over to her back. "If you want me to continue to be awesome, I'm going to need to recover."

"It's good to be a girl."

"I'll take your word for it." He sat up. "I'm going to go get rid of this condom and when I get back, we'll see if I can't make you even more happy to be a girl."

"I look so forward to it, Sir."

He was gone for only a few minutes, but in that time she felt utterly alone in his large bed. She couldn't fathom why. The only thing she could attribute it to was The Taskmaster. God, she hated that man. At least, she thought it was a man. No, it was more; what she felt was beyond hate for whoever it was. Not only for what they were doing to her, but because they had now cast a shadow on what had been an amazing night.

"You okay?" Luke climbed in the bed and pulled her close.

She relaxed in his arms, chiding herself. She didn't want him to think she regretted anything. And she certainly didn't like the fact she'd thought about The Taskmaster so much while he was gone. "Just lonely without you."

"I was gone for five minutes, tops."

"It felt much longer."

He started to speak, then hesitated.

"What?" she asked.

"I was just wanting to make sure you were okay with spending the night."

Was she? Hell, yes. But would it be smart? In their haste, they'd agreed to one night, sure, but should she? Where would that leave them in the morning?

"Will anyone be worried if you don't go back to your place tonight?"

She laughed. "My plants."

He nibbled on her ear. "I meant what I said earlier. If we only have tonight, we should take advantage of the *whole* night."

"Mmm." She'd never leave if he kept that up. "When did you get so smart?"

"When I accepted your invitation to dinner." His fingers teased the back of her neck. Fuck, he'd remembered. All those years and he hadn't forgotten how to drive her crazy.

"Sir," she whined, pushing her hips against him. "Please, please, please tell me you're recovered enough." He had if the bulge she felt told her anything.

"Probably," he said, but didn't move.

Well? she bit back.

"Probably, I have, but there's something I want to do first."

As long as he stayed naked and didn't get out of the bed, he could do whatever he wanted. "What?"

"I want to see if you taste as good as I remember."

She moaned as he lowered himself between her legs. She might not survive until morning.

Chapter Six

The next Friday night, Meagan eyed the secluded house that looked more like a hunting lodge, and then turned back to Abby. "Are you sure it's okay that I'm here?"

Abby all but rolled her eyes as they got out of the car. "It's fine. And you were the one saying you needed to get out more."

"I could just go to the bed-and-breakfast." It was what she'd planned to do before Abby invited her to the "Girls' Night In."

"You'd be by yourself. That defeats the purpose of getting out."

"Dena's husband doesn't mind all these women sleeping at his house?"

"You, me, Julie, and Sasha are hardly 'all these women.' Besides, Dena said Jeff was more than happy to spend the night at Daniel's."

"If you're sure."

"I am." Abby waved at the car that pulled up behind them. "Look, there's Sasha."

They waited while the other woman parked and got her overnight bag. She smiled. "Hey, Abby, and Meagan, right?"

"Yes, that's right." The last time Meagan saw Sasha, the evening ended with her soon-to-be Master punishing her for coming without permission. But now, she couldn't help but notice the gorgeous collar the brunette wore in place of the thin leather band she had on the last time. "Love your collar."

A look of complete bliss covered Sasha's face and she lifted one hand to trace the necklace. "Thank you."

Ah, new love. Had she ever looked like that? "I can't wait to hear about your hot Brit."

"I'm surprised Cole let you get away tonight," Abby said as they made their way to the front door. "Isn't Friday when you two start your more structured time?"

Sasha ducked her head, but not before Meagan saw her cheeks flush. "Yes, but he had to travel into New York City tonight to meet with his editor and some people she brought in. He said it'd be late, so he'd stay overnight and come home in the morning. Otherwise, I'd planned to just stay for a few hours."

She sounded a bit wistful, as if she really wanted to be with Cole, but was trying to tell herself that it was just fine she was staying at Jeff and Dena's. No, Meagan decided, she'd never experienced anything like that before.

A dark-haired man with a gentle smile opened the door. "Hello, ladies. Come on in. Julie's already back in the bedroom with Dena." His gaze stopped at Meagan and he offered her his hand. "Jeff Parks."

His touch was strong and sure. "Nice to meet you, Jeff. Meagan Bishop. I'm a friend of Abby's."

"Technically," Abby said. "She's my boss, but for tonight, we're just friends."

Understanding crossed Jeff's face. "Her boss, you're the one—"

"Come on, let's go see Dena," Abby interrupted, grabbing Meagan's hand and pulling her down the hall before Jeff could finish his sentence. "'Bye, Jeff."

They left a frowning Jeff standing at the front door. Meagan peeked over her shoulder. He stood watching them, his arms crossed. "Uh, Abby. Jeff doesn't look very happy."

"I am *not* going to go into what happened at that club. That was months ago."

"He was there?" When Abby's first post went up at the news station, it was an unprecedented success and Meagan had taken her to a BDSM club to celebrate. An old Dom friend asked Meagan to dance and later to play. She'd agreed because he assured her he'd taken care of Abby. But he hadn't and she'd almost been assaulted.

"He was the one who saved me," Abby said. "And I'm not talking about it anymore."

They'd made it to the bedroom where a gorgeous and very pregnant blonde was sitting up in bed, surrounded by pillows and giggling at something the brunette beside her was saying. They looked up at their entrance.

"Hey, guys," Abby said. "This is my friend Meagan. Meagan, that's Dena in the bed and Julie beside her. Julie owns Petal Pushers with Sasha."

Meagan nodded and said hellos, but she couldn't help but feel out of place. These ladies all knew one another and had shared history. She should have gone to the bed-and-breakfast.

She was even more sure of that when Jeff entered the bedroom. He made a beeline to Dena and sat beside her on the bed. "I'm going to Daniel's. You let me know if anything happens."

Dena lightly stroked his cheek and gave him a sweet smile. "Yes, now you go have guy fun. The little miss and I are fine."

He leaned forward and kissed her. "Love you." He kissed her belly. "Love you, too. Stay put a few more weeks."

When he stood up, he spoke to Abby. "Call me if she so much as sneezes."

Behind him, Dena picked up a pillow and aimed it at his head.

"I see you," he said.

"Damn, you do have eyes in the back of your head," Dena said, but put the pillow down.

"Nah, just a well-placed mirror." He nodded to the far wall. Instead of leaving though, he turned to Meagan. "Any friend of Abby's is a friend of mine. If she's made peace with you, I won't hold the past against you either."

No one said anything until he left.

"That was cryptic," Sasha spoke first.

"Not talking about it," Abby said.

"I should go." Meagan shook her head. "This was a bad idea."

"No," all four women said at once.

Meagan hesitated. It *would* be nice to be part of girls' night. "I don't know."

"I'm deciding for you," Abby said. "You're staying."

Meagan turned her Domme face on her, but Abby just laughed. "Don't even."

The group seemed to think the discussion over. Sasha walked up to the bed. "How many weeks are you?"

Dena rubbed her belly. "Twenty-eight."

"I miss being pregnant."

All eyes shot to Abby. She held her hands up. "Not that we're doing anything to change that. I mean we are *doing it*, but not to get pregnant or anything. I just, you know, enjoyed being pregnant."

"You should have a third," Julie said.

"Easy for you to say," Abby replied. "You don't even have one."

"Not yet."

"Are you . . ." Sasha started.

"No, but we've talked about it lately."

Everyone agreed this was A Really Good Thing and before she knew what was happening, Meagan found herself getting caught up in the laughter and teasing of the group.

Two hours later, Abby, Meagan, and Julie finished off their second bottle of wine. Dena didn't drink any for obvious reasons. Sasha said she couldn't drink without Cole's permission and he hadn't replied to the text she'd sent asking.

Meagan glanced to where Sasha sat frowning at the silent phone. "Kinda makes you want to grab them by the balls and give a good yank, doesn't it?"

Sasha laughed. "Yes, but yank Cole's balls? Nope. Never going to happen. But it would be nice if he at least replied."

"He's probably in a meeting or driving or something." Julie nodded. "But yeah. Hell to the no to the ain't gonna happen, on ball yanking."

Meagan tried to picture messing with Luke's and had to agree. "Right, bad choice of words. Yeah, I could just see me doing that with . . ."

She trailed off as four pairs of eyes looked her way.

"I didn't know you were involved with anyone," Abby said softly.

"I'm not. I mean, it was one night." She blew a piece of hair out of her eyes. "One really, really amazing night."

"The photographer?" Sasha asked.

Meagan nodded, remembering Abby told her Sasha was the one who found the old magazines.

"Oh my . . . *fuck*," Abby said. Meagan was surprised at how pale she looked.

"Abby?" Meagan asked.

"I just didn't think you were ever getting back with him." She groaned. "Shit."

"What is it?"

"I'll tell you later. When I've had less wine."

"There we go." Sasha put her phone down with a sigh. "He said no. He wants my head to be clear. Though I don't know why. It's not like he's here."

"Julie," Dena said. "Before I forget, will you let Bo and Ace out? They need to go out one more time for the night."

"Sure." Julie hopped up. Not quite as gracefully as she had before the wine, but still steady.

"Sasha," Abby said. "Are you okay? Is something wrong?"

"Remember how you once told me Doms had a reason for everything they did?" Sasha asked.

"Yes."

Sasha stood up and put her hands on her hips. "What could possibly be his reason for not letting me drink tonight? I mean, he's not here and it's not like I get together with you guys a lot. It feels like he's just doing it to be a pain in the ass."

"I doubt he's being a pain in the ass," Abby said.

"Maybe I'll have a glass. He'll never know and you guys won't tell."

Dena laughed. "Girl, they always find out."

Sasha sighed. "True. Ugh. It's like he has Dom ESP or something."

Julie returned from letting the dogs out, but she wasn't alone. Cole stood behind her and since they were both behind Sasha, she didn't see him. Meagan tried to get Sasha's attention, but Cole held his finger up to his lips. He was just intense enough looking that Meagan obeyed.

"Seriously, he's worse than Santa Claus. I wouldn't be surprised to find out he's got elves stationed everywhere as spies." She sat back down with a huff.

"In that case, why don't you come sit on my lap, so you can tell me if you've been naughty or nice?" Cole asked, an amused expression on his face.

Sasha gasped and as Cole approached her, she came up to kneel and bowed her head. "Sir. I wasn't expecting you."

"Obviously." He ran his fingers through her hair. "I decided I didn't want to spend the night in the city. I came by to see if you'd like to go home like we originally planned. If not, you can stay and drink."

"That's why you wouldn't let me have a drink?"

"We've never played intoxicated. We're not going to start tonight." He rocked back on his heels. "Assuming you come home, that is."

Though she had seemed content with staying overnight with the girls, Meagan couldn't help but see the delight in Sasha's expression—heck, her entire being—at the prospect of going home with Cole.

"Let me get my things." She stood up and kissed his cheek. "Take me home, Cole," she said in not quite a whisper.

"Don't you want to stay? Visit with your friends?"

"I want you."

He gave her a sultry grin and then in a surprise move, he grabbed her around the waist and dipped her low, giving her a long and passionate kiss. "I'm not going to argue with that," he said once he had her back upright. He glanced at Dena. "Tell Jeff we'll come by and get her car tomorrow."

Dena sniffled and waved her hand at the couple. "Damn pregnancy hormones. Go. Don't worry about the car."

Sasha quickly told everyone good-bye and good night and though the other women hugged her and said they were happy for her, Meagan could tell Sasha had one thing on her mind: get home with Cole. He stood off to the side, waiting patiently while she got her things together. Sasha gave Julie an extra-long hug and nodded at something she said. Then she turned toward Cole with an infectious smile.

"Let's go home, Sir."

He snaked an arm around her waist, pulling her close, and giving her a quick kiss, before saying to the group, "Good night, ladies. I'd say I'm sorry for stealing Sasha away, but I'm not."

When they heard the front door close, Julie broke the silence. "I would never in a million years have thought they'd be good together, but every time I see them, I can't imagine them with anyone else."

"She grounds him," Dena said. "I haven't known him for as long as Daniel, but she soothes him, for lack of a better word. There's a peace with him he's never had before. Even with Kate."

"Kate and Cole were in a twenty-four/seven relationship for eight years," Abby told Meagan.

"I think it's because she accepts who he is and doesn't try to change him or make him something he's not," Julie said. "And he does the same for her."

"That's so important," Abby said. "If you go into a relationship trying to change that person, you'll never be content."

It was a simple truth, one Meagan had heard numerous times before. But for some reason, hearing Abby say it thrust it in an entirely new light. How many times had she gone into a relationship with that mind-set? Granted, it was never as cut-and-dried as "He's okay. Let me fix XYZ and he'll be perfect," but the intention was there.

And how many times had she been in a relationship when the guy tried to change her? Too many to count.

If Sasha and Cole had found in the other person someone who accepted them, she was thrilled. And jealous.

Her phone buzzed and she pulled it from her pocket. *Luke.* She'd told him she was going to the bed-and-breakfast, but hadn't told him about her change of plans.

"Hey," she said, answering.

"Hey." He didn't sound right. Not really as though he was angry, but there was a hint of something in his voice.

"Something wrong? You sound off." She prayed silently that he hadn't found out about The Taskmaster.

"I'm at a bed-and-breakfast someone told me they were going to be at, holding a bottle of wine, cheese, crackers, and a rope. Guess who's not here?"

"You went to the bed-and-breakfast to see me?" Meagan glanced up and saw that no one was talking; rather, they were all staring at her. "I changed my plans. Abby invited me to a girls' night thing. I'm at Jeff Parks's house."

"Abby West?"

"Yes."

"She's a sweetheart. And so much for my surprising you."

Meagan's head spun quickly, trying to figure out how she could meet him, but she couldn't find a way.

"If I had a way to get there, I'd come meet you." She couldn't hold back the sigh. "Abby drove me."

"That's okay. Maybe we can do it another time."

Why was he going to the bed-and-breakfast when they'd agreed on one night only? She wanted to tease him about his plan to seduce her, but didn't feel comfortable doing so with all the ears listening.

"We're still on for tomorrow?" she asked.

"Yes."

It would be their first session since they slept together. She'd be lying not to admit how much she still wanted him. But it wasn't anything she was going to talk about. Especially not with an audience.

"I'm looking forward to it." Looking forward to having his hands on her body. Looking forward to her knees turning to jelly when he gave her a command. Suddenly the next day couldn't come soon enough.

Meagan didn't make it home the next morning until nearly eleven. She'd planned to get back by eight, but Jeff showed up around seven and cooked breakfast for everyone. He looked so relieved that Dena was fine and insisted everyone stay to eat. She'd looked over at Abby and neither one of them had the heart to turn him down.

Which meant she didn't have much time to prepare for the session with Luke. Not that, technically, there was much to prepare other than her mental state. She was still floored he'd traveled to the bed-and-breakfast last night.

Before she got ready for Luke, she needed to check her e-mails. She'd forgotten her battery charger the night before and her phone died shortly before midnight.

Once she made it home, she plugged it in and booted up her laptop. There was an e-mail from Guy.

Hey, Meagan,

You left last weekend before we had a chance to talk.
What's your schedule like this coming week? Let's do lunch!

Ugh. Let's not. She clicked out of it, but didn't delete. She'd think of a reason to decline later.

Next up were several work-related issues. She read through them, but didn't reply. The next e-mail made her physically ill.

Hello, slut,

It seems like I was right and you didn't need any advice about getting close to Luke. Since you're doing so well, it's time for you to once again do something for me. I want you to find where Luke keeps his pictures.

You have a week to find out.

Don't even think about saying no. I'm bigger and stronger than you, and I know where you live.

The Taskmaster

Her whole body shook when she finished reading the e-mail. This had to stop. She couldn't do it. Getting information about a new club was one thing. But digging through his personal stuff? She couldn't think of a legitimate reason to ask him where he stored them. And she wasn't about to go looking without him knowing. That would be wrong.

But even if she asked Luke about the pictures, if he ever found out she was being blackmailed, he'd hate her. He'd think she only went out with him, only slept with him, in order to get close to him. She couldn't stand it if he thought that. She'd just have to make sure he never found out.

And why the hell had this person decided to get to Luke through her? She leaned back in her chair. There had to be a connection between the three of them. Was it a given The Task-master knew her and Luke personally? That was scary.

She turned it around every way possible until her head hurt, but came up with no answers other than one. For this after-noon, she'd have to ensure Luke had no reason to think any-thing was up.

"Okay," Luke said, hours later. "Tell me what's going on."

They'd been working on the first bondage scene shoot for over an hour and so far he had nothing he could use. Nothing. Every-thing was perfect and working like it should. Everything except Meagan. He knew something was wrong the minute he saw her.

Oh, she tried to hide it, and maybe she would have fooled someone who didn't spend a good amount of their time watch-ing people. But watch people he did, through his lens as a photo-grapher, in his club as a business owner, and while taking his pleasure as a Dom. Since he'd done all three with Meagan, she was only lying to herself if she thought he didn't know better.

She looked up from where she was kneeling with her hands clasped behind her back. "What makes you think anything's up?"

"Don't make it worse by lying."

She took a deep breath. "Sorry. I'm just not in the right head-space today. I didn't get much sleep last night."

Last night when she was at Dena's with some of the ladies from Wilmington, and Abby.

Abby.

Damn it. *That's* what the problem was. She'd been with Abby all night and, with other submissives present, they'd probably started talking about scenes. And it would have been nothing for his name to come up. Especially since he'd played with Nathaniel and Abby on multiple occasions. He hadn't even thought about the times he'd been invited into the Wests' playroom until right now.

Meagan probably thought he'd been keeping it from her on purpose. It'd slipped his mind she was Abby's boss.

With a sigh, he put the camera down and started untying her.

"Wait," she said. "What are you doing? We aren't finished, are we?"

"We are for now," he said. "Let's talk."

Her face grew unnaturally pale. *Fuck, what had Abby told her?* He nodded over to a love seat against the far wall and, without him saying anything, she stood up and walked over to it. She sat with her head down, picking at her nails. He took a seat close, but not touching.

"I'm sorry I didn't tell you about playing with the Wests first," he said. "You shouldn't have had to hear it from Abby."

Her head shot up and from the "O" of surprise her lips made, whatever had been bothering her didn't have anything to do with him and Abby.

"Shit," he said. "That's not what was on your mind, was it?"

"You played with Abby? And Nathaniel?"

"Er, umm." Damn it all. Wasn't this just great? He couldn't very well deny it now, could he? "Yes, a few times. It wasn't like a regular scene. Nathaniel's not one to share. But yes, I've dominated Abby. I've just never had sex with her."

Meagan appeared to be thinking this over. "That explains why Abby got so flustered when I mentioned you."

But Abby never told her anything. Nope. He'd taken care of that all by himself.

"I hope this doesn't make things awkward between you," he said.

She tilted her head. "No, I don't think it will. We're all grown-ups."

"Good. I would hate to come between you and an employee."

"Will it be awkward for you?" she asked.

"No, I don't think so." He tapped his finger on his knee. "You know, it was actually Abby who inadvertently opened the door for this book."

"How is that?"

"I took some pictures of her and Nathaniel months ago and they allowed me to post a few of the ones that don't show who they are. Rick saw them and asked me if I'd be interested in the book he was publishing."

"Did he want Abby to be the model?"

"No, he asked me who I thought would be the best person for the job and you were my first choice."

"Why me?" she asked.

He couldn't lie to her, so he told her the truth. "You were made to be in front of the camera. I knew that the first time I took your picture and the years haven't changed that."

That information lightened the dark expression she'd had all day. But, unfortunately, if she hadn't been thinking about him and Abby during the session, there was something else bothering her.

"Since I messed up reading your mind," he teased, "why don't you tell me what was bothering you during the scene just now?"

She took a deep breath and drew herself up straight. "Work stuff. I'm not going to think about it now. I'm ready to get to work."

He wasn't sure he totally believed her. Maybe he needed to

change things up and force her mind to be focused on him alone. "Yes, let's get back to what we were doing."

She stood up.

"Sit down."

A look of confusion crossed her expression, but she sat down.

"I'm going to try something else for the shoot. The book is on artistic BDSM so, if you agree, I'll run this more like a scene and less like a photography session."

She nodded wordlessly.

"If you agree, strip and crawl to the middle of the room and wait for me on your knees."

Lust flashed in her eyes and she quickly undressed and dropped to the floor to start crawling. Luke took advantage of the angle to snap a few shots of her ass. She made it to the middle of the room and waited on her knees. He let her stay there for a bit to get in the proper mind-set; then he took his camera and joined her.

"For the next hour or so, you are mine to control," he said. "Do you agree?"

"Yes, Sir."

She was a beautiful woman, no question about it. But on her knees, allowing herself to be dominated, she was stunning.

"What's your safe word?"

"Red."

"Noted." He put the camera down and picked up some silk rope. It wasn't what he would use for an actual scene, but it worked well for photographs. "Stand up with your hands behind your back."

She stood. Her compliance must have triggered something in her mind, because she no longer looked troubled. All previous evidence of worry had been replaced by an expression of peace and contentment. And he knew no matter what happened with the two of them in the future, no matter what they did or didn't do, for this time, right now, she was his. From the look of bliss on her face, she wouldn't want it any other way.

He took his time drawing the rope around her arms. Done properly, bondage was an art, and though he wanted good pictures for the book, more than that, he wanted to pay homage to Meagan's body by decorating and restraining her to the best of his ability.

When he'd introduced her to bondage years ago and watched the emergence of her submissive side, he'd thought that she was awe-inspiring. But as he stepped back after binding her arms behind her and seeing the submissive she'd become, he was even more awestruck.

He took his time walking around her, trying to capture with his camera just a touch of the beauty that was her submission, but knowing it was far too vast to ever be conveyed by a mere photograph.

He found he didn't want to stop. He wanted all of her in his ropes. But, he had reached their agreed-upon time limit.

"Meagan." The decision would be hers. "That's our time for the day and I got some beautiful shots. If you want, I'll untie you and we can wrap up. Or, if you agree, I'd like to continue and see how the rest of you looks bound by my hand."

"I want more, Sir."

"If you're sure," he said.

"I'm enjoying this. There's so much freedom to be found like this. I can shut my mind off. It's so refreshing not to have to think."

Instead of a verbal reply, he answered by covering her lips

with his. It was a kiss he fully controlled. One he took. Bound as she was, she couldn't touch him, and though she could have taken a step back, she didn't. She remained still, allowing him to kiss her and letting him know how much she wanted it by kissing him back.

He ended the kiss and slipped a black blindfold out of his back pocket. "To further help you shut your mind off."

She nodded, but she didn't have to. She knew he'd stop only if she said her safe word. He secured the blindfold around her head and stepped back.

"Thank you, Sir," she said in a breathy sigh.

"You like when I take your sight away?"

"Yes, Sir. It frees me even more."

Yup. She was fucking stunning.

He ran his hands over her body. "You okay with me touching you like this?"

"So okay, Sir."

He smiled and continued brushing his hands along her body. "I'm going to decorate this gorgeous body of yours with my ropes. It's silk, so it'll feel so good against your skin. And when I'm finished, it'll look fucking fabulous."

Like before, he bound her slowly, and whispered while he worked. Telling her how sexy she looked, how much it turned him on to have her in his ropes, and how it was going to take him so long to bind her properly, she'd probably still be feeling his silk on her body tomorrow.

"Can you feel them circling your breasts?" he asked.

"Yes, Sir."

"Think of the ropes as an extension of my hands. If I could, I'd be like this silk, touching you everywhere. Making sure you

felt me all along your body. There's not a place I wouldn't touch."
He slipped a hand between her legs. "Fuck, you're soaked."

"Mm, I really, really like bondage, Sir."

"I'll say." He teased her clit. "Fortunately, I really, really like
putting you in bondage."

Once he finished the upper part of her body, he took more
rope and started on her lower half.

"Are you okay in the position you're in?" he asked.

"Yes, Sir."

Since she was standing, he wasn't going to put her legs in any
wild and crazy positions. He'd save that for later. When he had
her in his bed again.

Oh yes, he would definitely have her in his bed again. There
was no way he wouldn't move heaven and earth to get her there.
It didn't matter that he'd said he'd wanted only one night. One
night wasn't nearly enough.

As he worked the silk around her legs, he peppered kisses along
her thighs, feeling pleased as her skin pebbled in gooseflesh.

"You look like a goddess in this silk."

"Thank you, Sir, but if I look good, it's only because you
make me that way." She sucked in a breath as his lips drew closer
and closer to the juncture of her thigh and torso, but whined
when he backed up.

"Not yet," he said. "I'm not quite ready to reward you for
being such a good girl."

He finished his rope work on her legs, then stepped back to
look. He'd been right. She was a different person in bondage.
Soft and pliable. The hardened TV executive was gone and in
her place was the most amazing submissive he'd ever worked
with.

Satisfied with the way she looked, he picked up the camera

and took pictures. He knew as he took picture after picture that the second part of the shoot more than made up for the lousy beginning. But even as the photographer part of him rejoiced in the quality of shots he was taking, the Dom part knew he'd achieved the greater victory.

Meagan wasn't one to easily give her submission. She was guarded and trusted only a few with that precious gift. She'd never said as much, but he knew without being told. The fact that she submitted to him so perfectly and easily was heady knowledge. A man could get drunk on that knowledge. And a Dom wouldn't rest until he'd claimed it completely.

Hours later, Luke woke to feel Meagan stir. After he'd untied her, he'd carried her to his bedroom where he wrapped his arms around her and told her to sleep. She'd given a few half-hearted protests, but even she knew she was in no state of mind to drive. Within minutes, she was snoring.

Luke had always been a light sleeper, so it came as no surprise to him that when Meagan extracted herself from his arms, he woke instantly. What surprised him was the fact that she sat up and moved to the edge of the bed. Even though his rational brain reasoned she might just be getting up to use the bathroom, his intuition told him it was something more. He kept his breathing deep and even so she'd think he was still asleep.

The bed shifted slightly and he felt the weight of her stare. She was watching him. Trying to see if he was sleeping? He focused on his breathing and willed his body not to move. After a few seconds, the bed shifted again as she stood up. Was she leaving?

He cracked one eye open. She wasn't putting her clothes on and for that he was thankful. He really didn't want to wake up to find a note where she should be. Besides, she didn't come across as the type of woman who would leave before dawn and not say anything.

The last time she spent the night, she'd wrapped up the next morning in an old robe he had. Since she was still naked after the rope scene, and he hadn't put anything on her after, she walked on tiptoes to the master bathroom and took the robe from the hook he had it on. Then she crept back through the bedroom and out into the hallway.

She was probably going to the kitchen for a little snack. He grinned. He was feeling a bit hungry, too. Though it wasn't food that would satisfy him. He'd sneak into the kitchen and turn tables on her. Maybe he'd hoist her *onto* the table. Yeah. That was the best way to take care of middle-of-the-night hunger pains. His cock agreed and stirred to life.

He slid out of bed, not bothering to put any clothes on. After all, she had only a robe and he wasn't planning on her wearing that much longer. He planned it all in his head. She'd have the refrigerator door open. He'd come up behind her and put his arms around her. She'd turn around. And then up on the table she'd go. He walked faster.

But when he stepped into the hallway, it wasn't to see her entering the kitchen, but his office.

His office?

He stepped into the room near the office, so he could watch her undetected. She was going through his desk drawers looking for something. Obviously not finding what she was looking for, she attacked his filing cabinet next. Whatever she was looking for, she was on a mission. Not once did she look up to see if her absence had been noted.

She sighed as she closed the last drawer. Her back was still to the doorway and he kept waiting for her to look over her shoulder, but she never did. Did she want to be caught? Or was she that intent on looking for what she wanted?

He couldn't imagine what she was after and he'd just taken a step forward to ask her what the hell she was doing, when she made a small noise and lunged at the photo boxes he had on a shelf behind his desk.

Photographs? What the fuck?

He ducked back into the room right as she turned around. He stayed still for five seconds and when he peeked again, she was going through his pictures. Her head was down and she was focused as he'd never seen her before as she flipped through the stack in the box. Being caught was clearly the last thought in her head. As silently as he could, he crept back to the bedroom and crawled into bed. Made sure he rolled onto his side so he wouldn't be facing her when she came back. What had he just witnessed?

According to the clock by his bed, merely five minutes passed before she returned to his bed. He knew he should confront her, but he wanted to wait. He wanted to see if he could determine which pictures she was looking for. Perhaps she only wanted to see the ones he'd taken of her. It struck him as he lay perfectly awake that he hadn't shown her any of the shots.

That had to be what it was.

He'd just convinced himself of that when he heard her sniffle. He held perfectly still, thinking maybe he'd heard wrong. But no, she twisted in the bed and from the sound of her breathing, she'd turned away from him. Though she tried to stifle it, she was obviously crying.

Fuck.

He was caught between angry and upset and worried. It was a completely new place for him and he didn't know how to handle it. He could pretend her coming back to bed had woken him up, but in his current state of mind, he doubted he could pull it off.

He could confront her. Ask her what the hell she was doing going through his office at two in the morning. But he felt perhaps he was too upset to talk rationally about it and with her already in tears, he would probably only make things worse. He'd just gotten her back in his life; he didn't want to push her away.

In the end, he did nothing. He stayed on his side of the bed, listening to her cry not-so-silent tears, and wondering what the fuck had just happened.

And what he was going to do when he found out.

No more crying, Meagan told herself. She'd done enough of that last night. Thank goodness Luke had been asleep at the time and her eyes were no longer puffy and red when they got up and had breakfast. She didn't hang around Luke's for long after. Just being in his presence made her feel even guiltier than she already was.

On the way back to her apartment, she took a detour. Later tonight she'd send an e-mail to The Taskmaster, but first she had to do something she'd rather not: visit her brother. She tried to stop by every few months to check on him, but she admitted it was more out of obligation than anything else. It'd been four months since her last visit and she'd promised her dad before he died that she'd keep an eye on him.

She shouldn't dread seeing her brother. That wasn't how families were supposed to work. Unfortunately, that was the way it was with her and Jake.

He was a year younger than her and, according to her grand-parents, had been an "oops" baby. When she was younger, she was often jealous at the attention he received from everyone. As she got older, she told herself it was simply that he was the baby of the family. But she remained jealous. Now, however, she was thankful she hadn't been treated the way he had been. In a word, he was useless.

She pulled up to the run-down condo he lived in. She hadn't bothered to call. It was a Sunday afternoon, after all. He'd be watching football.

She heard the announcer's voice from the television through the closed door. And, if she wasn't mistaken, other male voices as well. Great, now not only would she have to deal with her deadbeat brother; she'd have to deal with his deadbeat friends too. She thought about turning around and going back home without seeing him, but that would mean she had to e-mail The Taskmas-ter and she'd rather put that off for as long as possible. With a sigh, she rang the doorbell.

The sound was turned down and footsteps approached the door.

"Are you happy? I turned it down," her brother said, flinging open the door. He did a double take when he saw her. "Meagan. What are you doing here?"

"Nice to see you, too, Jake."

He looked as though he'd just rolled out of bed. And judging by his smell, it'd been several days since he'd showered.

"Yeah, whatever," he said. "Why are you here?"

"I came by to see how you're doing. Aren't you going to let me in?"

He didn't want to—that much was obvious by the pointed

stare and refusal to move out of the doorway. But she knew this game well, so she stood her ground and lifted an eyebrow.

With an exaggerated sigh, he stepped out of the way. "Don't say anything about the mess."

She pressed her lips together, but didn't say anything as she stepped over the threshold into the pigsty that was his apartment. Just inside the entranceway, piles of clothes filled one corner of the room, fast-food wrappers and bags were strewn everywhere, and the air held a hint of mold. Jesus, how could he stand to live like this? Her skin itched and she knew as soon as she made it home, she'd be taking a shower.

A guy she didn't know sat on a threadbare couch, watching TV. He nodded at her, but didn't acknowledge her in any other way.

"Ray, this is my sister, the TV exec. Meagan, this is my roommate, Ray."

"Pleasure," she said, and he just grunted.

It was a mistake to come today. She didn't want to talk with Ray around and she sure as hell wasn't going to sit down on anything.

"How's work going?" she asked Jake. Last time she'd talked to him, he was stocking groceries, but granted, that had been over four months ago and he rarely kept a job that long. "Still at the grocer?"

"Nah," he said, scratching his chest. "I quit. They wouldn't work around my schedule."

"What schedule?"

"I told you, I'm writing a book. The muse wouldn't talk to me with all that structure and shit. I have to be free."

Structure and shit? Did he mean life? She shook her head. In the past, she'd given him money, but she'd stopped that years ago. "So where are you working?"

"I told you, I'm writing."

"You found someone to give you an advance?" She thought that very unlikely. For one, his idea was probably something preposterous about aliens battling ape people, and two, he couldn't write for shit.

"No, but I will. I just need time to finish." He snapped his fingers. "Hey, do you think you could loan me some money for rent? Ray's been covering most of the expenses. I want to do my share."

"And your *share* is hitting your sister up for a loan? I have an idea. Why don't you get a job? Do something meaningful."

"I'm writing a book."

"For five years."

"Art takes time." He looked at his roommate. "You get that, don't you, Ray?"

Ray took a swig of beer and belched. "Your sister's hot."

She wrinkled her nose. "Please."

"In fact." Ray lowered his hand to his crotch and gave himself a slow stroke. "If you'd like to contribute to your brother's share, I'm sure we could work something out."

Yes, she'd miscalculated. The Taskmaster would have been the better option. She leveled Ray with her best Domme glare. "Bring anything of the sort up again in my presence and I'll tie your balls in a knot around your dick."

"Meagan, really?" Jake asked.

"You're seriously going to let him talk to me that way?"

"A lot of girls like him."

She stared at him in shock. "You're an ass."

He shrugged. "It's the truth."

"Obviously, talking with you is out of the question." She hugged her purse close to her body and turned. "I'll show myself out."

Before the door closed behind her, she heard Jake tell Ray, "She's always been an uppity bitch."

"You asshole," she mumbled as she walked toward her car. "I should have let the police have you."

On her way back home, she thought back to that summer.

Chapter Seven

Seventeen years ago

"There was another fire last night." Meagan's father set the newspaper down on the table and took a long sip of coffee. "No one's been hurt yet, but it's only a matter of time. Whoever's doing this is escalating."

"You think so?" Meagan asked.

"He got lucky this time, or rather the homeowners did. An off-duty fireman happened to see the fire and he was able to dispatch a crew. If he hadn't been there . . ."

"That's scary." Meagan shivered. "I don't even want to think about it."

"It was worse this time. The family was inside. I sure hope we can find out who's been doing this."

"No clues?" Since her dad worked for the fire department, he would know.

"Not anything I can talk about."

"You'll find out who it is."

"Maybe not," Jake said, strolling into the kitchen, his hair still wet from his shower. "Not if they're good. Not if they don't fuck up."

Her dad gave Jake a pointed stare. "Watch the language."

Jake rolled his eyes. "Whatever. The truth is, I bet you never find him."

"Don't be a dick. Of course they will," Meagan said.

"Language," her father repeated.

She decided to ignore her dad. "Jake, I'm leaving for school in three minutes. If you don't want to walk, I suggest you get your ass in the car."

Her father sighed. "Meagan."

As she walked past the table on the way to the garage, her eyes fell on the discarded newspaper. "Oh my God. I know that house." She grabbed the paper. "Jake, isn't that Melissa Coop's house?"

Jake took a granola bar from the pantry and squinted at the paper. "Might be."

"It is! Oh my God."

"Meagan, calm down." Her father took the newspaper back. "The family was okay. I promise we'll find out who's behind this."

She was still shaken as she got in the car and drove to school. Jake was unusually quiet, not complaining about her taste in music or the way she drove. He drummed his fingers against the door handle, and then picked something out from his nails.

"I can't believe someone set Melissa's house on fire," she said when they were halfway to the high school. "I mean, what do you think? Didn't you ask her out?"

"Yeah, but she turned me down."

"I wonder if she'll be at school today."

"Don't know. Like I said, she turned me down when I asked her out. I really don't know if she'll be there or not."

"Doesn't it bother you that this happened to someone you know? Someone you liked?"

"Not really. I mean, she's fine, right?"

"The paper said they got out in time. It doesn't mention if she was hurt."

"If she was, the paper would have said. They aren't going to let a moneymaker like that slip by."

"How is the fact that she's injured going to sell a bunch of papers?"

But Jake was finished talking. He focused on the passing scenery, probably lost in his own thoughts. She looked down at his fingers still drumming on the car handle.

"Jesus, Jake! What happened to your hand?" A long red gash ran across the top of his hand, surrounded by several smaller cuts.

"Oh, that." He ran his finger along the line. "Cut myself in the garage last night."

"Doing what?"

"Fuck off. None of your business."

"Excuse me for caring. It looks like you needed stitches."

"Well, I don't." He jerked the sleeve of his jacket down in an attempt to cover the gash.

Damn. And people said women were moody.

The rest of the ride to the school passed in silence and when she parked the car, Jake jumped out and hurried into the main building. Meagan shook her head as she watched him disappear in the crowd.

"You heard about Melissa's house?"

She turned to find one of her friends, Penelope, walking toward her.

"Yeah," Meagan said, remembering Penelope lived across the street from the Coops. "Saw it in the paper this morning. Horrible."

"I heard they lost everything."

"I really hope they find the bastard who did this."

"Me, too. Do you know if Jake saw anything?"

Meagan wrinkled her brow. "Why would Jake have seen anything?"

"I saw him outside in the area earlier last night. Thought he might have heard or seen something."

She planned to wait until her parents weren't at home before confronting him, but even though they were out that night, Jake was, too. The next night they were all sitting down to dinner when a call came in about another fire. Her father rushed out to head to the station and the next time she saw him, he was in the hospital, hours away from death due to the injuries he'd sustained as a result of the call.

There weren't any more strange fires after that. Then again, she had to lose her father to get them to stop. She never thought it was a fair trade.

Chapter Eight

B ack at her apartment, Meagan took a long, hot shower and then pulled out her file containing all the news articles she'd clipped about the unsolved fires.

She'd been so certain she'd done the right thing all those years ago in covering for her brother. Back then, she'd told herself if she went to the police, it'd make her dad look bad. For sure, he wouldn't get the promotion he'd been talking about for the last eighteen months.

And, there was a part of her that wanted to help her brother. If she kept quiet, maybe he'd recognize he'd been given a second chance and he'd straighten up. She reasoned with herself that no one had been hurt, other than her father, and it was only property damage. Plus, her father had asked her not to tell.

All those years, she'd kept her brother's secret and as time went on, she felt she could no longer come forward. It was much too late. In all honesty, she was now as guilty as he was. It really hadn't done her any good anyway; someone had obviously known the entire time. Which brought up again: how did The Taskmaster know?

And again the questions came that she had no answers to: had he always known or had her brother let something slip in a recent conversation? Was he there when it happened? If so, wasn't he as guilty as they were? Not to mention the one question that wouldn't leave her alone: what did he want with Luke?

She knew what she had to do and before she could change her mind, she turned on her laptop and typed an e-mail to The Taskmaster.

> *I know where he keeps his photos, but it doesn't matter because I'm not doing anything else for you anymore. I'm done. D.O.N.E. Done. I don't care what you do or what you say or what you threaten. Find someone else to do your dirty work, this bitch is done.*

The reply back was almost instant.

> *HAHAHAHAHAHA.*

Which only made her angry. She typed back a reply, but thought better of it and deleted it before sending. He wanted her angry. He wanted a reaction. She'd be damned if she'd give him the satisfaction.

Instead she typed a quick text to Luke.

> **Dinner tomorrow night at my house?**

His reply was almost instant.

Love to. What time?

7 okay?

See you then.

She smiled as she put her phone down. There. That was much better than going off on a man who could potentially ruin her. Dinner with Luke. Two weeks ago, she'd never have thought it possible. Especially when she'd convinced herself he was an ass and she wanted nothing to do with him.

Now she could admit that she wasn't sure she'd ever gotten over him all those years ago. She should probably thank The Taskmaster for forcing her to reconnect with him. Had it not been for him, she and Luke would still be strangers. She'd have completely missed out on discovering what an incredible man he'd become.

Not to mention the insanely good sex.

Speaking of which, she needed to straighten up the house and put clean sheets on her bed. And figure out what she was making for dinner tomorrow night.

On second thought, scratch that. She needed to figure out where she was getting takeout from.

The next day Luke showed up at her apartment at five minutes till seven. Of course he was punctual, of course he was. Meagan was still running around, trying to decide which shirt to put on.

"Coming!" she yelled at his knock, dragging a short-sleeve silk blouse over her head. "Be right there."

He was smiling when she opened the door.

"Hello," he said. He looked devilishly handsome in blue jeans and a T-shirt.

"Come in." She held the door open wide so he could pass through.

He dropped a kiss on her cheek before stepping over the threshold. "Thank you for having me tonight."

She smiled at the potential double meaning. "It only seemed fair, seeing as how you had me the night before last."

He laughed softly. "Nice place."

Meagan looked around her apartment as if seeing it for the first time. It was neat and tidy, perhaps overly so. But that was just the way she was. She had a tendency to stress-clean. And between her brother, Luke, and The Taskmaster, there had been a lot of cleaning going on. The decor was more contemporary than traditional, though the one thing she insisted upon was comfortable furniture.

Her place wasn't very large, so it took only a few minutes to show him everything. She ended the tour in the kitchen, where the fresh-baked smells of the lasagna she'd picked up at a local Italian restaurant filled the air.

"Something smells good," Luke said.

"Lasagna."

"You made lasagna?"

"I didn't so much make it as I picked it up from a nearby restaurant and reheated it."

"Either way, it smells delicious."

Once more he was charming and down-to-earth. He had a breezy, nonchalant air about him. She liked that; it buffered her more type-A personality. They talked over dinner about their families, their current careers, and where they wanted to be in five years.

As they were finishing up eating, Luke grew serious. "I feel the need to apologize for what happened all those years ago."

"You don't have to," Meagan said. "I get it. You didn't like me then."

"What the hell? Didn't like you? I liked you *too* much."

She snorted.

"Don't do that. Listen to me." Luke took a deep breath and started. "After that remarkable weekend we had together, I spoke with a close friend of mine. He was older and more experienced, and I trusted him. I was so happy after that weekend and I wanted to be with you so much. I was so young and naive, I thought we would always be like that."

As he spoke about it, the memories of that time came back to her. She remembered the joy and elation after they had spent the weekend together. And her heartache and despair when he ended it.

"But my friend told me I was walking on thin ice. To have an affair with the model in my shoot? Especially one of my first models? In that day and time, he told me I was only asking for trouble."

She remembered when they'd broken it off. She'd thought she'd just move on, but days after, she went to another shoot with a different photographer. She'd forced herself to be all smiles and giggly and happy, but it didn't take long to see that something wasn't right. The guy was different, standoffish, almost cold, borderline indifferent.

Meagan, in her insecurities, thought she had done something wrong. For the duration of the shoot, she wondered what it could've been. Was she acting odd? Was the guy just having a bad day? Or was it more? Had word spread about her and Luke?

Her heart pounded. Did the photographer expect her to sleep

with him? That was why he acted so strange. Then she realized it would probably always be that way. The men she worked with would just assume she'd sleep with them. Suddenly, modeling didn't appeal to her anymore. Though she'd thought she'd cried herself all out over Luke before, she remembered crying herself to sleep that night, and for many more to follow. She mourned what she saw as the loss of her modeling career.

"Don't apologize." She reached across the table and took his hand. "Yes, you hurt me, but that's part of growing up. The truth is, you left me with much more than you took away."

"How's that?"

"If it hadn't been for that weekend, I'd have never explored my submissive side. Thank you for that." It occurred to her she'd never thanked him for that before.

"You're too good, Meagan."

"No, not really."

"You know what I would like to do?" he asked.

"Wash all the dishes for me?" she teased, just because she liked seeing his smile.

"Not quite. But I would like to see what we could be together." He spoke quickly as if he expected her to interrupt. "I'm not asking for forever. Not even a solid commitment. Just these few weeks while we're working together. I'd like to explore us."

No-strings fun with Luke? It was better than nothing and she'd be a fool not to take what she could get. "Would there be sex involved?"

His eyes grew dark. She still held his hand and he squeezed her fingers. "Count on it."

"I'm in."

He lifted her hand to his mouth and his lips brushed against her skin. She sucked in a breath. "Should we wash the dishes now?" he asked.

She thought he was teasing her back. She hoped he was teasing her. He continued to brush his lips back and forth across her hand. Each pass of his lips sent shock waves of lust throughout her body. He was watching her intently, like he *knew* what effect his mouth had on her. And he was asking about dishes?

She almost told him yes, just for kicks and giggles and because the question was so ludicrous, it deserved a likewise ludicrous answer. But right as she opened her mouth to reply, he bit, *fucking bit,* the fleshy mound of her palm at the base of her thumb and she was gone.

"Hell, no," she said, and he chuckled.

"Don't you think it's better to wash them now instead of letting them sit?" he asked, but was still holding her hand.

"That's what the dishwasher's for," she managed to get out and then stifled a moan as his teeth scraped the delicate flesh on the inside of her hand. "Fuck."

"Let's at least put them in the sink," he said.

"Honestly, you're concerned with dishes?"

"It'll be bad if they get sticky."

"Sticky can be good."

"How's that?" His teeth had left her hand and he was now nibbling his way up her arm.

"If I got some caramel and put it on your cock and then licked it off."

Mischief danced in his eyes. He dropped her hand and went searching through the kitchen cabinet drawers. She tried to peek over his shoulder to see what he was doing, but his shoulders were too broad. "What are you looking for?"

He turned around and had a thin fabric napkin in his hand. "This."

"A napkin?"

"Or a makeshift blindfold."

"Kinky."

"Not yet but give me a few minutes. Turn around."

This could be fun, Meagan thought. Being blindfolded in her own kitchen. He didn't bring any toys with him tonight, and he didn't ask where hers were. He must plan on using his hands. Or, maybe he was going to be creative and use some kitchen utensils. Regardless, she was very curious, so she turned around.

Within seconds the makeshift blindfold had covered her eyes and she could see nothing.

He pushed her shoulders. "On your knees."

She carefully made her way to the floor, thankful she had mopped it not long ago. She almost laughed, thinking of mopping the floor when she was kneeling in front of Luke.

"Okay," said Luke. "I want you to open your mouth and hold out your tongue. I'm going to give you something to taste, and if you get it right, you get a reward. An incorrect answer? Well, we'll have to see about that."

She heard him rummaging around in the refrigerator and her mind worked frantically to try to remember what she had in there. Not much. She didn't often cook, so most of the items were just for snacks. The refrigerator door closed and she heard Luke walk to stand in front of her.

"Open."

She opened her mouth and stuck out her tongue. A cold, round object was placed inside.

"Bite."

The grape exploded in her mouth, deliciously sweet and somehow even better because of the position she was in.

"Like that?" he asked.

"Yes, Sir."

"Open."

This time when she opened her mouth, it was filled, not with food, but with his thumb. She sucked it deep into her mouth.

"That's it, sweetheart. Suck that thumb." His voice was thick with need. "Damn, you feel so good. So hot. You like sucking that thumb, pretending it's my dick?"

She couldn't talk with his thumb in her mouth, so she simply nodded.

"I thought so," he said. "Suck it good and I might let you taste my cock."

She moaned, wanting it, wanting him, badly. She ran her tongue around the tip of his thumb and relished his soft groan in reply. How she loved bringing him pleasure. The knowledge she could take this strong man and turn him on, make him moan simply by twirling her tongue around his finger? Heady stuff.

"Fuck," he said when she scraped his skin with the edge of her teeth.

She expected him to pull away and drop his pants. After all, that's what she assumed the purpose of him sticking his thumb in her mouth had been. But apparently, either that wasn't the case or he changed his mind.

One minute, she was kneeling on the floor with his thumb in her mouth and the next, he'd hoisted her up on the counter-top. She had no idea he could move so quickly. She barely had time to register where she was when his hands were at her waist and he unbuttoned the top button on her pants.

"There are times I like watching you strip for me. See the slow reveal of your delicate skin. Then there are times like today when I want to undress you for myself." He unzipped her pants. "It's like opening the best Christmas present ever. Made all the better because I know what lies underneath is all mine."

He gave a hard tug and her pants came off. She wished she wasn't blindfolded so she could see his expression. All she had on from the waist down now was a tiny lace thong.

"Holy fuck," he whispered, running a finger along the upper edge. "You look so damn hot."

"Thank you, Sir."

He dragged a finger along the lines of the lace, following the edge down between her legs. She didn't need her sight to know how wet she was. She could feel it. And apparently, the evidence of her arousal turned him on.

"Someone likes getting dirty in the kitchen," he said.

She opened her mouth to agree with him when his finger began to rub back and forth over the dampness on the silk fabric and whatever she was going to say died in her throat. She bucked her hips in an attempt to get his fingers where she wanted them.

He slapped her inner thigh. "Naughty girl. I know where I want my fingers. You stay still and take what I choose to give you."

She grumbled in disappointment. Now that he knew how badly she wanted him, odds were good he'd take his sweet time giving it to her.

"None of that, now." He hooked his fingers in the legs of the thong and slowly pulled it down and off. "You know I'll make you feel good."

She found her voice. "Yes, Sir. I know you will. I'm just wondering how long you're going to make me wait until you do."

"With an attitude like that, I might tease you all night long. What do you think of that?"

"I think I'll die from pleasure overload, Sir."

"I doubt anyone's ever *died* from pleasure overload."

"How many people have you teased all night long?"

"You'd be the first."

"There you go. You tease me all night, it'll be your fault when I pass out dead. Be kind of embarrassing to explain it to the police, don't you think?"

He laughed. She loved that they could be so carefree together, even in their respective roles. So many of the Dominants she'd played with in the past took everything much too seriously. Not Luke. He could be serious, but he was also playful and funny.

"You know what I think?" he asked, tracing circles right above her clit.

I know what I think. I think I want your fingers just a touch lower.

"I'm afraid to ask, Sir."

"I think you talk too much."

She clamped her lips together, expecting him to get on her about her chatter. *So much for playful Luke.*

"Yes," he said. "You talk entirely too much. I think you need a distraction to help you be silent."

He didn't make her wait long to find out what he meant by that. Before she had time to think, she felt him move between her legs and his mouth was on her. She was so surprised, she let out a yelp before she could stop it.

"Mmm, not quite silent, but definitely no chatter." His breath was hot against her skin. She'd had a wax the day before and she was hypersensitive there. She clenched her fist to keep from grabbing his hair and pushing him to where she wanted him to be.

Deep breaths, she told herself. *You know that he'll make it better than what you could do on your own.* She took another breath and felt her body relax more.

"Your submission isn't something you hand over lightly," he said. "Thank you for trusting me with it."

He was sexy as all fuck, but when he said things like that, he came very near to stealing her heart. The meaning and truth of his words, and who he was, swept over her, and she relaxed further, knowing he had her best interest at heart. That he wanted only her pleasure.

"I like you like this." His chin was rough on her skin. "So accepting and compliant."

She couldn't help it when she replied, "Don't get used to it, Sir."

His laugh was muffled by the fact he'd just sucked her clit into his mouth. Her body tensed with the effort not to come.

He pulled back. "Don't hold back tonight. I want to hear all your sounds and I want you to come as many times as you're able."

"You're going to be the death of me, Sir."

He didn't reply, but went back to his slow, teasing torture with his mouth. Freed from having to withhold her release, she let her orgasm sweep over her. She thought he'd stop then, but apparently he wasn't finished. It wasn't until she came a second time that he stepped away.

"Lift your shirt. Let me see those gorgeous breasts," he said.

From her place on the countertop, she arched her back and slid her shirt up. She wished she could see him, could see his eyes. That way she'd know what he was thinking.

Which was probably why he'd blindfolded her. So she wouldn't. It wasn't her place to think right now.

"So fucking gorgeous," he said, running his hands over her chest. "I could feast on you."

She jerked when something cold dribbled across her nipples.

"Mmm," he said. "Now that looks delicious."

She wondered what it was that he had put on her. She tried to remember what she had in her refrigerator, and she hoped beyond hope that it wasn't expired. That would not be good.

"Uh, Sir?"

"Yes."

"You might want to check the expiration date on whatever that was." Damn, that was embarrassing to admit.

"You have expired food in your refrigerator?"

"I'm saying the potential exists that there could be expired food in my refrigerator."

He was silent for several seconds. Heavens, what could he be thinking? Was he looking in the refrigerator? Again, she tried to think about what could be in there that he could possibly have used.

"Okay," he said. "Here's what we're going to do. I'm going to check the expiration date on this caramel sauce, and if it's good we'll continue. If it's bad, I'll have you write an essay on the dangers of expired food. And I'll probably spank you."

The caramel sauce. How long had that been in there? She thought it had been there for quite a while, but didn't those things have a long use time? Writing an essay sounded boring as hell.

She heard the refrigerator open again. She wished again she wasn't blindfolded. That she could see was happening. Then the refrigerator closed.

"You're in luck. It's all good." He licked a nipple. "But you are still a very naughty girl for making me worry like that."

She arched her back as he continued his assault on her breasts.

He was true to his word and made a feast of her. His teeth, his tongue, and his lips. They were everywhere, and yet they still weren't enough.

"You're still sticky," he said. "I'm going to make you take a shower after I fuck you. Maybe I'll take you in the shower. Or maybe I'll have you suck me off."

At the moment, she would agree to almost anything if he would keep touching her.

"But for now . . ."

He didn't say anything else; he simply pulled her to the edge of the counter, spread her legs wide, and entered her with one hard thrust. The feeling of being possessed was made all the more intense by not being able to see. It had been far too long since she had been with a Dom who knew what he was doing as well as Luke did.

He alternated his movements between hard and deep, and slow and shallow. In doing so, he hit parts of her she didn't know she had. And the spots were very, very happy he found them.

"Holy shit, yes," she muttered when he hit a particularly sensitive area.

He redoubled his efforts, until his pounding was almost punishing. And still she wanted more. She didn't think she would ever get enough of him, and though that made her slightly worried, she wasn't going to think about that at the moment.

He slipped a hand between them, to circle her clit. It took only two swipes of his fingers across the sensitive area for her to come completely undone. She screamed her release as he gave one last hard thrust and gave in to his own.

He reached up and undid the blindfold. He ran his hands up her body, pulling her down off the countertop until she was standing and pressed against him.

"How is it possible for you to keep taking my breath away?" he whispered, and pressed his lips against hers in what began as a soft kiss, but grew in intensity until they were both panting for more.

"I don't know," she said. "But you do the same to me."

"Your kitchen is a mess."

"I don't care," she said in between kisses.

"Shower?"

"Yes, someone got me all sticky."

"I didn't hear any complaints." He bent his head and licked her nipple. "Mmm, caramel's my favorite."

"Next time I put the caramel all over you."

He chuckled. "We'll have to see about that. Which way to the bathroom?"

She held out her hand. "Come with me."

She had never been more thankful of her tendency to stress-clean than she was when she led Luke into the bathroom. How embarrassing it would have been had the bathroom been dirty. Fortunately, both the bathroom and the kitchen had been well cleaned before his arrival.

"Nice place." Luke looked around the bathroom as they stepped inside.

She loved her bathroom. Bigger than what you could normally find in the city, she'd had the space redone to include a large shower and double vanities. She modeled it after a spa, with the thoughts that it would be comforting after a long day's work. Truthfully, she never thought about inviting a man into it.

Ever the Dom, Luke made himself right at home, turning on the water, and taking two towels from the towel rack to place on nearby hooks.

He peeked inside her shower. "I bet you only have girly soap, don't you?"

"The alternative would suggest I make it a common occurrence to have men in my shower."

She didn't miss the flash of jealousy that was apparent in his eyes for just a brief second.

"When you put it that way." He shrugged.

"Kind of makes you like girly soap, doesn't it?"

"I'll never have been happier to smell like a rose," he said with a grin.

She dug through her cabinet drawers until she found a neutral scent she'd picked up at a hotel. "Lucky for you, I'm all out of rose."

"Bless you."

"I have to admit, I'm not overly fond of my man smelling like a rose."

His grin grew larger. "Your man?"

Did she say that? Was he upset? He didn't look upset, but on some men it was hard to tell.

"I, uh, mean, you know. Is that what I said?"

No, he didn't look upset at all. In fact, he looked the exact opposite of upset. He started walking toward her and his movements reminded her of a tiger she once saw in the zoo: confident with a hint of cocky. The corner of his mouth lifted up. "Oh yes. You definitely said it."

With one quick move, he captured her in his arms. "You said *your man.*"

It was on the tip of her tongue to deny it, but before she could, he covered her mouth with his. "Turns me on so much to hear you say that," he said when he broke the kiss for air. "To think of you as my woman."

Just that quickly, all thoughts of soap, cleaning the apartment, and denying him anything flew out the window. And in that second, she wanted to be his woman, and even more so, his submissive.

In the back of her mind, there was the nagging voice telling her she couldn't be his anything with The Taskmaster between them. But she refused to dwell on that while she was in Luke's arms, kissing him, with his hands promising all sorts of sensual pleasure. She wanted to freeze time and stay in this moment forever, because surely nothing could beat naked Luke in her steamy bathroom.

He pulled away. "We'd better get in the shower if we don't want to run out of hot water."

"Always so practical."

"It's more than being practical. It's about keeping you naked and wet as long as possible."

"I see. So it's really you just being perverted?"

"I assume that's a rhetorical question."

She laughed, enjoying the easy banter between them, and decided for the rest of the night she wasn't going to spend one second thinking about The Taskmaster. At the moment, there was only space for Luke in her thoughts.

And right now he was stepping into her shower and his ass looked so fine. . . .

"You're staring at my ass, aren't you?" he asked.

"I don't know why you would assume that." She was only slightly perturbed he'd known what she was doing.

"I can tell by the sound of your voice that I'm right."

"You don't always have to be right, you know. Or get the last word in."

"Meagan?"

"Yes?"

"Get your ass in here."

She mumbled halfheartedly for a few seconds about how bossy he was, but as soon as she stepped into the shower, he stopped her with a kiss. His lips were urgent, like he hadn't gotten enough of her in the kitchen. She was only vaguely aware of the hot water washing over her. Luke had moved into her mind, leaving little room for anything else.

"You look so damn hot covered in water." His gaze traveled up and down her body. "I may keep you in the shower indefinitely."

"That would be hell on your camera and equipment."

His lips were back on her, and she tipped her head to give him greater access as he nibbled his way down. "Who needs cameras when I've got you naked and wet in my arms?"

"Know what's even better?"

"Nothing."

She laughed. "Me naked and wet and bathing you."

"That might do me in," he said, but in all fairness, he looked pretty damn hot himself.

"Let's see, shall we?"

She took a clean cloth and worked the hotel body wash into a rich lather. Starting at his neck, she took her time, squeezing the soapy water over his shoulders and scrubbing. Surprisingly enough, he remained still, letting her explore his body while she washed it.

"Turn around," she said.

She loved his back. It was all strength and muscles, and she couldn't help but taste him. She licked him right between the shoulder blades and delighted in the groan he gave in return.

"Like that?" she asked.

"Fuck, yes," he moaned when she went a step further and lightly scratched him with her nails. She catalogued all his responses, wanting to commit to memory everything he liked.

Before when they were together, she was so caught up in him and experiencing submission for the first time, she hadn't paid close attention to his body.

Now, she suddenly realized, she could. Especially with her experience as a Top. Until the impromptu shower with Luke, she'd never thought about using the Domme side of her to enhance her service as a submissive. Funny, she thought, since she'd always been quick to tell others how being a submissive helped one to Top.

She didn't know she'd laughed out loud until Luke turned around and she realized she'd stopped washing him.

"Is my backside humorous?" he asked. He tried to look behind him. "I mean, I always thought it was rather average-looking, but now I'm worried. Especially if the sight of it makes you laugh right when you were in the middle of doing something else."

"Oh, no." She shook her head. "I wasn't laughing at your backside."

He took a step toward her and pressed her against the tile shower wall. "Thank goodness. What was so funny, then?"

She ran her hands down his chest, delighting in the way he sucked in his breath. "It's not overly humorous. Just something I found interesting."

He nibbled on her ear. "Tell me, before we run out of hot water."

"I've already washed you. If we run out of water, you'll be fine. I'll be the one who's still sticky."

"Point taken. I'll wash you while you talk." He didn't wait, but lathered up body wash and started on her shoulders.

"You know, it's really hard to remember what I was thinking about with you doing that."

He brushed her nipple. "Too bad. Talk."

Trying to concentrate on what she'd been thinking about before Luke got his hands all over her body, she took a deep breath. "You know how they always say it's good for a Dominant to have experience as a sub?"

"Yes."

"Out of curiosity, have you ever been a submissive?"

"Yes." He nodded, but seemed entirely fixated on his task of washing her. "Early in my training, I spent some time with a Domme."

Interesting. Maybe she'd ask more detailed questions about that later. "Do you think it helped you to be a better Dominant?"

"Yes, certainly."

"I feel the same. In fact, I've often told Dominants that they should be in a few scenes as a submissive."

He worked the body wash across her back, and she paused for a long moment, simply taking pleasure in the surroundings and what was happening. The steam. The hot water. Luke. It was a perfect moment, and she wished she could stop time to make it last longer.

"Is that what you were thinking about that made you laugh?" he asked. He'd moved on to her hair, and she closed her eyes as he massaged her scalp.

"That feels so good," she said in a half murmur.

"That's what I'm aiming for."

He took his time washing her hair. She guessed because she'd mentioned how much she enjoyed it. His fingers worked magic against her scalp, and she actually groaned a few times. Who knew hair washing could feel so good?

"You're incredible. I should pay you to come wash my hair every day."

"Having you naked in the shower is payment enough."

"You're too easily pleased," she teased.

"Trust me, I'm not. I just have a weak spot for you." He gave her scalp once last hard massage. "Okay. Time to rinse."

As he rinsed the shampoo out, she picked up the conversation again. "Anyway, like I was saying, I was washing your back and it hit me: why haven't I thought about it working the other way?"

"The other way?" He was behind her, so she couldn't see him, but she could hear the question in his voice.

"Right. The other way. If being the submissive in a scene or two can make you a better Dom, doesn't it make sense that being the Top in a scene or two could make you a better sub?"

"Hmm. Interesting." He didn't say anything else for a while, and she appreciated that. It meant he was thinking it over, not just agreeing with her. "I think it might be more . . . I'm not sure of the word. Easy isn't right. Practical is better, but not quite it either. Might be *simpler* for a Dom to be a submissive for a few scenes than the other way around. And simpler isn't the right word either, but you know what I mean?"

She frowned. "I think so." Then she had a flashback of Melissa and Master C, and she knew exactly what he was talking about.

"It may be harder for you to imagine since you're a switch. But I'm trying to think of Abby being a Top." He turned her around so they were face-to-face. "I can't see it."

"Me either, but let's not talk about my employee when I'm naked and in the shower."

He grinned. "Are you jealous?"

"Oh, hell no." And she wasn't. She didn't think. "I'd just prefer not to bring other women into the shower with me."

He backed her against the tile again, but his time, he lifted her left leg and hooked it around his waist. "There is no one else in this shower or in my thoughts at the moment. Just you and me and what I'm getting ready to do to you." His fingers lazily stroked her wetness. "Do you believe me?"

"Yes, Sir." She bit the side of her cheek as he pushed two fingers into her.

"Oh, fuck." He sounded upset.

"What? What's wrong?" She looked around, trying to find the source of his displeasure, but came up empty. After all, what could go wrong in the shower?

He sighed. "No condom."

She almost told him it was fine. That she was clean and on the pill and that she trusted him. But she didn't. She knew part of it was him protecting her, and she respected that.

"Damn it," she said. "They're right in the bedroom. In the nightstand."

He grabbed her leg and kept it wrapped around him. "You're not leaving this shower."

"But the condom . . ."

"Can wait." The look in his eyes kept her from arguing further. "I'm going to get you off with my fingers, and then you're going to kneel here in the shower so I can come in your mouth. We'll dry off, and then maybe we'll see about finding those condoms."

He didn't wait for her approval, but slipped two fingers inside her, pressing against her G-spot. Which effectively put a stop to her ability to say anything. She was thankful he had her back to the tile, because she knew her legs weren't enough to support her.

"Yes, oh, oh," she panted as he pumped his fingers in and out of her.

"That's right. Come on my fingers." With every inward push, he stroked that sensitive spot deep inside, and she couldn't have held back her orgasm if her life had depended on it. As she came, he leaned his head down to whisper in her ear, "You're so damn sexy when you come."

He only let her catch her breath for a few minutes before he pushed her to her knees. "My turn."

She opened her mouth and greedily sucked him inside. Though she tried to set the pace, he fisted his hands in her hair and held her head still. "Feels so good in your mouth. I'm not going to last long."

She didn't want him to last long. She wanted to drive him so crazy with pleasure, he lost control and became unable to hold himself back. When he thrust into her mouth, she ran her tongue over his length, and once he was all the way inside, she tried to suck him deeper.

"Fuck, Meagan," he said with a half moan the second time she did it. The third, he held still, deep in her mouth, and came with a hard thrust that brought tears to her eyes as she worked to swallow his release.

He was breathing heavily as he helped her to her feet. He looked totally spent, but gave her a sexy smile and turned the water off. Before getting in the shower, he'd hung towels nearby. She hummed in pleasure as he wrapped one around her and watched as he dried himself off.

"Ready to find the condoms?" she asked.

"You're going to be the death of me—did you know that?"

She blinked innocently. "It was your plan. I'm just repeating it. But if you'd rather not—"

Her words were cut short by his lips taking hers in a crushing kiss. She'd brought up the condoms to tease him. The truth was, she could do with some recovery time as well, but his kiss rekindled her desire to have him take her again, and she melted into his embrace.

He finally pulled back. "You may be the death of me, but I'll go with a smile on my face."

Chapter Nine

The weekend of Dena's baby shower was a bit chilly. Because she was on bed rest, the women agreed to throw the shower at the Parkses' house. Since it would be an early morning and she didn't live in Delaware, Abby invited Meagan to spend the night. Meagan had been to the Wests' house in Wilmington only once before and she was surprised to see Lynne there. She had met the woman previously at the club, before Luke bought it. And while she had heard Lynne had moved away, she had no idea she was the Wests' new nanny.

Nathaniel put the kids to bed early, and shortly thereafter, he went out with Cole and Jeff. As soon as he left, the women gathered in Abby's kitchen. Abby got out a bottle of wine and three wineglasses and they all sat in the living room.

"What a surprise, Meagan," Abby said. "I didn't know you knew Lynne."

"Yes, we knew each other before Lynne moved away."

Lynne settled herself on the leather couch, tucking her feet underneath her. She took a sip of wine. "I can't believe you remember me," she said. "Simon and I only went out to the club that one time."

"I remember you." Meagan swirled the flavorful wine in her glass. "This is good, Abby."

"Thank you," Abby said. "It's my favorite."

Meagan turned back to face Lynne. "So why did you decide to move from New York?"

"The law firm I was working at had a bad year. There were a lot of layoffs and I wasn't sure what I was going to do. I'd always wanted to be a teacher and when I heard Abby and Nathaniel were looking for a nanny . . ." She shrugged. "I called Abby, met with her and Nathaniel. The next weekend, I met Elizabeth and Henry. They're such great kids. And the rest is history."

"Do you still want to go back to school?" Meagan asked.

"Yes, eventually, I think."

"But not until the kids are in school," Abby said with a laugh.

"This probably isn't the right time," Lynne said. "But I was thinking, if I could work on my teacher certificate some during the summers, I might be able to homeschool the kids."

"That is such a good idea." Abby drummed her fingers on the couch. "I'll check with Nathaniel, to see if we can set something up in order for you to get your certificate."

"Oh, thank you."

"Now for a harder question," Meagan said.

"Is this about Simon?" Lynne asked.

"I was just wondering what happened. I rarely saw him with anybody before you, and I haven't seen him at all the last couple of months."

Lynne hesitated before replying. "He said he didn't think I

wanted to do anything with the lifestyle. I tried telling him I was new and only needed time, but he took it the wrong way and broke up with me. I was so upset. It wasn't that I didn't want the lifestyle—it was just so much, so soon, and I needed to take a step back." She sniffled. "I really miss him. Abby, does Nathaniel ever talk to him?"

"I'm not sure. I don't think Nathaniel talks to many people from our New York group." Abby poured more wine. "He's been so busy here in Delaware. Do you want me to ask him?"

Lynne's eyes grew wide. "Oh no."

"Are you sure?"

"Yes." But she didn't seem sure.

"Lynne?" Abby asked.

"I thought I might look online. Join a BDSM chat group."

"Why would you do that?" Abby asked.

"I thought it would be best to get some more information. Learn a little bit more. Then maybe at some point, I can approach Simon again."

"You liked him, didn't you?" Meagan asked in a whisper.

Meagan knew all too well what it was like to have the guy you were interested in walk away. She had a feeling the look she saw on Lynne's face was the same she'd possessed after Luke had left her fifteen years ago. And she didn't wish that on anyone.

"Yes." Lynne's voice was so soft, Meagan barely heard her.

"You know"—Abby had a wicked grin—"if you'd like to get together with the Delaware group, Nathaniel and I can arrange it."

Lynne looked a little unsure. "I don't know. Let me think about it."

Abby seemed satisfied and looked over to Meagan. "So tell me about you and Luke."

Meagan sighed deeply. "I don't even know where to start.

We're working on these photos for this book and it's supposed to be work only, but it's not. And I'm just scared, you know? We've been down this road before and it didn't end well."

"But you're both older now," Abby said. "And you have a lot more experience. Not to mention, you both know what you want and what you don't."

"True." Meagan could see her point, but knew it wasn't that easy. "I just don't know how Luke feels."

"Have you thought about asking him?" Abby raised an eyebrow.

"It's not that easy."

"That's because you make it harder than it should be."

"Says the woman who's been married for ten thousand years."

Abby laughed. "Says the woman who has learned the hard way that things are easier when you talk about them."

"I know you're right, but it just seems so hard. To expose yourself like that. To put yourself out there, and not know how it'll be received."

"But surely it beats not knowing anything at all about how he feels."

"I guess so." Meagan sighed.

A silence followed, everyone thinking their own thoughts about what had just been said. Meagan thought maybe she should talk to Luke. After all, she would never know until she asked. Perhaps, maybe, Luke wanted more than a no-strings relationship, too.

"Is anyone staying with Dena tonight?" Meagan finally asked, breaking the silence.

"I think Julie and Sasha are staying with her," Abby said.

"That's good. I would hate for her to be by herself."

"I seriously doubt Jeff would let that happen."

"How many weeks is she now?" Lynne asked.

"Thirty something," Abby replied. "I think they want her to at least be thirty-three or so before they induce labor."

"They aren't going to let her go full term?" Meagan didn't think so, but she hadn't heard for certain.

Abby shook her head. "No, they said the danger was too high to let her go much past thirty-three."

"And so far everything has been okay with the baby?" Lynne got up and poured more wine.

"Yes, Dena said everything so far has been perfect with the baby." Abby got a wistful, faraway look in her eyes. "I'm so happy for them both—they both deserve all the good things."

Meagan remembered that Jeff had been the one to save Abby at the club. She also knew that he had played a few times with Abby and Nathaniel. She wondered what Dena thought of that. Did it bother her? Or did she not care? She knew Abby had played in a roundabout way with Luke. While what was in the past didn't bother her, she wasn't sure she'd like it if it happened again. Similarly, Meagan didn't think Jeff had played at all with anybody since he and Dena got married.

For just a moment, Meagan allowed herself to think what it would be like to be married. To have that companionship. That support. That love. She didn't realize until that moment how lonely her life was.

Sure, she had her work friends. And her brother, although you really couldn't count him. But at the end of the day, she didn't have a significant other. She allowed herself to look into the future and all she saw was loneliness. An empty house. An empty bed. An empty life. And for the first time in a long, long time, she was sad.

Meagan stretched. Suddenly she didn't feel like talking anymore. "I'm beat. I'm going to go to bed."

Abby raised an eyebrow and Meagan was certain she saw straight through her. "Are you okay?"

"Yes, just a little tired."

"Okay, I guess we'll see you in the morning."

"Good night," Lynne said.

Meagan said her good nights and went upstairs to her room. The baby shower the next day started at ten o'clock. She was going to ride with Abby and Lynne, and she wouldn't make it back to her own house until late in the afternoon.

She wondered what Luke was doing tonight. Was he thinking of her? Did he miss her? They weren't going to have a session tomorrow because of the baby shower. Luke said they were ahead of schedule, so it really didn't matter. Suddenly next Saturday seemed so far away.

She made it to the guest room and remembered she'd turned her phone off. She couldn't stop the grin that came over her face when she saw the text from Luke.

What are you doing?

He had sent it fifteen minutes ago. There was a good chance he was still awake. She quickly typed her reply.

Just getting ready to turn in.

He typed back instantly.

By yourself?

She knew what he meant, but she decided to play with him a little bit.

No, I'm cuddling up with Nathaniel and Abby. And later, their nanny is going to join us.

She imagined the smile on his face as he read her reply.

Ha ha ha very funny.

What?

I meant was there anybody in the room with you.

I knew what you meant.

Someone is being a very naughty girl.

And . . . what are you going to do about it?

You'll have to wait and see.

Scary.

There was a pause before his next text came in.

I miss you.

I miss you too.

And I'm really sad that I won't see you tomorrow.

I was just thinking the same thing. Next Saturday seems so far away.

Right? I don't think I can last seven more days.

Me either.

Next best thing?

Meagan smiled, having a good idea of where he was going. **And that would be?**

Take your clothes off.

Even though they were just texting, Meagan still felt like being playful. **What makes you think they're on?**

Funny. Take them off.

Yes, Sir. Will you take yours off too?

Eventually.

Meagan didn't reply until she had stripped completely. And then, just to tease him, she took a picture and sent it to him.

All done.

Nice. Now get in bed on your back.

Arousal began to grow low in Meagan's belly and she did as Luke asked.

Ready.

Good girl. Now touch yourself. Any way you want.
But don't come.

Meagan almost whined. **Ass.**

I'll remember that.

No doubt.

Get busy.

It was so easy to picture his smile and she couldn't help but smile in return. With his face in her mind, she let her fingers drift down her body. They were his hands and he was being so gentle. Teasing. She moaned in pleasure, knowing this was just the beginning.

She brushed her thumbs over her nipples, pinching lightly. And that felt so good, she did it again, harder. That's what Luke would do. He would tease her, right up to when she thought she couldn't take it anymore. And then he would stop.

Her phone buzzed with an incoming text.

Having fun?

It would be more fun if you were actually here.

Agreed. I wish I could see you. Wish I could touch you.

What would you do?

You'll have to wait and see. For now, act like your
hands are mine and do what you wish, but don't come.

I don't like this no-coming rule.

Why do you think I made it?

Because you're a sadist.

Ha Ha Ha. You have no idea. Get busy.

Yes, Sir.

She closed her eyes and let her hands skim across her body. They were Luke's, and he was teasing her again. Her hands drifted lower, breezing near her clit because she knew Luke wouldn't touch her there yet.

With one hand she brushed her breast and with the other, she stroked the insides of her thighs.

In her mind, she thought of the things Luke would be saying to her.

Feel that? Do you like it? Do you want more? So greedy.

And she would reply, "Yes, yes, yes."

But he wouldn't give it to her just yet. Oh no, he would make her wait. Keep her right on the edge and not let her fall over until he was ready. And it would be so, so long until he was ready.

Her phone buzzed again.

Close?

Getting there.

Run your fingers down your slit. Tease yourself.

The ass. What did he think she had been doing? **I am.** She refrained from using an exclamation point, knowing if she did so, it would only add to whatever he had planned for her.

Nice self-discipline, he replied.

He knew her so well, almost too well. How was it possible that he knew what she was thinking? Was she that transparent? Or was he that good?

She decided not to dwell on it, wanting more of the fantasy. Wanting more of him, even if it was only in her mind for now.

She played with herself the way he asked and in her mind, he was with her. He was the one touching her. He was the one bringing her so close. It was almost impossible how close she was. She had barely touched herself. And yet with Luke, almost anything seemed possible.

Thoughts of Luke, paired with the feeling of arousal that her fingers created, had her nearly panting with want. She reached for her phone.

Now?

No. His reply was almost instant.
What? Why? she replied.

Are you questioning me?

She couldn't help the snark that came without her thinking.
I believe that's what the punctuation I used meant.

Oh sweetheart. You'll never learn, will you?

That didn't sound good, but she replied anyway. **Probably not.**

Now it's time for you to go to bed.

But what about, she started typing. Before she could finish her sentence, he wrote back.

Do not come. Do not ask. Go straight to bed.

Her fingers hovered over the a. Ass, she wanted to write. She decided not to, though, thinking maybe he would change his mind if she followed directions.

Yes, Sir, she wrote instead.

Good night, Meagan.

Good night.

Though she had been tired before texting with Luke, she found after they ended their conversation she wasn't tired at all. Not only that, but she needed release badly. She debated what she should do. Going to sleep would be her best option. That didn't seem likely, though. She could get herself off, even though he told her not to. Yes, she decided, that was actually the best option. After all, how would he know?

She lay back on the bed, letting her knees fall open wide. Her fingers drifted to exactly where she wanted them. This time she didn't think of Luke. How could she, when she was doing what he commanded her not to? With her eyes shut tight, she quickly brought herself to completion. And though she felt relief, it was not a satisfactory orgasm.

Afterward, she was wide-awake. Eventually, she heard Abby and Nathaniel in the hallway. There were soft murmurs at the opening and closing of a door and finally, silence.

Sleep didn't come easily, and it was well after one a.m. before she drifted off.

She still felt guilty the next morning. It wasn't like her. Guilt was a new emotion. The last time she remembered feeling guilty was the debacle with Abby at the club. She was glad she wouldn't see Luke today, because she didn't think she could hide what she'd done the night before.

Nathaniel cooked breakfast for everybody. Apparently, this was not a common weekend occurrence. Meagan remembered Abby had told her once that she normally wore his collar on the weekends. She supposed that meant Abby normally cooked. But this morning, Abby's neck was bare.

Abby and Nathaniel's two children, Elizabeth and Henry, joined them for breakfast. They were both precious. Meagan had never spent too much time with them, but they were so much fun to be around. In fact, they had her rethinking her stance on being childless. Perhaps, maybe, she did want children one day.

Lynne came down to the kitchen right as Nathaniel was plating the French toast. He wished her good morning and made her a plate as well. Once again, Meagan thought Abby was a very lucky woman.

"How did you sleep?" Abby asked.

Meagan decided to be honest. "Not too well, but I blame that on Luke."

Nathaniel raised an eyebrow. "Luke?"

"We sent some texts back and forth last night."

"Ah, texts," Abby said. "Done that before."

"And it wasn't the most relaxing ending." Meagan didn't want to say any more, since there were children present. Hopefully, the adults would understand what she was trying to say.

Nathaniel chuckled in understanding. "Done that before," he said, copying his wife.

"Done what, Daddy?" Elizabeth asked.

"Teased your mother," he said.

"Not nice, Daddy," Henry said.

Nathaniel ruffled his hair. "I know. And your mother was quick to tell me the same thing."

"That I was," Abby said. "For all the good it did me."

Nathaniel winked at her.

Yes, Meagan thought. Abby was a fortunate woman.

When they pulled up to the Parkses' house a few hours later, Meagan was surprised to see a familiar car. What the fuck was Luke doing here?

"I didn't know Luke was invited." She asked Abby, "Since when do men come to baby showers?"

"I know Nathaniel was invited to this one," Abby said. "But since Lynne was also coming, he decided to stay home with the kids."

"Okay, but since when do Luke and Jeff know each other?"

"I think Jeff is working with Luke on security."

Right. Luke had mentioned hiring someone to revamp the security system at the club. And, while she knew Jeff was into security, she had no idea he knew Luke. This could be trouble.

But there was nothing she could do about it now. She would

just try to act normal, like nothing happened last night, and most certainly that she did not have an orgasm without his permission.

Her resolve lasted as long as it took to open the door, step into the house, and take one look at Luke. Because the truth was, she couldn't actually look at Luke. She looked everywhere except Luke: the couch, the exposed wooden beams of the ceiling, the wrapped baby presents on the table.

"Meagan?" Luke asked. "How are you? Sleep well?"

"No, I didn't actually," Meagan said. "I just had the same conversation at Nathaniel and Abby's house."

"And what was the general consensus?"

"That Nathaniel was a meanie to tease Abby."

Luke gave her a knowing smile. With slow measured footsteps, he kept her in his sights, as he walked toward her. Once again, Meagan found she couldn't look him in the eye.

When he finally stood before her, he lowered his head toward her ear, and whispered so that only she could hear, "You came last night, didn't you?"

She didn't answer the question; instead she asked, "What makes you say that?"

"Avoiding the question, I see."

"Not necessarily."

"Look me in the eye, Meagan." Luke's voice was very serious. "And tell me you didn't come."

She looked him in the eye, but she knew she couldn't lie to him. "I came."

"Someone was a very bad girl."

"I'm sorry, Sir."

"Be that as it may, sorry just isn't good enough."

"I don't see what the big deal is," Meagan said. "I mean, you're not actually my Dom."

"Oh, Meagan, Meagan, Meagan." Luke pulled back, took her chin in his hands, and forced her to look him in the eyes. "It would have been much better had you not said that."

She figured as much, but that didn't stop her from saying it. "It's the truth."

"No, the truth is, I gave you a command last night. To which you replied, *Yes, Sir.*"

"But that doesn't mean—"

"Hush. The best thing you can do right now is be quiet."

Why did his forcefulness turn her on so much? His hands were not gentle against her skin. There was a strength he rarely showed in his touch and that strength made her shiver.

"Good girl," he said when she didn't argue any further. "Now tell me, am I right?"

She couldn't very well deny that he had acted as her Dom last night, especially with what he probably saw in her eyes, and the way she reacted to his touch, as well as his command.

"Yes, Sir," she whispered.

"Here's what we're going to do," Luke said. "After the shower, we go by the Wests' house to get your car. Then we're going to my house, because it's closer than yours. We won't have a photography session, but I will deal with your disobedience then. Any questions?"

"No, Sir."

"Good girl." He dropped his hands from her chin. "Now, let's get this party started."

Meagan couldn't relax for the entire duration of the shower. Fortunately, she believed only Luke was aware of that. Every so often she would happen to glance behind her and she would see him staring at her. Each time their eyes met, he would smile slightly as if he knew exactly what she was thinking.

He probably did.

Luke kept his eye on Meagan the entire baby shower. It was funny—when Jeff first asked him to attend, he almost turned him down. After some quick thinking, and the realization that Meagan would be there, he had accepted.

And now, he was glad he did. It was so much fun to tease and torment Meagan. When he gave her his command the night before, he knew there was a good chance she would disobey. And he knew as soon as she walked through the door and saw him that she had. Crazy how easy it was to read her.

Of course, that didn't mean he was going easy on her. She had disobeyed, after all. And since she was a sub, she was well aware of the consequences such an act carried. So aware, in fact, that it didn't appear she thought of anything else during the entire shower.

He wondered if she would try to prolong her departure from the shower. Or did the thought of his discipline turn her on? He knew Jeff had a playroom, and he was very tempted to take her into it. But what he had in mind required a bit more privacy.

When Dena had opened all the presents, all the food had been eaten, and the first few people left, Meagan looked his way. He nodded. It was time to go.

Meagan hastily said her good-byes, hugging all of the women, and whispering something he couldn't hear to Abby. He thought about asking her if she was ready, but she moved so expeditiously, he didn't have to.

Meagan had accepted pleasure from his hands. Now he would see how well she handled correction.

Two hours after the end of the shower, they pulled into the driveway of his house. Though she'd seemed eager to leave the party, he could sense a tiny bit of trepidation when she got out of her car.

Instead of moving into the house, he stood in the driveway, arms crossed, watching her. She looked even more uncomfortable. Good. She needed to know that his commands were to be obeyed.

"Does it feel like I'm your Dom now?" he asked.

"Yes, Sir."

"Good. I want you in the bedroom, naked, kneeling in the middle of the room. You will wait for me. Any questions?"

She shook her head.

"Words, Meagan."

"No, Sir. I have no questions."

He nodded his head in acknowledgment and unlocked the front door, holding it open for her to pass. He didn't tell her how long it would be before he entered the bedroom. He didn't want her to know. He wanted her to anticipate it. Think about it. He wanted her body and soul to hum in anticipation of what he was going to do.

She made her way down the hall and disappeared into his bedroom. Leaving her with her thoughts for now, he went to the kitchen and got a glass of water. While he drank it, he checked his voice messages and his e-mail. He decided to leave his clothes on for now. Glancing at the clock, he saw that about twenty minutes had passed. Plenty of time for Meagan's mind to be in a tailspin.

He entered his bedroom quietly, and was pleased to find her

waiting the way he had asked. Though she was not facing him, she knew the minute he walked in the door. Her body tensed slightly and her breathing hitched, just a bit.

"Why are you here this afternoon, Meagan?"

"I disobeyed you last night, Sir."

"How?"

Yes, he thought, answering the question in her head. I'm going to make you say it.

Her hands fisted. This wasn't a position she was used to, nor was it one she liked. Neither of which mattered to him at the moment. Today was a lesson. One she would not forget. He would see to it.

But she still didn't answer. "Tell me, Meagan. Now. Your delay will only make things worse."

"I disobeyed you, Sir. You told me not to come and I did."

"I wonder," he said, "what you would do in this situation, to one of your subs. How would you handle it?"

"So far, Sir, the exact way you are."

"I don't issue commands lightly. And I don't think I give too many of them. However, I do expect that when I give one, it is obeyed. Do you understand?"

"Yes, Sir."

"Tell me what you should have done last night." This was something he normally did before he disciplined a sub. To reiterate the wrongdoing as well as the expected behavior.

"After we said our good-byes"—she spoke softer than normal, perhaps a little worried now that she was in his bedroom—"I should have gone straight to bed and not touched myself. And I most definitely should not have made myself come."

"I don't enjoy this part of play," Luke said, which was the truth. There were those Doms who did, but he was not one of them. However, it was necessary on occasion. "I would much rather you be here for pleasure. And I'm sure you feel the same."

He didn't pose it as a question and she didn't answer. He waited a few more minutes, letting the silence and the gravity of the situation sink further into her consciousness. And to allow them both time to get into the needed headspace.

"I want you to stand and bend over the bed."

She moved quickly and got into position. He half expected some smart-ass comment and the fact there was none spoke volumes. Good. She was taking this seriously.

When she was in position, he came up behind her. He lightly stroked her bottom and was surprised that she didn't flinch. "We'll start with my hand and go from there. No need to count."

Her faint nod was all he got in acknowledgment. Frankly, it was all he expected, since he hadn't asked her a question.

She was tense; it was obvious in the way she held herself, the way she didn't move under his touch. "This will be easier if you relax," he said. Which she knew, of course, being a switch and having played both roles.

She took a deep breath and her muscles relaxed slightly. Without waiting for her to do more, he started to spank her. Lightly at first, just warming up her skin. It would almost be pleasurable, if she didn't know what was coming next. But of course she did, and her body anticipated it.

He slipped his hand between her legs, feeling the wetness there. So she wasn't completely scared; her body betrayed her. There was a part of her that liked this.

"Such a naughty girl," he whispered. He gave her butt a pinch. "This turns you on, doesn't it?"

"I think that much is obvious, Sir."

He chuckled. "Still a bit cheeky, I see."

"Sorry, Sir. I can't help it. It just comes out."

"Yes. And that's one of the reasons I like playing with you so much." It was true—he liked her feisty nature, her sass and spunk. He didn't want that to change, didn't want to change her.

He didn't say anything else, but started again with her spanking. This time going a bit harder, alternating his strokes, so they didn't land in the same spot. Gradually, her pale skin grew pink and then redder as he continued. He could tell when the strokes began to hurt, because she started flinching slightly.

"What did you do last night?" he asked.

"I disobeyed you about coming." Her voice was tight, as if she spoke through her teeth.

"And what happens when you disobey?" He punctuated his question with another slap.

"I wind up bent over your bed and not in a good way." She paused just a moment. "Sir."

"Oh yes." He couldn't help but laugh. "I do like your spunk."

He picked up the paddle he'd laid out earlier. She hadn't seen it, so it would be unexpected. He struck her ass with it once and she grunted. Twice and she winced. He added more, stopping when he felt she'd had enough. She was breathing heavily when he put the paddle down, but remained perfectly still. That was, until he ran a hand between her legs.

"My, my, my," he said. "Will you look at this? Someone is very turned on by the spanking I gave her. Too bad disobedient subs don't get to come."

She whined.

"None of that," he chided. "You came last night. This was a naughty pussy, wasn't it?"

"Yes, Sir."

"Hmm." He acted as if he was in deep thought. "I think that means your pussy needs to be punished."

"Oh no," she said.

"Oh yes. Widen your stance."

She moved her feet a few inches apart.

"Wider." He kicked them, so she was fully exposed to him, and ran a finger along her wet entrance. "Mmm, look at this naughty pussy, just begging to be punished."

He gave it a slap and she moaned in pleasure. Fuck, what it did to him to see her like this, so sexy in her submission, so eager for his touch. He stroked her again. "So wet at the thought of what I'm going to do. Makes me hard as hell. When I finish whipping this naughty pussy, I'm going to push you to your knees, fist my hands in your gorgeous blond hair, and thrust my cock into that hot mouth. Then you're going to suck my dick until I come down your throat."

When he ran his fingers between her legs again, she was even wetter, and he grinned as he slapped her there. At her moan, he picked up a mini flogger and brushed it lightly against her thighs.

"Oh, what, wait," she started, but he didn't stop. Instead he lifted his arm and brought the flogger down on her sensitive flesh. She yelped.

He didn't hesitate, but flicked it down, over and over, until her body trembled with the effort to stay still. Finished, he put the flogger down, took her by the shoulders, and turned her around. Her eyes blazed with desire and the fierceness was almost enough to have him change his mind and let her release, but he forced himself to push down on her shoulders.

"Now you're going to take me." With quick fingers he undid his pants and shoved them down. Just as quickly, he grabbed her hair and pushed himself into her waiting mouth. He gasped at how deep she took him.

"Yes, fuck, Meagan." He thrust again and closed his eyes as her warmth surrounded him. Damn, but he wasn't going to last long. She felt too good. His hands tightened in her hair, which made her suck him harder. He groaned and held her head still while he pushed deep inside her one last time, coming so hard he saw stars.

It took him a few seconds to compose himself and when he finally opened his eyes, Meagan was kneeling demurely at his feet.

"Fix my pants," he managed to get out.

She straightened him up, even kissing the tip of his cock before tucking it inside his boxer briefs. He reached down and pulled her up, noticing her slight wince at her backside.

"I'd like nothing more than to push you to your back, slip between your thighs, and return the favor, but since you came last night, you aren't allowed to come today," he said.

"I understand, Sir."

He dropped a hand to her ass. "How's your backside?"

"Sore enough that I won't be tempted anytime soon to have an orgasm without permission."

"I meant every word," he told her. "I don't like punishing submissives."

She snorted. "Right. That explains the massive erection you shoved in my mouth."

"Watch it." He slapped a bare butt cheek. "That came from seeing how wet I made you."

She wisely didn't argue.

He took a robe from the foot of the bed and placed it around her shoulders. "Come sit down," he said. He took her hand and led her to a nearby love seat. Once he sat down, he pulled her into his lap.

"Ouch," she said, wincing at the pain from the movement.

He adjusted her so she sat more comfortably on his lap, but he didn't apologize. And he knew she wouldn't expect him to. "Would you like some water?"

"No, I'm good like this for now." She snuggled deeper into his embrace.

Though he would have happily gotten her some water, he wasn't too upset that she wanted to snuggle. He didn't like what he'd just had to do, and he wanted nothing more than to simply sit and hold her.

She was soft and pliable in his arms. In fact, for some reason, she seemed more affectionate than normal. He ran a hand down her back, enjoying the heat radiating from her skin. He dropped his head so he could easily smell the shampoo in her hair. He couldn't place the scent; it was a combination of something citrusy mixed with a hint of spice. He wasn't sure he'd ever smelled it before, but now, if he did, it would always remind him of Meagan.

He held her until he felt her grow restless. "Ready for some water now?"

"Yes."

He gently helped her to her feet and took her hand. "Come with me. I'll get you something."

After he had settled her in the kitchen chair, and she had finished half of her water, he asked another question. "Can you stay tonight? Or do you need to get back?"

She didn't answer immediately; in fact, she seemed torn. Surprising, since she'd been so happy to be in his arms just moments before. For some reason, he desperately wanted her to stay, but he knew it was her choice and he wasn't going to pressure her one way or the other.

"Yes," she said, finally. "I'll stay."

"Do you want something to eat? I can throw something together real quick."

"No. I didn't get much sleep last night. I think I'll take a shower and head off to bed."

He nodded. "You can use my bathroom."

"Thank you."

She finished drinking her water, excused herself, and disappeared down the hall. Minutes later, he heard the sound of running water. He decided to use the guest bathroom to take his own shower. That way, maybe they would finish at the same time and they could talk before going to sleep.

But when he finished and made his way into his bedroom, she was already curled up under the covers, sleeping. With a soft sigh, he joined her, settling himself behind her. He soon found that sleep didn't come easy and for several hours he lay awake, thinking. He had just started to drift off to sleep when she started moaning.

He tightened his grip around her, afraid she was having a nightmare. However, it wasn't long before he became aware that she did not moan out of distress. Oh no, when she started rubbing against him and grinding her hips, it was obvious she was having a sex dream.

Suddenly, he wasn't tired anymore. He was the exact opposite of tired. He was wide-awake and very, very hard.

"Meagan, sweetheart."

"Mmm."

"You're dreaming."

"Yes, Sir. About you."

He thought he was turned on before, but hearing that she was dreaming about him, especially with the seductive sounds that slipped through her lips, made him even harder. He slid his hand between her legs, delighted to discover how wet she was.

"Wake up and turn around," he said. "And I'll make it worth your time."

"Sir?"

"I do like it when you call me Sir," he whispered. "It makes me so damn hard."

She jerked awake more fully and he could sense her confusion over his statement.

"How?" she asked. "I thought you said . . ."

"I said you couldn't come today. Look at the time." He knew what she would find when she looked. Fifteen minutes until one. "It's tomorrow."

She turned around, as if to judge by his eyes if he was lying or not. "Does this mean . . . ?"

She didn't finish her question, but he answered it for her anyway. "Yes, this means I'm going to do what I wanted to do before."

"You're going to . . . ?"

He found it just a little humorous that she couldn't complete her sentences. "Yes. Now spread those thighs so I can taste that sweet pussy."

The following Monday, Meagan asked for Abby to come in to work. She didn't come every Monday, because of the drive, probably only once or twice a month. To be honest, Meagan didn't think she would tell Abby everything, but perhaps talking to her friend would help clear her mind.

"Knock, knock," Abby said, standing in the doorway.

Meagan looked up and couldn't help but smile at her vivacious friend. Abby always had that air about her: friendly, open, down-to-earth. Just someone you felt like you could talk to. "Hey, girl, come on in, and close the door if you don't mind."

Abby must have picked up on her unease because her normal jovial face showed just a hint of a frown as she closed the door behind her. "What's up?" she asked as she sat down.

Meagan dropped her head into her hands and rubbed her scalp with her fingernails. "I don't know, Abby. I just don't know."

"This sounds serious. Did something happen with you and Luke after you left the shower?"

Did something happen after she left the shower with Luke? She forced herself to swallow the chuckle that threatened to burst out of her throat. Yes, she wanted to say, something had most definitely happened between her and Luke after they left the shower. But Meagan wasn't about to tell her that Luke had her bent over his bed while he spanked her. Nor was she going to tell her how he took her twice in the middle of the night.

"Have you ever kept anything from Nathaniel?" Meagan asked.

Abby shook her head. "I do not like the way this is going."

"I know. I don't either. I've just got myself in a mess." Meagan drummed her fingers on her desk. "Though perhaps *mess* is a bit of an understatement."

After she made it back to her place from Luke's, she found she had an e-mail waiting from The Taskmaster.

> *I don't know why you think you have any say about when this is over. You don't have a say in anything. So I'm going to be nice and pretend like I didn't get your last e-mail.*
>
> *Now, that photographer of yours took some risqué*

shots of an actress not long ago. I want those pictures.

And you're going to get them for me, know why?

Because I can break every bone in your body one by

one and do it in such a way, you'll be begging for mercy.

But I won't give you any.

You have two weeks.

Even now, days removed, she shivered, remembering the e-mail.

"I don't even know if I want to ask what's going on," Abby said.

"Let me alleviate some of that worry," Meagan said. "I won't give you details."

Abby sat back in her chair, crossed her arms, and for several long seconds, she studied Meagan. "Does this have anything to do with the e-mail I got with a picture of you? Because now that I'm thinking about it, things started to get a little strange with you and Luke right after that."

Meagan didn't want to lie to her friend, but she didn't see how she could tell the whole truth either. "Yes and no."

"Did Luke have something to do with the naked picture?"

Meagan could see the wheels turning in Abby's head. She knew her friend. If Abby thought Luke had done something to harm her, she wouldn't stop until he made amends. And she couldn't have her friend thinking poorly of Luke. "Oh no. It's not like that. Luke had nothing to do with sending the naked picture."

Abby still had one eyebrow raised. Obviously, Meagan had not been sincere enough in her reply. "Believe me, Abby. It is not Luke. He is innocent in all this."

"And what exactly is 'all this'?"

"I can't tell you everything," Meagan started and then hesitated. How much did she want Abby to know? Abby would keep her secret; she knew that. She sighed and rubbed her head again.

"You know you're going to start losing hair if you keep doing that?"

"Okay, here it is. My brother got into some trouble a long time ago, but no one knew except me. Or at least I thought." She looked up at Abby. "And now, it seems as if somebody did know. And if word got out, it would hurt my brother and me, and tarnish the reputation of my dad. I promised him on his deathbed I wouldn't let that happen."

Abby was silent for several minutes. Meagan could see her processing the information she had just been given. She was a smart woman, who would sort the pieces out, and put them back together.

"A naked picture of you. Someone knows something they shouldn't know. And someone doesn't want that information to get out." Understanding dawned in Abby's eyes and she leaned forward. "Are you seriously telling me that you're being blackmailed?"

It was the first time Meagan had heard the words said out loud and she shivered.

"You don't even have to confirm it," Abby said. "I can see it on your face. I'm guessing you haven't told the police, or else you wouldn't be talking to me about it. What I don't understand is how Luke is involved."

"Luke has information. Or in this case, pictures."

Part of Meagan couldn't believe she was actually admitting everything, especially to Abby. But she had to tell somebody something or else she'd go crazy.

"You have to tell the police."

In all honesty, Meagan could not have anticipated Abby saying anything else. Perhaps that was why she felt comfortable talking to her about it. Of course, there wasn't a snowball's chance in hell she would go to the police. She just needed to share her burden with somebody. However unfair it was to give that burden to Abby without her consent.

In her heart, Meagan knew she was a selfish, deceitful woman. She had once promised she would never hurt Abby again, and here she was giving her information that would worry her.

"I am a rotten, awful friend." Meagan didn't deserve a friend like Abby. And she most certainly didn't deserve Luke. "I just don't know what to do."

"Have you talked to your brother?"

"Do you have any siblings?"

"No, I'm an only."

"Well, I might as well be. My brother is an ass. No, scratch that—*ass* is too nice of a word for him." Damn that promise to her dad.

"Really?"

"Put it this way: I saw him not long ago, went by his apartment. Now you have to understand, he isn't working a real job, and he's mooching off his roommate. So when I wouldn't give him money, his roommate suggested I work off his debt."

Abby's horrified expression confirmed she understood. "Are you serious? And you're going through all this turmoil to protect him?"

"Crazy, isn't it?" Meagan took a picture from her desk drawer. It had been taken when she and her brother were children. "I still see him like this in my mind. We were young. There was so much promise in him."

"But he's an adult now. You are, too."

"My dad . . ." She blinked the tears out of her eyes. "He died protecting Jake. If I let this Taskmaster guy tell what he knows, it's like he died for nothing. And I can't stand that."

Abby just nodded and squeezed her hand. "I know," she whispered.

Chapter Ten

Days after that conversation with Abby, Meagan still didn't know what to do, but she was down to a week before her deadline was up, so she needed to decide soon. Should she go to the police? Should she talk to her brother first? But as soon as that question popped into her head, she immediately dismissed it. No, she wasn't going to talk to her brother about anything.

Maybe she should bring it up with Luke. After all, he had the information The Taskmaster wanted. But just as quickly as she had dismissed talking to her brother, she also dismissed talking to Luke. Because she knew if she talked to Luke, he would think the only reason she did anything with him was because of The Taskmaster. And while that may have been the case in the beginning, it was far from the truth now.

Maybe . . . Maybe she would tell The Taskmaster that Luke had moved his pictures or that he had deleted them. What if she did that? He couldn't very well retaliate if there wasn't anything to give him, right?

She pulled up to Luke's house Friday night still undecided about what she was going to do. She knocked on the door and, while she waited for him to open it, decided not to think about it for the next few hours. Tonight was just her and Luke. They weren't even going to take pictures. Luke had called her earlier in the week and asked her to come over for dinner.

"Just you and me," he'd said. "Dinner and whatever else we want to do. We can worry about the pictures later."

Meagan knew they had just about finished the shoot for the book anyway. She thought they might have one or two more sessions to do. The one thing she knew, however, was that she didn't want to stop seeing Luke when they finished. And she had a feeling Luke felt the same.

So there was no way she would mess that up by admitting her initial contact with him was because of The Taskmaster.

"Meagan, sweetheart," Luke said, as he opened the door. He reached over and kissed her cheek softly. "Come on in. How are you?"

"Better now," she said. Which was the truth. Why did everything always seem much better when she was with him?

He gave her a big smile and held out his hand. "You look fabulous tonight."

Her heart fluttered at his words. The truth was she had spent an inordinate amount of time in her closet trying to decide what to wear tonight. She had finally decided on a simple off-white sheath dress. She took a second to look him up and down. He had on khaki pants and a light blue polo shirt. "You don't look too bad yourself, handsome."

"Made your favorite," he said, leading her inside to the kitchen.

"And how do you know my favorite?" she teased.

"Every time we go out, you always order the same thing. Salmon. So I decided that tonight I would cook you my version of salmon. It's one of the two things I cook."

She had no idea she always ordered the same thing. Though, looking back, she did always seem to order salmon. "I like fish. And it's good for you, too."

"Agreed."

They stepped inside the kitchen and she was surprised to see the table was not set. Luke noticed her confusion.

"I thought we'd change things up a little bit tonight. Eat in the dining room."

The dining room? That sounded . . . formal. He led her through the kitchen and into the connecting room. He had certainly been busy this afternoon. Lit candles were everywhere and the table was set with fine china.

"China?" She ran a finger along the gold edging of a plate.

"It was my mother's," he said. "And I never use it, so I thought why not use it tonight?"

Why indeed? Was it because this was one of their few dates that didn't involve taking pictures before or after?

"I didn't mean for it to freak you out." Luke seemed to misinterpret her silence.

"I'm not freaked-out, just surprised." She sat down in the offered seat. "I've just never known a bachelor to have such fine china."

"True. But I'm not your average bachelor."

That was an understatement. "So you made salmon?"

"Yes, and it'll be ready in about two minutes."

True to his word, five minutes later he set a delicious-looking plate of salmon and vegetables in front of her. She eyed everything. "This looks delicious."

"Thank you. Let's hope it tastes as good as it looks."

She nodded, but she couldn't imagine something that smelled so divine not tasting good. Luke poured them both some wine, and she almost giggled when she noted the label. It was the same red that Abby liked.

But all her giggles faded away as soon as she took her first bite. "Oh, wow," she said as soon as she swallowed. "You missed your calling. You should be a chef."

"Nah, I don't enjoy cooking that much."

"Shame." And that was all she said because she was much more interested in eating than discussing why Luke would never be a professional chef.

Their conversation started out light and easy, but midway through dinner, Luke grew serious.

"I'll admit," he said, "there was something I wanted to bring up tonight."

She waited. Was it possible he knew she was being blackmailed? Had Abby told him?

"Don't look so scared," he said. "I think, well, I hope, that you'll like what I'm thinking."

She could have kicked herself for being so easy to read. "Do tell."

"The short of it is, I've really enjoyed spending time with you over the last few weeks. I know our time is almost up on the book. I believe we can wrap it up in one more shoot. But I don't want that to be the end of us. I'd like to keep seeing you." He spoke quickly, but sincerely, almost as if he wasn't as sure as he seemed of her response. She found it delightfully endearing.

And beyond her wildest dreams.

He enjoyed spending time with her. He wanted to spend more time with her. It was the exact same thing she wanted and yet the very thing she was also afraid of. Afraid because she wasn't sure how she would keep the blackmail issue away from him.

But she didn't have to think too long before answering. "I would like that, too."

His face broke into a grin. Lord, he looked so handsome when he smiled. It made her smile in return. He reached out and took her hand from where it rested on the table.

"Thank you. Thank you for giving us a second chance," he said.

"How could I not? You've always been the one my heart's wanted." It had been a hard admission to herself and even harder to voice aloud to him. But he deserved the truth; they both deserved the truth.

"Meagan." He spoke her name reverently while still stroking her hand. For several long seconds they simply enjoyed the silence, their hands touching, the warmth that surrounded them, and the possibilities that lay before them.

Finally Luke broke the silence. "Will you stay the night?"

She didn't have to think about her answer. "Yes."

He dropped her hand long enough to walk over behind her chair and pull it out; then he reached down again and took her hand. "I want you."

"Yes," she repeated, wanting the same.

He pulled her close into his arms and, pressing his nose against her hair, whispered into her ear, "I'm going to keep you up all night. I'm going to explore every inch of your body. And when you think I'm finished, I'm going to do it all again."

She ran her nails down his back, enjoying the way he moaned

in pleasure. "Then I'm going to explore your body. Every inch."
She shifted her hands to the front of his body and gently cupped
him. "Every. Last. Inch."

"Damn, woman, I'm not sure I have the strength for all of that."

She lightly squeezed his erection through his pants. "I'm sure
you'll find a way."

He hissed as her grip got tighter. "I'm sure I will."

"Maybe." She started undoing his pants. "Maybe I'll start in
here. Tell me. Has anyone ever sucked you off in your dining
room?"

"No. Are you going to be the first?"

"Are you going to let me? Or does that go against some Dom
rule?"

Mischief danced in his eyes. "The only rules are the rules I
make up and I'm thinking, the new rule is, anytime we eat in
the dining room, you have to suck me off."

She let her hands trail down his body as she lowered herself
to the floor. "That's a rule I could get behind."

"Or more accurately, would it be a rule you could kneel for?"

She slowly took his pants down, releasing his cock. "All day.
Any day. And twice on Sundays."

"Do it." His voice was hoarse, stretched tight with desire.
"Wrap those lips around me. Take me into your mouth."

She willingly and happily obeyed. She loved the taste of him.
Loved being on her knees for him. Though she liked the gentleman Luke, it was the Dom Luke who really turned her on.

Unfortunately, he didn't allow her much time. It seemed
way too short before he was pulling her up to stand.

"I wasn't finished," she said.

"Be that as it may, I'm not going to be the first one to release
tonight."

"Lucky, lucky me."

She started toward the bedroom, but he put a hand on her shoulder to stop her.

"I've never had anybody strip down naked in my dining room before either."

She lifted an eyebrow. "Is that an order?"

"It is now. Take them off." He stepped out of his own pants. "I want you completely naked, except for the heels. The heels stay on."

She slipped out of her dress and underwear. "Like the heels, do you?"

"I like them a lot."

The admission made her almost giddy. She'd bought the shoes with him in mind. They were ridiculously expensive—red, strappy, and very high. "When I bought them, all I could think about was you fucking me in them."

"Is that right?" he asked. At her nod, he continued. "Then I think as your Dom, it's my duty to make that fantasy come true."

His words heated her, ran through her body like lava, making her even hotter as she pictured the scene. And, of course, he picked up on that fact right away.

"I can tell how much the thought of that turns you on. Walk in front of me as we head to the bedroom so I can see that fine ass." As if to emphasize his point, he gave her right butt cheek a slap.

She giggled, but started walking toward the bedroom, looking over her shoulder as she did so. He saw her looking and gave her a wink. She swayed her hips as she walked, satisfied with the fact he couldn't keep his eyes off her. "Like what you see?"

"Sweetheart, when it comes to you, I like everything."

Satisfied, she turned around and walked into the bedroom. "Where do you want me?"

"That's a loaded question." He unbuttoned his shirt, slowly, as if he knew she was watching him and enjoyed what she saw. "Where do I want you? I want you everywhere."

"Shall we start on the bed?" she teased. "Maybe then move to the bathroom? Or the shower? We haven't tried your shower yet."

"Maybe." He was thinking now, and that made her a tiny bit apprehensive. Because now it seemed as if he was going to try something different. Of course, with Luke that would be fun. She trusted him completely, which was more than she could say about some people she had played with in the past.

"No matter what you decide, the first thing that should happen is you getting naked." She made a move toward him. "Let me help with that shirt."

"No, I think you should stay right there." He turned and walked toward the bathroom.

"Where are you going?"

"I decided we're going to start in the bathroom."

"But if we start in there, I have to take my shoes off."

He turned around, and narrowed his eyes. "First of all, you keep forgetting you're not in charge. Second of all, I didn't say we were starting in the shower. I said the bathroom. Thirdly, you'll keep the shoes on until I tell you differently. And lastly, keep trying to Top from the bottom, and I'll spank yours."

Damn, it turned her on so much when he got bossy. Or maybe it was the fact that he was going to fuck her in the bathroom, with her shoes on. Of course, it could've been the threat of a spanking. "Yes, Sir."

"That's more like it." He disappeared into the bathroom and didn't say anything else, but she heard him moving around and the opening and closing of drawers. "While I'm getting everything ready in here, I want you to play with yourself. Any way you want, as long as you don't come."

"Yes, Sir."

"And you're going to tell me what you're doing."

"Right now, I'm playing with my breasts." She cupped them, running her thumbs over her nipples.

"Nice, a good place to start. But are you just brushing them?"

"Yes, Sir."

"Pinch those nipples. Hard. Because you know I would make them hurt."

She moaned because she knew it was true. She ran her hands over her breasts again, this time pinching the nipples between her thumb and forefinger. "I'm pinching."

"Harder."

She pinched them even harder, rolled the tip between her fingers. "Okay," she said, and her voice was more strained than it was before.

"Good girl. I can tell by the hitch in your voice that you did what I asked." He was no longer rustling around the bathroom. "Now run your hands down your body and slowly brush just the entrance of your pussy. Tell me how wet you are."

She didn't think she would be too wet, but Luke apparently knew better because when she reached down, she was more than ready. "Very wet, Sir."

"Good," he said. "You need to be wet for what I have planned."

Holy fuck. What did that mean?

But he continued on, as if he hadn't just said something shocking. "Rub your clit. Rub it to where you're just on the edge, and when you feel like you're going to come, you may enter the bathroom."

She wanted to take her time, to ease herself into arousal. Drag it out little by little. Make him wait. But she was on the edge and so vastly curious about what he had planned. With one hand she rubbed her clit, and with the other kept pinching her nipples. She found herself fighting off orgasm sooner than anticipated.

When she entered the bathroom, Luke stood in the middle of the room. Thank goodness he had taken his clothes off, because he was damn fine-looking naked. If she hadn't been aroused, the sight of him naked, erect, and waiting would have done it.

He took one look at her and fisted his cock. "I wish I had my camera. You look so fuckable in those heels."

She almost told him he was a fine one to talk, but her gaze landed on the countertop and she sucked in her breath at what she saw. Luke followed her line of sight and grinned.

"I've never had your ass."

No, he hadn't. In fact, she couldn't remember the last time she had anal sex.

But Luke seemed unaffected by her hesitation. "Go bend over and place your hands on the edge of the tub."

His tub was a large, freestanding number that would provide plenty of support. She took a deep breath and followed his instructions. However, when she was in position, she started having second thoughts.

Luke walked behind her and cupped her backside. "You're nervous."

"Slightly, Sir."

"You know I would never hurt you."

"Yes, Sir."

"Your brain knows that, but your body is a different story."

He proceeded to caress her, using his knowledgeable hands to slowly stroke that spark of arousal back into a flame. "So what I need to do is to get your body to that point. To where it trusts me. So that it accepts whatever I choose to give it."

And what are you going to give it tonight? she wanted to ask. Instead, she closed her eyes and placed herself in his experienced hands, because she knew in doing so, he would take care of her, he would pleasure her, and it would make him happy to feel her surrender.

"There we go, sweetheart," he said as she relaxed her body. "Your submission is so sweet, so sexy. Thank you."

She did tense briefly when she felt his slick finger against her anus.

"Easy." He pressed a little farther. "Nice and easy. I'll be gentle."

She knew he would, so she took a deep breath and bore down against the pressure, allowing his finger to slip inside her. She was unaccustomed to the fullness. Anal sex had never been her favorite.

"I'm not going to fuck you here tonight." He removed his finger and replaced it with a small vibrator. "But I will soon, so I need to get you ready."

The vibrator was bigger than his finger and her entire body trembled in anticipation of what was to come. She had a feeling he wasn't going to remove the vibrator anytime soon.

"You're so tight. How long has it been?" he asked.

"A long time, Sir."

"Definitely something to look forward to in the future." She felt him take a step back, but he kept hold of the vibrator. "You look so damn hot. Bent over the tub in those heels, your ass offered to me, and your greedy, wet pussy aching to be filled."

Yes! she wanted to shout. Because she needed to be filled so, so badly. But he wasn't doing it just yet. No, with the vibrator inside her, he was playing her. His hands once more traveled all across her body. Taunting. Teasing. Tormenting.

"Please, Sir."

"Are you trying to tell your Dom what to do?"

"No, I just need—"

He gave her butt a hard slap. "Don't tell me what you need. I'm your Dom. I know what you need. I know what you want. But you only get what I offer. Understood?"

She took a deep breath to keep from whining. "Yes, Sir."

He chuckled, perhaps realizing her struggle. Seconds later came the rustle of a condom package. Finally he was pressed against her, but didn't enter.

"Can you feel me? Seconds away from pushing into you? Do you know how tight you'll feel with that vibrator in your ass? So damn tight." He pushed just a little into her. "Do you feel it? Your body stretching to accept me?"

"Please, Sir." She was caught between the desire to have him inside her and just a bit of anticipation because she knew it would be a tight fit. It was probably going to hurt, but she knew it would feel so, so good after a few seconds.

"You're imagining it, aren't you?" He held still. "How it'll feel when I push my way inside. The initial burn that'll make you worry I'll split you wide-open. The gradual acceptance of my cock as I fuck you deeper and deeper. And you're so stretched and so full, you don't think you can take anymore."

He started pushing into her again, his wicked whispers making her crave more and more.

"What do you think I'll do when I finally get my cock buried inside you?" he asked.

"Fuck me, Sir?"

"Before that."

How the hell did he expect her to think when there were so many sensations running through her body? She wasn't sure what her name was. She didn't know what year it was. If the room caught fire, she probably wouldn't notice because it'd be minor in comparison to the fire he created inside her.

A hard slap on her ass reminded her he'd asked a question she hadn't yet answered.

"I don't know, Sir. Please."

Please what, she wasn't sure. Please fuck me? Or please let me come? Just please something.

His voice was hot against the back of her neck. He fisted her hair and with one last thrust of his hips, he made it all the way inside her. She yelped.

"Do you remember the question?" he asked.

There had been a question? "No, Sir."

"What do you think I'll do now that I'm inside you as deep as possible?"

God, she was so stuffed, so full. She needed him to move even though she was afraid if he did, she'd explode into a million pieces. "I don't know, Sir."

"Poor girl. I'll just show you." And before she had time to think about what that meant, the vibrator started buzzing.

She tried frantically to grab on to something, but the side of the tub was too slick. Luke began to fuck her in earnest and the feeling was so overwhelming, she saw stars. The buzzing combined with his movements . . . Damn it all, she wasn't going to last long.

"I can't hold out," she said, but it came out in an almost squeal and even she wasn't sure what she was saying.

He grunted and pulled almost all the way out, but there was no reprieve because he adjusted his hips and thrust into her again. This time threatening to make her lose balance.

"Damn it." He spoke in a half pant, half groan. Seconds later the buzzing stopped and he slipped the vibrator out of her.

Her brain was too foggy to understand. Why had he stopped?

"Sir?" she asked when he pulled out as well.

"Not enough support here to take you as hard as I want."

She wasn't sure she could stand, but as it turned out she didn't have to worry. Luke gathered her in his arms, picked her up, and carried her to the bed. He placed her on her back and for that she was glad, because it allowed her to watch him. Right now he was looking at her so intently it made her want him all the more.

"Let's see," he said. "How do I want to go about this?"

Keeping his eyes on hers, he lifted one leg and placed it on his shoulder; then he took the other one and did the same on the opposite shoulder. Holy shit. She was so exposed in this position, he'd fill her completely.

"Oh yes," he said. "I see that look in your eye. You know exactly what I'm going to do, don't you? You'll be so tight like this. I'll be able to sink so deep."

He moved his hands from her legs but left her legs on his shoulders. He gave them a gentle pat before he dropped his hands, and gave her a look to tell her she'd best leave her legs where they were. She was only vaguely upset he wasn't going to use a vibrator, when he took a large plug and lubricated it.

"I see that look, too. You know exactly where this is going, don't you?"

"Yes, Sir."

She closed her eyes as he pushed the large anal plug inside

her. The stretching was uncomfortable, but just for a minute. And though she had never been a fan of anal sex, she couldn't help but want to have Luke take her that way.

"There you go," he said. "Take it all."

She grunted as the plug settled into place. And then yelped when he gave her a slap on the ass.

"Now, where were we?" He positioned his cock at her entrance. "Right about here."

But he didn't enter her; instead he took the tip of his cock and rubbed up and down her slit, teasing and taunting her. Mother fucking hell, would he not just fuck her already? The question shouted in her head, but she held it inside. And she didn't want to beg either; she had already done that and it did little good.

"The anticipation is heady, isn't it?" he asked.

He pushed the tip of his cock inside her and she was even more stretched than she was when he had the vibrator in place. And still he didn't take her. He pumped in and out with just the tip for what seemed like forever. And his whispers . . .

"I can't wait to sink inside you. Feel your warm heat as you let me in."

I'm not going to beg. I'm not going to beg. I'm not going to beg.

Maybe if she kept repeating that, she'd actually keep her mouth shut.

"So quiet all of a sudden?" he asked. "Tell me what you want."

"I want you to fuck me." Belatedly, she added, "Sir."

He took a deep breath, lined himself up once more, and entered her with one long, hard thrust. "Hell, yes," he said in a half moan. "You feel so good."

She could barely comprehend what he was saying, she felt so full, but why wouldn't he move? He was buried completely inside her. She knew it had to take an inordinate amount of self-control to keep from moving. Was he just letting her get used to him?

Then ever so slightly, he started to move. Slowly at first, before gradually lengthening his strokes and thrusting deeper and harder.

"Yes," he panted as he pounded repeatedly into her. "Take me."

He took her legs from his shoulders and bent them so they were close to her chest. The new position made her feel even more exposed. He redoubled his efforts, slamming into her over and over and soon it became too much to hold inside. She was unbelievably full and with every thrust, his cock would shift the plug just enough to send a pulsating need to have him *there* as well.

Her climax sneaked up on her and she clenched her muscles to keep from coming. "Please, Sir. May I come?"

He must have been nearly as close as she was, because he surprised her with a "yes." It was all she needed. She let her body relax and the orgasm swept over her. Unlike times before though, this time she kept going and coming and he kept pounding and pounding. She wasn't sure if it was one really long orgasm or several small ones, but she never wanted it to end. Luke stiffened inside her, but he kept on thrusting after his own release, setting off another one for her.

By the time he pulled out and lay down beside her, she was spent. She was vaguely aware of Luke getting up from the bed to get a washcloth. Of his hands gently removing the plug and cleaning her. His strong arms as he pulled her close. Only then did she allow herself to drift off to sleep.

Meagan awoke slowly, surprised to see it was still dark. She propped up on one elbow and looked over Luke's body to the clock on the nightstand. Three thirty. Way too early for her to be up. Her mind immediately went back hours before. Though she would not have thought it possible months ago, she could no longer picture life without Luke.

Which meant she would have to do something about The Taskmaster. Maybe she should get the picture for him. No. She couldn't do that to Luke. The actress in the picture would have chosen Luke because of his discretion. To have that picture become public could be a career breaker for him. Did she even want to see if she could find the picture?

Yes. Yes, she did. For some reason, she had to know if the picture even existed. Maybe she wouldn't be able to find it and that would be the end of it. And a small part of her thought if she did find the picture, maybe The Taskmaster wouldn't ask her for anything else.

From her exploration of his office weeks before, she knew where the pictures would be. She slipped out of bed and into the bathroom first. That way nothing would seem suspicious to Luke if he woke while she was still in the bathroom. The thought ran through her mind that this was it. There would be no more getting anything for The Taskmaster. She'd have to meet with her brother and tell him the truth. Let him know that his actions had not gone unnoticed.

She dreaded that conversation, but the truth was, he was now an adult and being an adult meant having to accept your past and deal with it. As for her role in the matter several years ago? She was also an adult. It was time for her to put on her big-girl panties and deal with whatever ramifications followed.

She looked at herself in the bathroom mirror. Yes, if she wanted a relationship with Luke it was time to grow up. She smiled at her reflection. Tomorrow was going to be a new day. She would not worry about The Taskmaster or her brother. She would focus on herself and Luke and what they could be together.

When she stepped back into the bedroom, she almost went straight to the bed. But at the last minute she decided to go down the hall, just to see if the picture was where she thought it would be. She wasted no time scurrying to Luke's office. She didn't even look behind her to see if he was awake. He wouldn't be. He was snoring when she left the bedroom.

She knew which drawers held the club pictures and which one held the more private ones. This one, the one of the actress, would most definitely be with the private ones. It surprised her he didn't keep this door locked, but then again, he probably wasn't expecting anybody to dig through his office, especially at three thirty in the morning.

She found the folder she was looking for. The file was neatly dated and labeled with the actress's name. She didn't open it or in any way look at the pictures. After all, they weren't hers to look at. She simply slid it back into its location in the drawer. Now she could honestly tell The Taskmaster she had looked for the pictures, but didn't see them. Win, win for everyone.

Interestingly enough, she still wasn't tired. Must have been the amazing sex hours before. So she didn't go back to the bedroom; instead she headed to the kitchen. She poured herself a glass of water while looking out the window overlooking the gardens.

She really liked Luke's house. It was so much more comfortable than her own apartment. Though she often joked with Luke about always going to his house, his place was the nicer of the two. For a few minutes, she allowed her mind to wander down paths she'd previously refused to go down.

What would it be like to live with Luke?

To live in this house with him day in and day out. And night after night. Her commute to work would be longer, but she thought she could deal with that. After the night they had spent together, anything seemed possible. She wanted to wake Luke up and discuss the future. She looked at the time. Probably not a good idea to wake him up at four a.m.

Besides, they had all the time in the world.

Chapter Eleven

Luke was wide-awake and seething when Meagan came back to bed at four fifteen. She had been in his office again. He'd brushed it off the first time; he could not do so this time. But at the moment, he was too angry to think straight.

Damn it, Meagan, he thought. *What the hell are you thinking and what the fuck are you doing?*

Meagan, of course, had no idea he was awake. He didn't follow her, but she hadn't been as quiet as she probably thought she was. What was she looking for? And why?

He stayed in bed, thinking until her deep, rhythmic breathing told him she had gone back to sleep. Suddenly, he couldn't get out of the bed fast enough. No, he didn't know what was going on with Meagan. And he needed to calm down before he decided what to do.

After freshening up in the bathroom, he wrote her a short note and placed it on the pillow.

Meagan,

*Had an emergency pop up at the club. Not sure when
I'll be back. Don't wait.*

I'll call you later,
Luke

He drove to the club. It would be deserted this early in the
morning, making it a good place to sit and think. He'd gone
through half a pot of coffee when a car pulled up to the front door.

He wasn't expecting anybody, so he went outside to meet
whoever it was. The tall, muscular man getting out of his car
looked familiar and as he came closer Luke recognized him. Fritz,
the gentleman he and Nathaniel had contracted for the new club.

"Fritz, hello." He stood and waited for the other man to
make his way up to him. "You're out and about awfully early."

Fritz smiled and shook his hand. "The same could be said for you."

Fritz had been born and raised in Germany, and though he
now traveled around the world, his heritage was evident in his
accent.

"Just not able to have a good night's sleep," Luke admitted.

"That's what normally happens to me when I'm having woman
trouble."

Luke snorted. "Isn't it always woman trouble?"

"Nine times out of ten."

"Come on inside. I made some coffee."

Fritz agreed and the two men each got a cup of coffee and
sat in Luke's office. Fritz said that he had come by to look at the
outside of the club.

"I thought Nathaniel said you couldn't start anytime soon," Luke asked.

"He is correct and nothing's changed. I just had some free time and thought I'd stop by."

"You work too much."

"Says the man already at work with half a pot of coffee gone before eight."

"It goes back to what you said before. Woman trouble." Luke wasn't sure why he felt comfortable opening up to Fritz. He knew the man to be a Dom because he'd attended the opening of the New York club as a guest of Cole's.

"Anything in particular?"

"I don't think she's being entirely honest with me. I've caught her sneaking out of bed twice. Well, perhaps *caught* isn't the right word. I haven't confronted her yet. The first time she went to my office and looked through my files. I didn't follow her last night, but I'm sure she did it again."

"And you don't want to ask her why?"

"No, I'd much rather she confront me with what she's doing."

Fritz smiled. "This is just my personal opinion, but sometimes subs need a little help."

"What do you mean?"

"Do you happen to have a time set up to play with her again?"

"As a matter of fact I do, next weekend." It would be their last photography session. He thought back to the night before and how before they went to bed, everything seemed to be headed in the right direction.

He'd been momentarily stunned when she admitted she wanted to continue seeing him. He was surprised she didn't pick his jaw up off the floor and hand it to him.

"We normally start at ten and go for as long as we want." There was no way to know how long this last session would take. Sometime before Saturday, he needed to pull all the photos together to ensure he had what was needed for the book.

"I have a way to get unresponsive subs talking," Fritz said. "If you want, I can outline it for you, or if you'd like a third, I'm willing to help."

"Yes, I'd love to hear your thoughts." He looked down at his desk and at the mess he called his calendar. Meagan's name was listed every Saturday. He didn't want to think about how lonely his Saturdays would be without her. Screw that. How lonely all his days would be without her.

What the hell, Meagan? What the hell? he asked himself for what seemed like the five thousandth time.

For the life of him he couldn't figure out what she was doing in his office. His mind went wild trying to decipher her motives. Was she trying to sabotage him?

He couldn't fathom that notion. Not after the previous night. If these past few weeks had been an act, she deserved an Oscar. She'd been too genuine in his arms. He prided himself on knowing when a sub was pretending. He'd bet his house that she was not pretending last night.

Some small part of him tried to convince the rest of him that maybe she was only wanting to look at the pictures of herself. After her first midnight visit to his office, he'd pulled her close and brought up in a roundabout way that he wanted her opinion on the photos he'd taken so far.

He listened as Fritz discussed his plan. It was unlike anything he had ever done before. It was beyond anything he'd ever contemplated. It was perfect.

Luke knew Meagan would probably figure out something was up. While no one had ever said he wore his heart on his sleeve, it wasn't hard to know how he felt. He hadn't called her all week, and they'd exchanged a few texts back and forth, but nothing in detail. Nothing to do with their feelings for each other.

On Saturday she watched him with curious eyes, looking for something, anything. He schooled his features so he wouldn't give anything away. In order for this to work, she needed to be completely caught off guard. She complied with everything he asked her to do quickly and with no complaint. Any other day, he would be thinking of ways to reward her. But not today.

Fritz waited in the room off the studio. There was a two-way mirror, so he was able to see the entire session. Luke wondered if he was able to pick up on Meagan's unease. He probably could; after all he was a very experienced Dom. He thought ahead to the scene Fritz had planned. Was it the right thing to do?

He wasn't sure. But he knew he had to do something about Meagan's visits to his office.

You could just ask her, he told himself. But he knew Meagan. It wasn't that she would be dishonest, but he wanted to ensure he was told the entire truth.

The day before he had looked over the pictures he had from their previous sessions. There weren't that many he needed to take today. Which was a good thing. He wasn't sure how long he could keep up the "everything's great, everything's fine" facade.

As he took the final shots for the book, he mentally prepared himself for the scene to come. *You have to do this,* he told himself. *You have to know.*

"I think that's it for the bondage scenes." He took a deep breath and scrolled through the last few pictures he had taken.

"Is that all? Should I get dressed?" She was naked at the moment, and Fritz did not want her to start out that way.

He nodded to a hanger he had on the far wall. "Go put a robe on."

She raised an eyebrow at his odd request. Normally, he would have her remain naked or else he'd have her get dressed. To have her put on a robe suggested something else would follow the session. If she was smart, she would pick up on the fact that something was different today.

But again she didn't hesitate. Not the Meagan of today. The Meagan of today was off balance enough that she didn't want to misstep. She quickly put on the robe and went back to kneel in the middle of the room.

"As you probably imagined," he said, "we aren't quite finished for the day. In fact, I have invited someone to run the next scene."

He didn't miss her sharp intake of breath or the way her body tensed.

"What's your safe word, Meagan?"

"Red."

"Very well. There is a room off to the side. On your right. The gentleman joining us is already in there, waiting."

"May I ask a question, Sir?"

"Yes."

"Are you going to be in the room, Sir?"

"No, but the room has two-way glass, so I can see. And I'll be able to hear."

Meagan glanced warily at the closed door and bit her bottom lip. Luke considered calling off the scene for a second. But only for a second. He needed to get to the bottom of this. And in doing so, to let her know that deceit had no place in their relationship. Assuming, of course, that they'd still have a relationship after today.

She threw her shoulders back, held her head up high, and walked through the door.

Her heart was about to pound straight through her chest. Meagan was certain it was beating so loudly that anyone within a six-foot radius could hear it. She came to a stop as soon as she passed through the door.

What the hell?

A man faced her, one hip leaning against a desk. Tall and lean, but with an air of self-assurance and strength. She didn't know him, but he looked vaguely familiar. Her mind scrambled to try to place him. *Opening night. Luke's club. He talked with Nathaniel after Cole left with Sasha.* She remembered a German accent.

"Ms. Bishop," he said, and she'd remembered correctly. He was German. "Come in and have a seat. My name is Herr Brose."

She didn't know why she was so scared. Honestly, he was a rather good-looking man. In fact, *good-looking* might be an understatement. In his tailor-made dark suit, he was downright dashing. But there was something in his demeanor, a hint in his expression, that told her the suit was simply the sheep costume and underneath, he was a very dangerous wolf.

"What exactly are we doing, Herr Brose?" The words were difficult to get out since her mouth was so dry.

"You are not the one to be asking questions. That is my job. I'm not one to let things slide; however, we've never met and I can tell you're apprehensive. So this will count as my good deed for the month. It won't happen again." He nodded toward the chair. "Go sit down."

Her legs shook so badly, she was surprised they carried her, but she walked over to the chair and sat down. He moved toward her with a grace that surely had to be at odds with his height.

"Arms on the armrests," he said. "Palms up."

Her fingers trembled as he bound her by the arms.

"Legs spread."

She instantly obeyed and wasn't shocked when he tied her legs to the chair legs. When he finished, he stood up and looked down at her. "Such a lovely robe." His fingers trailed along the collar and she shivered. His hands were warm; she'd imagined them cold. "I'll let you keep it on for now."

She glanced at the window she knew Luke was watching through, but couldn't see anything. He was watching, wasn't he?

Fritz turned around. "Shall we begin?"

She nodded.

"Words, Ms. Bishop. When I ask a question, you are to answer me with words."

"Yes, Herr Brose."

"Lovely," he said, and turned the lights off.

For what seemed an eternity, she stared into the darkness, unable to see anything. Not even a light from under the door. She pulled against her restraints, but she was bound too tightly and couldn't budge.

A light over her head flickered on and she was momentarily blinded. But he didn't wait for her eyes to grow used to the light before he began.

"We'll start easy," he said. "What is your name?"

"Meagan Bishop."

"And your occupation?"

"I'm an executive at NNN."

"Do you enjoy your work?"

"Most days." She took a deep breath. This wasn't too bad. It looked a bit scary at first, but this was nothing she couldn't handle.

"When did you last have sex?"

"Last weekend."

"How many times did you come?"

"What?"

"Wrong answer." He moved from the desk into the light and took off his suit jacket, all the while keeping his eyes on her. "Each wrong answer earns a punishment."

She watched in awe as he rolled up his sleeves. It was his accent, she decided, that made him sound so scary. Fuck, his arm muscles were huge. His hands took the material of her robe and with one jerk, the garment ripped into two pieces, exposing her from neck to waist.

"How many times did you come last weekend?"

"Umm, twice." She couldn't remember.

"Four." The corner of his lip quirked up. "Punishment time."

He went back to the desk and returned with a riding crop. "Four swats on each breast."

Fuck no, she almost shouted, but bit back her words. She took a deep breath and waited for him to strike. He surprised her by instead kneeling and cupping her right breast with his free hand. His touch was firm, but gentle and his mouth curved into a smile at the small gasp she couldn't hold back.

"Such pretty skin." His fingers lightly danced over the top of her breast.

She swallowed.

His touch grew rougher and he rolled her nipple between his thumb and forefinger. He pinched it and an electric shock traveled down her body from where his hands were to the space between her legs that ached to be filled. He repeated his actions on her other breast. She held back her moan; she hadn't thought anything about this setup would have turned her on, but it did.

When she was very nearly writhing in her seat for him to touch her more *damn it,* he stood and, without waiting, brought the flogger down first on one breast and then the other.

Fuck, that stung.

He rubbed his thumb over both nipples again and then quickly flogged them again. The combination of pleasure and pain made her more aroused than she'd thought possible when she first walked into this room.

Was Luke watching? Did her response to Fritz turn him on? The German Dom repeated his actions, but when he stood for the fourth and last time, she saw his fingers tighten on the handle of the flogger.

As expected, the last strike held no pleasure, only pain, and unlike the others, afterward he didn't caress her. Instead he took a step back.

"I suggest you take me at my word when I tell you that you don't want that particular punishment on your pussy."

She nodded.

"Words, Ms. Bishop."

"Yes, Herr Brose."

Satisfied, he turned away and walked back to the desk, put the flogger down, and faced her, leaning his hip on the edge of the desk. "Tell me, Miss Bishop, why are you here?"

"I'm sorry, Sir. Can you elaborate on what you mean? Here in this room, or here at this house?"

"Apologies. Why are you here at this house?"

"Today Luke and I had to finish the photo shoot, Sir."

"And when you were here last weekend?"

A slight feeling of unease started to creep into Meagan's body.

She couldn't put her finger on exactly why, but something was off. Once more, she tried looking through the two-way glass. Nothing. For all she knew Luke wasn't even watching anymore.

"Eyes on me."

"Yes, Herr Brose. I came over last weekend."

"Why?"

"Because Luke invited me to dinner."

"And you stayed all night?" he asked.

"Yes, Sir."

"Was this the first time you spent the night?"

"No, Herr Brose."

The unease she felt earlier began to lessen a bit. From the way it sounded, Luke was interested only in her feelings for him. Nothing more. They would finish this scene, and then she would kick his ass. Honestly. An interrogation scene? To get to the bottom of her feelings? It was almost pathetic.

Some small part of her brain chimed in that Luke was not pathetic or anywhere close to it. There was probably another reason for the interrogation scene. She flexed her hands, urging him mentally to hurry up.

"I'm not going to ask you how many times you've spent the night before."

Meagan sighed in relief. She was afraid that because of the circumstances, her head wasn't clear enough to correctly determine the number. Fritz watched her intently from his place by the desk. His stare almost made her feel guilty. But what did she have to feel guilty about?

Oh no.

Oh no. Oh no. Oh no.

"Interesting expression, Ms. Bishop." His eyes momentarily flashed with victory. What was that about?

He pushed away from the desk, taking a ruler with him. He walked toward her slowly, slapping the ruler against his palm as he did so. In the otherwise silent room, the sound resonated. And though she was expecting it, each slap made her jump slightly.

"So skittish." The ruler slap against his palm again. "Are you starting to figure out why you're here? Here in this room, that is."

"Not really, Sir."

He didn't acknowledge her answer. "You're so vulnerable in this position. Every inch of you exposed and offered to me." He stood by her side and ran a finger down her arm to her palm, where he gently swirled his forefinger at the base of her thumb. "You've been a naughty girl, Ms. Bishop. Tell me what you've done. Confess and I will go easy on you. Deny anything and I will punish you thoroughly."

Her heart started to pound. Did Luke know? If so, how much? Was he aware of the blackmail? Maybe he wasn't sleeping when she got out of his bed after all. Had he set up this elaborate scene to get her to confess?

No. There was no way he could know. No possible way.

But Fritz stood there with a knowing expression on his face. Fuck. He knew something.

"Come now, Ms. Bishop." His voice was softer, but somehow that made him seem only more dangerous. "Let us be reasonable. There's no need to make this hard on yourself."

"I, uh, I'm, *shit*."

He picked up a black pair of gloves from the top of the desk and ever so slowly put them on. All the while watching her. He shrugged and wiggled his now gloved fingers. "Of course, it doesn't matter one way or the other to me, you see. In fact, I often find I enjoy a stubborn suspect."

Suspect. He knew. They both did.

"How much do you know?" she asked.

"I believe I already gave you a warning about asking me questions, Ms. Bishop. You will atone for that mistake in a few minutes."

"If you already know, why are you doing this?"

"Another question? My, my, my, you are a naughty one, aren't you?"

She clamped her mouth shut to keep from saying anything else. He sat perfectly still, never taking his eyes off her. Finally, he stood.

"I didn't hear a safe word or a confession." He stood and crossed the floor to stand before her again. He leaned down and his breath was hot against her ear. But when he spoke, he spoke in German and it sounded scary as fuck.

"I don't understand, Sir."

"You weren't supposed to." He took a knife from his pocket. She stopped breathing, her eyes never leaving the blade as it sliced the ropes around her ankles and wrists. "Go bend over the desk."

She wondered what he would do next. Was he still trying to get information out of her? Or was he just going to punish her? She reached the desk, and as her hands slid across the top, she noticed how they trembled.

Behind her came the sounds of opening and closing doors, a large thump, the trickling of water, and something electronic being turned on that filled the silence with a low whirling sound. Her breathing increased and she felt as if she was going to throw up. She couldn't do this. She couldn't be in this room. Not with that man and not like this.

She jumped when his gloved hand touched the back of her neck. The cool leather sent her over the edge. "Red."

His hands dropped and immediately Luke entered the room. She glared at him. "Was this really necessary?"

He folded his arms across his chest. "Yes, I want to hear it from you."

She took a deep breath. "I'm being blackmailed. I was told you have some pictures they wanted. If I provide the pictures, they won't hurt me or do anything with the information they have on me."

Luke's dropped mouth and wide eyes suggested he didn't know as much as she thought he did. "You're with me because you are being blackmailed?"

"You set up this elaborate scene and you didn't know what was going on?"

"Damn it, Meagan, answer my question first." There was something more than shock in his voice. There was anger, yes, but there was also sadness.

"Only in the beginning."

He flinched at her words, but she was the one who felt as if she had been punched in the gut. His expression . . . She couldn't bear to look at him.

"Get out of my studio."

She held out her hand, as if to touch him. "Luke?"

He took a step back. "Don't touch me. Get the fuck out."

"Just let me explain." If she could only make him see that even though she was with him in the beginning because of the blackmail, that was no longer the case. She wanted to be with him. And only him.

"I don't need or want your explanation." Now when he looked at her, there was no surprise, no shock, and no sadness. Only anger. "I get that you wanted to get back at me for what I did years ago. I can understand you being angry about that. But for you to invade my privacy, to sneak into my office, and to take my pictures." He shook his head. "I need you to leave so I can think."

Hot tears filled her eyes, but she knew now was not the time to reason with Luke. She would call him later, when he'd calmed down. She nodded. "I'll just get my things."

He didn't reply.

Chapter Twelve

Two days later, Abby invited Meagan over to their New York penthouse. She said she and Nathaniel were staying in the city, doing a bit of shopping, and just hanging out, but he had a meeting in the afternoon and would she like to come over? Nathaniel's aunt had their two children. Apparently, Lynne was taking a short vacation.

Meagan had been to the penthouse only once. That was several months ago, when she had to apologize to Abby for the nightclub incident. The club that was now Luke's.

Damn, it hurt just thinking his name.

During the last two days, he had not attempted to contact her. Nor had she been in touch with him. She tried to tell herself it was okay, but the truth was she missed him. She missed his lazy smile, his easygoing attitude, and even his voice when he'd issue a command. Now that he wasn't in her life, she realized how lonely she was.

Thank goodness for friends like Abby, who invited her over to hang out. She hadn't told Abby about the breakup yet, but maybe she'd tell her today. Maybe her friend would have some advice on what she should do. She knew what she wanted to do: tell The Taskmaster to fuck off and leave her alone. Every time she thought about it, it sounded better and better. The only thing keeping her from doing it was her brother. She didn't want to mess up his life any more than he'd already messed it up by himself.

And then she'd think, why should she worry? He was a grown man; he could take care of himself.

Because she'd promised her dad. She cursed herself for making that promise.

Round and round her mind went, and since she couldn't decide what to do, she did nothing. Which made her only more restless. Something had to give. And soon.

Abby was all smiles opening the penthouse door. "Hey, come on in."

When she stepped inside, she heard male voices and raised an eyebrow at her friend.

Abby waved her hand as if shooing a fly. "Nathaniel decided to have his meeting in the living room. Said the office here wasn't large enough for everyone."

"I thought he had an office in the city?" Not that she minded. It was Nathaniel's house; he could do anything he wanted.

"He does, but this is private, personal business. About the new club. Luke's here."

They'd been walking down the hall while they talked and the exact minute Abby said "here" was the exact moment they made it to the living room and Meagan came face-to-face with Luke. To be fair, Fritz and Cole were also sitting with Luke and

Nathaniel, but she couldn't look anywhere except at Luke. He was just as surprised to see her as she was to see him.

Other than Fritz, she didn't think anyone else knew what had happened between them. She could only hope he wouldn't say anything now.

"Excuse us, gentlemen," Abby said, totally oblivious to the shock their entrance had caused. She nodded at Luke. "We're just passing through."

Damn it. She should have told Abby about the breakup.

But of course, Nathaniel, being Nathaniel, reached out and grabbed Abby as she passed and pulled her into his lap. "Glad you could stop by," he said with a grin.

Abby made a noncommittal noise.

"I'm glad Nathaniel waylaid you," Cole said and looked over to Meagan. "You, too. We have a few questions and since none of us are women or submissives, we need your help."

Meagan risked a quick peek at Luke. His lips were pressed together tightly, and from the looks of it, it was taking all his strength not to speak what was really on his mind.

"We'd love to help," Abby said from her spot on Nathaniel's lap. "Wouldn't we, Meagan? Look, there's a seat beside Luke— you can sit there for a few minutes."

And there was nothing she could do in response to that other than sit beside the man who now hated her. She schooled her features as best she could, knowing she wasn't going to be any- where near *I'm totally okay with this,* but hoping she wasn't giving off the *Please God let there be a hole in the floor and let me fall right through it* vibe either. But as soon as she sat down and Abby looked their way, the smile disappeared from her face and she knew it hadn't worked. Either the expression on Luke's face or her own told Abby everything she needed to know.

Meagan cleared her throat. "What can we do for you? I'm a woman, but I don't identify as a submissive. I'm a switch."

There was nothing from Luke. No words. No movement. She wasn't sure he was breathing.

Of course by now, everybody had noticed the tension between her and Luke.

Cole cleared his throat. "Switch works."

Across the room, Abby looked as though she was bursting to ask what was wrong with Meagan. Instead she turned to Cole. "What are your questions?"

"We were discussing the new club. For the dressing rooms, should we separate by gender or by role?"

"If you do it by role," Meagan mused, "where does that leave switches?"

Nathaniel raised an eyebrow at Cole. "She makes a good point."

"So we go by gender," Cole said. "Do you think everyone would be okay with submissives and Dominants sharing the same room to change in?"

"I'm okay with that," Abby said. "I'd rather share with a Domme than a man."

"How would same-sex players feel?" Meagan asked.

The men nodded and Nathaniel replied, "We'll have to take that into consideration."

Meagan really hoped that was all the men wanted to know. Normally, she wouldn't mind discussing a new club, but with Luke right beside her still not moving and still not talking, she wanted only to escape as quickly as possible.

"How is your New York club set up, Luke?" Cole asked.

"The dressing rooms are set up by gender." Luke's voice was tight. "But there are separate role-specific rooms as well."

Meagan knew for a fact there weren't any rooms designated for switches. Any other time, she would be jumping all over Luke to bring that up. Not today.

"Do you have a room for switches?" Nathaniel asked. Beside her, Luke tensed even more and Abby whispered something into her husband's ear. Meagan would bet money it was about her, but Nathaniel only nodded and didn't give any indication as to what his wife had spoken to him about.

Luke responded with, "No."

"How does that work?" Cole looked at Meagan. "If there's not a room designated for switches, which one do you use?"

Meagan balled her hands into fists so tight, she knew she'd have nail marks on her palms. She shot Abby a *let's get out of here* look. However, Cole had asked her a question. "I know before I get to the club which role I'll be in for that particular night. I dress appropriately at home, and use the corresponding room when I arrive at the club."

"Thank you," said Cole.

"I think we could set up something similar," said Nathaniel. "Luke?"

"I don't see why not."

An uncomfortable silence followed, and she felt as if everybody was watching her even though she knew that wasn't the case.

Abby gave her husband a kiss on the cheek. "If you guys don't have any more questions for us, we'll be on our way."

"Thank you," Nathaniel said.

Meagan stood up and followed Abby out of the room. As soon as they were outside of earshot, Abby turned to her. "So, what the hell happened between you and Luke?"

Luke braced himself for the questions as soon as the ladies left the room and he wasn't surprised when Nathaniel spoke first.

"Luke? Is everything okay?"

No, he wanted to shout. Everything was not okay. It could not be further from okay. At the moment, though, he wasn't sure he wanted to explain everything to the gathered men. Especially not to Nathaniel, who had never cared for Meagan and simply put up with her because Abby worked for her and genuinely liked her.

It shouldn't have made a difference. He shouldn't care what people thought of Meagan. Yet somehow he did. He cleared his throat. "Meagan and I have been working on a project and it's over now. In more ways than one."

Sitting in a chair near Nathaniel, Fritz remained silent. After Meagan had left a couple of days ago—well, after he kicked her out—Fritz had seen how upset he was and didn't push the issue. He left after telling Luke to call him if he wanted to talk. At the time, talking was the last thing on Luke's mind. But maybe talking now would be beneficial.

"As you probably know, Meagan and I were together for a short period of time several years ago." He stopped, trying to decide how much he wanted to share and making sure Meagan wasn't within earshot. "We've been working together on a project of mine, a BDSM-themed, erotic photography book, and we ended up going beyond the original agreement."

He wasn't going to tell them about the blackmail. He glanced over to Fritz and the man nodded, his indication that he would play this conversation however Luke wanted.

"The short of it is, we were right all those years ago to end it. We aren't good together."

"If you ask me"—Cole watched him carefully—"I say you both looked miserable just now. In fact, I recognize the expression you both had."

"And what was that?" Luke asked.

"It's the same look I had when I was trying to convince myself I didn't need my Sasha." Cole shook his head, remembering. "I only made us both miserable."

"I remember," Nathaniel added. "That night at the New York club, when you said it was too soon for either of you and that anything beyond her training wasn't in the plan."

Fritz laughed. "Cole told me the same thing. 'Fuck the plan,' I told him."

Cole pointed at the other Dominant. "You can stop right there, Fritz. You're a fine one to talk."

"I don't know what you're talking about."

"Oh, really?" Cole looked as if he was having too much fun teasing his friend. "Do you think it somehow escaped my attention that you have a thing for my ex?"

Fritz didn't deny anything. "You know I would never do anything to take your slave away from you."

"Of course I do. But she's no longer my slave and yet, here you sit, not having made any type of move."

"The time isn't right."

"The time will never be right." Cole's eyes widened and he snapped his fingers. "I know. Sasha mentioned hosting another tea party. I can invite you and Kate over."

"Seriously?" Nathaniel chimed in. "Your collared submissive serving tea to your ex-slave? That takes balls, man."

Cole thought for a minute. "Yeah, Sasha would probably have my balls. But don't worry. I'll think of something."

Luke was thankful the conversation between Cole and Fritz

kept everyone's attention away from him, but as soon as Cole stopped talking, they all looked at him.

"No. Never," he said. "Meagan and I are finished. Forever this time."

Thankfully, the office Abby led Meagan to was far enough away from the men that they couldn't hear their conversation. Why did it seem as if every time she visited Abby, *he* was there?

"I'm so sorry," Abby said as soon as they were in the office and the door closed. "Did you and Luke split? I didn't know."

"It's much worse than that." Meagan knew she needed to say the words, but they wouldn't come.

"He found out." Abby said them for her.

"Worse, he only had an idea something was going on and he set up an interrogation scene with Brose out there."

Abby shivered. "Damn. I don't even want to think about that."

"Believe me, it wasn't much fun doing it."

"What did he say when he found out?"

Meagan closed her eyes against the tears that threatened to spill. "He told me to get the fuck out of his studio and out of his house. He wouldn't listen to me or let me explain."

Abby leaned forward and took her hand. "I was afraid it would come to this when you didn't tell him. I'm so sorry."

"There's no way to get him back, either, is there?"

"Trust once lost is difficult to get back." She squeezed her hand lightly. "But it is possible. I know it is. But I don't want to give you false hope. I think that's worse than no hope."

"I just wish I knew what to do."

"Have you been in contact with whoever is blackmailing you?"

"No, not yet. He gave me more time with this. I have until the end of the week."

"What are you going to do?"

Meagan thought about what she wanted to do: curl up in a ball and cry, lock herself in her house and never come out. But those weren't options. She had a life and she had to live it. Even if that life now stretched out before her, looking more and more lonely every day. "Maybe I'll get a dog," she tried joking. "Surely, I can't mess that up."

"Seriously, though." Abby's voice sounded soft and soothing. It was a balm after Luke's tirade.

"I'm thinking about going to the police and telling them everything. Then I can contact the blackmailer and tell him to fuck off."

"Or if you go to the police, you could give them the details and let them go after him."

Meagan thought about both possible options. While there would be satisfaction in telling The Taskmaster what he could do with himself, she knew deep down that it would be for the best if she let the police handle it. They were more capable than she was, and in doing this she could wash her hands of the entire situation.

"Yes," she said, agreeing with Abby. "I should probably go to the police. My one big concern, though, is whether he has any more naked pictures of me. I feel so . . . violated. I'd hate for one of those to get out."

"If you go to the police, and give them all the information you have, maybe they can take care of it for you."

Meagan just wasn't sure she was ready to do that.

When she got home, she booted up her computer and sat looking at the blank screen for several long minutes. She knew it wouldn't be possible to reason with The Taskmaster and he had already proven that he was unwilling to negotiate. That vastly limited her options. Plus, she had probably lost Luke forever, so whatever she did, needed to be for her. It was too late to get him back.

She took a deep breath and started an e-mail.

Taskmaster,

In my life, I have done several things that I regretted. Most of them are small, and have little to no bearing on either my life or my future. But there is one that I deeply regret. And that was falling prey to your demands.

I'll give it to you—you knew exactly which buttons of mine to push. Which fears to play upon. And where to hit me at my weakest. But those aren't the main reason I'm so angry. The main reason is that you involved Luke.

Part of me thinks I should be happy. After all, your little plan put me back in contact with him. And I will forever hold those times dear. But you took what was dear and made it something I was ashamed of. Something I couldn't enjoy without feeling guilty. But most important, something that hurt Luke. And that is something I cannot forgive.

I'm not playing your game anymore. Do what you want, I don't care. Nothing you can do will come close to hurting me any more than you already have.

Regards,
Tired of Your Shit

After composing the e-mail, she drummed her fingers on the desk. Not because she was unsure about sending the e-mail, but because she was trying to decide if she should copy Luke. When she realized it might be her last chance to contact him, she put him on blind carbon copy, closed her eyes, and hit SEND.

She expected him to reply immediately as he'd always done in the past. After sitting and staring at the laptop screen for five minutes, it became obvious he would not. She couldn't decide if that was a good thing or a bad thing.

Eventually, she turned off her laptop and put it away.

Now that she had ended the situation with The Taskmaster, she had to decide her next step. She didn't think she was going to the police. No, that would be too easy, and she needed to make a statement. She wanted to send a loud and clear message, not only to The Taskmaster, but also to Luke. Though she didn't think there was any chance of them ever getting back together again, she couldn't help but hold out some sort of hope he still wanted her.

His feelings for her had been real; she knew that. Surely, there was no way those feelings could simply disappear overnight. She held on to the hope that he was simply angry and perhaps one day he might forgive her.

She was restless for the rest of the afternoon, but she'd decided on her next step and she made a few phone calls in order to line it up. Thinking it would help clear her mind and pass the time until she heard back from The Taskmaster, she decided to go to the pizza place where Luke had stopped before their picnic.

She walked outside with the intention that she'd get takeout and eat in Central Park. But halfway to the restaurant, she knew she couldn't do it. Too many memories of Luke. Instead, she would simply eat alone, in the restaurant.

A lady was working the hostess stand when she entered. She was glad; this way she wouldn't be recognized. She wasn't in the mood to answer any questions about Luke.

The waitress had just taken her order when a familiar voice rang out.

"Teresa," a man said who sounded very much like Luke. "Did Angeleno kick you out of the kitchen?"

The hostess laughed. "He knows better."

"Just picking on you. How about a table for two?"

A table for two? He was with someone. Was it a date? She didn't dare look over her shoulder to see. She felt like sinking into the booth and wished she still had the menu to hide behind.

The hostess took Luke and his date to the other side of the room. Fortunately, a plant kept Meagan out of his line of sight. However, if Meagan looked between the leaves, she could just make out his table. Her heart sank when she saw he was with a woman.

And not just any woman. She was beautiful. Most definitely a model.

The waitress brought her food, but she didn't feel like eating. She forced herself to take a few bites, though it may as well have been cardboard. Laughter drifted her way from Luke's table and though she couldn't hear what was said, the message was clear.

She had been replaced.

She left as quickly as she could, not even taking her leftovers home. She didn't want to wait for a box; she just wanted to leave and get home. To get on her pajamas and curl up on the couch and think about anything other than how quickly Luke had found comfort in another woman's arms.

And because she was a glutton for punishment, she checked

her e-mail one last time before going to bed. There were two new messages. She read Luke's first.

> *Don't bother copying me on any further messages. They will be deleted unread.*

She couldn't stop the tears that ran down her cheeks. If that wasn't a sound good-bye forever, she didn't know what was.

That left the e-mail from The Taskmaster unread. She opened it, knowing no matter what it said, there was no way it would be half as painful as Luke's.

> *You only think you've won, you uppity bitch. Just you wait. When you least suspect it, I'll make you pay. And it'll make those pansy-ass spankings from Luke feel like child's play.*

Reading the e-mail should have frightened her. There in black-and-white was a bold threat. But her eyes could barely make it past the first sentence.

Uppity bitch?

There was only one person who had ever called her that.

Her brother.

She reread the note. And he knew about the spankings. Was it someone from a club? Did her brother even know she was into kink? And again, how and why was Luke involved? As far as she knew, only people in the kink scene would even be aware that she and Luke knew each other.

The more she thought about it, the more sense it made. There was no way anyone other than her brother could know about the details of that year. And Jake always needed money. He probably saw blackmail as a way to get her to pay without coming out and asking her for money. Plus, as much as she hated to admit it, he was horribly intelligent when it came to computers. It wouldn't be hard for him to hack into the system at work.

Still, it didn't sit right. While she could see Jake blackmailing her, she couldn't picture him taking nude photographs of her. That was sick. And then she realized—Jake *was* sick. Forget money or handouts. He needed help. He needed therapy.

But again, how would he know about Luke? And about her involvement with BDSM?

She picked up her phone and called him. He answered on the second ring.

"Hello?"

"It's me," she said, and he grunted in reply. "What the hell do you think you're doing? You think I wouldn't figure it out?"

Silence was her only answer and she knew she had him cornered.

"Do what?" he finally asked.

"I don't know how you found out about Luke, but you can stop it. I was serious. I'm not playing your game anymore."

"What game and who's Luke?"

She rolled her eyes. *Figures.* "Be a man for once and own up to it."

There was a muffled sound as if he covered the mouthpiece and garbled talking.

"Jake!" She raised her voice. "Damn it, I'm not finished."

But the only thing she heard was more muffled talking and then the beep, beep, beep as the call was dropped.

She shoved the phone into her purse. "You think it's that easy to get rid of me?"

Chapter Thirteen

The next day, Guy surprised her at work by stopping by her office midmorning.

"Guy." She stood up as he walked in. "How are you? What brings you to this part of the building?"

He flashed the grin that had gotten him into the hearts and living rooms of the city's inhabitants. "Why, you, of course."

"Have a seat." She waved toward the chair across from her desk.

"No, that's okay. I can't stay long. I just wanted to see if you were free for lunch."

She froze halfway down into her seat. "You could have called for that," she finally said, sitting down.

"Yes, but I thought if I showed up in person, you'd be a lot less likely to turn me down." His smile dimmed somewhat. "And there's a position I'd like to discuss with you."

A position? She frowned. "I don't know."

"Come on," he said. "It's just lunch."

But that, of course, was the problem. It was just lunch and from there, it would turn into just dinner. She'd known Guy for years. She knew how he worked. And damn it all, there was a part of her that wanted to say yes. Sure, Guy was a player, but she'd know where she stood.

And he was vanilla. She was sure of it. Maybe it was time she dated a vanilla man. There could be safety in a vanilla relationship. She was getting older. Maybe it was time to put the kinky stuff in the bottom drawer.

Across from her, Guy waited.

Everything about a relationship with him would be easy. She was so tempted. He was nice and if she ignored or accepted the player side of his personality, word had it he was a lot of fun.

She opened her mouth to say "Yes" but what came out was "No."

No, she didn't want vanilla. No, she didn't want easy.

And hell to the no, she didn't want Guy.

Luke didn't really feel like talking to Nathaniel about the new club in Delaware. But he and Abby were in New York City for the week, so it only made sense to have a meeting when they were all in the same town.

Abby opened the door and was all smiles when she saw him. But he could tell there was something hidden behind her jovial expression that she didn't want him to see. He'd been a photographer and Dom for too many years not to notice such things. Most days he was okay with it, but today he thought it really would be nice to be a little less observant.

"Hello, Abby." He didn't even try to make his voice sound

happy. Abby was Meagan's friend and employee and he knew the two were close.

"Luke." She stepped aside. "Come on in. Nathaniel will be here in a minute."

"Thank you."

She led him into the living room and the silence was deafening. She definitely knew something and it took all his strength not to ask how Meagan was doing.

"Can I get you something to drink?" she asked.

"No, I'm fine."

They were saved from making further attempts at small talk by the appearance of Nathaniel. He walked in and looked at the two of them sitting. "Something wrong?"

Luke waited for Abby to say something. When she didn't, he replied, "The better question is what's right?"

Nathaniel looked at his wife. "Abby?"

Abby shrugged. "I can only assume he's talking about Meagan."

"Ahh." He nodded when Luke didn't either confirm or deny Abby's statement.

Luke couldn't help it—he had to know. He looked at Abby and asked, "How much do you know?"

"Likely more than you." She looked at her husband. "I know you wanted me to stay and talk about the club, but I need to discuss this with him first."

Nathaniel nodded. "Shall I stay?"

"Please do," she said. "I'd like your opinion on a few things."

"You realize," Nathaniel said, "we're not discussing my favorite person."

"I have never known anybody to hold a grudge for so long."

"You were almost assaulted."

"That was months ago and I wasn't."

From the way the conversation was going, it appeared this was not the first time they'd had this discussion.

"I put up with her because she is your boss and you like her, for whatever reason I certainly don't know."

Luke couldn't help but notice the smile Abby had opened the door with was long gone. "You and I," she said to her husband, "will pick up this conversation later." She turned to look at Luke. "What did Meagan tell you?"

Luke took a deep breath. He wanted to discuss Meagan even less than he wanted to discuss the new club. It was obvious Abby had something on her mind and she wasn't going to move on until she had her say.

"I know she was being blackmailed. And that was the main reason she agreed to do the photo shoots with me." He looked up, silently wishing that Abby would tell him he was wrong. That he had misunderstood and Meagan had wanted to be with him from the start.

But Abby simply nodded. "That's true," she said. "In the beginning."

Luke snorted. "I suppose now you're going to tell me that after I took a few pictures of her, she fell madly in love with me and couldn't imagine life without me. So much so that she kept the fact that she was being blackmailed a secret."

He glanced at Nathaniel. The other man clearly had no idea what his wife was talking about. And he didn't seem happy about it.

Abby must have sensed the same thing. She turned to him. "It wasn't my place to tell you. It really didn't concern me."

"Either way." Nathaniel shook his head. "You should have called the police. Something."

"I did what I thought best for my friend. And I wouldn't change it at all."

Nathaniel opened his mouth to speak, but then closed it. Obviously, the conversation wasn't over. It just wasn't going to continue at the moment.

Abby shifted her attention back to Luke. "Yes, it started that way. But as time went on, she grew more and more attracted to you. And she was afraid to tell you about the blackmail because she thought you'd act exactly like you are now."

"Of course," Luke said. "How else would she expect me to act?"

"Can you see her point at all?" Abby asked. "Seriously, what would you have her do?"

"I'm going to go out on a limb here and say, tell the truth?"

"She was protecting her brother and her father."

Luke laughed. "Her brother is an ass. Why the hell would she want to protect him?"

"It was more than that. Whoever it was also threatened her."

That was the first Luke had heard about a possible threat. The thought of someone hurting Meagan made his blood boil. He clenched his fist. "Damn it, she should've told me. I could protect her."

Abby's right eyebrow cocked up. "Really? Maybe you would have known if you'd let her explain instead of kicking her out of your house."

A punch to the gut would have felt better. Damn it. Was his ego so fragile that he couldn't have heard her out that day? Had she been so frightened for her safety that she felt she couldn't talk to him?

He knew how it looked. Like he wanted to have his cake and eat it, too. It was the Dom inside him who was bound to protect at odds with the man who'd had his heart broken.

He shoved his hands through his hair, finally admitting the truth to himself. "I was an ass. I care for her. I do. What happened hasn't changed that." He sighed. "I just don't know if I can trust her."

"Have you never made a mistake?" Abby asked.

"Abby," Nathaniel said, a slight warning in his tone.

She held up her hand. "No, he has to understand that we all do stupid things when we're in love."

Luke felt as if someone had punched him. Love? Was it possible Meagan loved him? It didn't seem possible. You didn't keep things from people you loved.

But as soon as the thought popped into his head, he dismissed it. Of course you did. People kept things to themselves all the time. Yes, Meagan had been wrong to keep the blackmail from him, but if he looked at it from her point of view . . .

He'd broken her heart years ago. He saw just recently how much their breakup back then had impacted her. If, in her mind, things were going well between them—and they had been—it stood to reason that she feared telling him about the blackmail might drive him away again.

Hell, it had. He was here now, wasn't he? Away from her. And he'd replied to the e-mail telling her not to contact him again. Damn. He was an ass.

Granted. It didn't get her off the hook. She'd fucked up and fucked up big-time. But she was human and if there was a chance she loved him, didn't he owe it to her, to *them*, to forgive her?

She'd given him a second chance. Didn't he owe her the same?

From her chair across from him, he saw Abby's smile begin to return. His expression must have shown what he was thinking.

"I knew you'd come around," she said.

"I don't know if I'd say that just yet," he admitted. "We still have a lot of issues to discuss and work out. But, I'm willing to work on them. Willing to listen."

"Damn." Nathaniel looked at him with a strange expression.

"What?" Luke asked.

"You're really in love with her."

He felt light for the first time in years. "Yeah, I suppose I am. Is it that obvious?"

Nathaniel nodded. "When I first came in here, you looked like someone had kicked your puppy. Now, all of a sudden, you look like you could go off and fight dragons."

"He looks blissfully in love," Abby agreed. Her phone vibrated with an incoming text and she reached for it.

Luke slapped his hands on his thighs. "Nathaniel. Abby. I know we were supposed to talk about the new club, but if you'll excuse me—"

"Looks like you may need to start fighting those dragons sooner rather than later," Abby said. When she looked up from her phone, she was frowning.

"Why? What's wrong?"

She held up her phone. "Meagan just sent a text. She figured out who was blackmailing her."

His heart pounded so hard, he could hear it in his head. "Who?" *Tell me. I'll fucking kill him.*

"It's her brother." She shook her head. "I don't like the way this sounds. She said she's going over to his place to confront him."

In a perfect world, Luke wouldn't have to worry about Meagan talking with her brother. After all, he was family. But the truth remained. He had threatened her and the possibility existed he might follow through with his threat.

"Shit," Luke said. "I don't know where he lives."

Nathaniel stood up. "Give me his name. I'll find him for you."

Meagan pulled up to her brother's apartment, noting his truck was parked near the front door. She'd almost thought to call before showing up, thinking maybe he'd be working. Then she decided that it would be more likely for him to publish his book than for that to happen, so she didn't call. Besides, she didn't want to give anything away.

She rehearsed in her mind what she was going to say. And, after she said it, she was going to insist he get some help. His refusal was not an option.

She tapped her foot while she waited for him to answer the doorbell. If all went according to her plan, this visit shouldn't take very long and then she'd work on getting Luke back.

"Yeah?"

It wasn't Jake who answered the door. Nor was it his roommate, Ray. She didn't recognize this man, but something about him looked familiar.

"I'm here to see Jake," she finally said.

He stepped to the side and waved her inside. "He's passed out in his bedroom, but you can wait for him to wake up if you want. He shouldn't be out too much longer."

Waiting with a stranger for Jake to wake up wasn't very high on her list of fun ways to spend a few hours. But she didn't have anything else to do and now that she was at his apartment, she really didn't want to make the trip again.

Like her visit before, she wasn't about to sit on any of the nasty furniture. She switched her purse to the other arm and tried to get as comfortable as she could.

The strange guy sat on the couch, watching her with a faint

amused expression on his face. It was annoying. Like he was in on a joke she didn't know about.

Why did he look so familiar?

Finally, she couldn't ignore it anymore. "What?" she asked him.

"You," he said. "Standing there like you're too good to sit down."

"I'm sorry," she said. "I don't believe I caught your name. I'm Meagan, Jake's sister."

He kept on smiling. "I know who you are, Meagan Bishop."

The hair on the back of her neck stood up. Something about this guy was off. She took a step closer to the door. "Funny. I don't have a clue who you are."

"I'm a friend of your brother's." He nodded to the couch. "Sit down and I'll tell you more."

"That couch is filthy. I'm not about to mess up my clothes by sitting on it." The couch in question had several dark stains. They didn't look fresh, but even if they were dry, there was no telling what else was on that thing. "Some kid could probably do a science experiment on what's growing on it."

The amused expression left the guy's face, quickly replaced by an icy stare that chilled her. "You little bitch. You think you're better than me, don't you?"

"No, I just think I'm cleaner." She tilted her head. "Scratch that. I know I'm cleaner."

He sat there smiling and it was, hands down, the creepiest thing she'd ever experienced. She sighed deeply and then regretted it as the smell of unwashed male assaulted her nose. And still he watched her. That was enough. She had to get out. It didn't matter that she would have to come back later. Anything was better than staying in the nasty apartment with that creepy guy.

"I'm going to go." She took another step toward the door.

"Tell Jake I came by and I'll call him later." And she'd make damn sure the next time she came by that creepy guy wouldn't be here.

"Are you going to see DeVaan?"

Her hand stopped halfway to the doorknob and the uneasy feeling she had grew stronger.

"So funny," he said. "You see, I got this e-mail from someone I'd been corresponding with and she told me to fuck off. I've been spending the last few days trying to decide what I was going to do about it. How I was going to punish her. And now I don't have to. Because she simply walked right into my hands."

She froze, trying to process his words. They didn't make sense. None of it made sense. She spun around, facing the man who had to be The Taskmaster. "Who are you?"

He stood up and she moved closer to the door, wanting to leave, but in the same breath, wanting to know why and now, even more, who.

"You wouldn't know me. You never actually saw me that night. You were too busy with V."

When he stood up, he looked much bigger than he had sitting down. And he stunk; it was worse as he drew closer.

"I wanted a piece of the brunette who came with you, but that Parks man messed it all up and then your precious DeVaan threw me out of the club. My reputation is ruined and I'm not welcome anywhere."

She gaped at him. *This* was the man who almost assaulted Abby? And then she knew where she'd seen him. At the club she Topped at. That night with Master C.

"So," he continued. "I decided to ruin *him* by selling his celebrity photographs to the highest bidder. And who better to aid in his distraction than the woman he never got over? And as a bonus, it also happened to be the woman who brought the brunette in the first place. You were never my original target, but once I discovered who you were, I decided your life should be ruined as well. It was easy, you know. Just followed you both for a while, made friends with Jake, and got the goods on you."

Puzzle pieces started to fall into place and Meagan took a step backward. "Jake?"

He gave a short laugh. "I couldn't believe you thought it was Jake. I was over here when you called. He didn't know what the hell you were talking about. Of course, he doesn't have the brain-power to do anything other than get high."

"What did you do to Jake?"

He waved his hand. "He's fine. Or I guess he is. Sleeping off his last hit. The question you should be asking is, *what am I going to do to you?*"

Heart pounding, she turned and headed for the door, but he was surprisingly quick and beat her there. In one smooth move, he had his arms around her and pushed her against the wall. "Did you seriously think I'd let you go that easily?"

She struggled, but he was too strong. He was pressed against her and she closed her eyes in disgust. "Let go."

"No way. I finally have you here and you're going to work off what you owe me since you didn't get that picture for me." His lips grazed her neck and she shivered. "A whore like you shouldn't have a problem with it."

"Jake!" she yelled. "Jake! Wake up!"

He slapped her. "Stop that. It won't work anyway. He'll be out for hours."

"Help!"

He slapped her again. "Shut up."

She jerked her shoulders, struggling to get away, trying to

kick him. It was useless. He pushed her harder against the door, banging her head into it, and she saw stars. From somewhere he took a dirty rag and tried to shove it in her mouth. She spat at him, earning another slap in the face.

A sharp rap sounded on the door. They both shouted at the same time.

"Help!"

"Go away."

There was a silence, and then came the sweetest sound she'd ever heard.

"Meagan?"

"Luke!" she called, seconds before The Taskmaster punched her in the stomach and she dropped to the floor. She curled into a ball and squeezed her eyes tightly, trying without success to make the pain go away. It hurt to breathe. He hadn't broken a rib, had he?

The deep breath she attempted came out as a wheeze and she braced herself for another blow. But what followed was a resounding crash as the door at her side gave way and splintered beside her.

"Are you fucking out of your mind?" The Taskmaster asked from somewhere above her.

"Where's . . . Why is she on the floor?" Luke sounded pissed. "Did you *hit* her?"

There was a thud as something—or someone—hit the wall, followed by a groan.

"Fucking touch her again and I'll rip you apart from limb to limb," Luke said.

Meagan rolled over to see what was happening. Luke held her blackmailer with one hand around his throat while he punched something into his phone with the thumb of the other.

"Are you okay, sweetheart?" he asked when he saw her watching.

"I'll live."

"I'm calling the police. Is this your brother?"

She shook her head. Her lungs still ached, but she managed to reply, "No, his friend."

"He's the one? Not your brother?"

"Right. You actually kicked him out of your club. Long story, but he's the guy who attacked Abby."

Luke slammed the guy into the wall. "Is that true, fucker?"

Jake. She sucked in a breath. Jake was passed out in his bedroom. She should go check on him. She pulled her knees under her body and sat up.

"Where are you going?" Luke asked.

"Got. To. Check. On. Jake," she said, punctuating each word as she slowly stood.

She had to find Jake and make sure he was okay. There was no telling what he'd taken. It wasn't until she was halfway down the hall that it hit her.

What was Luke doing here?

She almost turned around to go back to the living room to ask, but Jake's room was closer. And, if she was honest with herself, until he told her differently, she could pretend Luke had forgiven her.

She found Jake snoring in his bed. Ugh. He smelled. No telling when his last bath was. At least his room was relatively clean. And by that she meant there weren't any fast-food wrappers scattered on the floor.

"Jake." She made it to the edge of his bed and shook him. "Wake up."

He mumbled something and rolled over.

"Now. The police are on the way."

One eye cracked open. "What?"

She breathed a sigh of relief that he was awake and coherent. "The police. They'll be here any second. Your asshat friend has been blackmailing me."

He didn't move.

"Come on. Get up and get dressed. After the police leave, we're getting you cleaned up. It's time to be a man."

Two car doors closed outside the apartment. She looked out the window. "They're here."

She made sure Jake was up and getting dressed before she left to join Luke in the living room. From the voices she heard, the officers were inside. It was time not only for Jake to grow up. It was time for her to do so as well.

"Meagan?" Luke called.

"Coming," she replied, and walked down the hallway toward her future.

It took a hell of a lot longer than Luke anticipated for everything to settle down. The Taskmaster, or Ted, had been belligerent to the police. After the police took him away, Jake took a shower while he and Meagan straightened up the apartment. Then he drove Meagan and Jake to a nearby rehab facility where Jake enrolled himself for treatment. Luke waited in the car while they took care of everything and couldn't help but notice the peculiar look on her face when she came back to his car. He wanted to ask her what the cause of it was, but they had so many other things to discuss, it didn't seem like the best time.

Without asking, he drove to her place. It wasn't what you

would call neutral, but he thought it was a better option than his place. For her part, Meagan was simply silent.

It wasn't until he followed her to her door that she voiced any concern. "Are you coming in?" she asked with a lifted eyebrow.

He nodded. "We need to talk."

Her lips tightened, but she opened the door and ushered him through. She didn't stop in the living room, but continued on toward the kitchen. "I don't know about you," she called over her shoulder, "but I need a drink. Wine?"

"I'd like something a bit stronger," he admitted. "But wine will do for the moment."

She handed him a glass when she made it back from the kitchen and sat down as far away from him as possible. "What did you want to talk about?"

"I'm sorry for how I acted when I found out about the black-mail."

She shook her head. "You don't need to apologize. It was all me. I should have told you."

"Maybe. But who's to say how I would have reacted? It might have turned out a lot differently and then we wouldn't have these." He reached into the messenger bag he'd brought in with him and pulled out the pictures.

She may have been hesitant to talk to him, but she was insanely curious about her photos. She shifted a bit closer to him. "Are those . . . ?"

"The pictures I've selected for the book. Yes. Come have a look."

He spread them out on the coffee table so she could see them easily. One at a time, she picked them up and studied each one. He'd been around models enough to know there were two types: the ones who found fault with everything about their bodies and those who thought themselves flawless. He hadn't been around Meagan years ago when she'd seen her pictures of their shoot. He wondered which camp she fell into.

She put the last one down. "Not bad."

"That's all you can say?" He picked up one from the night she had the formal gown on. With the moonlight and her wistful expression, it was a stunning portrait. "This is fucking fantastic."

"You did an amazing job."

"Thank you, but I had a lot to work with."

Her delicate smile was enough to let him know she wasn't as unaffected by his praise as her next words would have him think. "The thing is, when I look at these pictures, I see a woman who was keeping secrets."

Her response left him momentarily stunned. But of course that would be what she saw. "Meagan . . ." he started.

"No." She shook her head. "Don't make excuses. I was wrong. I just . . ." She blinked away tears. "I just didn't want to ruin what we had and instead I messed it up even more."

"It might have been messed up, but it's not unfixable."

She looked up in surprise. "You want to fix it?"

"I'd like to try." He stood up and walked to where she sat and took a seat beside her. "I think what we have is worth a second chance. Let's face it. I haven't been a saint in this entire ordeal."

"Yeah, but at least your screwup was years ago. Not like mine."

"You were being threatened and you wanted to protect your brother. I can't fault you for either of those things."

"Funny thing, that." She took a long sip of wine. "Wanting to protect Jake."

"What's funny about that?"

"I told him about the blackmail while we were waiting for him to be admitted today. You were in the car."

And it had taken damn near forever. He thought she'd never get back to the car. For a minute, he thought maybe she'd decided to admit herself for something. "Right. I remember."

She finished the wine in her glass and told him about the fires. He sat silently, just listening.

"Ted got him drunk one night," she said, after she'd told him almost everything. "It was the anniversary of Dad's death, but Ted didn't know. Jake was miserable and feeling guilty and told him everything. Cleansed his soul, he said. Fucker e-mailed me the first time the very next day."

Luke thought it odd that Jake had been so bothered by it, but he never talked to the one person who knew he'd set the fires. As far as he knew, the two siblings had never discussed it. "Why didn't he cleanse his soul with you?"

"Oh, you know. I was the perfect one. With the awesome job and great house. I had it all together. I didn't need anything of the sort." She winced.

"There's something else, isn't there?" he asked gently.

She nodded and he waited for her to tell him. Finally, she took a deep breath.

"My father died because of the last fire Jake started." She got only those words out before stopping and looking at him. He was shocked speechless and simply nodded for her to continue. "I was able to talk to him, at the hospital . . . before."

He reached over and took her hand. She squeezed his in a silent *thank you*.

"He told me he knew what Jake had been doing. He covered it up because he didn't want people to know his son was the one starting fires. Then he made me promise to look after him. And I've tried. Heaven knows, I've tried. I'm just . . ."

He stroked her hand with his thumb, afraid if he said anything, she'd stop, and from the way it sounded, she needed to tell someone what she'd been keeping inside all these years.

"What else could I do?" she asked. "I had to keep quiet. My father died a hero and if I'd told people what really happened, he won't be seen as that."

"And Ted decided to use your guilt as a way to get to me." He hated the man even more. "I'm sorry, Meagan. Not only for not listening before, but for what your father did to you. That's a lot to put on a teenage girl."

She sniffled. "My mom didn't even know. It feels so good to finally tell someone."

He pulled her into his arms and whispered, "I promise from now on, you can tell me anything and I won't judge you or hold it against you."

She nodded. "Thank you."

He held her for several minutes, basking in the simple joy of having her in his arms again and how thankful he was he hadn't lost her. When she pulled back, he reluctantly let her go.

She bit her lip and glanced out the window. "Is it bad that I still don't want it public? I don't want to tarnish his memory at the station. Not for something that happened so long ago."

He'd always prided himself on being truthful. Honesty was the best policy and all that. But sitting next to Meagan, he questioned the usefulness of being completely honest in regard to this issue. So many lives had already been impacted by Jake's actions and things were looking as if they would finally settle down. What would be the point in resurrecting it?

"No," he finally said. "I don't think it's wrong."

She let out a deep breath. "If you think I should pursue it, I will."

"I think you should let it be. The only regret I have is that Jake didn't tell you he'd confessed to Ted. If he had, maybe it wouldn't have gone as far as it did. You would at least have known who you were dealing with. Maybe you could have stopped it earlier."

"True. But like you said before"—she picked up the picture he'd held up to her earlier—"not only would we not have this picture, this book, but we wouldn't have memories of the night this was taken."

He allowed himself a smile. "That was an awesome night."

"Right? The pizza in Central Park was divine." She said it with a straight face, but she was laughing at him with her eyes.

"Woman, if the pizza was what you remember about that night, I may never take you on another picnic."

Now she laughed for real. "Ah, the male ego. So fragile."

"I should spank your ass for calling me fragile," he said in a mock angry voice.

"Did I say fragile? I meant strong and fierce."

He inched closer to her. "Strong and fierce, hmm?" He let his lips trail across her collarbone. "That's more like it."

"Point proven."

He pulled back. "Tell me you didn't just say that."

But instead of denying it, she laughed.

"Now you're going to get it," he said.

"I'm trembling."

"Not yet, you aren't. But you will be when I finish with you." He pulled back with a groan. "We shouldn't do anything today. You've been through a lot, physically and emotionally."

He could tell she wanted to protest, but she had to know he was right.

"I know you're right and I'm glad you recognize I'm not in the place or mind frame to restart anything physical," she said. "But, damn, I wish you weren't."

He leaned over and before his lips touched hers, he whispered a promise: "Soon."

Soon turned out to be almost a week later. Unlike years before, though, this time he wasn't silent. They talked on the phone every day, and each night before she went to sleep, he would text her dirty fantasies that had her yearning for when they would be together again.

The Saturday following the fiasco with Ted, Meagan pulled up to Luke's house, surprised to see a car in the driveway. Was he having someone over? She tapped her foot as she waited for him to open the door, thankful she had changed her mind about showing up in only a raincoat.

"Meagan." Luke dropped his head to give her a quick kiss. "How are you doing?"

"Good. Do you have company?"

"Nathaniel and Abby came over to discuss a few things concerning the new club."

She lowered her voice to whisper, "Will they be leaving soon?"

He laughed and the low, seductive sound sent shivers down her spine. "I'll ensure they do."

"Excellent."

He took her hand and led her into the living room, where they found Nathaniel standing and an animated Abby on the phone.

"I can't get there anytime soon. I'm with Nathaniel at Luke's place. We're heading into the city to pick up the kids from his aunt and tomorrow we're all seeing a play." Abby glanced toward the door and a smile broke over her face when she saw Meagan. "Meagan just showed up. I'll beg her to bring me."

Meagan wasn't sure where Abby wanted to go, but unless it was a matter of life and death, she didn't see it happening. She cocked an eyebrow at Luke, but he shook his head. Apparently, he wasn't sure what was going on, either.

"Meagan," Abby said, sliding the phone in her pocket. "I know you just got here, but I have a big favor to ask you."

Meagan didn't want to come across bitchy, so instead of saying, "Hell to the no," like she wanted to, she forced a smile and asked, "What do you need?"

"That was Julie." Abby's entire demeanor pulsed with excitement. Meagan was going to feel bad letting her down. But just thinking about being with Luke was enough to assure her she wasn't going to feel *that* bad. "Jeff called her. Dena's in labor!"

"What?" Nathaniel said, while at the same time, Luke asked, "It's not too early?"

Abby shook her head. "They're monitoring everything and so far, both Dena and the baby are doing well." She looked over at Meagan. "Will you drive me to the hospital? Nathaniel has to be in the city."

"I can rearrange things, love," Nathaniel said.

"It's not a problem," Meagan said. "I'll drive you." Dena having a baby wasn't a matter of life or death, but it definitely took precedence over sexing it up with Luke.

"I have a better idea," the man in question said. "How about I drive you both?"

"Would you?" Abby asked, and then looked at Meagan. "And you don't mind?"

"Not in the least," Meagan assured her.

Once it was decided, everyone moved quickly. Abby kissed Nathaniel good-bye with a promise to drive into the city first thing in the morning so they could make the play. Luke made a few phone calls and pulled Meagan close for a hug.

"You're an amazing woman," he said in a low voice.

She gave him a kiss. "When we get back here tonight, I'll show you just how amazing."

The drive to the hospital was lively, with Julie sending periodic texts letting them know how Dena was doing.

"This is so exciting," Abby said, reading the latest news from Julie. "She's almost fully dilated." Her smile faded into a frown. "Oh, shit. Her mom just showed up."

"And that's bad, why?" Meagan asked.

"Dena's dad is an ass and didn't approve of her marrying Jeff. He hasn't talked to her since they got engaged and her mother's been the same way. Why she decided to show up at the hospital, much less how she found out Dena was even in labor, is beyond me."

"I'm sure the impending arrival of a grandchild has something to do with it."

"True, but did she just now realize it? Where's she been for the last nine months?"

"At least she's showing up at all."

But Abby didn't look convinced. "I hope I don't run into her."

They arrived at the hospital to find out from Julie that Dena's mother had, in fact, just left.

"Jeff told the staff to call security," Julie said, after explaining that she hadn't heard anything from him in the last few minutes. "He said that woman better be gone by the time he came back."

"I hope the lack of news means the baby's here," Abby said.

"Me, too," Julie agreed.

Meagan took a seat beside Luke and put a hand on his thigh. He placed his hand on top, giving it a little squeeze. "Wasn't exactly how I planned to spend the afternoon," he said.

"Me either, but what's the saying, 'Anticipation makes the heart grow firmer'?"

He looked at her as if she was crazy. "It's *absence* and *fonder*."

"Actually." She inched her hand up his thigh. "I was right about everything other than the heart part."

"Is that right?" He stopped her hand.

"Yes, it makes something firmer, but it's not the heart."

"You'd better watch it," he said. "I've been thinking about you all week. I can't promise I'll be able to restrain myself much longer."

"Funny." She wasn't ready to stop teasing him yet. "If either one of us were to be restrained, I'd have put money on me."

"Meagan," he warned.

She wasn't able to reply, because at that moment, the waiting room opened and Jeff entered the room. No one said anything and even though his huge smile reassured them, the very air seemed to hush.

"It's a girl. We have a daughter." Tears streaked down Jeff's cheeks and he choked out, "And she is perfect."

The room dissolved into joyous chaos with everyone asking questions at the same time. Jeff held up his hand. "Six pounds, eight ounces. Twenty inches long. We named her Mireille Kennedy Parks. Dena is doing great and as soon as everyone's settled, they'll let you go back." He took a step back, clearly happy to have shared his news, but looking down the hall as if some invisible force pulled at him. "Now, if you'll excuse me . . ."

"She's beautiful, Dena," Meagan said about an hour later. The sleeping infant was bundled in her mother's arms and her father stood nearby, silently watching over his family with a look of such fierce love, it nearly took Meagan's breath away.

"Thank you." Dena kissed her daughter's head and then ran her fingers over the downy black hair the baby must have inherited from her father.

"And I love her name," Meagan said.

"We had some *discussions* over that," Dena said with a laugh and an upward glance at her husband. "We finally went with Mireille for *miracle* and Kennedy after the lady who rescued Jeff from the streets years ago."

Meagan thought that was sweet. "I like it when names have meanings."

"I wanted to go with Mireille Ophelia Parks. Ophelia was the lady's given name. Kennedy was her last name."

"And I said that would mean her initials would be MOP and I wasn't doing that to her," Jeff said.

"I eventually saw his point and we agreed on Kennedy." Dena sighed. "But I love the name Ophelia."

Frankly, Meagan thought it sounded too old-fashioned, not to mention tragic. She thought Kennedy was a much better name.

"It's a good, solid name," Luke said from near the door. "She'll grow into it."

"Thank you for bringing Abby," Dena said. "And I'm so glad you were able to come, Meagan."

Meagan was happy she went with her gut and came to the hospital. "I'm glad Nathaniel and Abby were at Luke's when Julie called. It worked out perfectly since I was there."

"Speaking of which," Luke said, pushing back from his place on the wall. "We probably should be leaving soon."

He gave her a knowing look she felt all the way down to her toes. It was a look that told her he still had plans for her that night and he was ready to move forward with them. And really, she wasn't about to argue with *that*. Especially since she wanted it, too.

"Do we need to take Abby anywhere?" he asked.

"No." Meagan shook her head and stood up. "Daniel and Julie are going to drop her off."

They said their good-byes and headed to the parking garage. Luke took her hand and for a few minutes, they walked in silence. That was fine by Meagan. She had so many thoughts running through her head after the eventful day.

She now knew where she wanted to be in five years. She wanted to be settled down. Married. She still wasn't sure if kids would be in the picture, but she figured she had enough time to work through that and didn't have to decide now.

She thought back to the conversation she'd had with Guy only days ago. He'd actually called her about the position he'd mentioned when she'd turned down his request to have lunch. Meagan had purposely put the entire conversation out of her head, telling herself she'd think about it later.

She thought about it now and suddenly she knew she needed to take it.

Luke opened the car door for her. She hesitated before getting in.

"Everything okay?" he asked.

"Yes. It's just—can we go to my place instead of back to yours?"

He motioned for her to get in the car and when he'd buckled himself in, he asked, "It'll take longer to get there, but sure. Any particular reason?"

"I need to call Guy and after I do that, I'll probably need to e-mail him some things."

He pulled out of the hospital parking lot and headed to the interstate. "Let me get this straight. You want me to agree to go to your house instead of mine so you can not only call some other guy, but so that you can *work*, too? Hell, no."

"It's not like that."

He didn't take his eyes off the road, but he lifted his eyebrow. "Then tell me how it is."

"I realized a few things today and I want to move forward on them."

"Things like what?" he asked.

She peeked at him. He appeared to be genuinely interested. Or at least he was willing to listen.

"Things like it's time for me to look into a job I want and not one I'm settling for. Guy gave me information on a correspondent position and I've decided I'm going to go for it."

"Will you be working with Guy?" he asked.

"Are you jealous?"

"No."

Suddenly she had a flashback to the pizza restaurant a few weeks ago. "Yes, you are. You're jealous. Interesting, since I've told you I have zero interest in Guy. Besides, you're one to talk."

"How do you figure that?"

"I happened to be at a certain pizzeria near Central Park a few weeks ago when you showed up with a date." She'd actually wanted to bring it up earlier, but after everything that happened with Jake and Ted, the timing hadn't felt right.

"What? No. I haven't been on a date . . ." He started to protest, and then he must have remembered. "Oh, *her*."

"Yes, her. And if you're going to be all jealous over Guy, you should at least tell me *her* name so I can annoy you properly."

"Her name's Louisa."

Louisa? That was worse than Ophelia.

"Louisa? Really?"

"Yes, but I call her Lu."

He would have a pet name for her. Meagan wondered how long they'd known each other. And for some reason, he was finding this conversation funny. He looked straight ahead, but she could tell he was holding back his laughter.

"Does Lu have a last name?" she asked.

"Yes."

"And it's what?"

He wasn't even trying to hold back his amusement now. "DeVaan."

She wasn't certain she heard him clearly. "What?"

"Lu DeVaan. My sister. She lives in New Orleans and happened to be in town for the weekend. To be honest, that wasn't my first choice of places to eat, but I'd taken her there once before and she said she couldn't be in New York and not eat there."

"Oh," was all she could think of to say.

He was smug now. The bastard.

"I think I like you jealous," he said, then reached over and squeezed her knee. "I'm sorry if that made you feel bad. Seeing Lu and thinking I'd moved on. Trust me. I hadn't."

She placed her hand over his, thankful for his warmth and his strength. But most of all, for his forgiveness and that they were together now and the dark days were behind them.

"I like it when you're jealous," she said. "It makes you go all caveman."

"Caveman, huh?"

She nodded.

"I'll keep that in mind," he said, but he didn't mention it for the rest of the drive to her house.

She'd have forgotten about it altogether if he hadn't picked her up with one swoop and thrown her over his shoulder as soon as they'd made it inside her house and she'd locked the door.

She beat on his back. "Put me down. What are you doing?"

"I'm going to show you just how much of a caveman I am." To prove his point, he gave her ass a hard slap. "And you're going to take it."

Chapter Fourteen

"Uh-oh." She didn't sound too concerned, but her hands stilled.

"*Uh-oh* is right." Luke smiled to himself as he carried her down the hall into her bedroom. "I thought you were a Top. Where are all your toys?"

"I'll never tell."

He put her in the middle of the bed so she was on her back and he hovered over her, his arms on either side of her body. "I can call and have Fritz come over."

"Hall closet. Top shelf."

"That's more like it." He brushed her cheek with his lips. "I'll be right back. When I make it back to the room, I want you naked."

He climbed off the bed and found her box of toys in the closet, just like she'd said. He looked over her collection with an appreciative eye, and then selected a few items to take back to the bedroom.

She was naked, like he'd asked, and sat on the edge of the bed. "What did you find?" She craned her head in an attempt to see what he carried.

"Meagan, Meagan, Meagan. We've been over this numerous times." He gave a sigh as though he was exasperated. "Who's the Top right now?"

She frowned. "You are."

"Right. So who gets to ask the questions?"

"You do, O High and Mighty One."

"You have your sass back, I see."

"Never really lost it, Sir."

"I do like you sassy and I like you addressing me with respect, but I think I heard a bit of sarcasm in your reply."

"No, Sir." She shook her head.

"No?"

"You didn't hear a bit of sarcasm—you heard a lot of it. And if you think for one minute I'm going to sit here and let you use *my* toys on me, you're delusional." She finished by crossing her arms and nodding her head.

"Is that so?" He liked it when she played the brat; it made everything so much fun. "Does that mean you're going to try to stop me?"

She tilted her head in thought.

"I'll take that as a *no*." Then, before she could argue, he pinched one of her nipples and slid on a clamp he'd taken from her closet.

"Fuck! That hurt!" She tried to bat his hand away, but he was already working on her other breast.

"Then I suggest you prepare for this one," he said as he placed the second one on.

She sucked in her breath. "Damn it."

"Now, be nice and I won't go back and get the clit clamp."

Apparently, that was the only warning she needed because she didn't say anything further; she simply nodded. She hated the clit clamp. That was good to know.

"Am I delusional now?" he asked.

"No, Sir."

"Take my cock out." He crossed his arms and waited for her to obey.

He didn't have to wait long. She quickly undid his pants and fished his cock out of his shorts.

"Does that feel delusional to you?" he asked.

"No, Sir."

"Suck it."

She dropped her head and took him in her mouth. He watched as he disappeared past her lips and then closed his eyes as the pleasure overtook him. The only downside to this position was he couldn't play with the clamps. Next time, he'd have to remember to get a chain.

He smiled, knowing that there would be a next time.

"Know what I'm going to do tonight?" he asked, while he worked her mouth with slow and purposeful strokes.

She mumbled something around him.

"Right, you can't talk with your mouth full. That would be bad manners and bad manners will get you punished. You just keep sucking that cock while I tell you my plans."

He dropped his hand to rest on her head and fisted her hair. She bobbed up and down on his shaft a few times before he held her still.

"Enough. Take me all the way in. I want to feel the back of your throat."

She took a deep breath, and then he held her head steady while pushing his way fully into her.

"Yes. Damn. That's good." He thrust a few times, finally pulling back to allow her some air. "And this is just the beginning." He entered her mouth again. "Tonight you're going to offer every part of your body for my use and I'm going to thoroughly fuck each one of your holes."

She moaned in pleasure and redoubled her efforts on his cock. It made him even harder knowing his plans turned her on.

"Right now, I'm using that sassy mouth of yours and, in a few minutes, I'll fill that wet pussy. It is wet, isn't it?"

She nodded around his cock.

"Then, when I'm so hard I can't think straight and I can't last another second, I'm going take your ass and ride you to completion." He bit back a moan as her lips tightened around him. "And only then are you allowed to come. Only then, when I'm buried deep inside your ass, will I let you come."

He had to pull out of her mouth or else he'd lose it right then and there. She fell back to rest on her knees while he finished undressing. Once he was naked, he motioned for her to get on her back and he pressed his body down on hers, holding himself up slightly so his full weight wasn't on her, but enough that she could feel him.

He bent his head and gave her a kiss, noticing when he pulled back that there were tears in her eyes. "Meagan?" Had he hurt her? Or been too rough? "Are you okay?"

She gave him a smile that melted his heart. "Perfect, Sir."

He brushed a tear away with his thumb. "Why are you crying?"

"I've spent my entire life feeling like something was missing and that I didn't belong. And tonight I realized I've been looking in all the wrong places." She ran a hand up to cup his face. "It's been right here all along. I found it in you."

"Meagan," he whispered. "You'll never feel lost again. Not while there's breath in my body." And then he kissed her with enough passion to take hers away.

Epilogue

ABBY
Six months later

Luke's New Jersey club was packed. It wasn't surprising that I didn't know most of the people in attendance. What was shocking was the number of vanilla people who crowded into the kink club for the party marking the release of Luke's book. Of course, it was Meagan's, too, but she had requested her identity not be revealed. Even if you knew her, you would never know she was the model unless she told you.

Just like you'd never know she now considered herself primarily a submissive.

Tonight she looked stunning in a glamorous pale pink gown, standing beside her Dom as he signed copies of *The Muse*. Every so often, Luke would look her way and the two of them would share a smile that increased the temperature of the room by several degrees.

"I'd tell him to get a room, but since he owns the place . . ."

Nathaniel said, coming up beside me and slipping his arm around my waist.

"Right?" I leaned into him. "She looks beautiful, doesn't she?"

"If you go for the tall blond type."

I laughed. "Smart man."

"I've been married long enough to know the proper answer to *that* question."

"She's blissfully happy," I said, thinking back to how she'd changed in the last few months. Being with Luke grounded her. She was more mellow and not as high-strung. She was also no longer my boss, as a result of a promotion she took. Though I hated not reporting to her anymore, I knew she was thrilled with her new job as a morning news anchor.

"I'm happy for her," Nathaniel said, and I knew he was telling the truth. "Who's that beside her?"

To her right was a man I'd never met, though I'd heard a lot about him. "That's her brother."

Nathaniel lifted an eyebrow. It wasn't a secret Jake had recently been released from rehab. I'd been wary when Meagan told me he was coming, but she assured me he'd done a one-eighty in therapy.

"He's applying for a job at Luke's downtown gallery." Meagan had told me hours ago when she pointed him out to me shortly after he arrived.

"Not here?" Nathaniel asked.

"I doubt Meagan wants her brother to see her here with Luke, when they aren't as . . . *put together*."

"Put together?" he whispered in my ear. "As opposed to when he has her naked and tied up for being a mouthy brat and is working on her ass with a flogger or two?"

"Yes," I choked out. "That exactly."

In fact, we had been at the club the night before and he'd been doing just that.

"I see your point." He looked around the club. "Have you seen Lynne?"

Lynne had approached us a few weeks ago, asking for a recommendation for joining our BDSM group. We had agreed, with a provision that she attend tonight's party first to meet Luke and some of the other members. We explained she needed to meet everyone first in an environment that wasn't a play party.

I stood up on my tiptoes. "She was over at the bar the last time I saw her. I don't know if she's still there or not."

"She is." Nathaniel had a better view of the bar, being so much taller than me.

"Is she alone?"

"Looks that way."

I sighed. "I'd really hoped she'd meet some people. I worry about her. Especially since she spends so much time with Henry and Elizabeth. I mean, it's not like she has a happening social life."

"I hope we haven't done her a disservice by hiring her." Nathaniel spoke the fear I'd been hesitant to voice.

"Me, too." But she was so good with the kids. I didn't want to lose her. And she'd already made plans to attend some classes online in order to work toward her teaching degree. "Maybe we should make more of an effort to get her out."

"As long as we keep in mind she's a grown woman, capable of taking care of herself and making her own decisions."

I rolled my eyes at his warning. "I have no intention of being her mom."

"It's not your motherly instincts I'm worried about." He must have seen someone he recognized because he nodded at them.

"It's not?"

"Hello, Nathaniel. Abby."

I turned to find myself looking at Simon, Lynne's ex as well as her one and only attempt at a D/s relationship.

"Hello, Master Simon," I said, my mind spinning with possibilities.

"No, definitely not your motherly instincts." Beside me, Nathaniel sighed. "It's your matchmaking ones that have me worried."

Turn the page for a first look at

Master Professor,

the first book in Lessons from the Rack,

a new series by *New York Times*

bestselling author Tara Sue Me

coming out in April 2017 from Berkley.

In the history of dumb and stupid ideas, Andie Lincoln couldn't shake the feeling that her current endeavor was the dumbest and stupidest idea of them all. She stood beside the large glass window in her Oregon hotel and wondered when exactly it was that she'd lost her mind.

She shouldn't even be in Oregon. She should be spending her summer working as an intern chef in a Seattle restaurant like she'd told her parents she was. It still bothered her that she'd lied to them. But seriously, what was the alternative? Tell them she was entering an exclusive BDSM school because she'd begged Terrance to find a way to get her in?

Hell, half the time, she didn't believe it herself.

And they would never believe that it was her idea. Oh no, they'd think he had somehow brainwashed her into going. They would never understand that she wanted this. Wanted to be trained in the BDSM world as a submissive.

Her phone rang, pulling her away from the window and thoughts of her parents. She smiled when she saw the display.

"Hey, Terrance," she said.

"How's my girl?" he asked.

The noise in the background confirmed he was still on the movie set. He must have had a break and used it to call her.

"I can't believe I'm here on the West Coast—finally, I might add—and you're on location in Pittsburgh."

He laughed. The softly seductive sound that never failed to make moviegoers swoon. She pictured him raking his fingers through his blond hair, and her heart sped up.

"I swear, if it wouldn't upset the production schedule and put the entire thing behind, I'd be with you right now." His voice was deep and determined, and she had no doubt he was speaking the truth.

"I understand," she said, because she did. "Besides, it's not like I'm going to be here long anyway. Tomorrow morning I head over to the academy."

"And how awful is it I'm not there for you?" He sighed. "Damn it, Andie. It's not right."

She loved it when the protective side of him came out. The side she knew would always put her first. It was a big part of the reason she asked to be trained for him.

They had been friends forever. Even Terrance leaving and becoming a household name hadn't dampened their friendship. And as time went on, the friendship had grown into something more. He said he loved how she wanted him for him and not who he was. And she loved him because he was kind and patient and made her laugh.

Then *that* night had happened. The night they both realized there was more between them than friendship, and he'd sat her down and told her he had things to tell her. Things he must tell her before they went any further.

He'd confessed he was a Dominant and wasn't going to give that part of himself up. She'd heard of the term, but really had no idea what it meant, so later, when she was alone, she did her own research and . . . Holy hell. Her vibrator had had one hell of a workout.

"You can't help it," she assured him. "I know you'd be here if you could, and I completely understand why you aren't."

"It still doesn't sit well with me."

"In that case," she teased. "I'll allow you to make it up to me the next time you see me."

"That I'll do." He laughed. "Call me tomorrow when you get settled."

"I will."

"How are you feeling? Are you nervous?"

That was another thing—ever since he'd brought up being a Dom, he was always asking about how she felt and what she was thinking. It took some getting used to. At first she thought he was asking just to be nice or because that was what he was supposed to do. Eventually, though, she realized he really cared.

She let out a deep breath. "I've moved beyond nervous, but I'm not quite at the scared-shitless stage. It's just hard to wrap my head around the next few months. I mean, I'm not a prude, but I am a virgin. And when I think about what enrolling at the academy will mean . . ."

Another one of those *What the fuck am I doing?* thoughts hit her, but she shook it off. When she took the time to really think about enrolling in the academy, she was more excited than anything. Thoughts of submitting to Terrance fueled her fantasies. She dreamed of the day she could give her whole self to him.

"Are you having second thoughts?" he asked, concern in his voice. "You don't have—"

"I know. I want to." How many times would she have to assure him? "I think it's completely normal to feel anxious, but I'm not having second thoughts."

"I've known Lennox for years," he said, speaking of the academy owner and headmaster. "He's a great guy, and I trust him and his staff completely. I have to, or else I'd never even think about you being there."

She twisted the curtain covering the window. "I know. And it makes me feel safe and protected when you say that."

"That's my job," he said. "Even though we're apart, I want you safe and protected."

There was a slight murmuring over the phone, and she knew before he spoke that break time was over.

"I have to get back to the set," he confirmed. "I'll call you tonight before it gets too late."

"Okay. I'm going to go for a walk and grab something light for dinner." Maybe she'd call her parents, too. Assure them she was fine and everything was covered. That way maybe she could go a few days without calling again. She didn't want them to suspect anything.

They said their good-byes, and Andie slipped her phone into her purse, determined not to let her nerves get the best of her.

Fulton Matthews knew he was going to have to tread carefully with his boss, Lennox McLure. After all, the man had just promoted him a month ago. At the time, Fulton had been thrilled with the new responsibilities, but he was starting to see they came with their own set of problems.

The door to Lennox's office opened, and his boss waved him inside. "Come have a seat, Master Matthews."

Without waiting to see if he'd listen, Lennox walked over to his desk, sat down, and templed his fingers. Fulton crossed the room and took a seat in the leather chair across from his boss.

"I know why you're here." Lennox nodded toward the papers Fulton brought in. "Those are the papers I gave you yesterday, aren't they? Andie Lincoln's application packet."

"Yes." And that was one of the questions he had. He was in charge of the new enrollees who would be arriving tomorrow, and one of his duties was to create a tailor-made curriculum. Why had Lennox waited until the last minute to give him the information?

"Go ahead," Lennox said.

He was a smug bastard—Fulton gave him that. Of course, he had reason to be. He'd single-handedly made the academy into what it was today: an elite BDSM learning center, known and respected throughout the kink world. Lennox himself was just as respected, although Fulton had never seen him participate in a scene. He'd once asked another staff member why that was, and the person shook his head and told him to leave well enough alone.

"My first concern is why I was only given this yesterday," Fulton said. "The other enrollees have had their curriculum set for months."

"I have my reasons. And I know you'll have her curriculum ready by the time she arrives tomorrow."

Not if I can help it. But he kept that thought to himself.

"What else is bothering you?"

"To be perfectly honest, I'm wondering why she's here. She's not our typical student, and several red flags came to mind twice while I was reading through her file."

"You've heard of Terrance Knight?"

Fulton frowned. "The actor?"

"Yes. Terrance and I go way back. Ms. Lincoln is to be trained to be his submissive."

The situation was worse than Fulton had thought. He tried to think of a way to discreetly tell Lennox he had a potentially fucked-up mess on his hands, but he couldn't come up with one. Not one that wouldn't get him fired, anyway.

"It appears to be a really bad idea," he decided on.

"Which part?"

"All of it." He took a deep breath. If Lennox wanted reasons, he was going to give him reasons and damn the consequences. "Ms. Lincoln is a virgin with zero BDSM experience. And apparently she's only interested in submission because her hot-shot Hollywood boyfriend is a Dominant."

"Is that all?"

Was that all? Hell, he was serious. "Isn't that enough?"

"No, unfortunately, it's not." Lennox pushed back from his desk. "Ms. Lincoln arrives tomorrow. I want you to do her initial interview and assessment. And I'd like to see the curriculum you design for her by five o'clock today."

And just like that, Fulton was being shown the door. Heading to his own office, he resisted the urge to crumple up the papers he still held in his hand.

Don't miss this bonus novella
in the Submissive series!
Turn the page for Abby and Nathaniel's
romantic wedding
and a honeymoon too hot to believe in

The Chalet

The
Chalet

A Submissive Series Novella

Submitting her body was only the beginning.

Abby King didn't know true passion until she gave herself to Nathaniel West, one of New York City's most eligible bachelors and desired Dominants. Now, on the eve of her marriage, she realizes all her dreams are coming true. And with a romantic honeymoon getaway planned at a secluded Swiss chalet, she's sure Nathaniel will find even more fantasies to fulfill. . . .

Nathaniel never thought he'd settle down until Abby broke down his barriers and changed his plans. With their wedding only weeks away, he can barely wait to possess her completely—heart, body, and soul—and show her the true meaning of being both a wife and a submissive.

Only, Abby has one more challenge in store before she becomes his: no sex and no collar for one month before the wedding. Nathaniel is willing to give it a shot but he has one scandalous stipulation—once that month is up, anything goes. . . .

To Adam and Steve.
Gobble, gobble, gobble.

Acknowledgments

There are so many things I could say about this novella, but I'll keep it short since it is a novella and the acknowledgments really shouldn't be longer than the story.

Adam and Steve, I don't know where I'd be without you guys. Thank you for your expert knowledge, your dedication, and your unwavering professionalism. I am blessed to have you in my corner.

Danielle and Rebecca, thank you for the multiples (multiple reads, that is). You make me work to be better and I truly appreciate it.

Mr. Sue Me, I couldn't do it without you by my side through "all things."

And to all the readers who asked about Nathaniel and Abby's wedding and honeymoon, I hope you enjoy this little peek into their Happily Ever After.

Chapter One

ABBY

Nathaniel looked at me as if I'd sprouted horns. "You think we should *what?*" he gasped.

Exactly the reaction I'd expected. I took a sip of my red wine and repeated myself. "I think we shouldn't have sex the month before the wedding."

"I was afraid that's what you said." He tilted his head. "Why?"

I picked up my napkin and pretended to wipe my mouth in order to hide my smile. *Why?* This from the man who had been so scared to talk about anything at the beginning of our relationship. Quite a change from the one who sat across the table from me now. The one who felt the need to discuss the *whys* and *why nots* and even the *I don't care, whatevers* about almost everything.

"I know the napkin trick," he said with a smile of his own. "I'm just a bit curious as to why you would suggest a monthlong period of abstinence when you have long-term sexual deprivation marked as a hard limit."

"I suppose the smart-ass answer is what's the definition of 'long term'? To see your face a few minutes ago, you'd think your definition is a week."

"A week for me *is* long term."

I laughed. "Then let's just say this is me pushing your limits."

"Pushing limits is *my* job," he said in a serious tone of voice, but his eyes were lit with amusement.

"I'm pushing mine, too, you know. Seriously, a month with nothing after one of our normal weeks?" I tried to count on average how often we had sex during a typical week, but gave up. Between our everyday lives during the week and our weekend lives when I wore his collar, well, there was a lot of sex.

"It's not as if I've never gone a month, you know," Nathaniel said. "And by abstaining, do you mean just us together or can we get off individually?"

I couldn't help it; I laughed again.

"What?" he asked.

"Just you being you. Trying to establish the rules of something we haven't even agreed to yet."

"I want to make sure I'm making an informed and well thought-out decision," he said in typical Nathaniel fashion. Always the planner. Always with backup plans. Hell, I bet even his backup plans had backup plans.

"You're smiling at me again," he said.

I reached across the table and took his hand. "Just smiling at you being you."

He lifted my hand to his lips and placed a small kiss on my knuckles. "So tell me why we should do this monthlong thing." He took my hand and traced the line at the base of my thumb. I shivered. "Because I'm thinking a month is a really, really long time." He brought my palm up to his mouth again, but this time nipped the skin just a bit. He smiled at my moan. "Wouldn't you agree?"

I shifted in my seat. "When you put it that way."

"I don't know if it's possible for me to keep my hands off you for an entire month." His lips danced along the top of my hand. "Much less my other parts."

My mind blanked for just a second at the touch of his lips on my skin and the images his words evoked. Why had I thought not having sex for a month before the wedding was a good idea?

Across the table, he looked at me with his *I'm waiting* expression.

I cleared my throat. "Well, I just thought a month would, you know, give us something to look forward to."

"I see. Because marrying me? Eh, you can do that any old day. Nothing to look forward to there."

He was kidding, right? I loved and hated that it was still hard for me to tell sometimes.

"You know what I mean," I said, deciding he was joking.

He let go of my hand. "Somewhat. I also think our wedding night is something to look forward to no matter what we have or haven't done the month before."

"But think about how"—I searched for the right word—"*intense* it'll be after we haven't done *anything* the month before."

His eyes darkened. "I guarantee you I can make it intense without having to abstain for a month."

"Nathaniel," I half whined, half begged.

He sighed. "You really want to do this?"

"Yes."

"And it's really important to you?"

"Yes."

"And I can't jerk off in the shower?"

"You can't jerk off anywhere," I clarified for him with narrowed eyes, just in case Mr. Rule Book decided to throw in my face two weeks before the wedding that I'd only specified he couldn't jerk off in the shower.

He leaned back in his chair, exhaling. "Damn. You've been around me too long."

"Impossible, but somehow true at the same time."

"You can't come either," he said. "No playing with yourself."

I nodded.

"And speaking of playing, what do we do about weekends?"

I'd thought about that, of course. Ideally, I would still wear his collar. Submitting to him wasn't entirely sexual, though sex did play a major role in our weekends.

"There's plenty we do on the weekends that doesn't involve sex," I said. "I think I should still wear your collar."

"True, but there's a sexual undercurrent in just about everything we do," he countered. "You don't have a submissive personality outside the playroom; it's part of your sexual nature. Serving me during the weekend turns you on. We need to think about whether having you serve me the month before the wedding, even in a nonsexual manner, will be a source of irritation. For us both."

He had a point. I tried imagining serving him all day on a Saturday, but without sex. If we stayed out of the playroom, I could easily see us both becoming increasingly sexually frustrated. With our emotions probably already running high as the wedding approached, collaring me might not be the wisest idea.

"No sex and no collar the month before the wedding," I said. "We'll probably both implode."

"As long as we don't take it out on each other."

"But on the upside, think about how awesome the honeymoon will be now."

"Abby," he said softly. "The honeymoon will be awesome regardless. But you know, we haven't talked about whether you'd like to wear your collar at all during our honeymoon."

"Yes, I think so. Not all the time. Probably not even most of the time. But for a day or two?" I thought about how it would feel the first time he collared me as his wife. When I would be Abigail West. My belly tightened just thinking about it. "Maybe more than a day or two."

Nathaniel nodded. "We'll keep it flexible."

"Another thing. I know I won't be wearing your collar on our wedding day, but I've decided I'm not going to wear any type of necklace."

"Oh?"

"This part of me"—I brushed my neck—"is for your collar. If I'm not wearing it when I become your wife, I'm not wearing anything."

His eyes grew dark and he gave me a sultry smile. "I'd thought about buying you a necklace for our wedding, but it would have been just that. A necklace. Your idea means so much more."

I was glad I was sitting down. His look would have made my knees weak, had I been standing.

"I'm looking forward to collaring you for the first time after the wedding. When you're Abigail West."

I squirmed in my seat, thinking about our honeymoon plans.

We were going to Zermatt, Switzerland, for two weeks following the wedding. Nathaniel had reserved a stunning chalet. We could step right outside and ski, or stay inside and do . . . other things. At first we discussed going somewhere tropical, but the more we thought about it, getting away to a snowy location sounded perfect.

Snow, after all, had been one of the driving forces in our

relationship. I believed we would have still wound up together, had it not been for the week we spent snowbound in his house, but there's no telling how long it would have taken to get to that point. Somehow it seemed fitting that we honeymoon with snow. Besides, damn near nothing beat Nathaniel naked in front of a roaring fire.

"Abby?" the man in question asked. "Did I lose you?"

"Sorry," I said. "Just daydreaming about the honeymoon."

"Well," he said, pushing back from the table. "The way I see it, we don't have much time before our self-imposed month of celibacy." He walked over to me and held out a hand. "Let's not waste it."

"I have to say, Abby," Felicia said the next day, spinning slowly and looking over the old chapel, "this place is perfect."

Because Nathaniel and I wanted to get married before the end of the year, we only had three months to plan the wedding. With that timeline, every possible venue in New York City and the surrounding area was booked. It wasn't a big deal to us; we simply wanted to get married and had tentatively planned for the ceremony and reception to be held at Nathaniel's estate.

He had friends and business associates everywhere, though, and earlier in the day he'd received a call that the wedding booked at the small chapel had been canceled. Since Felicia hadn't returned to her teaching job following her marriage to Jackson, I asked her to come look at it with me. Felicia and I had been friends since our childhood days in small-town Indiana. We went to college together and even roomed together for a short period of time.

Early in our relationship, Nathaniel had mentioned that his

cousin, Jackson, a professional football player, didn't have a date for an event the entire family was attending. On a whim, I mentioned my best friend, Felicia. They went to the event together and were married less than six months later.

The chapel we were at, just outside the city, was over one hundred years old and the sanctuary had an almost medieval look to it with rustic wooden pews and stone walls. I could easily imagine how beautiful and romantic it would be bathed in candlelight.

"It is perfect, isn't it?" I said in response to Felicia. "Since we're not inviting anyone other than close friends and family, there'll be plenty of room. Any bigger and there would be too many empty seats."

"And the space is so beautiful, you don't need much in the way of decorations."

"That's what I was thinking," I said. "Just candles and maybe a few flowers." Nathaniel had said he wanted cream-colored roses with just a hint of pink at the tips.

"Now you just need a reception space to open up."

I sat down on one of the pews and pulled out my planning notebook. "We could still have it at Nathaniel's if nothing becomes available."

She sat down next to me, her expression serious. "How long do you think it'll take before you start seeing the estate as yours?"

Her question caught me off guard. I'd honestly expected her to ask me about the food or music or something. "I do," I said. "Lots of times when I'm talking I'll say 'our house' or something similar. Sometimes it just comes out as 'Nathaniel's' though. I guess if you think about it, it's been his place longer than it's been mine."

"I haven't said this and I'm sorry I've waited so long, but I think he's good for you." Felicia tucked a strand of red hair behind her ear. "Whatever it is you guys have with each other, it's obvious that it's working."

It was the closest she'd ever come to saying she approved of our lifestyle. I couldn't help it, but I looked at her in shock.

"Don't look at me like that," she said. "I simply got curious and Googled a few things."

"You Googled 'BDSM'?"

"You know we're having this conversation in a church, don't you?" She shot a look over both shoulders, though she didn't have to; the place was empty.

"Should we step outside? I will if it'll make you more comfortable."

"No, we can stay here. I just thought it was odd to be talking about stuff like that in church."

I smiled. "Stuff like that? Say it, Felicia. Say 'BDSM.'"

She punched my arm. "Stop it, perv."

"Me? You're the one Googling kinky sex." I wiggled my eyebrows. "Did you find it exciting?"

Though we could discuss just about anything, she'd never wanted to talk about my need for submission. Unfortunately, the early part of my relationship with Nathaniel hadn't done much to endear her to the lifestyle. Especially considering the shape I'd been in when I left him.

"I guess I can see why someone would like it," she said. "And I read that it's more than kinky sex."

"I told you that."

"I know, but I wanted confirmation."

"Right, because everything on the Internet is true."

"Admit it—you just like giving me a hard time."

I winked at her. "Yes, partly. But really I'm just glad you finally see it's a need I have that Nathaniel fulfills."

She sat back in her seat and suddenly looked very self-satis-fied. "Nathaniel said as much once."

She was dying to tell me. I could see it in her eyes. Since I wanted to hear what she was talking about, I played along. "Really? When?"

"That time you were in the hospital."

"That was ages ago." In actuality, it hadn't even been a year, but so much had happened since then.

"Feels that way, doesn't it?" She shook her head. "Anyway, that night you were in the hospital, I went out in the hallway one time to tell him what I thought about his sorry ass. He told me then that whenever you were together, it was always your needs first."

"Really?" I'd always wondered what it was the two of them had discussed that night, because I noticed their relationship had changed afterward; neither one of them had ever told me.

"Yes, and I didn't believe him. I thought it was all about him since he was the Dominant." Her eyes grew quizzical. "It's true, though, isn't it? Even though you're the submissive, he's always thinking about you and what you need."

"Right, but conversely, *he's* my focus when I'm wearing his collar. I'm always thinking about him."

She thought about that for a few seconds. "Interesting. Like you balance each other out."

"Something like that, but honestly, when I'm wearing his collar, I'm not thinking about how balanced and equal we are. I'm thinking only about him and what he's saying."

"Which is why I'd make a horrible submissive."

I shrugged; she was probably right. "It's not for everyone and that's okay. Obviously what you and Jackson have works for the two of you."

She gave a hearty smile at the mention of her husband. "I'll say."

"Speaking of Jackson," I started and then stopped, unsure I really wanted to know the answer to my question.

"Yes?"

Oh well, I decided, might as well know once and for all. "Does he know about our lifestyle?"

She laughed. "I wondered how long it would take you to ask."

"And?"

"Yes, he knows. We were watching TV one night and they did a story on the increased public interest in BDSM. He looked over at me, I looked at him, and I finally said, 'Yes, I know about them.'"

That Jackson knew really didn't surprise me. I'd always assumed Nathaniel's cousin knew. Honestly, he had spent enough time at the house. Nathaniel kept the playroom locked, but it was possible Jackson had been over a time or two when it wasn't. Especially during the time he stayed over following my breakup with Nathaniel.

"And he knew you meant us?" I asked Felicia.

"Neither one of us came out and said it for a while. I guess for me it was that long talk you gave me on confidentiality. I didn't want to be the one who told Jackson his cousin was kinky."

Before I'd gone to see Nathaniel the first time, when I was talking with Felicia about what I was going to do, I'd pounded into her head how important confidentiality was. "Thank you for that. I really appreciate it."

"You're my dearest friend. I'd never betray your trust. I finally told Jackson I was your safety call. He nodded and said he figured I knew about Nathaniel since you and I were best friends."

"How long has Jackson known?"

"He said he had a suspicion for a long time, but it wasn't until after you guys broke up and got back together that he knew for sure. We really didn't talk much about it after that." She looked around the still-empty church. "If you're finished looking over this place, I think we should leave. All this kink talk in church has me afraid lightning's going to strike me dead."

It was amazing how quickly time passed. Of course, it didn't help that we were planning a wedding in less than three months. There were many times I wondered what we had been thinking when we selected our wedding date. How did we think it would be possible to set everything up so quickly?

I'll admit, once in a while, we let the stress get between us. There was so much to do, to set up, to schedule, and there never seemed to be enough time. We had started spending weekends at Nathaniel's penthouse in the city, just to be closer to everything and everyone we needed to meet with.

It wasn't until the third weekend in the city that I realized how much I'd come to count on escaping the hurried pace of Manhattan for the tranquillity of our country estate in the Hamptons. Granted, the penthouse was spacious enough, but you only had to look outside to see reality. As someone who had spent years living in the city, it surprised me how much I needed to step away from it on a regular basis.

"Next weekend, we're staying home," I said the third Sunday night in the penthouse.

Nathaniel looked up from his e-reader. "Can we do that? There's nothing here we need to be doing?"

"I don't care. I need some space, and room to think and breathe, and I want to walk outside and not bump into half the population of the United States."

He'd let me do the majority of the planning. I appreciated the thought behind him doing so, but at times it grew overwhelming.

I probably should have hired a planner, but I'd had the crazy idea I could handle it myself.

"Abby?" he asked, his forehead wrinkling.

"I'm just ready for it to be here already. For life to settle down."

He set the reader down and walked over to where I sat. He put his hands on my shoulders and slid behind me. My eyes closed in pleasure when he started a soothing massage. He knew just how and where to push and stroke.

"You're tense," he said, working on a particularly tight spot.

I simply hummed in response. His hands felt so good.

He dipped his head to whisper in my ear, "I think this calls for drastic measures."

We'd had a trying weekend. Between balancing wedding planning and playtime, I was exhausted.

"I don't think I'm up for drastic at the moment. I think a glass of wine and bed is just about all I can handle." I sighed. "Maybe just bed."

His hands never stopped. "I was thinking a soak in the tub with a glass of wine, then bed."

"I don't even have the energy to run a bath."

"You don't have to," he said. "Let me take care of you."

My eyes drooped with every pass of his sensual hands. "If I can stay awake."

"If you fall asleep, I'll make sure you make it to bed."

I yawned. "Deal."

"Stay here and let me get everything ready."

"Like I can move." I felt all warm and relaxed after his massage. Like a puddle on the couch.

He brushed my cheek and left the room. I curled up in a ball and snuggled deeper into the soft leather.

"Abby," he whispered some time later.

The shadows in the room had changed. I must have fallen asleep unknowingly. I stretched and my sore muscles reminded me of our weekend play.

"Bath time?" I asked.

"Unless you'd like to skip it and go on to bed."

"Bath."

I sat up, but he whispered softly, "No, you don't," and scooped me up in his arms to carry me down the hall to the master bath.

Like his bathroom at the estate, this one also held a massive soaker tub. Nathaniel had placed lit candles around the room and an open bottle of wine that sat on the floor alongside a lone wineglass. The tub was filled with lemongrass-scented bubbles.

"I'm going to set you down," he said, and gently put me on my feet.

I tried to unbutton my shirt, but my fingers were clumsy.

He batted my hands away. "Let me."

In almost no time, my clothes were on the floor and he was helping me into the tub.

The water was the exact right temperature and I sighed as I slipped in up to my shoulders in bubbles. Nathaniel grinned and poured a glass of wine.

I took the glass when he offered it to me. The sight of him standing there, watching me, perked me up. Maybe the nap had helped more than I realized. "You going to join me?"

"I was thinking about it."

I scooted forward, all traces of fatigue gone. "Stop thinking and join me."

He needed no further encouragement and within moments, he had stripped and was sliding behind me. I closed my eyes as his arms came around me.

I passed him the wineglass. "This is the best idea you've had all weekend," I said just to tease him.

"Is that so?"

"Mmm," I hummed when he started rubbing my shoulder. "That thing you did last night was good, but this is definitely better."

He laughed. "That thing I did last night had you screaming my name as you climaxed for the third time."

I stretched back against him with a knowing smile. "Third? Are you sure? I only remember two."

The wineglass had somehow made it back into my hands and his fingers were inching down my sides. "Your memory is faulty because of the immense pleasure you were experiencing. It was definitely the third time you climaxed."

"Nah. Can't be. I'd have remembered that."

"The first two times you came you were told to be silent. The third was when I finally allowed you to be vocal. I remember, because I had to threaten you with the gag right before the second and I said if I had to use it, there would be no third time."

Of course I remembered the entire night. How was it possible anyone could have forgotten any of that?

His hands rested on my upper thighs and were slowly making their way further up between my legs. "In fact," he said. "I believe I also told you that if you made a sound during the second, you couldn't have my cock for a week."

"Right," I said as if I was just remembering. I sucked in a gasp of breath as his fingers started stroking and dipping ever so slightly into me. "And since it's one month and one week before the wedding, I wasn't about to disobey you."

"Exactly."

"Speaking of cock." I put the wineglass down on the floor

beside the tub and twisted around. "I'd like some please. Straight up. Hard and deep."

If I shifted just the right way, I could feel his erection. Unfortunately, he'd decided it was his turn to tease.

"I don't know. Since you had such a difficult time remembering last night, maybe I want to keep my cock to myself. Besides." He tilted his head. "You're tired."

I ran a hand down his chest. "I'm not *that* tired."

"Still, best not to push it."

"Push it." I took him in my hand. "Push it inside. Now."

"No. I don't think you're adequately prepared for me to do that."

"Well, then." I gave his cock a good squeeze. "What are you waiting for? Prepare me."

"No. I think you owe me for pretending to forget the massive number of orgasms I gave you last night."

"Not fair." I stuck my lip out in a fake pout, but he wouldn't budge. "Okay. Fine. What do you want me to do?"

"Simple," he said with an evil look in his eye. "Prepare yourself."

I sat back with a splash. "What?"

He folded his arms across his chest. "Now."

I closed my eyes for a second as his words swept over me and sank inside. Fuck, I loved it when he took control. Tonight I felt a little playful, too. "You're so mean."

"Yes."

"And evil."

"Yes."

"And you've taken your collar off me."

"Maybe," he said. "But I'm the one with the cock and I'm keeping it to myself unless I get to watch."

I narrowed my eyes. "Evil bastard."

"I think the water's cooling off. Maybe I'll get out of the tub."

"Fine. Be that way." Acting like I was very irritated, but knowing he was well aware of how much of a turn-on this was, I hooked my legs on both sides of the tub. "Maybe I'll just decide to finish myself off after I prepare myself adequately," I said.

"If you think your hand and fingers are an acceptable substitution for the real thing, by all means, help yourself."

I fake glared at him, but stroked my breasts with one hand while trailing the other between my legs. Some of the bubbles had popped, leaving him with a clear view of what I was doing. For added effect, I laid my head back and closed my eyes as I pinched a nipple.

"No, you don't." His voice was rough. "Eyes open and on me."

My heart pounded faster at his command. I didn't have to listen to him. It was a Sunday night and his collar was off. But even so, I opened my eyes and met his gaze. For whatever reason, knowing I had the power to tell him 'no,' but obeying him anyway, turned me on further.

"That's it," he said. "Play with that pussy. Get it ready for my dick, because I'm going to make sure this is one fuck you won't be forgetting anytime soon."

I whimpered.

"Whimper all you want. You need to get prepared."

He'd only exerted that sort of control over our sex lives a handful of times with his collar off. Perhaps he knew that its rarity made it more of a turn-on. It did make me wonder, though, how it would be to wear his collar more often.

His eyes were dark with desire and he nodded with satisfaction as I stroked myself harder. "Show me how much you want it."

Slowly, I worked myself to the point of shaking with need. I kept my gaze firmly locked on his as I moved my fingers over my body and teased my aching flesh.

He stroked himself. "Almost."

I circled my clit with a finger, not sure I could hold out much longer. His name was a plea. "Nathaniel."

"Yes. I think you're finally ready. Keep your legs there."

I groaned.

His smile was evil. "Got to make sure I satisfy your request for deep."

He was over me and between my legs within seconds.

"Now," I said. "Please."

With one hard push, he buried himself inside me. I climaxed immediately around him.

"Oh fuck." I gasped for air.

He placed a hand on either side of my head and began thrusting in and out of me. In the position I was in, I felt every glorious inch of him as he moved.

"Eight days," he said with an inward push. "Eight days until we start the self-imposed month of celibacy."

Bad idea, I decided. How could we possibly go a month without sex?

"I just might call in sick and tie you to the bed this week," he said, and his breath was coming in pants. "Fuck you night and day."

"Best. Idea. Ever."

"Damn," he said. "If you're still able to talk, I'm not doing my job properly."

He redoubled his efforts, pulling out and pounding inside me once again. Then, when he was buried within me, he thrust his hips and went even deeper. Pretty soon, I wasn't able to form coherent words in my head, much less speak them. Still he kept on, over and over. He slipped a hand below the water and teased my clit.

"Do you have more for me?" he asked with a shaky breath.

I mumbled something as another climax swept through my body. He thrust deeply and held still, caught up in his own release. Almost as soon as he was spent, he framed my face and kissed me slowly and intently. His kiss was full of promises of passion yet to come.

I tightened my arms around him as I tried to unhook my legs from the edge of the tub. "Ow."

"Let me." He pulled back and took my legs, massaging them before placing them on either side of him. "Better?"

"Much."

"I don't think I did much in the way of helping you relax."

"I don't know about that. I'm feeling pretty good right about now. Besides." I ran a finger down his chest. "I haven't thought about the wedding, or planning, or anything for at least the last hour."

"Imagine how well I could distract you in the month before the wedding if you'd forget about this no-sex thing."

I pushed against his shoulder. "Is that what this was about? Trying to get me to change my mind?"

"Change your mind?" he asked with a look of fake surprise. "Never. I was just helping you relieve some more of that tension you were feeling in the living room."

"Nathaniel."

"Okay. I thought maybe I could get you to think about changing your mind if I proved how well I could distract you." He wiggled his eyebrows. "Did it work?"

I sat up and reached for a towel. "No, but I wouldn't turn you down if you wanted to distract me again in bed after we've dried off."

He flopped back in the tub with a splash and a sigh. "I suppose I'll take what I can get."

"Eight days," I said, shaking my ass. "Better get busy."

It turned out to be a long month. Numerous times, I thought about giving in and changing my mind about the no-sex idea. Fortunately—or unfortunately, depending on which side you looked at it from—whenever I was tempted to give in, Nathaniel held firm, and whenever he asked if I'd change my mind *just this once*, I was able to say "no."

In seemingly no time, it was two days before the wedding and I was headed out with Felicia and Elaina for my bachelorette party.

I kissed Nathaniel goodbye when they stopped by the penthouse to pick me up. "Aren't you a little worried about what they have planned?"

"No." He returned the kiss. "I trust them."

Felicia snorted. "That's your first mistake."

"Nah," Elaina said, rubbing her belly. She and her husband, Todd, a childhood friend of Nathaniel and Jackson, were expecting their first child. "It's at least his third."

"I don't think so," he said, pointing at her. "You're pregnant. And you"—he pointed to Felicia—"if you do anything too crazy, the paparazzi will be all over it."

"Not if I wear a disguise," Felicia said.

"You've been around Jackson too long," Nathaniel said. "Although, I'm not sure he has a disguise that could cover up all that red hair."

"Come on, let's go," Elaina said. "We promise we'll bring her back in one piece."

We left him and took off down the private elevator, giggling as we made our way to the garage. Felicia grew all serious as we walked to the car.

"There's one thing we forgot to mention," she said.

"What's that?" I asked.

"You have to be blindfolded so you can't see where we go."

"What?"

"Oh, come on," she said. "I'm sure you've been blindfolded a time or two with all that kinky stuff you guys do."

"Felicia Kelly Clark," I warned. "That sort of talk is off-limits."

"Tell me I'm right and I'll shut up."

I stood beside the car and crossed my arms. "I'll do no such thing."

"I told you I Googled this, right?" she asked, undeterred by my defiance.

I cocked an eyebrow at her.

"Read this interesting article on gags," she said. "We could talk about those, too."

"Or not." I wasn't sure where Felicia was going with this, but it'd been almost a month since I'd had any type of sex. Plus since she'd once said she didn't care to hear the specifics of how Nathaniel and I worked, I wasn't inclined at the moment to discuss it with her.

"I'll call Nathaniel," she threatened.

"Go ahead." I shrugged. "In fact, I'd like to see that. Give me your phone. I'll dial."

"Come on, you two," Elaina said. "Felicia, I've known Nathaniel for most of my life and he's never spoken a word to me about his sex life." She turned to me. "And you, lighten up. It's your bachelorette party."

Felicia looked slightly abashed, but I shook my head. "I haven't had sex in almost a month. I'll lighten up during the honeymoon."

Elaina groaned. "Tell me he didn't do that no-sex-for-a-month-before-the-wedding mumbo jumbo."

It was my turn to look abashed. "It was actually my idea."

"Oh, girl." She put her arm around my shoulders. "You should have checked with me first. Todd and I did that. Worst idea ever. He lasted all of five minutes our wedding night."

"Five minutes?" I croaked.

"Get inside." She opened the driver's-side door and slipped behind the wheel. "And I'll tell you all about it."

I walked around to the passenger's side and Felicia hopped into the backseat. Within minutes, we were on our way to wherever it was they were taking me. We had a spa day planned for tomorrow. I, for one, was looking forward to some serious girl time before the wedding.

"So anyway," Elaina said. "Todd had this grand idea that we shouldn't have sex the month before our wedding. At the time, I thought it was so romantic."

"See? That's what I thought," I said.

"It sounds better than it actually is," Elaina said. "We finally made it to the hotel room at one in the morning and all I wanted to do was sleep. Todd, though? Well, you know men."

Felicia snorted. "We didn't even do the month-before thing and Jackson was like that."

I turned around to look at her. "You and Jackson got married the day after you met. You didn't have time for the month-before thing."

She cocked an eyebrow. "I still have the gag."

I stuck my tongue out at her and turned back to Elaina. "So what happened?"

"I told Todd I wanted to sleep and he laid this huge guilt trip on me about how it was our wedding night and how we had waited and how the next day would be busy because we were flying out of the country and blah, blah, blah."

Another benefit to Nathaniel's private jet—we could pretty much decide when we left. We'd scheduled to take off in the afternoon the day following the wedding, which would allow us plenty of time to do whatever we wished to do after the ceremony and reception.

"I'm guessing from what you said before that you went along with him and didn't sleep right away?" I asked.

"I might as well have gone to sleep—he was worse than a teenager. One month we'd waited and like I said, he lasted five minutes. I'm not even sure we'd taken off all our clothes." She giggled at the memory. "Nathaniel's older, though. I'm sure he has the control thing down pat."

I certainly hoped so. How horrible would it be to have waited for a month and for our wedding night to be over before it started?

"Funny thing," Elaina said. "We were living together before we got married and the night before the wedding we talked about calling an early end to our pact. Ended up all we did that night was sleep; we probably should have given in." She looked over at me. "Maybe you and Nathaniel should give that some thought. End your month tomorrow night."

I shook my head. "We're not even going to be together tomorrow night. I'll be at the penthouse and he'll be at the estate."

"Maybe you should rethink that," Felicia said.

"I'm sure it'll be fine." I bit my bottom lip.

At least I hoped it would be.

Chapter Two

ABBY

When I woke the morning of my wedding, the sun wasn't out yet, so I stretched, enjoying what would probably be the last quiet moment of the day. My eyes fell on my engagement ring and it hit me: I was getting married today. To Nathaniel. My Dominant. By the day's end, I'd be his completely. I was so ready.

I took my time and leisurely climbed out of bed, slipping into my robe and padding over to the window. Light flurries were still falling, swirling in the streetlight. I sighed with happiness, watching as they floated this way and that.

My cell phone rang and I scurried to the nightstand, smiling when I saw who was calling.

"Good morning."

"Good morning," Nathaniel said. "I didn't wake you, did I?"

"No." I made my way back over to the window. "Just watching the snow fall."

"It stopped here an hour ago."

I looked at the alarm clock. "An hour ago was five fifteen. Weren't you able to sleep?"

"Not without you."

I didn't sleep too well without him, either, but instead of saying so, I decided to tease him. "I hope that doesn't mean you'll have to go to bed early tonight."

His voice changed, growing low and gruff. "I'm going to bed exceptionally early tonight."

"You are?"

"Oh yes, and you are too. And I'm keeping you in bed for an inordinate amount of time."

Waves of yearning swept through my belly. "How do you plan on doing that?"

"Because I'm bigger and stronger than you and you're going to be under me, with me claiming my bride in every way possible."

I groaned just thinking about it.

"By the time I'm finished, you'll be so thoroughly fucked, you won't be able to leave the bed for days."

I slipped a hand between my legs and circled my clit through the material of my gown. It had been too long. One month too long. "Mmmm."

"I'll let you sleep for a few hours then and when you wake up, I'll take you again, but I'll be slow and gentle."

I closed my eyes, imagining it. Nathaniel and I. Cool, crisp sheets. A fireplace with a blazing fire. My finger circled faster. It'd been so long.

"Abigail?"

My eyes snapped open and my fingers stopped. "Yes."

"I've been trying to get your attention. What are you doing? You aren't touching yourself, are you?"

I looked down at my hand. *Shit*. "Um, yes."

"Did you come?"

"No," I said, glad that he'd gotten my attention in time.

"Need I remind you this abstinence idea was all *yours*?" His tone grew lighter. "This from the woman who claimed she wasn't into long-term sexual deprivation."

I laughed. "What can I say? It seemed like a good idea at the time."

"It'll be your fault if I don't last longer than five minutes tonight," he said, joking about what I'd told him concerning Todd and Elaina.

"In that case, you'll just have to spank me," I said.

My only reply from him was a low moan and a mumbled curse.

"Want me to change the subject?" I asked.

"Yes, please."

"What time are you leaving the house?"

"About an hour," he said. "I'm meeting Jackson and Todd for breakfast. I've also invited your dad to join us."

My father still lived in Indiana, where I grew up. We weren't very close. I'd always been closer to my mom. She'd passed away several years ago, though, and I'd been trying to have a better relationship with my dad.

"Thank you. He'll like that. I think Felicia's stopping by in an hour. We're going to meet Linda and Elaina."

Linda, Nathaniel's aunt who raised him after his parent's death, and Elaina were going to meet up with us at the spa where I was getting my hair done. They were going to spend the morning making sure the church was ready for tonight. Since Nathaniel and I only had three months to plan the wedding, it'd taken a lot of work on everyone's part to get everything together.

It was hard to believe the day had finally arrived. After all the nonstop planning and worrying and picking out this and deciding on that, it was time. I just hoped the last few hours passed quickly.

"That didn't sound like a happy sigh," Nathaniel said.

"It was an impatient sigh," I said, not even remembering sighing in the first place. "I'm ready to be your wife."

"Six o'clock won't come fast enough for me."

"Me, either."

"It's not too late," he said. "We could just elope."

"You should have suggested that back in September. If I'd known then what I know now . . ."

"Yes?"

"I'd have been Mrs. Nathaniel West months ago."

"Don't tell me that," he said. "I'll start thinking about all the fun we could have been having in the last month."

"Okay then. I wouldn't have changed my mind; I'd have done everything the exact same."

He sighed. "Is it six yet?"

"Not even close. Do I get to see you before I walk down the aisle?"

"Not if Linda has anything to do with it. She won't admit it, but she's horribly superstitious."

I glanced out the window and saw it was snowing harder. "Note to self, either stay away from Linda or keep her occupied."

His chuckle was warm and low. "Good luck with that one."

"The good news is that no matter what, I'm seeing you at six o'clock."

"Then, starting tomorrow, it's nothing but you and me for an entire two weeks."

As I got ready, it felt like two thousand butterflies were throwing a party in my stomach. It was almost dreamlike to think I was marrying Nathaniel. All those years ago, I would never have believed there would be a day like this that would bind us together forever. And when I left him months ago, I never thought I'd see him again.

Fate had a different plan though, and our hearts couldn't be content without each other. Finally, after all our struggles, here I stood, hours away from becoming his wife. I couldn't remember a time I felt happier. I closed my eyes and tried to commit the feeling to memory.

"Ready for me to lace you up?" Felicia asked.

I knew I was probably grinning like an idiot when I turned toward her and nodded. She simply smiled back, perhaps remembering her own wedding day.

"I'm so happy for you." She hugged me. "And I love this gown."

It was nothing like the gown I'd imagined getting married in, but I knew the moment I'd put it on that it was mine. The sweetheart neckline accentuated my chest, making the most of my small size. A full skirt flowed elegantly from the tapered waist. But it was the top that had sold me. The top was made like a corset, with tiny pearls and crystals sewn in between the lace.

Nathaniel had me wear a corset a few times during our weekends. He loved the sight of me in one and I had to agree. They made me feel elegant and sexy and completely feminine all at the same time. To find a wedding gown that would both make me feel that way and leave Nathaniel speechless? I was sold.

I held still while Felicia did the laces and I shivered with the knowledge of who would be undoing them. I imagined his fingers, slowly working on the ties, his lips grazing the back of my neck, the whisper of cool air as my skin was exposed, and the rush of heat as he claimed me forever.

Chapter Three

NATHANIEL

There's something to be said about being the last of your friends to get married. Being the first is hard. I remembered how horrible Jackson and I were to Todd when he and Elaina got married. Of course, we were much younger then, and we assumed no man could get married without a proper bachelor party.

We had mellowed out by the time Jackson got married. Plus the fact that Abby and I were following along less than a year later toned down the hysteria a bit as well. As it turned out, the prewedding party boiled down to the three of us hanging out at a local bar.

Much better, I thought to myself hours before the wedding. I stood in a tiny back room of the church, too full of nervous energy to sit down, but not able to walk the halls because according to Linda, doom and gloom would be sure to follow if I laid eyes on Abby before she walked down the aisle.

Jackson was outside talking with someone about the reception on his phone. Todd had left earlier to run some unknown errand for Elaina, so for the first time in hours, I finally had a moment to myself.

Not far from where I stood in the tiny church, Abby was waiting, preparing to become my wife. I closed my eyes against the wave of emotion that thought brought with it. We had traveled so far, crossed so many miles to get to this point. Yet I knew within my heart that the twisted path we had taken to reach this day had been worth every minute, every heartbreak. Our journey had not been easy, but every difficult step had drawn us closer and we'd become better people for it. My heart was full, knowing our journey was just getting ready to start in earnest.

I wondered what she was thinking. At this exact moment, what was going through her mind? We'd been together long enough for me to have a pretty good idea of what she was thinking based on her expression. If I could just get a quick look at her right now, it would put my mind at ease.

I took a deep breath to calm my mind and focus. Everything was fine. Not too long from now, we'd be married. Tomorrow we'd take off for two weeks alone.

I didn't want to think too much about our honeymoon. It would be horrifically embarrassing if I had to walk down the aisle with a hard-on. But after a monthlong period of abstinence, I couldn't help but imagine collaring her for the first time as Abigail West. My fingers itched to lock my collar around her neck, push her to her knees, or bend her over the bed.

Better think about something else.

I glanced out the window. The snow had stopped, but left everything with a thin film of white. Numerous cars and taxis had pulled up outside.

"You ready?" Jackson asked, coming up behind me and clapping me on the shoulder.

I captured him in a one-armed hug. "Never been more ready."

"I stopped by and saw the women."

"How's Abby?"

"Beautiful, happy, and ready to become Mrs. Nathaniel West. Which she'll be in about an hour."

I looked at my watch. "Thirty minutes. I asked for an abbreviated ceremony, but I'm not sure the minister understood. I don't think he understands English all that well."

He laughed. "There's a church full of people waiting for you guys."

I straightened my jacket. "Let's go."

I'm sure the church was lovely. Abby had worked hard to make certain everything was perfect. But my eyes barely took in the stone walls, candles, and roses. I didn't pay attention to the gathered crowd either. My eyes were locked on the front of the church, focused on the spot where Abby would become mine forever.

The minister, Jackson, and I made it to the front and I rocked back on my heels and waited. Before long, the music changed: the soft strands of a harp and violin replacing the piano. The doors at the back of the church opened and I straightened my shoulders.

Felicia walked down the aisle, but I didn't give her more than a glance. My focus was on one thing: Abby. She was waiting at the back of the church, waiting to become my wife.

It was almost absurd to think it possible.

And then she stepped into the doorway and my breath caught. She was exquisite. As she made her way toward me on her father's arm, I'm sure I was grinning like an idiot and I didn't even care.

Her dark hair was piled on top of her head with a few way-ward tendrils escaping. I longed to reach out and touch one, tuck it behind her ear. Her neck, of course, was bare.

I felt fiercely possessive as she walked toward me. I couldn't take in her beauty all at once; it overwhelmed me. Her gaze locked on mine and I finally had the answer to the question I had wondered about earlier. She was fine. She was beyond fine. She was radiant.

Finally, Abby and her father reached the front of the church. Though we didn't touch, the energy between us seemed tangi-ble. I tried my best to listen to the minister as he began the cer-emony, but I kept glancing out of the corner of my eye at Abby.

When it came time for her father to give her away, he kissed Abby's cheek and shook my hand. Then he placed her hand in mine.

"You're a good man, Nathaniel," he said. "Take care of my girl."

"With my life," I promised.

I took both of her hands in mine, awed by the love I saw in her eyes.

"Abby," I whispered, rubbing the top of her hand with my thumb.

Her eyes glistened.

We had decided on traditional vows and as we stood with our family and friends, repeating the words that would bind us forever in the sight of God and man, I felt a deep peace within my soul.

She slipped my father's wedding band on my finger, all the while looking into my eyes. As the ring settled in place, it was as if everything in the world made perfect sense. I took her wed-ding band of princess cut diamonds set in platinum and placed it on her finger. For a few precious seconds, we stood gazing into each other's eyes and I felt her love and desire sweep over me. I knew she found the same passion reflected in mine.

The minister stepped forward. "By the authority vested in me by the state of New York and our Heavenly Father, I pronounce Nathaniel and Abby husband and wife. Those whom God has joined together, let no one put asunder. Nathaniel, you may kiss your bride."

I pulled her to me. "Finally," I said before my lips pressed against hers in a kiss.

I'd never felt more alive, more in love, more *more*.

"I love you," I whispered against her lips.

"Ladies and gentlemen," the minister said when we pulled away, "it is my pleasure to present Nathaniel and Abby West."

Holding hands, we turned and greeted our family and friends as husband and wife.

Chapter Four

ABBY

The day couldn't have been more perfect. Everyone we cared for and loved was in attendance to share our day. But best of all, Nathaniel and I were finally married.

I'm not sure I'd ever seen Nathaniel look more handsome. It wasn't the tux or his gorgeous eyes and chiseled jaw; it was the emotion visible in his expression: the love, joy, and overwhelming look of bliss. He was merely handsome the day I met him. Today, he was breathtaking.

We held hands as we walked to the back room of the church where I'd gotten ready. Everyone else was on their way to the reception hall in the city, but we had a few minutes before our hired car arrived to pick us up.

When we made it into the room, he closed the door behind us, turned the lock, and pushed me against a wall.

"Abby West," he almost growled.

"Mmm." I trailed a finger down his chest. "Say it again."

"Abby West," he repeated before teasing me with a soft kiss.

My hand made it to his waist. "Now say it the other way."

His eyes grew dark with pent-up desire as he spoke the name he used when I wore his collar. "Abigail West."

My knees threatened to give way. Holy hell, what it did to me when he called me Abigail.

"How long until the car gets here?" I asked, desperate to have his hands on me.

"Not long enough. Just enough time for this."

He dipped his head and his lips met mine in a kiss that was long and deep and gave a hint as to what would follow. He entwined our fingers, and pulled our hands above our heads. His lips were strong and insistent, but I knew mine were just the same.

"We could skip the reception," I suggested when he finally pulled back.

"Don't tempt me," he said. "As it is, that gown is temptation enough. Is that a corset?"

Sweet, sweet victory.

"It is." I gave him a teasing smile. "I hoped you'd like it. Felicia had to lace me up in it."

His finger danced along the bodice. "Is that so?"

"Yes. In fact, I doubt I can get out without help." I batted my lashes at him. "Think I'll be able to find someone willing to give me a hand?"

"Oh, trust me, I'll get you out. It'll be like unwrapping a present."

"If I had a decent change of clothes, I'd let you do it right now."

He shook his head. "If I did it right now, there's no way we'd make it to the reception."

"You say that like it's a bad thing."

"Come on." He slipped a wrap around my shoulders, then took my hand and led me outside. "If we miss the reception, we'll regret it when we're old and gray."

One of Nathaniel's business associates owned a large penthouse he rarely used that included what could only be described as a ballroom. It was the perfect place for the reception: private, with a stunning view of the city. When he heard we weren't getting married at our country estate, he'd offered to let us use it.

I'd given Felicia free rein over the decorations, telling her I only needed to know the barest minimum. She had flawless taste, so I wasn't worried at all.

Nathaniel and I rode in the back of the limousine to the penthouse, sipping on the ice-cold champagne that had been waiting for us. The driver was separated from the passenger section by a glass partition, so we had our privacy. We sat side by side and I laid my head on his shoulder while I twisted his wedding band around his finger.

"What time do we need to leave?" I asked. I still didn't know where we were spending the night. I'd given him my overnight bag earlier.

"No specific time." He grinned. "I know exactly what you're doing and it's not going to work."

"I wasn't trying to get information out of you. I was just wondering."

He gave me his *I don't believe you one bit* look.

"Okay," I admitted with a smile. "Maybe I was trying to find out just a little."

He kissed my forehead. "You'll have to wait and be patient."

"I used up all my patience during the last month."

"Mr. West," the driver's voice buzzed in on the intercom. "Sorry to interrupt, but there's a call for you."

"It's my wedding day. I'm not taking calls." He had told me earlier he'd left his phone in his carry-on luggage. Unless it was an absolute emergency, he wanted to be unreachable.

"It's your pilot, sir."

We looked at each other. His pilot? The one taking us to Switzerland tomorrow? This didn't sound good.

Nathaniel picked up the handset in the back of the car. "Yes."

His expression didn't change the entire time he listened. That in and of itself told me something was wrong. Nathaniel asked a few questions, which confirmed my fears, especially when he said, "What are our other options?" Then he told his pilot he'd call him right back, and hung up.

He turned to me with a sigh. "There's a major winter storm coming. We either need to leave tonight and beat it or wait until it passes." He frowned. "I'm sorry. I checked the weather last night. Everything was supposed to go north of us."

I placed my hand over his fist. "How long would that be?"

"The storm will be over in a day or two. But it might take longer for the airports to be operational."

"And if they're not?"

He grimaced. "No honeymoon."

While it wouldn't be the worst thing in the world to not have a honeymoon, it was something I'd really been looking forward to. Two weeks alone with Nathaniel in a country where no one knew us, where we had no responsibilities but each other. That was too hard to give up. Would I risk that for spending more time at our reception?

I looked up, caught his eye, and lifted an eyebrow. The corner of his mouth uplifted in a half smile.

No, it wasn't a risk either of us wanted to take.

"There's no decision to make," I said.

"That's what I thought. We leave tonight."

Nathaniel spent the rest of the car trip on the phone with his pilot making arrangements. From the way it sounded, we were going to have to cut down our time at the reception. I took hold of Nathaniel's left hand and checked the time. Just past seven thirty.

He hung up with a sigh and ran his fingers through his hair. "We need to take off no later than ten. That gives us just an hour and a half at the reception," he said just as we arrived at the penthouse.

"So we eat quickly, talk to a few people, and then leave."

"I hate that we'll have to spend our evening watching the clock."

"It's okay with me," I said. "If that's what it takes to ensure we have a honeymoon, I don't mind keeping the chitchat to a minimum tonight." I slid closer to him. "I have plans for the next two weeks and nothing about them involves New York."

He cupped my face. "You always know just how to look at something to make it seem completely all right."

"Honestly, choosing between a honeymoon with you for two weeks and an evening with a group of people I see all the time?" I kissed him softly. "Not much thought had to go into that one."

He smiled and took my hand. "I just wanted today to be perfect."

Stepping out of the car, I took his arm as we made our way inside the building. "We're married. Nothing could make this day less perfect."

Chapter Five

NATHANIEL

Abby, of course, had been correct. The reception was simple, but perfect, and if anyone thought it a bit rushed, they kept it to themselves. The small crowd pulled us apart shortly after we arrived and we spent some time chatting with our guests. As I accepted congratulations from a colleague, I scanned the crowd looking for Abby. She stood in the center of a group of women I recognized from the library. Everyone was *ooh*ing and *ahh*ing over her ring.

I doubted she'd had much, if anything, for lunch, so I excused myself to get us a plate. I chuckled at the first food station I came to and filled our plate with tapas. I was sure there was still a smile on my face when I approached the group Abby was speaking with.

"Ladies," I said with a nod to them all. "I hate to interrupt, but I'm going to steal my bride away for a quick bite and hopefully talk her into a dance."

Everyone was all polite with smiles and "yes, of courses" and "don't mind us." I led her to the head table, pulled her chair out, and pushed mine close enough for our knees to touch. I figured we probably had between five and ten minutes before well-wishers approached us again.

I held up a banderilla. "You didn't tell me we were having tapas."

"You didn't ask," she said, with a wicked gleam in her eye.

Tapas was our favorite playroom snack. Usually, I'd have her feed me first, and then I'd serve her. She might have caught me off guard slightly by having it at our reception, but I planned to turn tables on her.

She reached for a skewer of vegetables.

"Put it down," I said in a low voice, and her hand stilled. I picked up a skewer, slid a cucumber off, and held it to her mouth. "Open."

Her lips parted and I slipped the vegetable inside. She placed a kiss on my fingers. Next I offered her a meatball and then nodded toward the plate. "We only have a few minutes."

She took some bread and lifted it to my lips. "When I planned the menu, we had more time to do this. I just wanted a discreet way to honor our weekend time."

I wrapped my hand around her wrist, my chest full of awe at how she'd planned our reception. Once more, the need to have her in my collar pulled at me. "I wish we had more time so we could serve each other adequately. Why don't I get someone to wrap this up for us so we take some of it with us? That way we can properly enjoy it on the jet."

Joy filled her eyes. "Thank you."

I leaned forward, meaning to kiss her, but before I could, someone slapped my back.

"First dance, man," Jackson said. "Felicia said for me to get you two on the dance floor."

"Shall we, Mrs. West?" I asked.

She rose to her feet. "Of course, Mr. West."

"Jackson," I said, taking my bride's hand. "If you can find a way for us to pack up some food, I'll let you and Felicia enjoy the honeymoon suite I had booked."

Someone might as well use it.

"I'll see what I can find," he said.

The crowd around us grew silent as we made our way to the dance floor. I took Abby in my arms as the soft, familiar piano melody started to play. It'd been way too long since we'd had any sort of intimate contact. My erection was uncomfortable against my pants, though thankfully the folds of her dress hid it well.

"I'm glad the suite won't go to waste," she mused. "Though I never thought I'd be spending my wedding night in an airplane."

I cringed. Not that the jet wasn't nice; it just wasn't the place I wanted us to spend our first night as husband and wife. And with that being the case . . .

"You know, I'm thinking," I said.

"Something not very pleasant from the look on your face."

"I'm thinking we should extend our month of nothing until we get to Switzerland."

Her mouth dropped open. "Another night?"

I smoothed her hair back and looked into her deep, dark eyes. "I don't want our first time as husband and wife to be shared by a pilot and his crew."

"We've done plenty of things in your jet. Why not tonight?"

"It's just different. I gave you a month. Can you give me one night?" I traced her lips with my finger.

She kissed the tip. "If you can guarantee me one thing."

"Anything."

Her teeth scraped the skin on my finger and I felt the touch all the way to my groin. "Promise me you'll last longer than five minutes when we make it to Switzerland."

I wrapped my arms around her tighter and, to the delight of the watching crowd, dipped her low. "Have I ever left you unsatisfied?" I pulled her back up and gave her a passionate kiss, just to prove my point.

When we finally broke away, she was breathing heavily, but she kept her gaze steady. "I remember a weekend or two I was definitely unsatisfied."

"Let me rephrase." I leaned in and whispered, "Have I ever left you unsatisfied during the week or on the weekend when you weren't being punished for being a bratty submissive?"

Her eyes flashed with longing and desire and she replied with her own whisper, "Not if you word it like that."

"I'm confident I'll do the same in Switzerland."

"Remember that weekend you promised to take me five times in one night?" she asked.

"You were naked that entire weekend. I'll never forget it."

"I think we should try for six."

Before I could gather my thoughts to make a coherent reply, there was a tap on my shoulder.

"Best man cutting in for a quick dance with the bride," Jackson said.

I realized then that the song had ended and a soft jazz one had started. According to my watch, we had another thirty minutes before we needed to leave, so I disgruntledly handed Abby over to him.

I watched them as they made their way to the middle of the dance floor. Along the outer edges, other people joined in.

"Nathaniel," Felicia said from my side.

I barely covered my shock. My relationship with Felicia was complicated. I knew she didn't approve of the lifestyle Abby and I lived on weekends, though Abby had told me of the conversation the two of them had the day they looked at the church. For the most part, I still felt as if Felicia put up with me simply because she had to. Certainly, she never sought me out.

"Dance with me?" she asked in a voice edged with uncertainty.

This time I wasn't able to cover my shock. Not only had she approached and talked to me first, but she was asking me to dance? I merely nodded and led her onto the dance floor.

The first few minutes were awkward. Felicia was obviously as uncomfortable being in my arms as I was holding her. Her back was stiff and her body tense. It was only as we drew close to where Jackson and Abby danced that I could discern Felicia relax.

"She's glowing," she said.

Jackson was spinning Abby around the dance floor and they were both laughing. She looked stunning, as always, but there was something more about her today. It was as if joy filled her so completely, it radiated from her. She caught me staring and blew me a kiss.

"She is," I said in agreement with Felicia. "Thank you for standing up with us."

Felicia took a deep breath. "I need to tell you something."

I braced myself for the worst, though I couldn't imagine what could cause her to seem so troubled.

She looked uncertain for the first time, glancing away, looking at the wall behind me. "I won't say I'm sorry for the way I treated you in the beginning. I was acting in what I thought was Abby's best interest." She shook her head. "I won't apologize for that."

I was too stunned to say anything and we stopped dancing.

"But I will say I'm sorry for assuming the worst about you and what you and Abby do." She finally met my gaze. "It's nothing I'd want to participate in, but you're what Abby needs. I know now you're looking out for her and I thank you for that. I'm glad she has you and I was proud to stand up with you two today."

To call me flabbergasted would be an understatement. "Thank you, Felicia," I finally managed to get out.

She nodded. "One more thing. If you ever try to pull one of those public things like what you guys did at the Super Bowl again, I'm calling the cops. That's just wrong."

Her reference to my *go big or go home* method of introducing Abby to sex in public caught me by surprise and I threw my head back and laughed.

Chapter Six

ABBY

Thoughts of the honeymoon filled my mind as we drove to the airport. Once in Switzerland, if we wanted, we could spend entire days in bed. With two weeks together and no set plans, I hoped several days would pass in that manner. I knew he had my collar packed somewhere. Though we'd agreed I'd wear it some, we'd left open exactly when.

The pilot waited for us. "Mr. West." He nodded, then smiled. "Mrs. West. Congratulations."

Nathaniel shook the pilot's hand. "Thank you. Are we ready to leave?"

"Everything's ready—just been waiting for you."

We made our way into the main cabin. I loved Nathaniel's jet. It was comfortable and modern, with plush leather captain's chairs in the main cabin. Down a short hall was a small bedroom and bathroom. Most of our time in the jet had been spent on weekends, so I'd had his collar on. I wondered where he had packed it.

I walked over to the table between the chairs and opened the drawer Nathaniel usually opened when he collared me. The drawer was empty.

"What are you doing?" he asked.

"I've never been able to figure out where you keep my collar during the week."

"And you thought maybe I kept it on the jet?"

"No," I said. "I just wanted to pick on you." I had a good feeling he probably kept the collar in the playroom during the week. I'd never looked there. The playroom wasn't off-limits to me Monday through Friday, but I never felt quite right in there without Nathaniel being present.

I sat down and tried to buckle the seat belt. I had to readjust the strap twice before I got it to fit over the yards of lace and silk of my gown. When it finally locked in place, I looked over at Nathaniel and laughed at the picture we made. Dressed so formally and buckled up on a plane.

Nathaniel grinned at me and held out a hand. "Something funny?"

I stroked my thumb over his palm. "Just that when I woke up this morning, I didn't see myself jetting off in a wedding gown before the day was over."

"Nothing ever seems to go as planned, does it?"

"I'm starting to see why your backup plans have backup plans."

He ran his free hand through his hair. "I'm sorry, Abby. We rushed through cutting the cake. You barely got to talk with your father. And—"

"Nathaniel, don't. Don't think you're to blame for the weather. Even if you had known, what could you have done? Nothing. We're married and that's all I care about."

It wasn't until we sat down and stopped moving that I realized
how tired I was. I was tempted to fall asleep where I was, but
the gown was starting to get uncomfortable. When the plane
leveled off, I unbuckled.

"I'm ready to get out of this gown if you're still willing to
help me out of it."

"I suppose the only other option is to keep you in the gown until
we land in Switzerland and I'm thinking that's not a viable option."

I shot him a *not on your life* look and turned my back to him.
"I'm guessing now's not the time to tell you the only thing I have
to sleep in is the gown I'd bought for our wedding night. Everything else is packed in my main suitcases."

He started working on the ties on my gown's corset top.
"And I'm guessing now's not the time to tell you I didn't plan to
sleep in anything on our wedding night, so I'll be in bed naked."

I groaned. Thoughts of him naked were chasing away my
fatigue. "Not if you want to keep to the *wait until Switzerland* plan."

The gown slipped from my shoulders and he peppered kisses
along my shoulder blades. "I promise it'll be worth it."

I twisted out of his embrace. "You'd better not. I'm low on
self-control at the moment."

But minutes later when I slipped out of the bathroom and
joined him in the bedroom, I knew I wasn't the only one facing
self-control issues. I blamed my nightgown. I'd picked it out
because it was elegant while still being seductively sexy. Made
of sheer material, it covered me while at the same time leaving
nothing to the imagination.

His gaze followed me as I walked to the double bed and he
silently lifted the sheet and blanket so I could crawl in beside

him. I turned so my back was to his chest. He gave a sharp intake of breath when I brushed against him.

"Fucking hell," he said.

His erection was pressed against my ass. "Yes, exactly."

We lay in silence for several long minutes. Neither one of us moved, which only made it more obvious that neither one of us was moving. I tried to steady my breathing, but all that did was highlight the fact that Nathaniel was behind me totally naked. I balled my fist and told myself to think of anything other than how easy it would be to roll over. He was already naked, so I could have my hands wrapped around him in seconds. A quick hike of my nightgown and he'd have complete access. Then with a shift of hips—

"This isn't going to work," we both said at the same time.

He gave a tight laugh. "Damn, stupid idea."

"Yours or mine?"

"Both."

I rolled over to face him. "I don't think I can go another night. This entire time I've been thinking I'd be okay if I just made it to tonight. And now it's here and we're going to wait another night?"

"I agree. We have to do something."

"I hope by *something* you don't mean separate beds."

"Hell, no." He sat up. "Where's my phone?"

"You're going to call someone? Really?"

He raised an eyebrow at me, but didn't say anything. Instead, he rummaged through his carry-on bag and pulled out his phone. "You were worried about me lasting five minutes? Tonight, we have exactly five minutes to get each other off. Hands only."

He brought the phone to the bed and set the timer. "Starting now."

We were sitting on the bed and my hands were over his body in an instant. It took him just a bit longer to wrestle with my gown and yank it up. On any other given night, I would have helped him out a bit, but at that moment, my skin was hungry for him.

I kissed his scruffy chin. "I need to taste you."

"Later," he said, pulling back only so he could slip the gown over my head. Then his hands roamed over me, touching and exploring. He situated himself between my knees and I gasped when his fingers brushed between my legs. "I feel like I'm in high school."

I took his erection in my hand. "Like you're making out under the bleachers, trying not to get caught?"

"Something like that." He glanced at his phone. "Four minutes and seventeen seconds."

I put myself to work on pleasuring him. We knew each other's bodies well enough to know just how and where to touch. And while I'd learned in the last six months how to delay my orgasms, I hadn't frequently practiced rushing them. That's what I wanted tonight but suddenly I wasn't sure if I could do it.

I took his touch and drank it in like the thirsty woman I was. I allowed it to sweep over me and as my arousal built, I worked his cock faster with my hands. I knew very well just how long he could hold off his orgasm, but I'd never seen him rush it. Tonight we were both letting ourselves run uncontrolled by pleasure, and I had no idea what would happen. It was like a whole new level of mystery between us.

He lifted his hips up to my hand. "Fuck, Abby. You feel so good."

My mind was on the two fingers he had inside me and the way his thumb ran over my clit. "Oh, yes. Right there."

We were both so needy and our desire so urgent, it felt like no time had passed when my climax neared. He wasn't far behind me; I could tell by the way his cock twitched. A few more strokes and I came around his fingers, right as he spilled into my hand.

We collapsed onto the bed. The phone's timer immediately went off, and we both broke out in laughter.

"I don't think I've ever come that fast," I said, wiping my hand on the towel he gave me.

"Me, either."

"It took the edge off, though."

He pulled me into his arms. "Yes, but not quite enough."

"I feel so naughty," I said with a giggle. "Like I cheated."

"We better not talk about you being naughty at the moment." His arms tightened around me and his tone grew serious. "You know, I can't help but think that even though tonight and this evening didn't go as planned, the day couldn't have been more perfect."

I ran a hand along his arms. "You're officially mine forever and always. It doesn't get better than that."

I thought we'd spend some time talking; after all, it was our wedding day. But the crush of the day's events caught up with us, and we drifted off to sleep after a few minutes of whispers and soft kisses.

I woke up to soft sunlight streaming through the plane windows about an hour before we landed. It took me a minute to realize it was probably close to noon in Europe, even though my body thought it early morning. I'd never been a big world traveler, so time changes always did me in.

Zermatt, Switzerland, didn't allow cars to be driven into town. We flew into Sion, where we had to transfer to a helicopter. The short ride only took fifteen minutes, but I was captivated by the scenery. Everything was a crisp white and looked so calm and serene.

After landing in Zermatt, we took a taxi to our chalet. Nathaniel pointed out the Matterhorn in the distance, looming high above everything. I loved the fact that the ban on any vehicle that wasn't electric also meant the absence of any smog that would hamper our view of the majestic sight.

"Is that it?" I asked as a three-story chalet built into the side of a mountain came into view.

Nathaniel glanced at the taxi's GPS and looked again at the building. "Yes, that's it."

"It's magnificent."

"Looks even better in person than it did in the pictures I saw before I rented it."

From the information we had, we knew there was an indoor pool and sauna on the lower level, a living room and kitchen on the main floor, and the master bedroom on the top floor, with floor-to-ceiling windows looking out over the town. We were secluded enough so that our nearest neighbors weren't visible, but the village was just a short car ride away. And because of the location, we could walk right outside of the house and ski.

Nathaniel reached over and took my hand. "So glad we made it before the storm hit, even though we had to cut out early last night."

"I'd do it again in a minute," I said as we pulled into the driveway.

"Me, too."

The taxi came to a stop. Nathaniel sat back in the seat for a minute. "I don't know about you, but I'm in desperate need of a shower."

"A shower sounds perfect." Especially if he would join me.

"Why don't you go on inside and hit the bathroom? I'll bring the luggage in and make sure the kitchen's stocked the way we requested."

"You're not going to join me?"

"Not this time," he said. "I'll shower in the guest bath."

"Waste of water if you ask me." I crossed my arms over my chest.

He kissed my cheek. "We have plenty of time."

For someone who had been initially opposed to my suggestion of no sex for a month, he certainly had been patient about it for the last ten hours.

Well, if you didn't count those five minutes the night before.

Regardless, I left him to deal with the luggage and I walked inside the stunning home that would be our refuge for the next two weeks. The interior was an odd mix of log cabin and contemporary, but it somehow fit together to create a warm and inviting space.

I decided to do the bulk of my exploring later. Ever since he mentioned a shower I felt grimier with each passing second. I breezed past the living room and kitchen, up the stairs, and into the master bedroom.

From the third-floor windows, I could see down the mountain to the village. I felt almost vulnerable surrounded by all the windows even though I knew there was no way anyone could see me. Nathaniel had selected the chalet for its privacy.

I dropped my overnight bag by the bed and walked into the bathroom. Seconds later, I'd stripped my clothes off and was soon enveloped by the soothing warm water of the decadent shower. Outfitted with two rainfall showerheads and numerous smaller vertical ones, the shower could easily fit two people. Nathaniel and I would certainly put the space to good use over the next two weeks. For the time being, though, I simply closed my eyes and let the water and steam revive me.

My skin was wrinkly when I finally got out. I honestly hadn't meant to stay in for so long, but it had felt so good. I glanced outside and saw the shadows were growing long. I wondered if Nathaniel had finished doing all the things he wanted to do and if he was finished with his shower yet. Since I didn't know if Nathaniel had brought up my bag with my clean clothes, I pulled on a robe I found hanging on the bathroom door. I debated leaving my hair wet, but decided I'd regret it, so I dried it as quickly as possible.

He was waiting in the bedroom when I left the bathroom. He must not have spent the time I did in the shower. Not only was his hair still wet, but he'd pulled heavy curtains across the windows and lit candles. The room was decorated all in white. A huge bed made up with an inviting downy duvet and fluffy pillows faced the windows. At the moment, the candlelight cast the entire room in flickering shadows. Nathaniel had been sitting in a plush white chair, but stood at my entrance.

"There you are," he said. "I was afraid you might never come out."

He walked to me, *my husband*, and I swallowed around the lump in my throat at the thought that this man was mine forever.

"I couldn't help it," I said, taking in his bare chest and the way his pants hugged his hips just so. I could see the bulge of his erection in the front. "The shower felt so good."

He didn't say anything, but walked until he stood before me, framed my face with his hands, and kissed me. His lips were strong and insistent and I felt his need sweep over me. Combined with my own, it would have made my knees buckle except for the fact that I had my arms firmly around him.

"Nathaniel," I said in a soft sigh.

"Mmmm," he hummed, entwining his fingers with mine and then he quoted:

> *In that book which is*
> *My memory . . .*
> *On the first page*
> *That is the chapter when*
> *I first met you*
> *Appear the words . . .*
> *Here begins a new life.*

I pulled our clasped hands together. "Dante?"

He nodded and our foreheads touched. "It seemed appropriate. I never knew that day I saw you at the library so many years ago that you would be the start of my new life. But I wonder, did it truly begin then, or the day you walked into my office the first time—or when you accepted my collar the second time?"

His body was warm against me and his breath was hot on my skin. I lifted my head and kissed him. "I don't know."

"I think," he said, "that maybe it starts tonight. With us here like this. Coming together as husband and wife." He kissed my wedding band. "And renewing our vow as Dominant and submissive."

He moved to the nightstand and took something from the top. My heart pounded, knowing what it was, and I hurried to my purse to get its mate. He was back in front of the bed when I turned around and he watched me with dark eyes as I made my way back to him.

He held up a ring made up of three intertwined platinum bands. Its meaning was found inscribed inside.

Abigail, my lovely, my submissive, my heart

His voice was low and heavy with emotion. "Abigail, I give you this ring as an everyday reminder of my dominance. When you see it, may you remember that you are your Master's most treasured possession." He slipped the ring on my finger, leaned in even closer, and whispered, "Always."

I swallowed around the lump in my throat and held up his ring, which had been engraved in a similar manner.

Master, I am yours, body, heart, soul

I slid it on his finger and whispered, "Master, I give you this ring as an everyday reminder of my submission. When you see it, may you remember that you alone hold my heart, my body, and my soul."

He kissed my right-hand ring and then cupped my face in his right hand. "My dear Abby and my cherished Abigail, I love you."

There were no words I could give him that would capture the feeling of utter rapture his words brought to me. So instead I decided to give him myself.

I took a step back and kept my eyes on his as I undid the sash of my robe and slipped it from my shoulders. The move reminded me of another time when I'd done something similar. That day I'd asked him to love me. Now I knew he did, so I asked for something different.

"Take me, Nathaniel. Make me yours, Master."

Silently, he stepped out of his pants and when he took me in his arms again, there was no poetry. He used his hands and his body to say what words were inadequate to convey.

He kissed me again, moving us toward the bed. His touch became urgent as if he wanted to feel me everywhere, all at once. Or maybe like he couldn't get close enough to me. My hands moved in a similar way. Across his chest, down his back. After a month of denial, I had a physical need to touch him and I drank him in. The hurried five minutes the night before hadn't been anywhere near enough.

He laid me on my back and I sank into the downy warmth of the duvet. Then he moved on top of me and his mouth was on my skin, kissing a trail from my neck, across my clavicle, and down to my breast. I gasped and arched my back as he sucked a nipple deep into his mouth. He teased the tip with his tongue and nipped it with his teeth.

My nails scratched his back and he groaned.

"Fuck yes," he said. "Mark me."

"Bite me," I asked in return. "Make it hard."

He sat up and took a breast in either hand. "Watch."

I could do nothing else but stare as he palmed and kneaded my breasts. With each squeeze, he ran his thumb across the nipple. The touch sent a spark of desire straight to the spot between my legs where I ached for him.

"Yes," I moaned. "Oh, yes."

He bent his head and nibbled the tender skin on the underside of my right breast, ignoring for a moment my plea for more. Treating me as if I were a delicacy to be savored, he took his time tasting me. Then, right when I felt as if I would go crazy for want, he pulled back and resumed his kneading, his touch progressively growing stronger.

"Still want it hard?" he asked.

I lifted my hips, eager for more. "Yes. Damn it."

"I've been without you for a month. I doubt I can go slow and easy the first time."

"Then don't."

He let go of one breast to trail his hand down my side to land between my legs. Gently he pushed a finger inside me, testing my readiness, but not asking if I was sure. "I've missed how tight and hot you are when I first push inside you." He took the other hand and pushed my knees apart. "Spread your legs for me, baby. I need to sink in deep tonight."

Please. Please. I nearly pulsed with the need.

I kept my legs wide for him as he moved between them and took his cock in his hand, positioning it at my opening. With a control that seemed at odds with his words earlier about not being able to go slow, he ever so slightly eased his way inside.

"Yes. Fuck," he said, closing his eyes as he pushed farther.

When he was as far and as deep as he could go, he stilled and opened his eyes. "Feel that? Feel my cock claiming you?"

"Please." I squeezed my inner muscles around him. "Please. More."

He dragged himself back out slowly, allowing me to feel every inch of his retreat. Once he was almost out, he held still for just a second and then, as if at the end of his control, he grabbed hold of my upper thighs and started an almost punishing rhythm. Thrusting hard and deep, he fucked me relentlessly.

It'd been so long and he felt so good that within no time my climax started to build. I dragged my nails down his arms and arched my back, wanting him deeper. "Nathaniel."

"Coming?" he asked, thrusting in. He moved a hand between my legs and teased my clit. "Shout for me."

"Oh, fuck," I said as my release built and built. "Oh, *fuck*."

He kept driving deeper, all the while teasing me mercilessly with his finger. My orgasm stirred inside me and I bucked against him, trying to reach it. His expression grew darker and he slowed down, stroking long and deep.

The change in friction, matched with his finger on my clit, pushed me over the top and I came hard, with his name on my lips. A look of pure satisfaction overcame his expression and he sped up once again, moving toward his own release.

"Feels so good fucking you again," he panted. "Claiming you. Watching you come."

I squeezed around his cock each time he pulled out.

"Fuck. Abby."

Unable to hold back any longer, he pushed deep inside me and held still, his body shuddering as he released. For several minutes after, I enjoyed the feel of his satisfied body on top of mine, his weight a sensual reminder of our shared pleasure.

His breathing slowed and he took me in his arms and rolled us so we faced each other.

"I'll have to admit," he said, a look of amusement in his eyes. "That was fairly intense. Just like you said."

"Mmm," I hummed. "I'll say. I probably won't be able to walk tomorrow."

"Just as well," he said, arms tightening around me. "I'm not sure we'll make it out of bed."

Chapter Seven

NATHANIEL

She stretched out against me, sighing in delight at my suggestion. "All day in bed. That sounds wickedly decadent."

"We should make wicked and decadent the theme for our honeymoon."

"We're certainly off to a good start," she said, snuggling deeper into my arms.

"Start is definitely the right word. I feel like we've only taken the edge off."

With her soft body wrapped around mine, I knew it wouldn't be long before I took her again. But while the first time had been quicker than normal, I planned to take my time the second. The urgent need to have her had been sated, leaving behind the desire to enjoy her slowly. And growing stronger with every passing moment was the need to have her in my collar. To have her kneel at my command.

"Was everything stocked the way we requested?" she asked.

It took me a few seconds to understand what she meant. "How did you go from wickedly decadent sex to whether or not there was enough food in the fridge?" I swore, the female mind was beyond my comprehension.

She giggled and propped herself up on an elbow, facing me. "I was thinking about spending all day in bed and that led me to wonder what we would do about food. Then I realized we might not have anything if they didn't do like we asked and how awful would it be if we had to go grocery shopping today."

"You seriously were thinking all that?"

"Yes. So, do we shop or not?"

I pushed back the hair that had fallen across her forehead. "It's time for you to get out of your wedding-planning mode and remember I've got everything under control. There's no need for a grocery trip anytime soon."

"Thank goodness."

"Which means I can take my time and have you slow and easy, with no need to worry about how we'll keep our strength up for tomorrow." I ran my lips along her collarbone. "And trust me, we'll need our strength with what I have planned."

"Is that so?"

"Mmm," I hummed. "But for right now, we have all the time in the world."

Unlike my hurried actions previously, this time I planned to thoroughly enjoy her luscious body. I took her hands and pulled them above her head.

"Leave them there," I said. When she started to protest, I added, "You can have your turn later."

She was soft and pliable under me. My lips explored parts of her I hadn't tasted in a month. The hollow of her throat, the valley between her breasts, even the ticklish skin below her rib cage—I kissed them all.

"I'm never going a month without you again," I said as I nibbled along her belly button. "Ever."

She sucked in a breath as I trailed my hand lower. "It seemed like a good idea at the time."

I positioned myself between her legs and pushed her knees apart. She still had her arms where I left them, so I took her hands and placed one on either thigh. "Keep yourself open for me."

I started with soft kisses at her knee, slowly working my way upward. I nipped the tender skin of her upper thigh and she gasped, letting her legs move together.

I pushed them apart. "Going to make me break out the restraints so soon?"

"No, Sir."

My erection grew harder and I wondered if she realized what she'd said or if it just came naturally. It had not escaped my attention that she responded positively to the slight dominance I sometimes injected into our weekday play.

I didn't want her collared all the time and had no interest in a twenty-four/seven Master/slave relationship, but hearing her submissive reply to my words turned me on even more. Fuck, it always turned me on when she called me "Sir." We'd planned to have her wear her collar some during our honeymoon, but I wondered if we shouldn't experiment with a few other things.

For now, though . . .

"I've been waiting all month to do this," I said, lightly tracing her wetness, dipping a finger into her. I brought it to my lips and tasted the evidence of her arousal. "So damn sweet. A man could live off this."

She chuckled. "I doubt that."

"We'll have to see." I dipped my head and ran my tongue along her entrance, sucking her clit gently into my mouth. I teased her with soft nibbles and gentle caresses before gradually getting rougher.

Her legs started to tremble. "Need you."

I rubbed my chin against her. I hadn't shaved when I took my shower, so I knew the roughness would arouse her more. "You've got me, Mrs. West."

She jerked against me. "Please. Now."

I circled her clit with my finger. "Come for me and I'll give you what you want."

She whined, but I dropped my head and ran my tongue over her swollen flesh. She came with a whimper, panting lightly. I moved up her body, bringing her hands with me and placing them around my neck.

"Now?" she asked.

"Now," I said. I rolled us to our sides and she hitched a leg over my hips. "Abby," I sighed, pushing into her.

The position we were in didn't allow for me to take her deeply, but that was okay. I'd already had her that way earlier. Facing each other the way we were allowed our hands the freedom to touch and roam. As I stroked inside her, my fingers whispered against her skin and traced her curves.

Her palm rested on my upper hip, moving along with my slow, steady thrusts. Every so often, she'd move slightly and her nails would scratch me, driving me to the edge of need. I held back, though, and simply enjoyed being with her, connected in the most intimate way possible.

"I love you," she whispered, rocking into me.

"Love you so much."

She lifted her head and our lips met in a sweet kiss that echoed the way our bodies moved. When our climaxes finally came, they were quiet and tender, and the pleasure washed over us as we held on to each other.

We dozed for a while, after, and woke when the sun had set completely. I left the bed just long enough to grab some snacks. When I returned we had a naked picnic of apples, grapes, almonds, bread, and brie. We talked a bit about how we wanted to spend the next few days. Together, we agreed to spend tomorrow at the chalet and perhaps explore the village the day after.

"Or the day after that," Abby said in between bites of apple.

I raised an eyebrow. "That long?"

"I think maybe I'd like to wear your collar the day after tomorrow."

"Oh?"

She shrugged. "It's been a month. And when you threatened to bring out the restraints, I realized how much I missed it. How much I needed it."

I took a sip of wine, interested in knowing if she remembered what had happened next. "You know you called me 'Sir' right after that."

"I did? Really?" Her forehead wrinkled. "I don't remember that."

"I wondered."

She picked up a grape and put it back down on the plate. Her forehead was still wrinkly, like she was thinking about something that troubled her. "I've never done that before. Called you 'Sir' when I wasn't wearing your collar."

"It's okay. I mean, it's not like I minded."

"You don't think it's odd, that I'd say something like that, just out of the blue?"

"No, I don't think it's odd and it didn't just come out of the blue. I did threaten to restrain you."

She didn't look convinced. Her lips parted, like she was going to say something, but then she stopped and dropped her head.

"Abby, look at me." I waited until she met my gaze before continuing. "I think it's perfectly natural for the facets of our lives to spill over onto each other. I'd be surprised if they didn't start to blend a bit."

"You don't think it's blurring the lines?"

"They're our lines to blur, right?"

"I suppose," she said, but her expression told a different story.

"Neither one of us wants an around-the-clock collared relationship. Just because you happen to not call me 'Nathaniel' during sex or because I tell you to be still doesn't change that."

She thought about it a bit more. "You're right. I see that." A smile broke across her face. "So you didn't mind, huh? When I called you 'Sir'?"

I felt my own smile in response to her question. "Didn't mind at all. Quite the opposite, actually."

"I'll keep that in mind."

"You do that."

She grew thoughtful again. "Wonder why I said 'Sir' and not 'Master'?"

I shrugged. "Maybe you thought you were in the library?"

"Or on the kitchen table."

"Or maybe it was just a natural reply to what I said. Funny how the body reacts sometimes without us realizing it."

She eyed my growing erection. "I'll say."

I laughed. "Trust me, I completely realized that reaction. It's my body's natural response to you, especially when I think about your calling me 'Sir.'"

She took the plate and wineglass from my hands and placed them on the bedside table. "Let's see what other replies we can get from your body. Besides, I think I remember you saying it was my turn later."

"Is it later already?" I asked, growing even harder.

"Mm-hm." She pushed me to my back and pulled my arms over my head. "Keep them here."

I grew even harder at her words. Though she wasn't a sexual Dominant, every so often she enjoyed having the opportunity to issue a command or two. And I'd admit, I liked seeing her playful side. I decided to play a bit myself.

Letting her keep my hands restrained, I lifted my head and nipped her ear. "Think you can top me, Abby?"

"I think I can, because if you move your hands, I'm going to ignore your dick." She trailed a hand down my side and lightly brushed my erection. "Though that shouldn't be a problem. You've already come twice. You probably won't even notice."

Her hand hovered over me. I felt the heat from her skin, but it wasn't nearly enough. *Hell, yes, I'd notice.* "Fine. I won't move my hands."

The look she gave me was pure evil. "Good, because I want to see if I can still deep-throat you."

My cock throbbed at her words as I imagined it and my hips lifted involuntarily. To sink into her mouth again. To watch her lips part around me. *Fuck.*

"No moving," she warned, and moved away.

"Abby," I said in a gruff voice.

She sat up by my side and drew figure eights on my chest with her finger.

Lower. Move your hand lower.

"Know how you'll sometimes say you're doing something for me?" she asked.

Her hand drifted lower and my eyes nearly rolled to the back of my head. "Yes," I hissed.

"Well, this is all for you. So be still and enjoy." She shimmied down toward the edge of the bed, keeping her eyes on mine. "I'm used to sucking you off so many times a week, I lose count. Do you know how hard it's been to go a month without tasting you?"

"Probably about as hard as I am right now."

"You *are* looking really hard. Is that painful?"

"I know you can make it better." And I hoped she'd do it soon. I nearly ached with the need to be inside her in some way.

"Watch," she said, as if I could do anything else.

Her lips parted slowly, much too slowly for my liking, around the head of my cock. I wanted to thrust into her, force myself all the way in her mouth. Fuck, it'd been so long since her warm heat had engulfed me.

She took more of me inside her mouth, moaning as she did so. I expected her to take all of me, the way she'd said. Instead, she wrapped a hand around the base of my cock and started bobbing. Teasing.

"Need. More," I panted.

Clearly, she didn't care because she continued her bobbing. Every so often she'd pull back completely and lick down my shaft.

"Damn, evil tease," I said when she sucked me partway inside.

She lifted her head. "Says the man who a little over a month ago made me go all weekend without release."

The weekend in question had been part of her training. I'd kept her on the edge for two entire days. "I let you come on Sunday, right before I took your collar off. When you came, you screamed so loud, you nearly broke the dishes."

She didn't reply to my version of the weekend in question, but sat up and took me in her hand. "You talk about my taste. What about yours? I want you hard and seconds away from coming. That way when I finally have you completely in my mouth, I won't have long to wait before I taste your pleasure."

And with that, she released me from her grasp and lowered her mouth onto my cock. I hit the back of her throat, but she relaxed and I sank all the way in. It was too much: the sight of my cock sliding into her mouth, the wet heat I found inside.

"Fucking hell." I lifted my hips, thrusting deeper, and my release burst from me.

She drank it down almost greedily and when I pulled out, she licked her lips. "I think I lied."

I felt drained after that last climax and wasn't sure I could move. I managed to lift an eyebrow. "Oh?"

"Yeah, I'm pretty sure that wasn't just for you."

Chapter Eight

ABBY

As planned, we spent the next morning resting at the chalet. Much of our time was spent on the lower level, enjoying the indoor pool. In the afternoon we put on our ski clothes and went outside for a while.

It came as no surprise to me that Nathaniel was an expert skier. Fortunately, I wasn't half bad either. For a few hours, we explored the area surrounding the chalet.

"Apollo would love all this snow," I said as we made our way back inside. Apollo was the Golden Retriever Nathaniel had rescued years before we met. He was spending the next few weeks at Jackson and Felicia's house. Apollo liked Jackson and was friendlier toward Felicia than to most other people.

We took off our wet clothes and warmed up in front of the living room fire. Nathaniel went to check on the steaks he was marinating for dinner and when he came back to the living room, he sat behind me and pulled me to his chest.

I snuggled into his arms with a content sigh. Though the living room was furnished with several plush couches and chairs, I enjoyed sitting on the soft rug in front of the fireplace. Much like the bedroom, the living room had numerous floor-to-ceiling windows. Nathaniel had pulled the curtains before we left, so at the moment, the room felt intimate.

"Have you given any more thought to tomorrow?" he asked. "Should we check out the village or stay here?"

"I still think we should stay here and you should collar me."

He placed a gentle hand around my neck. "Just for the day?"

"Night, too."

"Okay, and we'll decide then what we want to do next."

"I think that's a good idea," I said. "But does that give you enough time to prepare?"

I knew how much thought he put into one of our normal weekends and that was at his house, where everything was familiar. I would think being in a new place, specifically one that didn't have a playroom, would be more challenging and he'd need longer to prepare.

He laughed softly. "Time to prepare? What do you think I've been doing for the past month? All I need is my toy bag and you. Private room preferred, but not necessary."

"What?" I asked, turning around to see his face.

He was smiling. "Just seeing if you were listening. I don't plan on playing in public while we're here."

"Maybe it's too bad we're not staying at a crowded resort," I said. "Think about all the fun we could have on the ski lift."

"Sounds dangerous."

"Just as well you're the one in charge. I'd probably get us arrested."

"Or killed."

"Nah," I said. "I wouldn't go that far, but incarceration would have been a definite possibility."

"Somehow, I think I could deal with prison if it was a result of something you'd planned for us."

"I'll keep that in mind," I said. After a few minutes of silence, I added, "So tomorrow?"

He kissed the top of my head. "Yes, tomorrow."

After breakfast the next morning, he told me to strip and go wait in the bedroom. Though I'd been expecting to be told to do so, my heart pounded anyway. It'd been a month, my less-than-rational side thought. What if I forgot everything? What if I messed up? How awful would that be? To mess up on our honeymoon?

I won't say I was as nervous as I'd been the first time we played; I wasn't. But there was a certain excitement that set my heart racing and made my nerve endings prickle.

He made me wait for a long time, or at least it seemed like a long time. Especially since by "wait" in the bedroom, he meant "kneel." While kneeling on the floor, I couldn't see the clock by the bed, but judging by the number of my breaths, more than ten minutes went by. My knees were out of practice with kneeling and they started to ache almost immediately. I resisted the urge to shift my weight; he could be watching, after all. I forced myself to be still and remain in the proper waiting position.

Then, just when I thought they'd never come, I heard footsteps on the stairway. Within seconds he was before me.

"Look at me, Abigail."

He spoke in the cool, controlled voice I knew so well, and almost instantly all my nervous excitement was replaced by aroused need. I lifted my head and met his fiery gaze.

My Master.

My playful husband and sensual lover were still there, but at the moment, there was no doubt the man in front of me was my unyielding and demanding Dominant. My knees didn't matter and the weeks we hadn't played melted away like they were nothing. And deep inside my soul, something whispered *Yes*.

"I have something new for you," he said, holding out a leather collar. "Your regular collar is fine for what we use it for, but this is a special occasion and needs a special collar."

A new collar? I hadn't expected that.

"Abigail West," he said. "If you accept this collar, it will brand you as mine for however long you wear it. Your body will be mine to tease and torment. And since it's been so long, I feel it only fair to warn you that I'm going to work you over hard. You have your safe words if you need them."

I was, not for the first time, thinking the monthlong-abstinence request might not have been the best idea after all.

"Knowing this, do you accept my collar?" he asked.

"Yes, Sir," I answered.

"Thank you, Abigail."

He buckled the collar around my neck and I swallowed. It felt tighter than my diamond collar.

"Feel okay?" he asked. "Not too tight?"

"No, Master. It's perfect." I rose up on my knees, eager for this next part. "May I serve you by sucking your cock?"

He stepped back. "I don't think so. Not yet."

It was the first time he'd ever said "no" after he collared me and I was caught off guard. I'd automatically leaned forward to undo his pants and had to catch myself before I moved farther.

He trailed a finger across my cheek. "I've missed seeing you like this, Abigail."

It wasn't my place to speak out of turn when I had his collar on, so I remained still and silent. He studied me for several long seconds and then turned.

I waited as he walked over to a short couch and sat down. It was then I noticed the tube sitting on the cushion beside him and I gulped.

"Come across my lap," he said. "I'm going to spend some time reacquainting myself with your ass."

He didn't often have me over his knees, knowing it wasn't one of my favorite positions to be in. I had a feeling I was in for a long day.

"How long has it been since I've spanked you?" he asked when I'd situated myself.

"I don't know, Master. Maybe five weeks?"

"About thirty-five days." He started rubbing my backside. "That sounds about right."

He continued with his rubbing, every once in a while dipping a finger between my legs, checking to see if I was wet. I was, of course, and every time he checked, he'd bring his finger to my mouth for me to clean.

"I've spanked you for your pleasure and I've spanked you for your disobedience." His hands got rougher. "Today I spank you because it pleases me to do so. It's been thirty-five days, so I'm going to spank you thirty-five times. Fifteen with my hand, fifteen with the paddle, and five with the leather strap. I won't make you count."

Apparently, he considered the rubbing a warm-up, because when his hand came down upon my flesh for the first time, it definitely wasn't a swat to prepare me. I grunted.

"Your ass has gotten soft," he said. "And it's my job to toughen it back up."

The first fifteen were hard, but nothing I couldn't handle. Especially since between swats, he'd play with my clit and drive me right to the edge of release. Even though he'd said I didn't have to count, I did so anyway in my head and I breathed a sigh of relief when he finished the first set. But he didn't pick up the paddle like I thought he would. Instead, I felt his slick fingers pressing against my anus.

"Five weeks since I spanked you," he said. "How long do you think it's been since I've taken you here?"

"Uh, two, mmm, two and a half months."

He hummed, pressing just inside with his finger. "And in those two and a half months how many times did you use a plug?"

Fuck. Fuck. Fuck.

"Abigail?"

"None, Master."

"None? Did it not occur to you that I'd take your ass this week?"

I swallowed hard and told the truth. "It must have slipped my mind."

He removed his finger. "I'm fucking your ass today whether it slipped your mind or not. And since you're not prepared, I'll have to prepare you my way."

I wasn't so sure I wanted to know what his way was.

"You brought this on yourself," he said as a large plug pressed against my tight opening and I flinched. "This is actually smaller than I am and I used plenty of lube. Bear down, take it, and be thankful I'm using it first and not just shoving my cock up your ass."

I relaxed as much as possible while he pushed the monstrous thing inside me. It stretched and burned going in, but he was right; it was better that he used the plug first. As much as I was gritting my teeth against the sharp pain, I knew it was nothing like what I'd be experiencing if I had to take him inside me first.

I let out a sigh when it slid in all the way, surprised at how full I felt. Ten weeks had made a noticeable difference.

"That's it," he said, slipping a hand between my legs and teasing me back into arousal. "Kneel beside the couch and think about how you should have prepared yourself."

I moved to my knees and into my waiting position while he walked off toward the direction of the bathroom. Water ran for a brief moment and in the silence that followed, I ran through all the opportunities I'd had to use a plug over the last ten weeks. It was true it had slipped my mind, and I knew it shouldn't have.

He came back into the bedroom and sat down on the couch, placing the paddle and strap beside him. "Look at me, Abigail."

I lifted my head.

"Did you do some thinking?"

"Yes, Master."

"And?"

"And I had plenty of opportunity to use my plugs. To prepare myself for you. I'm sorry, Master." It was the truth. In all my wedding and honeymoon preparations, I should have made sure I was adequately prepared. I almost added, "But I did wax," then decided against it.

"Apology accepted," he said. "But since you didn't prepare for the possibility of anal sex, I'm not going to allow you to orgasm as a result of it. When I take you, it'll be for my pleasure only. Do you understand?"

Damn it all. My orgasms stemming from anal sex were some of the most intense ones I had. "Yes, Master."

"I'm glad you see things my way. And just so we're clear, if you do orgasm without my permission, it'll be the last one you have for a long time. Understood?"

"Yes, Master." He'd withheld orgasms from me before, so I knew he wasn't joking, honeymoon or not.

"Very good." He patted his lap. "Now come back here so I can continue with your spanking torment."

Torment was a good word for what he did. My backside was only the tiniest bit sore from the first spanking, so he resumed his rubbing torture. And again he kept me right on the edge of pleasure by teasing my clit and stroking my needy flesh.

"No need to count," he said, right before bringing the paddle down the first time.

With the plug in place, I felt all kinds of full as it was. Add in his seeking fingers and the paddle that brought just enough pain to be pleasurable and before long I was squirming on his lap.

"That's a lot of wiggling for a forgetful submissive who won't be coming anytime soon," he said, halfway through the set of fifteen. "If you were smart, you'd be still."

He was right: there was no use in trying to get more friction where I needed it, since it'd be a while before he allowed me to climax. I didn't even want to think about what would happen if I came without permission.

"Sorry, Master." I planted my feet firmly on the floor and held on tightly to his calves.

"Seven more," he said, smacking downward so the paddle landed directly over the plug. It shifted deeper into me and I felt my hips rock against his thigh.

So good. It felt so good.

I closed my eyes as the last six fell. He set the paddle down and ran a finger between my legs.

"Such a wicked girl," he said. "So aroused after her spanking. I think we may start each day of our honeymoon with a spanking. What do you think?"

Was he really asking me that? How would that work since I wouldn't be wearing his collar every day? He didn't expect me to wear it for the next two weeks, did he?

"We'll have to have this discussion a little later," he said. "Now isn't the right time. For now, be very still. I'm going to remove the plug."

The damn thing was just as uncomfortable being removed as it had been going in. I think I may have cut off the blood circulation to his ankles at one point, I grabbed his legs so tightly.

When it was out, I lay panting across his lap with him stroking my hair. "Good job, my lovely. Next time you'll make sure you prepare yourself, won't you?"

"Yes, Master." Damn straight I would.

"Five more to go," he said. "I think I'll let you choose how you'll get them. You can either stay over my knees and suck my cock in thanks after or you can bend across the bed, but I'll spank your pussy with the strap for the last two."

Six months ago, I wouldn't even have considered it. Spank me there? With a strap? No, thank you! But he'd spent time working me gradually and now, while it hurt initially, the sharp wave of pleasure made it worthwhile. So it was tempting . . .

"I'll stay across your knees, Master," I answered.

"Very well," he said. "Kneel on the floor and tell me why."

It was, I swear, his new favorite thing to do, asking me to tell him why. I'd questioned him on it when he first started. His response was that it gave him insight into how and what I was thinking and also helped him know what I did and didn't like.

I slipped from his lap and knelt by his feet. Since he asked for a reply, I knew he wanted me to look at him while I answered.

"I don't like being over your knees, but I love having you in my mouth, so based on those two items alone, it's a wash."

He nodded. "Thoughts on option two?"

"You know I prefer to be over the bed, and I've come to like it when you take a strap to me that way."

"Yes," he said. "That's why I thought you'd go for the second option."

"But," I continued. "You also told me not to come before you gave permission or else I wouldn't come for a long time."

"Ah, I see." He stroked my hair. "You were afraid you might come from the strap?"

I nodded.

"Wise decision," he said. "Well thought-out with all options considered. And you did an excellent job of explaining your thought process to me. I think we've both made a lot of progress during the last few months."

It always made me feel warm all over when I pleased him. "I think so, too, Master."

He picked up the strap. "Come here and let's finish that spanking."

While I used to be frightened of the strap, as long as he wasn't using it for punishment, I wasn't anymore. I'd learned he knew how to wield it to bring pain-laced pleasure as well as plain pain. I went back across his lap, knowing only pleasure awaited me.

I was correct. The last five strokes, when combined with his expert fingers, brought the sharp pleasure I craved. I was panting with need when he finished the last one.

He kept me on his lap for a few minutes, rubbing a soothing cream over my sore flesh and telling me how much he enjoyed me and how he'd missed this time between us. When he finally told me to thank him with my mouth, I ached to have him in me in any way possible.

I figured he wouldn't finish in my mouth since he'd been so insistent about anal sex. As such, I took my time, undoing his pants and stripping him out of them. I palmed his balls and cupped him gently before ever so slowly taking him in my mouth.

I swirled my tongue around his tip, mimicking the way he'd teased my clit. And when I deep throated him, he sucked in a breath. After that, he kept his hands in my hair, ensuring I didn't take him too deeply. I assumed he was afraid if I deep-throated him again, he might come.

My suspicions were confirmed when, moments later, he pulled back and commanded me to bend across the bed.

"Missed this ass," he said, giving me a playful swat. "I'm never going two and a half months without taking it again. Hold yourself open."

I did as he asked, allowing him the room to prepare me. He'd brought the warming lube and I sighed as he spread it over and inside me.

"Like that?" he asked.

"Yes, Master. I've missed you taking me."

Unlike times past, he didn't use his fingers first. As soon as he finished with the lube, his slick cock was pressing against me. I tensed my muscles.

One of his fingers played with my clit. "Relax, my lovely."

"Sorry, Master."

"Are you okay?"

"Yes, Master. Please don't stop."

"I need you to relax. This might be for my pleasure, but I don't want you hurt."

His subtle reminder that he was still looking out for my needs and was doing what was best for me was what I needed to hear to relax further.

"There you go," he said, holding my hips and pressing into me.

His fingers slipped between my legs and he stroked me there as his tip passed inside me. He might have said this was for his pleasure only, but he was ensuring I got something out of it, even if that something wasn't an orgasm.

"Fuck, Abigail. You feel incredible."

I pushed my hips back toward him. "You don't feel bad yourself, Master."

He chuckled and gave me a swat. "Don't think flattery will get you an orgasm."

"I wouldn't dare."

"Yes, you would."

"You're probably right."

During our banter, he'd worked himself deeper, so with a final push and a coarsely spoken, "I know I'm right," he was buried inside me.

I bit the comforter as he pulled out and started a slow and torturous push and pull. Then he added his fingers back to my achy flesh and I started chanting.

"Fuck. Fuck. Fuck."

"Exactly," he said.

The feel of him inside me that way was exquisite in its pleasure. Anal sex always seemed so dark and forbidden, it never failed to turn me on. Though I tried not to, it wasn't long before I was begging.

"Please, Master, let me come."

"No."

I bit the inside of my cheek to keep from begging again and clasped the comforter in my fist. My eyes damn near rolled to the back of my head when his fingers started pumping into my pussy in time with the strokes of his cock in my ass.

"Please," I whined.

"Stop begging or else I'll pull out, gag you, and fuck you slowly for hours."

I didn't doubt him, so instead of focusing on what he was doing to my body, I recited the alphabet backwards. In German.

"Damn it, Abigail. If you're going to speak in foreign languages, at least say something interesting."

"Sorry, Master. I thought I was doing that in my head."

He thrust at an angle that made me squeal. "Well, you weren't."

His breathing was getting choppy and his thrusts harder and faster. I hoped beyond hope that meant he was close. I knew I sure was. And I knew I couldn't take much more.

Mercifully, he slipped his fingers from me and grabbed my hips. He rocked into me a few more times before blessedly climaxing. I breathed out a sigh of relief, thankful I had been able to hold back my own release.

He peppered kisses across my back, lightly stroking my arms before pulling us both up on the bed. He curled us up on our sides, spooning. His touch was gentle, all trace of teasing gone as if he knew how precariously close I was to orgasm.

"Ist alles in Ordnung?" he asked, and I laughed. He tightened his arms around me.

"Yes, *Meister*, I'm okay."

"Meister? Mmm, I like that, too." He pressed a kiss to my shoulder. "Still want to come?"

"Yes," I said, and thought about my answer some more. "But interestingly enough, I'll be okay if I don't."

"Really? Explain."

I ran my fingers down the length of one of his arms and placed my hand over his. "Right here, right now, I'm completely content. I still feel the need to come, but it's lost in the satisfaction I feel at knowing you're pleased with me."

He kissed the back of my neck. "So pleased. I know that wasn't easy."

No, it hadn't been easy, but I'd done it for him and would do it again in a minute if he asked. He held me for a time and I closed my eyes, enjoying the feel of being in my Master's arms.

Eventually, he kissed the back of my neck again and gave my butt a slap. "Break time's over. Go stand in front of a window."

A small part of me balked, a natural reaction I assumed for a person being told to go stand naked in front of a window. Of course I knew that no one could possibly see me, but my heart still raced as I moved off the bed and toward the edge of the room. I heard him walk into the bathroom and the sound of running water. It was several minutes before he returned.

"Hands above your head," he commanded. "And press yourself against the glass."

The glass was cold as I placed my hands above me and I pressed my forehead against it, hoping to help alleviate some of the heat I felt. Looking out the window I only saw white: the snow falling, the mountains around us, and the drifts below. In the distance, I caught glimpses of the village and, in the far distance, the towering Matterhorn.

I was so caught up in the beauty of the scenery, I didn't realize he'd come behind me until I felt the slap of a flogger against my butt.

"Look at you," he said, his voice low and deep. "All spread

out against the window." The flogger struck again. "Just think of all those people down below and what they would think if they could see you." The flogger struck my upper thigh. "Naked." It hit again. "Turned on by being flogged."

He continued his low murmurings, and as the blows of the flogger grew harder and harder, I found myself getting lost in a sea of white. The snow swirled around me, somehow tying together the sharp slap of the flogger and the sweetness of his fingers, touching me just so.

All the while, his voice was my anchor. He kept up a constant low murmuring, allowing me to focus on him while surrendering my body to the sensations he created. For that time, he was my lifeline as I floated in a swirl of pleasure.

The flogger was soft against my back and harder along my thighs. It danced seductively between my legs. And all the while he caressed me with his voice. It seemed like no time at all before the blows became slow and soft.

"Green," I said. He couldn't stop. It'd been too long since I'd had this feeling; I needed more. "Green, please."

"I don't think so, my lovely. You've had enough for now."

"Please," I whined.

"Later," he said. "Right now you're not in a place to make a sound decision."

I begged to differ, but as he slowed the flogger, his fingers picked up their speed. I ground my hips greedily against his hand. "You're right, Master. This is *much* better," I panted.

He laughed. "I still haven't given you permission to come."

"Oops." I stilled my hips.

His body pressed along the back of mine. "Maybe soon. Maybe I'll fuck you against the window."

I knew if I said anything, I'd just beg and he'd already warned me about the begging. So instead, I bit the insides of my cheeks and stifled my moan.

"Would you like that, my dirty girl?"

"Yes, Master. So much."

I heard the flogger drop to the ground. "Brace yourself."

It was all the warning I got because in the next second, he was sliding into me. I moaned as he entered me completely.

"Feels so good," he said, his hands coming to rest beside mine on the window. "I wish there were people outside. So they could watch me fuck you."

I pressed my cheek to the window and closed my eyes, enjoying the feeling of having him inside me. My breasts were hitting the window with each of his thrusts into me. The chill of the glass intensified the heat he was creating within my body. I balled my hands into fists as he pounded deeper and harder and faster.

"Please," I whispered again when I felt I was at my breaking point. "Master."

He slipped a hand between us and teased my clit. "Going to come against the window with my dick inside you?"

Oh, god. Was this a test? His hips rocked and I lifted myself up on my toes to allow for his penetration. "If it pleases you, Master."

"Oh, it pleases me, Abigail." He said with a thrust. "Come when you wish."

I lasted for only seconds before my climax claimed my body and I came in one long wave after another. He stiffened behind me and covered my body with his own as his release followed.

Afterward, we were both quiet and still.

"Thank you, Master," I finally murmured.

He scooped me gently up in his arms and carried me to the bed. "*Bitte schön*, my lovely."

I sighed and curled up next to him. He stroked my hair and pressed kisses to the back of my neck. "Didn't realize how much I missed that," I said.

"Neither did I."

Usually after a play session, I was tired and would have slept in his arms for an hour or so. Today, for some reason, I felt energized. I rolled over to face him and propped myself up on an elbow. "Can we talk for a few minutes, Master?"

A soft smile covered his face. "Of course."

"You said you didn't know how much you'd miss it. What's the longest you've gone without playing?" I knew it hadn't been the month we'd just had. Maybe it was the time we'd been apart.

"I suppose it would be when I dated Melanie."

"Right," I said. I'd actually forgot about her, the woman he'd tried to have a vanilla relationship with. It was shortly after breaking up with her that I interviewed to be his submissive.

"Why do you ask?"

"I just wondered if it surprised you when you played again. How much you missed it."

"It did," he said. "I think that's why I went against my gut feeling and invited Gwen to play."

"But that didn't work out." Gwen had been the opposite of Melanie and needed more pain than he was willing to give.

"Just because our needs within the power exchange didn't align. It wasn't that we didn't both want the power exchange itself."

Not wanting to discuss another woman on our honeymoon, especially one he'd played with, I changed the subject. "So why were you surprised today?"

"Probably because I've been enjoying our everyday time so much." His eyes grew playful. "Especially since that month thing is over."

"So you're so excited to have sex again, you'll take it any way you can?" I teased.

"Look who's being sassy with my collar on," he said with a smile.

"So you're so excited to have sex again, you'll take it any way you can, *Master*?" Normally, I wouldn't be so flippant while wearing his collar, but I felt so good and he was relaxed and easygoing.

Quick as a cat, he had me flipped to my back and loomed over me. "I believe, Abigail, that collar means I can have all the sex I want, anytime I want. Wouldn't you agree?"

His expression was so intense, I bit back the smart remark I had dancing on my tongue and replied with a simple, "Of course, Master."

The intensity of his face didn't change, but his eyes darkened with desire. "Damn straight," he said, seconds before his lips crushed mine in a kiss so full of passion, I forgot what we'd been discussing.

When he broke the kiss, he remained over me, his legs between mine and his hands on either side of my head. "Speaking of how long it's been since we've played, how are you feeling?"

At his question, I realized how sore I was, especially my backside and upper thighs. Now that my subspace high was wearing off, I was glad he didn't listen to me when I'd spoken "green." "Actually, I'm feeling a little sore, Master."

He nodded. "I think a long soak in the tub would work wonders on those achy spots."

A long soak in the tub would be even better if he joined me. Though I doubted how much it'd help my aches if he did.

"I know what you're thinking," he said, rolling off the bed. "And no, I won't be joining you in the tub. I think you've had enough for one day."

I stuck my bottom lip out.

"It's been a month—we need to ease back into it slowly," he said. "While some people believe in hitting the ground running, I've found all that's good for is causing shin splints."

I couldn't help it. I laughed. "Shin splints, Master? My shins are the least sore part of my body."

He gave my thigh a playful swat. "It was an analogy, you mouthy sub."

"You like me feisty."

"I like you, period." He held out his hand. "Can you walk?"

I scooted off the bed and took his hand. "I think so."

The master bathroom held a soaker tub big enough for both of us, but much to my chagrin, Nathaniel was serious about not getting in with me. He wrapped me in a soft robe and had me sit in the spacious room's chaise longue while he prepared the water.

Once it met his satisfaction, he had me stand and disrobe. I held on to him while I stepped into the water and sighed as I sank into the sweet-smelling bubbles.

I cracked one eye open. "Sure you don't want to join me?"

"I want to join you, all right, but I'm not going to." He twisted my hair up and pinned it on top of my head. "I'll be right back."

I closed my eyes again and sank deeper. "I'm not going anywhere."

He returned not long after, with a glass of ice water and two ibuprofen tablets. I popped the pills in my mouth and chased them down with the water, not realizing how thirsty I was until I'd drank half the glass.

I looked up at his chuckle. "Sorry, Master. Did you want some?" Frequently, we'd share one glass of wine, so I didn't know if he'd intended to have some of the water.

He took a washcloth and began washing my shoulders. "No, that's all for you. I'll get some later."

I drank the rest of the water and he took the glass. With strong, solid hands, he washed my body, massaging my back and being extra gentle with my backside and thighs. As he worked my muscles, I began to feel the normal aftereffects of our play. I hoped I wouldn't fall asleep in the tub.

"Someone need a nap?" he asked.

"Yes, Master, please," I said, surprised at how groggy I sounded.

"I just need you to stay awake long enough for me to dry you off."

He helped me out of the tub and he quickly dried me off and slipped me back into the robe. I tried to walk back into the bedroom, but he simply said, "No, you don't," and carried me.

I was asleep before he laid me on the bed.

Chapter Nine

NATHANIEL

While she slept, I sat in the bedroom and made plans for the next day. She would still be wearing my collar, but instead of staying inside and playing all day, I thought it'd be a good idea to be outside some.

Most of the time, our weekends were spent at the estate. I enjoyed that time, but wanted to be out and about more in public while she wore my collar. We had ventured out a few times during the wedding planning, but nothing extensive. Switzerland was the perfect place for both of us to grow more comfortable sharing our collared time with others.

I made a few calls to arrange everything and then checked on her again. She was still sleeping, so I headed into the bathroom to take a shower. While washing off, I replayed the day's events in my mind. I loved that she'd been more playful. When she felt comfortable around someone, I noticed she became more fun-loving.

It wasn't, I decided, that she didn't feel comfortable with me. We shared plenty of laughs during the week. Ever so slowly that side of her was coming out more and more on the weekends as well.

She was just starting to stir when I made it back into the bedroom. I checked the clock and found it was just about dinnertime. I thought about heading down to the village to eat, but decided against it since we'd be out tomorrow. Quiet dinner in, then.

She rolled over to her back and grimaced slightly. "Did I oversleep, Master?"

I brushed her forehead. "There's no such thing when you're recovering from a scene. You can go back to sleep if you'd like."

"No, I think I'd better not." She stretched her arms above her head. "Don't want to be awake all night."

"Oh?"

"If you're awake with me, Master, that's one thing, but I don't want to be tossing and turning in bed."

We'd agreed weeks ago that for our honeymoon, no matter how frequently she wore my collar, all nights would be spent in bed together. I didn't mind that she still used the submissive bedroom at times during the weekend, but this was our honeymoon and I'd be damned if she was sleeping separate from me.

"Point taken," I said. "Are you hungry? I can get dinner together."

All at once she became fully awake and swung her legs over the side of the bed. "No, Master. Let me serve you."

On a regular weekend, she did serve me by preparing meals. I wasn't opposed to it while we were here, but she was coming off of a scene and it had been a while since we'd played. I studied her.

"I don't mind," I said. "If you're still tired and sore."

She slid from the bed and came to her knees before me. "Please, Master. Let me serve you tonight. I promise I'm not overly tired or sore and I truly wish for the honor of serving you this way."

My chest swelled with emotion. Whatever had I done to deserve such a woman in my life? Especially to have her as my submissive and wife.

"If you're certain, Abigail."

Her head tipped up. "Very certain, Master."

I nodded. "I think we should have dinner in the living room, by the fire. You will join me."

Joy covered her face and she hopped to her feet. "Thank you, Master."

"Oh, Abigail," I called as she headed to the door. When she turned back, I added, "The robe stays here."

After breakfast the next morning, we took a taxi to the slopes I'd looked into the previous day. The terrain there was perfect for cross-country skiing.

"Cross-country in the literal sense," I told her as we started out.

"Really, Master?" she asked, adding the *Master* after verifying there was no one nearby to hear.

"Yes," I said, starting off. "We're going to Italy."

Her laughter followed behind me.

For the next few hours we skied, enjoying the scenery and the company. While Abby wasn't the most athletic person, she enjoyed skiing and we'd trained together in the gym for months before the wedding.

Not long after noon, we came to a stop in a little clearing.

"Welcome to Italy," I said.

Her breathing was just a bit heavier than normal, but at my words a smile broke across her face. "We're in Italy, Master?"

"Yes." I slipped off the backpack I'd brought and unzipped it. "Makes me feel like a spy."

"Makes me feel like I'm living *The Sound of Music*."

I took out two wineglasses and handed her one. "Except you're not a nun."

"Thank goodness."

I smiled and poured us wine. "Can you imagine?"

"Not even a little bit."

"To us," I said, lifting my glass.

"To us," she repeated, lifting her glass and clinking it against mine.

We took a sip of our wine and I thought about how perfect the day was. Both of us together, married, skiing across borders, and simply enjoying the day. Especially with her wearing my collar.

I inhaled the crisp, wintry scent. "Just about perfect, wouldn't you say?"

Her sly smile tickled the edges of her mouth. "I think it's missing one thing."

I had a fairly good idea of what one thing she meant. "Maybe, but I'm not about to get frostbite on my cock."

"Master," she chided. "I didn't mean that. I was talking about snacks. Did you bring something to eat in that backpack?"

"I don't know whether to be disappointed or not." I took out an apple and tossed it to her. "Good catch."

"All that backyard playing with Jackson helped." She narrowed her eyes. "Wait a minute—did you say that because you expected me to miss the apple? So what, you decided to throw it to me anyway?"

"Watch your tone of voice," I said. "Just because we're not in the playroom doesn't mean you can act any old way when you're wearing my collar."

She looked abashed. "Sorry, Master."

"I know you've been playing catch with Jackson. I'm there, too. I was complimenting your catch." I lowered my voice. "I'm going to let this instance slide because I'm in a good mood. Speak to me that way again while you're wearing my collar and I'll double your punishment."

"Yes, Master. I understand."

We stayed in the clearing for a while, enjoying our snacks and the surroundings. She had told me after Jackson and Felicia returned from their European honeymoon that she had no interest herself in the kind of country-hopping they did. I had felt certain, however, that she would be fine with skiing across borders.

We spent the rest of the day out skiing and made it back to the chalet after dark. I planned to take her collar off that night. After dinner she went to take a shower and when I finished with mine, she was curled up in bed, sleeping. I didn't want to wake her up just to remove the collar—that could wait until morning—so I pulled her to my side and fell asleep myself.

The next few days were wonderful. We spent time skiing and exploring the local area, but there were days we simply stayed inside and enjoyed each other's company. Honestly, we didn't have to leave the chalet. With the spa, pool, and library, everything we needed was close by.

About a week after arriving, we took a taxi into the village for our first fondue.

"I can't believe we've been in Switzerland for a week and haven't tried fondue," she said once we'd sat down.

"Shh," I said, looking around at the other diners. "Don't say that too loudly—you'll have us kicked out of the country."

She laughed. I couldn't help but smile in response. She was always beautiful, but her laugh warmed me from the inside out.

I stood up when she pushed back from the table.

"I'll be right back. I think I saw the ladies' room on the way in."

I sat back down and looked over the menu. It was written in French and I thought with a chuckle about suggesting to Abby she memorize it. Next time she was trying to hold her orgasm at bay, a French menu would be more entertaining than hearing the German alphabet backward.

"Can I take your drink order?" the waiter asked, interrupting my thoughts about Abby and the playroom.

"I'll have a Trois Dames Oud Bruin and my wife will take a glass of your house red." I probably didn't hide what I knew was a silly grin. I couldn't help it, though; it was the first time I'd referred to her as "my wife" out in public.

"Did you have a chance to look over the menu?" Abby asked when she returned and I'd helped her back into her chair.

"Yes, and it's in French. A shame we didn't decide on a German restaurant."

She kicked me under the table.

"What?" I asked. "Just trying to expand your foreign vocabulary."

She sighed and leaned back into her seat after we ordered. "Only one more week."

I didn't want to think about returning home just yet. Didn't want to have to think about the reality outside of our honeymoon haven. "It's going by so quickly. Is there something you specifically want to do next week?"

"You mean as in places to go, or things we could do in the chalet?"

I nearly choked on my drink. "I was talking about places to go, but if there are things we haven't done *otherwise* I'm open to those as well."

She looked over both shoulders. The restaurant was at capacity, but the tables were arranged to give privacy. We wouldn't be overheard.

"I've worn your collar two days so far. I'd like to wear it more."

I swirled my drink. "I can arrange that."

"Maybe another two days?"

"Monday and Tuesday?"

"I think that would work perfectly."

Playing early in the week would work out well since we'd be traveling home the next weekend and, as such, I probably wouldn't collar her.

"There's actually something else I wanted to talk about," she said. "But I'm not sure this is the right place."

"Something private?"

She nodded.

"You're probably right. This isn't the best place to discuss those types of things. Can it wait until we get back?"

She agreed and we spent the rest of the night eating, drinking, and laughing. After dinner we walked around the village some. From one spot, if you stood the right way and held your head just so, you could see our chalet. I pointed it out to Abby and wondered out loud if anyone had a telescope. She punched my shoulder.

Late that night, after we returned, I found her propped up

on pillows in front of the fireplace. Her hair was still slightly damp from her shower and she held a mug of coffee.

"This looks comfortable," I said, taking a seat beside her. "What are you thinking?"

"Remember a few nights ago when I called you 'Sir' and didn't remember doing it later?"

It was suddenly very clear why she hadn't wanted to have this conversation at the restaurant. "Yes."

"I've been thinking about that. How I like it when you take control during sex, even when I'm not wearing your collar, and what that means."

"And what do you think it means?"

"I don't know. That's why I wanted to talk to you about it. I know I don't want to wear your collar every day."

I loved the fact that our relationship was strong and open enough for us to talk about things we didn't want. Loved that we felt comfortable enough to simply talk. Especially when we didn't know something.

"I don't want you to wear it that often, either," I said. "So we both agree on that."

She had her robe on and was sitting facing the fireplace, hugging her knees. She was gazing into the fire with a look of utter concentration, as if she could find the answers she was looking for in the flames. I decided to take a different approach.

"Look at me, Abby."

She didn't even hesitate in shifting her focus from the fire to me.

"That right there," I said. "Why do you think you turned your head so quickly and without stopping to think about it?"

"I know you want me to say because I'm a submissive, but I

don't think that's the whole reason." Her head lifted just a bit. "I think most people would react the same way."

"Good point. You're right on that one." I thought for a second on how best to make my case. "Let's try this." I scooted closer to her and slipped an arm around her shoulders. "Let's say we're naked."

She pulled back slightly. "Are we just pretending or are we actually getting naked? Because if we're actually getting naked, I don't see this conversation lasting very long."

I bit her earlobe. "We'll just pretend for now. So in my scenario, we're both naked—"

"Am I wearing your collar or not?"

"You're not. And I'm kissing you kind of like this." I turned her to face me and I stopped whatever words she was about to say by crushing my lips to hers. I framed her face and kissed her long and slow and deep. When I pulled back, she was panting.

"I like this scenario," she said.

"It gets better." I inched a hand inside her robe and cupped her breast. "While I'm kissing you, I start to caress you like this."

"I'm torn between telling you to get to your point or to simply relax and let myself feel."

"Just relax and feel. I'll get to my point." I ran a thumb over her nipple. "Eventually."

"Mmm." She closed her eyes and I took the coffee mug from her and placed it on the end table next to where we were sitting.

"Let's say we're standing together and I'm kissing and caressing you, and I lean over and whisper in your ear, 'Touch my cock, baby. Stroke me and make me feel good.'" I took her free hand and placed it on my growing erection.

"I'm sure vanilla people say stuff like that all the time."

I didn't reply. "So you're stroking me and I'm telling you how good you feel and how I love having your hands on my body. And then I look at you and say, 'Get on your knees and suck me off.'"

She kept stroking me.

"Suck it," I commanded. "Fucking do it now, Abby."

Her eyes widened and her lips parted. She moved to undo my pants, but I stopped her. "There. Right there. In that second before you moved, how did you feel?"

"My heart started racing and I grew aroused." She narrowed her eyes. "So I get off when you get bossy. That still doesn't mean I want to be submissive all the time."

"You're missing the point."

"Then explain it to me."

"My dominance turns you on. It doesn't matter if you're wearing my collar at the time or not. And it turns you on because you're a sexual submissive. It's the way you're wired. It's not something you can turn off and on."

"I get that partially." She'd moved so her back was to the couch. "I guess I just thought if we did it over the weekend, the need wouldn't be there during the week."

"The need will always be there because submitting will always be what turns you on."

"So what do we do with that?"

"What do you want to do with it? We've already established neither one of us wants you in my collar all the time."

She was quiet for several minutes, silently thinking, I supposed. I reminded myself how relatively new she was to the lifestyle. I could give her my opinions and advice, but the truth was, she needed to come to her own conclusions.

"I think there's a lot of truth to what you're saying," she finally said. "Looking back over our weekday times, it's always been more intense for me when you've been more dominant."

I recalled vividly how strongly she'd react whenever I took control during sex. I supposed knowing how she'd respond had always been a given to me. Then again, I'd been a Dom a lot longer than she'd been a sub.

"I would wholeheartedly agree with that," I said.

"But you never said anything."

"It's something you had to figure out for yourself. And," I added, slipping my hand back inside her robe, "I showed you with action, which I think is always better than words."

She playfully swatted my hand away. "Wait a minute. I can't think with you doing that."

I moved my hand and silently hoped she didn't need much longer to think. The way the robe was hanging from her shoulders . . . just a mere touch and it'd slip off completely.

"What if you exerted a little bit more control in the bedroom on weekdays? I think that would work." She tightened the robe around her body. "It would only be in the bedroom, so it's not like it is when I wear your collar."

"I could definitely get behind that idea. And since you wouldn't be collared, you wouldn't call me 'Master.' That's only for when you wear my collar."

"Can I call you 'Sir'?"

"If you'd like. But I don't want to set up a lot of rules for our weekdays."

Her body shifted so she was facing me more and excitement danced in her eyes. "Can we start now? Like this week?"

"I don't see why not. In fact." I stood up. "You're going to suck my cock, Abby. But first, take the robe off."

Chapter Ten

ABBY

When he collared me that Monday, he gave me a writing assignment to complete in the afternoon. So for part of the day, I sat in our sunroom, surrounded by mountains and writing about ways to incorporate sexual submission into our everyday lives.

"Of course," he'd said with that wicked gleam in his eye as he gave me the assignment, "that means you first have to decide on your definition of sexual submission."

I'd spoken with submissives in our local group who thought writing assignments were punishments, but they'd never felt like that to me. I'd always felt that sometimes it was easier to think on paper.

When I picked my pen and journal up, it was as if the floodgates of my mind opened and allowed me to put into words what speaking and thinking alone couldn't do. Nathaniel, of course, noticed this right away. As a result, whenever there was a subject he saw I needed to come to terms with, he'd have me write about it.

He also knew that writing sometimes felt easier to me than talking to him. When I put my thoughts in my journal, I knew he had the right to read what I'd written. But he'd assured me that nothing I ever wrote would be used against me, so his eventual reading of what I wrote didn't worry me. I knew we would end up discussing it. But sometimes it was easier to start that conversation in writing.

He walked into the sunroom that Monday as I was finishing up.

"How's it going?" he asked, handing me a cup of hot chocolate.

"Thank you, Master." I took the mug and had a sip. He'd been making me the best hot chocolate since we'd gotten to Switzerland. "Mmm, this is so good. I'm almost finished with my writing."

He nodded and took a seat opposite me. "Will it bother you if I sit in here?"

"Probably not, Master. As long as you're quiet. Though if you'd like to distract me or if you want me to distract you, I won't complain."

"No distractions for now," he said with a soft grin. "I want you to finish."

I gave a mock sigh. "If you insist."

For the next thirty minutes, we sat in comfortable silence. I wrote and he read something on his tablet. When I finished with my assignment, I gathered my journal, placed it on his lap, and knelt on the floor at his feet.

"Finished?" he asked.

"Yes, Master."

"Did you find the exercise useful?"

When he asked me such a question, I was to answer honestly. If I hadn't found the writing useful, I was free to tell him so. At such times, only my dishonesty would be a disappointment to him. My answer today was a truthful "Yes, it was very useful."

He took the journal and placed it on the end table. "I'll read over this later. For now, tell me one thing you learned while writing." He knew that after I'd written about a subject, it was usually easier for me to articulate my feelings to him.

"As I wrote, I came to realize that sexual submission takes on many forms. And it can be played out and incorporated in a lot of ways. Whether one is a collared submissive or not."

"Sounds strikingly similar to a statement I made not so many nights ago."

"Yes, Master, but like you also said, it's a conclusion I had to come to myself."

He stroked my cheek. "And have you?"

We had been together, living a dual relationship for over six months. In that time, we'd come together numerous times as both Dominant and submissive and just as Nathaniel and Abby. I loved both parts of our lives, but looking back, the intimate moments I'd enjoyed the most were those when he took control in the bedroom.

"Yes, Master. And I came up with a few ideas on how to incorporate our special relationship into our weekdays."

"Excellent. I'll read over what you wrote and we'll discuss that later."

He was always very insistent that we not negotiate anything while I wore his collar. We would most certainly discuss my ideas, but I knew from experience it wouldn't be anytime today or tomorrow.

Frankly, I was looking forward to him taking a more dominant role in the bedroom. I thought back to a few nights ago in front of the fireplace, when he'd shown me by his words exactly how my body reacted to his commands. Every time I remembered him saying, "Fucking do it now, Abby," my insides tightened and a particular warmth spread over my body.

That night had been the first time he'd shown me exactly how he could be more in control, even when I wasn't wearing his collar.

"I wonder, though, Master," I started, and then stopped. "But maybe we should wait and discuss it later. When my collar is off."

"I don't mind having a discussion. As long as we both know nothing will be decided or agreed to until it's off."

I was still kneeling on the floor. I thought it doubtful I'd forget that long enough to haphazardly agree to anything. More than that, though, I knew he wouldn't want me agreeing to anything pertaining to our weekdays. That was key to my decision to tell him my thoughts now.

"We both have such intense head spaces during the weekend," I said. "And you, *you* have to do so much planning and preparation. How will that work on, say, a Tuesday night?"

He put one foot across his knee and thought before speaking. "I think we'll have to make the weekdays less structured. I won't be planning anything specific. The weekdays will be a time for it to just happen naturally."

I couldn't help it. I giggled. "The last time we let things happen naturally, we ended up with cold risotto and marinara sauce on a certain part of your anatomy, Master."

His laugh was playful. "You did an outstanding job of cleaning the sauce off, though. Can't say taking it natural is a bad thing."

I laughed along with him. "No, definitely not a bad thing."

I enjoyed that as our relationship grew and strengthened, we found it easier to have lighthearted moments during my collared days. During times like this, I found it hard to believe we'd ever hesitated to laugh and share everything together. I couldn't fathom I'd known him less than a year.

He was still smiling when he said, "I have, however, planned something for this afternoon. Go on into the bedroom. I'll be there in five minutes."

I hurried into the bedroom, curious as to what he had planned. The curiosity only grew when I saw the handwritten note at the foot of the bed with a blindfold beside it.

> *Abigail,*
>
> *Get in bed and put the blindfold on. You are not to take it off at any time.*
>
> *It is late in the evening. You are alone in the house. Earlier in the day you had the blinds open and you were pleasuring yourself. You didn't think anyone was watching. You were wrong.*
>
> *And you really should have made sure the front door was locked before you went to bed.*
>
> *Nathaniel*

My heart pounded. Role-play. I loved it when he created a role-play scenario. Loved the feeling of pretending to be someone else. It allowed me to act out some of my fantasies. Typically, though, what we did was more straightforward: workplace, deliveryman, or naughty schoolgirl. This sounded intense.

I didn't have long to prepare. He said he'd be upstairs in five minutes. I debated for a few seconds on whether I should strip or leave my clothes on. He hadn't said either way, and therefore, I could do either. Which way would be more fun?

I hastily took everything off and scurried under the covers. The blindfold simply slipped over my head and in no time I was silent, still, and waiting in the darkness. Always before when he'd blindfolded me, I'd prided myself on my heightened sense of hearing, so I thought I'd know when he came into the bedroom. This time, I yelped when my hands were yanked above my head and tied into place.

"You should have checked the lock before you got into bed." Nathaniel's voice was rough and gritty, but it was still his.

Knowing I was safe, I allowed myself to sink deeper into my role. "Who are you?"

"That doesn't matter. What matters is I saw that little show you put on earlier when you thought no one was looking."

"You saw that?"

"Yes, I saw what a naughty girl you were playing with yourself, fucking your fingers. I bet you knew I was there and it turned you on more, knowing I was watching."

"I didn't. I—"

He put a hand over my mouth. "Be quiet. If you speak without permission, I'm going to slap you. Your only job right now is to do what you're told and to make amends for this afternoon. Do you know how you're going to do that?"

I shook my head.

He took my jaw in his hand and squeezed. "Answer me when I ask you a question."

"No."

He squeezed so hard, it hurt. "You fucking know better. Address me correctly."

"No, Sir."

"Better not make that mistake again." He moved his hand

and pulled the sheet down. "I knew you'd sleep naked. Dirty girl. You were probably hoping someone would break in and give you what you want."

This was a new side of Nathaniel, a darker side. He was rough and demanding and I found it hot as hell. The fact I didn't have my sight only made it hotter.

"I bet if I . . ." He slid a hand between my legs and forced a finger inside me. "Just like I thought. Your little pussy is desperate for cock." He shifted on the bed and removed the remaining covers.

He was silent for a long time and I started to grow uncomfortable.

"Look at you all spread out on the bed. When I saw you earlier, I imagined you like this. Naked and aching. Watching you made me so damn hard. So now you're going to open those legs for me." He slapped my upper thigh. "Now."

I grew more and more aroused the longer he talked and when I spread my legs, I knew he could see exactly how much. I thought he'd slip a finger into me, but he pinched a nipple instead, causing me to moan.

"So wet for me," he said. "Good thing, because I'm seconds away from pounding into you as hard as humanly possible."

I felt him move on the bed again. This time settling between my legs. He pressed his cock right against my slit.

"Feel that? Feel how hard and thick I am?"

"Yes, Sir." I shifted my hips, needing him to move.

"Good." He pushed the head inside me. "Fucking hell, the sight of you taking me."

I wished I could see. Could watch as he claimed me. I groaned as he moved the slightest bit.

His hand covered my mouth. "You're not to move or make a

sound and you certainly aren't allowed to come." He pushed deeper. "Your only purpose right now is for my use and my pleasure."

As if proving his point, he thrust all the way inside me and, *holy shit*, it felt so good I had to bite the inside of my cheek. He withdrew and drove back in with a grunt. He muttered something under his breath, and then took my right leg and pushed it up so it touched my chest. He slid even deeper on his next thrust.

"That's it. Take that cock." His hips picked up the pace and slammed me into the mattress with every forward push. With his punishing rhythm, I knew I couldn't hold out for very long.

Under the blindfold, I squeezed my eyes tightly, but that didn't help very much. He shifted his hips and hit new spots. Desperate not to come, I inhaled deeply and held it.

"Breathe," he growled in my ear, his hips never stopping.

The air left my body with one loud *whoosh*. "Yellow," I panted. "I can't. I can't stop it."

Almost immediately the blindfold was taken from my face. His dark, need-filled eyes stared into mine. The intensity of his expression almost took my breath away again, but then he gently whispered, "Come, Abigail."

With those two softly spoken words, I freed my body and my orgasm engulfed me immediately. He held still while I constricted around him and then he pushed into me again and again, not stopping until, with a final grunt, he thrust deeply, allowing his own release.

He rested for only seconds before reaching up and untying my hands. One at a time, he kissed both my wrists and placed my arms at my sides. His familiar hands ran over my body and I sighed as he reclined on the bed and pulled me to him.

"Are you okay?" he asked.

"Yes, Master. I always enjoy role-play." I turned my head and kissed his chest.

"I know, but I need to be certain. We've never done anything resembling consensual nonconsent."

"We've talked about it before and I said I was interested. Now that we've touched on it, I'd like to do more." I shivered again just thinking about the way he'd talked, his rough and demanding hands, and, most of all, his mastery over me. "It's thrilling and exciting, but I know I'm completely safe with you."

"Look at me." He pulled me closer. "I want to fulfill all your fantasies and desires."

"And I want to fulfill yours."

"Oh, my lovely." He lifted my chin, gave me a soft kiss, and whispered against my lips, "You already have."

The Thursday before we left, he found me reading in the living room. We'd spent the day skiing and exploring the village a bit more. He'd disappeared shortly after we returned. I'd assumed he'd called to check on Apollo. Our honeymoon was the longest Apollo had been away from him and Nathaniel checked on him frequently.

When he returned, he strolled into the living room and took a seat beside me. "Reading anything good?"

I closed my book. While he had switched to e-books years ago, I still preferred actual books. To me there was just something about turning pages and—call me crazy—the smell of a book. Technology couldn't replace that.

"Pride and Prejudice," I said.

"Again? Haven't you memorized it yet?" He was smiling and his voice was playful, so I knew Apollo must be doing well.

"Haven't memorized the entire thing just yet. Maybe by the end of the weekend. It *is* a long flight home."

"Are you ready to go back?"

I gave the question some thought. Part of me was ready to get back home and see family and friends again. I especially missed Felicia, since we talked on an almost daily basis at home. And part of me was ready to go back to work. I knew I didn't have to work. Nathaniel had told me I could quit when and if I wanted to. But I enjoyed my work and the people at the library, plus I couldn't imagine what I'd do if I didn't work. I'm sure I could stay busy, but for the time being, it would be nice working and knowing I could quit if I wanted to.

Another part of me, though, was enjoying my time with Nathaniel and I knew when we returned home, he'd be busy catching up on his own work. I knew how demanding that would be. Our time together would probably be drastically reduced. I most certainly was not looking forward to that. A downside to marrying such a successful businessman was that I had to share him with too many damn people.

"I'm torn," I said in answer to his question. "I'm ready to get back home in order to see people and even get back to work. But I know you'll be extremely busy and I won't be able to see you that much. I've enjoyed having you all to myself for the last two weeks."

"I feel the same. Torn." He reached over and took my hand. "But I promise you that business will never come before you and our marriage. I've known too many men who have ruined their lives by treating work as the most important part of it, and I vow not to do that. In fact"—he smiled—"I give you permission to kick my ass if I ever get my priorities out of whack."

I snorted. "Like I need your permission to do that."

"True, I'd expect you to kick my ass. Permission or not."

"Your dad wasn't like that, was he?" I asked almost hesitantly.

He didn't talk about his parents often, but his prior statement made me curious.

Surprisingly, he didn't even pause before answering. "No, he definitely had his priorities straight. Always took time for family. Never missed an event that was important to me. And I remember he and Mom would go off on their own without me for a week or so, several times a year."

"Sounds like he was a good role model."

"He was. It goes without saying, but I hate that he died so young." He looked down at his wedding band. The one that had been his father's. "He had so much left to teach me."

I placed my hand over his. "I think he taught you a lot and I'm sure he'd be proud of the man you've become."

"Thank you." He leaned over and kissed me gently. "I wish they could have met you."

He'd said as much before. Since my mother had died when I was an adult, I couldn't imagine not having her with me while I was growing up. "I wish I could have met them, too. But you know, I see glimpses of them in you."

He sighed and put an arm around me. "I'd like to think that's true."

We sat for a few minutes, wrapped in our own thoughts and watching the snow fall softly outside.

"It's so beautiful here," I said, breaking the silence.

"Quite a bit different from New York."

"I couldn't live away from the city, but I really like it here. It's so different, even from the estate."

I'd really grown attached to the chalet in the last week, and the village had its own charm. I especially liked the no-car rule. And how many other places could you visit where you could ski across borders?

"And the food is outstanding," he said.

"Yeah, especially the hot chocolate you make here."

"I was just thinking about making some. Want a mug?"

"Sure, that sounds great."

While he left for the kitchen, I walked over to the window and looked outside. It suddenly hit me hard that we'd be leaving soon and that made me a bit sad. The chalet had been a haven for us and I knew I'd always remember the two weeks we'd spent here, both for the intimacy and pleasure we'd enjoyed and the insights I'd gained about my own nature.

We still hadn't discussed my journal writing. I supposed we did have the long flight back. The jet would allow us plenty of time and privacy to talk.

"One hot chocolate and a special delivery for a Mrs. Abby West."

I looked up to find him reentering the room carrying a tray holding two steaming mugs and an envelope with a silver bow.

"I got mail? Here? With a bow?" It didn't make any sense.

"Technically, I put the bow on it."

"Why would you put a bow on my mail?"

He nodded toward the couch and put the tray on the center table. "Have a seat and drink hot chocolate, and I'll explain."

I took my seat and picked up the mug, but it was too hot to drink. "Mmm, smells so good."

He took a sip of his own. "Needs to cool a bit." He picked up the envelope and handed it to me. "Here, open this."

His eyes were filled with excitement and a huge grin covered his face. I looked from him to the envelope and took it from him. "What's this?"

"Consider it a belated wedding present."

"From who?" I shook it. "Sounds like paper."

"It's from me and it *is* paper, silly woman. Open it."

"We said we weren't exchanging wedding presents, that we were just doing the rings. Now I feel bad. I didn't get you anything." I should have known he'd get me something. It really wasn't fair. Although I had to admit I was intrigued by what could be in an envelope.

"You gave me the gift of yourself by marrying me," he said with a quirky smile.

I cocked my head and narrowed my eyes. "That's sweet and all, but don't think I'm going to forgive you for getting me a gift after we agreed we weren't exchanging them."

"I guess I'll have to find a way to live with your wrath."

I took the bow off the envelope and placed it on his knee. "Silver?"

"It's my favorite color on you."

I blew him a kiss and opened the envelope. Inside were several sheets of paper, but I only read the first one. My hand flew to my mouth. "Nathaniel?"

"I hope you like it."

I looked up at him in shock. "I can't believe it."

"The timing worked out perfectly. I really didn't plan on this."

I quickly read the paper again. "You *bought* me the chalet?"

"Yes."

"I can't believe you bought me the chalet." I looked around the room. All this was mine?

"Now we can come back anytime we want. And a few years from now, when we're all tired and grumpy because the kids are driving us crazy, we can hop on the jet and get away for a few days. Linda would love the opportunity to watch grandkids. She's already bugging Jackson and Felicia about starting a family."

"Or when we're tired and grumpy and work is driving us crazy?"

"Or when we're tired and grumpy and we're driving *each other* crazy?" He winked.

I felt almost giddy as the disappointment I had mere minutes ago about having to leave was replaced by elation with the realization that I now owned the property. I put the envelope and papers on the table and straddled his lap. "Are we going to drive each other crazy?"

He dragged his fingers through my hair. "You always drive me crazy."

"You're a fine one to talk, Mr. West." I pressed my lips against his. "Thank you for my wedding present. It's perfect and I love it."

"I'm glad. I wanted us to have our own special place we could get away to and when the owner told me it was for sale, I knew I'd found it." He still wore the quirky grin. "Am I forgiven now for getting you a wedding present even though we said we weren't exchanging them?"

Of course he was, but I wanted to tease him a little bit longer. "I don't know. I think there's one thing you need to do in order to be totally forgiven."

"Oh?" He looked genuinely surprised.

"Mmm," I hummed, and then whispered in his ear, "you have *got* to have a playroom added to this place."

His laughter was infectious and as I was laughing, he rained kisses along my neck. "If you insist on adding a playroom, I know just the architect."

"Make sure it has lots of windows," I said, thinking about the day he took me in the bedroom in front of the windows and imagining it happening over and over.

"Going to start making demands about the playroom?" His lips had traveled lower and were grazing my collarbone.

"It's my chalet."

"It'll be my playroom."

I sucked in a breath as his hand slipped up my shirt. "Would it help if I said *please?*"

"We're going to have to do something about this exhibitionism thing you seem to enjoy so much." His other hand went up my shirt and within seconds my bra was unhooked. "I think maybe we should do a demo scene at a play party."

My body pulsed with desire at the thought of playing with people watching. Submitting to Nathaniel in front of the group. "Yes. Please. And thank you."

He lifted my shirt up and over my head. "I think the February party is scheduled to be held at our house. Think that sounds good?"

Less than two months? "Yes, Sir."

He growled and dropped his head even lower to suck a nipple into his mouth. "There you go, driving me crazy again. Makes me so hard when you call me 'Sir.'"

"Sorry, Sir. But not really, Sir." I arched my back as he drew me deeper into his mouth. "Does this mean we get a playroom with windows and we get to do a demo scene in February, Sir?"

He lifted his head. "Yes, my lovely, you may have your playroom with the windows and we'll do a demo at the party in February."

"Thank you." And just because, I added, "Sir."

"Remember when I said I was going to toughen that ass up?"

"Vividly, Sir." The familiar ache started to grow between my legs.

"I'm tempted to take you over my knee right now."

I fisted his hair in my hands, pulling at the dark strands as his lips traveled across the upper part of my body. His mouth left a trail of goose-pebbled flesh in its wake. "Only tempted? What's stopping you?"

"There are other things I'd rather do at the moment."

"Oh? Do tell."

"I'll do better than tell. I'll show you."

He slid me from his lap so I rested on the floor. I scooted away from the couch, stopping in the middle of the soft rug in front of the fireplace. I was already topless and felt the warmth of the fire against my back.

"The first thing you do is take the jeans off," he said.

With a lazy smile and moving in a speed that matched, I slowly made it to my feet. He was still sitting on the couch and his eyes grew dark with desire as I unbuttoned my jeans and took my time inching them past my hips and down my legs. I stepped out of them and kicked them to the side. "Now what?"

"You lose the panties."

I thought about taking them off right away, but decided to draw the game out a little bit longer. "When are you going to get naked?"

"Eventually."

"Eventually, like now or eventually, like later?"

"I haven't decided."

I sat back down on the floor and crossed my legs. "I'm not taking anything else off until you start getting naked."

He toed his shoes off.

I rolled my eyes. "Not even."

"You just said to start getting naked—you didn't specify what to take off."

"That's fine." I walked on my knees over to the coffee table and took my hot chocolate and drank a sip. "I'll just stay like this all day." I took another sip. "All night, too."

When he saw that I wasn't budging, he muttered, "Oh, all right," and pulled his sweater over his head.

I set the mug down. "That's better. Now stroke your cock for me."

"I thought you said you liked it when I took control sexually."

"I do. That doesn't mean I don't like to offer helpful suggestions every once in a while." It was true I enjoyed his dominant side, but I liked teasing him and playing with him as well.

"Helpful suggestion, I see," he said, but he unzipped his jeans and took his cock out.

I stood up and watched as he stroked himself for a few seconds. His voice was rough when he spoke again.

"Lose the panties, Abby."

I tossed my hair over my shoulder, and turned away from him so my back was to him.

"Cheater," he said.

"There aren't any rules that I was made aware of," I said.

"That's okay. I have a certain fondness for your ass."

Laughing, I peeked over my shoulder as I hooked a finger in the waistband of my panties and pulled them down. "Not sure why I brought these anyway. They never stay on."

"What's the fun in keeping them on?"

"Right," I said. "That's why I brought them. To tease you."

"And a damn fine job you're doing. Turn around, please."

His hand was still leisurely stroking his cock when I turned to face him. "My, my," I said. "Is that for me?"

"Any way you want it."

I walked over to him, making sure to sway my hips just so. I stopped in front of him and slowly dropped to my knees. "In that case, the first thing I'm going to do is lick the head of your cock to taste you. Then I'm going to pull you to the end of the couch and suck you into my mouth, as far as I can."

"Sounds like my kind of plan."

"I thought you'd approve." I took his hands and placed them on his upper thighs. "While I enjoy the taste and feel of you in my mouth and you know I love to suck you until you can't help but lose yourself down my throat, I'm warning you now that I won't be quite ready for you to come just yet."

"I had a feeling that would be the case."

"Yes, you're a very smart man and you know me very, very well." I kissed the still clothed part of his knee. "Right when you're getting ready to come, I'll stand up and straddle you. But before I move any closer, I'll ask you to check my pussy to make sure I'm wet enough for your cock. Matter of fact, let me check right now." I ran a finger between my legs and held it to his lips. "What do you think?"

He groaned, but took my finger inside his mouth and gave a gentle suck. "Almost, but not quite."

"When you check me then, you'll have to be very thorough."

"I'll double- and triple-check."

"Good, because you could really hurt someone with that thing if you weren't careful."

He gave a half snort, half grunt.

"And then, only when you say I'm ready, I'll lower myself down onto your waiting cock. Going slowly, to make sure I'm as ready and prepared as you said I was." I closed my eyes and could almost feel him at my entrance. "You feel so big and thick pushing inside me that I wonder, just for a minute, if I can take all of you. But then you take me by the hips and force yourself inside with one hard push."

"Fuck, Abby."

"I gasp at the sensation of having you buried so deep inside me, but you decide to take over and you hold my hips still and you thrust up and into me over and over. And you're fucking me as hard and as fast and as deep as you can and I'm locked in place above you, only able to close my eyes and take that massive dick pounding into my body."

"I'm getting ready to show you just how hard and fast and deep this massive dick can pound that dirty-talking body."

I loved it when I drove him to the edge, so with a wicked smile, I continued. "It feels so good and I whisper in your ear, 'Harder, I need it harder.' So you slow your thrusts down a bit, but only so you can control them better and make sure you're fucking me with as much force as you possibly can."

"Going to do you so fucking hard."

"And then I feel my orgasm approach and you reach between our bodies and rub my clit and I can't hold my release at bay anymore and I come hard right as you push one last time and come with a roar."

I was weak with desire and so aroused I feared a mere touch would set me off. Nathaniel probably felt about the same: his hands were back on his cock and he was breathing a bit heavier than normal. It took all my strength to turn from him and say, "I think I'll finish my hot chocolate now."

My hand hadn't reached for the mug before I was on my back on the rug with Nathaniel looming over me. Somehow, he'd managed to lose his pants. "Damn hot chocolate can wait. I have to be inside you right the fuck now."

He pushed into me with one solid thrust and didn't wait before he starting moving his hips, rocking deep inside me.

"Going to come this time hard and fast," he said as he kept pounding into me. "Then we're going to go upstairs and reenact that little scenario you just described." He was silent for several seconds, working himself in and out of my body. "I may decide to take a dinner break, because we'll need to regain our strength for after dinner."

My climax was hard and swift, building and cresting almost at the same time, and leaving me breathless, after. Nathaniel's must have been the same, because by the time my breathing returned to normal, he was rolling to his back, dragging me to rest on top of him.

"What happens after dinner?" I asked, propping myself up on his chest and running a finger around his nipple.

He took my hand and kissed each finger, one at a time. "After dinner is when I gather you to my side and kiss every inch of your body. And in the second before my lips touch your skin, I'll whisper so softly you won't be able to hear, nonsensical things that only our souls understand."

I lowered my head to his and our lips came together in a gentle kiss. A stark contrast to the urgent and demanding way our bodies had come together moments before.

"I like the thought of that," I said, pulling back slightly.

He tucked a lose piece of hair behind my ear. "Which part?"

"About our souls understanding each other."

"My soul understood yours the very first time I saw you. It called to yours softly, saying, 'One day we will be complete in each other.'"

I smiled, liking the idea of some part of our inner being recognizing the other. "And what did my soul say?"

"It said, 'Boy, you've got a lot of growing up to do.'"

I hid my smile in the crook of his neck. "It did not."

"Oh, yes it did. And mine said, 'I'll work hard to make myself worthy of you.' And somehow, deep inside, both of our souls knew that our journey wouldn't be the easiest, but that one day we'd have a night like this when everything finally came together. A moment just like this when everything is right."

I placed a hand on his heart, as my own chest swelled with emotion. "My soul is complete in you."

"And mine," he said, placing his hand over mine, "has finally found its home."

Tara Sue Me wrote her first novel at the age of twelve. Twenty years later, after penning several traditional romances, she decided to try her hand at something spicier and started work on *The Submissive*, and she soon followed that with *The Dominant*, *The Training*, *Seduced by Fire*, *The Enticement*, *The Exhibitionist*, and *The Master*. The series has become a huge hit with readers around the world and has been read and reread millions of times.

Tara kept her identity and her writing life secret, not even telling her husband what she was working on. To this day, only a handful of people know the truth (though she has told her husband). They live together in the southeastern United States with their two children.

CONNECT ONLINE

tarasueme.com